SACRIFICE

ADRIANA LOCKE

Sacrifice
Copyright (c) Adriana Locke, 2015
ALL RIGHTS RESERVED

All rights reserved. Without limiting the rights under copyright reserved above, no part of this publication may be reproduced, stored in or introduced into a retrieval system, or transmitted, in any form, or by any means (mechanical, electronic, photocopying, recording, or otherwise) without the prior written permission of both the copyright owner and the above publisher of the book.

This is a work of fiction. Any references to historical events, real people, or real places are used fictitiously. Other names, characters, places, and events are products of the author's imagination, and any resemblance to actual events or places or persons, living or dead, is entirely coincidental.

Cover Art:
Kari March, K23 Designs
www.facebook.com/designK23

Cover Photos:
Dollar Photo Club
www.dollarphotoclub.com

Editing:
Ashley Amigoni, Escapist Freelance Editing
www.facebook.com/AshleyAmigoniFreelanceEditor

Interior Design and Formatting:
Christine Borgford, Perfectly Publishable
www.perfectlypublishable.com

Also by ADRIANA LOCKE

The Exception (The Exception Series Book #1)

The Connection (The Exception Series Book #1.5)

The Perception (The Exception Series Book #2)

DEDICATION

To my children, affectionately known as the A-Team.

No matter what I do in my life, you will always be my greatest accomplishment. Your lives give mine meaning and a wholeness that can never be replicated.

You are my world, my heart, and my soul. For you, I would sacrifice it all.

Love you forever,

Mommy

Chapter ONE

CREW

THE SLUSH CRUNCHES beneath my boots, my breath billowing away from my body.

I bow my head deeper, pulling the hood of my sweatshirt out from under my jacket to cover more of my face. I toggle the paper sack in my other arm, hoping nothing spills out on the wet asphalt. Remnants of the last snow are piled beneath the trees and mound in the shadows of the large apartment complexes looming above.

The neighborhood is alive despite the bitter cold. People sit on the porches of their apartments and duplexes, some toking shit that sure as fuck isn't tobacco. Smoke rolls from the chimneys of the few single family houses in the area. Most of them are dilapidated, nearly rotting to the ground.

I grit my teeth.

I hate that they live here.

The apartment comes into view. A wooden chair is placed at the right of the door, a faded red and yellow striped pillow sitting on it. The steps of the porch are piss-poor and I have to sidestep the second one. The right side has a gash splitting the wood and I'm pretty certain if I stepped on it, I would fall through. I grimace and make a note to call her landlord. Piece of shit might not give two fucks about this place now, but he will.

I'll make sure of it.

I bang against the door with my knuckle. It is a cold fucking day, even for Boston at the end of February. It made for a long day unloading cargo at the shipyard. The afternoon warmed a little, but now that the sun is going down, the chill is biting through my Carhartt jacket. I bring my hands to my mouth and rub them together, blowing on them to warm them up.

I knock again, getting impatient. I hear music playing on the other side of the wood, the John Mayer stuff she's always loved.

A loud commotion, something like a piece of wood smashing something followed by a scream, comes from the apartment next door. Cold and irritated, I turn the handle to give it a flick, thinking the jingle will make her give in and open it. My jaw tenses when it begins to swing free. A chip of paint from the door falls to the tile below.

What the hell is she thinking?

I walk in, brushing the hood off my head and scan the kitchen. The music is playing from her phone on the counter and a pot of something bubbles on the old gas stove. I notice that she's got a sink full of dishes, which isn't like her. She's normally spot-on when it comes to details, taking care of everything she can control. It can be annoying as hell, but I figure it's some kind of reaction to all the shit she's *not* able to control in her life.

I plop the bag down on the table, rattling the basket of apples that sat upon it. When she comes around the corner, her brown eyes go wide as she grabs at the doorframe, obviously not expecting me.

"Damn it, Crew!" Julia says, clutching her chest with one hand. Her shoulders relax and a small sigh escapes her lips. I'm cautiously optimistic that maybe she's relieved to see me, but it's short-lived.

She throws her shoulders back and narrows her eyes. I don't know exactly what effect it was supposed to have on me, but it's a good thing I don't really care.

"Lock your fucking door," I growl, returning her glare. "You're lucky it's me and not some asshole from one of the apartments across the street."

"Lucky it's you." Sarcasm is thick in her voice as she shakes her head, her long black locks swinging side-to-side. She walks toward the stove and shuts off the music.

I crack the paper bag with the back of my hand, making her flinch. "I brought you some stuff."

"Stop bringing me *stuff*."

She keeps her back to me, picking up a lid and slamming it on a pot.

SACRIFICE

I know she's not happy to see me because she never is.

Tough shit.

"Where's the monkey?" I ask.

"In the living room."

Her words come out flat, but I'm used to it. I don't expect anything more from her.

I can't.

"Everleigh! Come here, baby girl," she calls.

It's such a natural thing, a mother calling her kid in for supper. It seems like just a normal part of an ordinary life. But I know the truth.

Appearances can be deceiving, but I enjoy the moment of deception. I'll take what I can get.

A few seconds later, the sound of little feet come running into the kitchen. "Uncle Crew!"

I kneel on one knee as she runs to me, her black hair flowing behind her.

"Uncle Crew!" she yells again and falls wildly in my arms, nuzzling her face into my cold jacket. I grab the zipper and yank it down, afraid the frozen metal will sting her little face.

My lips find her forehead as she wraps her arms around me. I hold her close, brushing back her hair, breathing in the smell of bubble gum that I've come to associate with my little niece. "How are ya, monkey?"

"I'm good," she giggles, pulling back and looking at me expectantly. "Did you bring me something?"

"Everleigh Nicole!" Julia reprimands her. "Have some manners!"

"But it's *Uncle Crew*." She bats her eyelashes at her mother, who rolls her eyes in response. "You did bring me something, didn't ya?" She looks at me again, a grin splitting her cheeks.

I could never say no to this kid. She could ask me for the fuckin' moon and I'd figure out a way to get it.

"Come on. You know I brought ya something."

Everleigh giggles and bounces up and down, her arms folded across the front of her Tinkerbell shirt. I reach in the bag and fish through the groceries and pull out a coloring book and a box of crayons. I really have no idea what the pictures are about, but it's the only one they had at the store.

"Yay!" she squeals, holding them up in the air so Julia can see them. "Thank you! I'll color you something beautiful and you can hang it at your house."

"You're welcome." I hold her gaze and give her a little nod to let her know our routine was still on. She tries to wink at me, but both eyes just flutter a few times. It takes everything I have not to laugh.

As soon as Julia turns her back, I slip her a banana Laffy Taffy and she kisses my cheek. She does her best sneaky walk back into the living room to avoid being caught with candy before supper.

I watch her go. Her long dark hair, just like her mother's, almost touches her waist. She's so much like Julia. She has the same heart-shaped face with high cheekbones, and the same graceful way about her.

Even so, there is so much about Everleigh that is like my brother. She's tall, like Gage, towering over most of her five-year-old friends. Her eyes are the same color, like the sky over the harbor on a really clear day. But the thing about my niece that reminds me most of my brother is her soul. Just like Gage, Ever is wise beyond her years. She's ridiculously smart and more mature than I probably was until I was in my twenties.

My brother loved her so damn much.

I release a sigh and lean against the battered refrigerator and feel it settle against my weight.

Julia ignores me, working at the stove. She's tied her hair back and I can see the stress in her shoulders, her posture defiant. She used to look that way in high school when she'd come to the house after a fight with her asshole parents. I hate seeing it now as much as I hated seeing it then. The only difference is now I have no one to blame but myself.

"You okay?" I ask, wondering if she will even respond to me. Sometimes she does. Sometimes she doesn't.

It's been a long two years since our worlds fell apart, but we've come to some sort of unspoken understanding. I've accepted that she's gonna hate me for the rest of her life. She's accepted that I won't go away. We've made some progress over time. She doesn't threaten me with a restraining order anymore. I don't get pissed at her refusal to cooperate. I just do what I'm going to do and she huffs but accepts it. Progress.

"Jules?" I ask again, watching her warily. I normally don't press, just drop off what I have and dash. Today, though, she seems more beaten down. I know she's probably missing him this week even more than usual, because I am, too. That makes me want to go get a drink, but I can't leave her without making sure she's all right. I owe her that much. "You okay?"

I see her set the spoon down and bow her head, and I brace myself for the unknown.

"Peachy."

Her voice is so low that I can almost not even hear her. She grasps onto the counter on either side of the stove and doesn't move.

I chew on my lip and watch her, wait on her to give me some indication as to what she's thinking. She gives me nothing to go on. "Need anything?"

"No, Crew," she said, whirling around on her heel, "I don't." Her eyes are on fire, blazing with some emotion I can't pinpoint. "And I didn't need my tires changed this morning either."

"What are ya talkin' about?" I ask, feigning ignorance. I know she's gonna bust my balls, but it's not like I had a choice. I couldn't take the chance of her driving Everleigh around on the roads with bald tires.

"So you didn't send Will to my office this morning to get my car? Nice of him to ask for my keys in front of half the department. Well played. How was I supposed to argue with him without causing a damn scene?"

I shrug.

"Stop doing this. *Please.* I can take care of myself."

We have a standoff, our gazes having the conversation neither of us wants to have. She's telling me she's not the little girl I once knew. But it's not like I don't know that. She might've grown up, but the woman she's turned into has a helluva lot to do with the decisions *I've* made.

There are so many mother fucking things I'd change if I could figure out how.

But I can't.

"How is she?" I ask with a nod to the living room, trying to change the topic.

Julia sighs, exhaustion flashing across her face. "She's okay. She wasn't feeling good this morning, so she stayed with Mrs. Bennett."

"Olivia? The neighbor lady?"

"Yes. She seems better tonight, though." She gives me a hint of a smile before her gaze drops to the floor. "Ever loves when you come by, so I'm sure she'll be happy tonight. *She* likes you."

The insinuation smacks me hard in the chest.

"She's been missing him a lot lately."

Our conversations don't normally make it to discussing Gage unless we're already arguing. The fact that she just brought it up shocks me and I'm not comfortable with it. I don't know how to take it. I feel my jaw pulse with frustration and scramble to change the subject again. "Why is it so chilly in here?"

Julia's smile disappears and she tugs her sweatshirt nervously. "I didn't know it was."

"How can you possibly not know?" I start to the thermostat across the room when she clears her throat.

"The heater isn't working right. I asked my landlord to come by and look at it earlier this week."

"And he hasn't been here yet?" I shoot her a look and she shakes her head. "He'll be here tonight." I dig my cell out of my pocket.

"Crew, don't. *Please*. The last time you called my landlord he was a complete jerk to me for a couple of months. I just got on good terms with him again."

I scroll through my contacts list, looking for his name.

"Crew . . ." I know her doe-eyes are pleading with me. I also know if I look up at her, I'll be somewhat inclined to give in.

So I don't.

Chapter TWO

JULIA

I FINISH ANOTHER fairytale about a poor princess meeting a benevolent prince. They are Everleigh's favorite bedtime stories. When I think back to my childhood, they were mine, too. I used to lay at night with my eyes squeezed shut, creating stories of a knight in shining armor coming to my rescue. He'd climb up the trellis outside my bedroom and knock four times on my window. I'm not sure why four times, but it always was. I'd rush to the glass and he'd guide me down and away from my parents.

Those stories are what little girl's dreams are made of. What they have yet to learn is when you have those dreams in the palm of your hand and they unravel, they are what nightmares are made of, too.

I plop the book beside me on Everleigh's sheets. She's beside me, fresh out of the bath, smelling like strawberry bubblegum. She snuggles in close to my side with the stuffed monkey she's had since she was born curled up against her. I brush her hair out of her face and she smiles up at me.

"Do you think I could meet a prince one day, Mommy? And I could be a beautiful princess and live in a castle?"

I smile at her innocence.

She'll learn soon enough.

"You never know."

"Are there real princes?" Her eyes glisten with excitement and I wish I could keep her this age, keep her this unaffected, forever.

"Sure, baby. There are still princes in the world."

"Like Daddy?"

My heart swells in my chest as she brings him up, not an uncommon topic for bedtime. There's something about the peace of the routine, the quiet moments right before sleep, which has her uttering Gage's name. She's been talking about him a lot recently, more than just at bedtime. Although I'm not sure why, I do know that regardless of the fact that it's been almost two years, it still never fails to bring tears to my eyes. Just the thought of my husband creates a cascade of emotions I've just *barely* learned how to deal with.

"Yes, sweetheart. Like your daddy."

"Do you think Butterscotch is in heaven with him?"

I nod. "Yes. I bet Daddy is taking care of your kitty." I smile at my little girl and force a swallow past the lump in my throat. "And I bet he's watching you right now and probably thinks you should be going to sleep."

She smiles at me, her crooked grin looking so much like Gage it physically hurts. "And Uncle Crew? He's a prince, too?"

It takes everything I have not to roll my eyes.

She looks down, playing with her monkey and I hope she's done with the topic.

Besides me, Crew is all the family she has. Her paternal grandparents are dead and mine will never know her. They're too in love with the bottom of bottles to ever trust around my daughter. I know the pain of seeing them get sloshed, the torment of listening to their verbal assaults, the burning sensation of having your arm squeezed so tightly you have to make up stories as to how you got the large bruises for weeks after. They haven't seen Ever since the week she was born. When they call on the rare occasion, it's because they need something. It's never because they want to see me or my daughter. Sometimes I wonder if they even remember Everleigh exists.

I watch her eyes get heavy and I yawn, snuggling down beside her and resting my head on the top of hers. My gaze catches the framed photo of Gage and Crew on her dresser.

They look so young and carefree in the picture, their gorgeous faces grinning at the camera. I remember snapping the picture after a long day at the beach and listening to my friends behind me whisper about how they could be models.

The picture is faded, the victim of many years and even more spilled

SACRIFICE

sippy cups. Everleigh used to push it around the house in her little shopping cart. When she outgrew that, she demanded it be in her room.

Her princes.

I can't help but grin as I close my eyes and remember seeing the two of them for the first time.

"They're coming over here," Lauren said, elbowing me in the ribs.

I felt my cheeks heat. I quickly turned my back to the boys walking our way. I spotted them earlier as we walked around Castle Island, an island in South Boston. We spent the day there, hanging out by the water, having picnics, and just generally being teenagers. I couldn't stop sneaking glances at them all day.

They weren't like most boys I'd seen before. Their bodies were harder, leaner, more chiseled than other guys our age. It wasn't just their physical appearance that captured my attention, but rather the way they carried themselves. They walked around the park with total confidence, like they weren't scared of anything.

My group of friends began to giggle and I turned my head slowly to see the two of them standing in front of us.

"Hey, girls," one of them said.

I snuck a quick look, breathing in the musk of their cologne which was tinged with the smell of sweat from the hot sun.

The one talking was slightly taller than the other. His hair was a darker shade of brown, his eyes a brighter blue. His grin was kind, his eyes wise.

The other one had close-cropped hair, a set of brooding eyes, and a cocky smile that made my knees turn to goo. His eyes glimmered and a shiver danced over my flesh, despite the heat.

"I'm Gage Gentry." The taller one smiled and I couldn't help but look away. They were too much. Just their proximity made me feel powerless, yet powerful at the same time. I'd never felt that way before . . . and I liked it.

"This is my brother, Crew."

Crew smiled at my friends and their giggling went up a few notches. I didn't giggle. I could barely catch my breath.

I gave him a quick once-over. He pressed his full lips together in an undeniable smirk. He raised his eyebrows as if to challenge me somehow.

That was a challenge I never should have taken.

"And Uncle Crew?" my daughter sleepily asks again.

I fight myself from telling my five-year-old daughter that her beloved Uncle Crew is anything but a prince. He's the exact opposite of Gage in almost every way. I know this firsthand.

Although they shared blue eyes and inherent charisma, Crew Gentry is reckless and hedonistic. He goes after the things he wants the moment he wants them with little regard to how it might affect him five years down the road or the people around him today. And even though he was once named the best up-and-coming fighter in the country, he's never fought for the right things.

Ever sighs and I feel my spirits sink a little with hers. I know she loves him. I know that, in his own way, Crew loves her, too. But I also know that with him, that just isn't always enough.

"Your uncle a prince?" I scoff. "Something like that, baby girl. You should go to sleep."

"I'll try. My belly still hurts though."

I kiss her on the forehead and pull the comforter up over our bodies. We lie quietly, the silence pierced by shouting from the street below.

I begin to hum a Maroon 5 song that we heard earlier in an attempt to drown out the commotion. I hate her living in this shitty apartment, but it was all I could afford since Gage's death. I wish we could've stayed in the little two-bedroom we bought in Cambridge, but with no life insurance to go on, it was impossible.

I never thought I'd be so attached to something materialistic, especially since I've never had anything in my life. But that little house was the one place that held our memories, a time capsule of our lives together. The house was the first thing we purchased together, the place we brought Everleigh home from the hospital. We shared kisses under the mistletoe in the hallway, Ramen dinners in the kitchen by tea-candle light.

With every box I packed when we moved, I added a bucketful of tears. Would the memories fade as time went on? Would I forget the smell of his cologne in the bathroom? Would I forget the dip in the mattress on his side of the bed? Leaving that house felt like I was leaving Gage behind. The only thing that got me through that time was knowing I had two connections to him—Everleigh and my wedding ring. And when I left the little house on Impala Avenue for the last time, I left a piece of my soul there.

Ever's breath evens out beside me. I should get up and clean the kitchen, but I don't. I know the sink is full and dinner is still sitting out, but I don't get up. My body is worn out and objects as soon as I even think about moving. Working all day at One Boston Place as a secretary and then a couple of weekly night shifts at Ficht's Diner has left me drained. But draining my energy into those dead end jobs is the only way we can continue to live, even in this crappy apartment.

The softness of the bed cushions my weary body and my eyes flutter closed. I see Gage's face immediately, as I always do. He's laughing, the timbre of his voice comforting me.

My body heats like it's wrapped in a warm blanket. I breathe and enjoy the memories of a time when my life was exactly what I wanted it to be. It was a time when my life was more than I ever imagined it *could* be. I felt safe. Loved. Prioritized. Gage made that possible.

The highlight reel begins—images of him swimming in the sea, cooking his favorite cheesecake recipe that he never shared with me, coming in from work in his suit and tie—all flash like fireworks.

I drift to sleep, my arms holding my precious daughter and my heart holding precious memories.

CREW

THE DOOR CHIMES as I open it. The interior of Shenanigan's, my favorite bar in Boston, is poorly lit and I give it a second to let my eyes focus. Jordyn, the redhead that works most nights, looks up as she pours a drink. She smiles and winks before turning her attention back to her job.

Green lights hang haphazardly along the glass behind the bar, Kings of Leon humming through the speakers. This place is laid back and out of the way, a hole-in-the-wall as far as bars go in this city. My kind of place.

I take a deep breath, letting the warm, thick air soothe my lungs. The handful of miles I ran before coming here really worked me over. Running five or six miles every day is an unshakable habit I've formed after years of training. It centers me, lets my mind take a break from the fuckery that is typically on auto-pilot streaming through my consciousness. It takes me back to a better time, to a time when my future was ahead of me. When anything was possible.

The clink of pool balls cracks through the small brick building. Mixed with the salty smell, it strangely puts me at ease. I make my way through the patrons and spot Will at our usual table in the corner. It's a little quieter back there and we have an unobstructed view of the television in the corner. I can still see the door and who's coming in and out from that position.

Will brings a bottle of some Craft beer to his lips, his arm tucked around a girl I've never seen before. Adam and Dane, a couple of kids in here all the time, are standing at the table, roaring with laughter at something Will said.

I nod at them. They're two guys I *can* tolerate because we have a lot in common. I don't know this because they told me. I know this because I can see it in their eyes. They have respect, the natural ability to know when to shut the fuck up.

You don't get that from a babysitter. You get that from the street. It's not something that's taught. It's something that's learned. You figure out how to navigate the world most people never see by keeping quiet and watching, listening, knowing who is in control of a situation.

"Heya, Crew." Will smirks while Blondie next to him plants drunken kisses on his neck, letting her tongue trail up his five-clock shadow.

"What's up?" I pull out a chair and sit. Blondie looks my way, eye-fucking me through her lashes.

"Hey, Crew," Adam says, feeling me out. "You watching the Pampa-Reyes fight this weekend?"

I shrug. Fighting is my passion . . . or it was. Sometimes I can watch it and enjoy it and sometimes it just tastes too fucking bitter.

"My money's on Pampa," Will says, his eyes going wide at something Blondie is doing to him beneath the table. He is a huge fighting fan and always knows what's going on in the fighting world. Back in the day, Will fought alongside Gage and me a time or two. He wasn't bad, but he had a mom and dad at home to report back to. That kept him out of a lot of trouble.

"Yeah, I agree," Dane says. "Pampa's ground game is strong. If he takes Reyes to the mats, I don't think he has a chance."

"Pampa will never get to the mats. Reyes will knock him out first." I grab a cigarette out of Will's pack on the table and work it over with my fingers. "Even if he doesn't, Reyes *needs* this more. He lost his last two fights in close decisions."

"Reyes, huh?" Another guy whose name I don't know appears beside Adam. "They both suck ass. Whoever wins will fight Davidson and that motherfucker is a beast."

Will and Adam both look at me immediately, waiting for my reaction.

"Easy there, Slick," Dane warns. "You're 'bout to step in a pile of shit and you don't even know it."

"That's fact as fuck," Will laughs.

Black, spiky hair and a diamond stud in one ear, Slick grins like he's just seen two whales fuck. This goofball is why I normally try to avoid the masses—too many motherfuckers runnin' around with a Hit-Me face that I *can't* tolerate.

I probably should've stayed home tonight, but I had to find something to occupy my mind. I dreamed about Gage last night. We were sitting on the beach, watching the waves come in, and he told me I needed to get my shit together. I laughed because it was something my brother always said to me. He took a handful of sand and let it run slowly through his fingers. I watched the grains drop onto the pile of shells below.

"Get your shit together, little brother. It's time you man the fuck up. I'm counting on you."

I'd woken up in a cold sweat. I didn't dream about Gage much, not at all, really. But there was something about the way he said it, the clarity of his voice, the intensity of his gaze that left me feeling light in my stomach all day. I couldn't shake it. I couldn't get the sound of his voice out of my brain.

I look up at Slick. He grins and tosses an arm around the shoulder of Dane. Dane sidesteps him and watches me nervously.

"Davidson? Is he a fighter?" I twirl the cigarette in my hand before flicking it to the table.

Slick snorts. "*Is he a fighter?* Are you serious? He's the baddest motherfucker I've seen in a *long* time. He doesn't just win fights, he wins by *murder*. They're saying he's unbeatable and I believe it."

I tilt my head and look up at him, chuckling.

"You're probably gonna want to shut your suck," Will smirks.

"My suck?"

"You know, your suck. Your mouth. Your *cock sucker,*" Will laughs. "Don't let your mouth buy something your ass can't pay for."

"Dude, do you even know who this is?" Adam interjects, shaking his head. "This is Crew Gentry, man. The only man to beat your so-called 'baddest motherfucker.'"

"No shit? You're Crew Gentry?" He laughs. "I thought you'd be bigger."

"Now is the time Slick stops running his suck and buys Crew Gentry a beer," I smile, a warning buried just under the surface.

His face pales. "Hey! Whatever Gentry's drinking is on me!" he shouts to Jordyn. He turns back and looks me up and down. "Yeah. I can see it now. You're still solid as a rock. Man, I still can't believe you didn't go Pro-"

"Yeah, I know," I say, cutting him off. I've been over it so many times in my head, not even counting the times I've spent reliving it through my trainers, or the doctors, or random guys that think they know something about fighting. I don't need to hear his jibberish about what went wrong or right or what-the-fuck-ever. It's obvious this punk knows nothing about fighting besides getting a foot up his ass.

"Let's go grab a drink," Dane says to Slick, clearly reading me like the street smart kid I know him to be. He can sense what's about to happen if Slick doesn't shut the fuck up. "Come on."

"I want to talk to Crew." Slick starts to pull a chair to the table and I look away.

"Trust me, man," Dane says, "no, you don't. Let's go."

I know Slick's watching me, but I don't look up. I don't want to chit-chat. Hell, I don't even wanna humor this guy. This kid's going to some Ivy League college, Mommy and Daddy payin' the bill. He's a silver spoon-fed asshole that thinks he knows something and I'm not interested in playing nice.

"Nice to meet ya," Slick says. He follows Adam to the front of the bar. I hear him whisper something about a legend and I roll my eyes.

"I was thinking you weren't gonna show," Will says, drawing my attention back to him. He turns his head from Blondie, but she grabs the sides of his face to turn him towards her.

"You wanna get out of here?" Blondie coos, her tone soft like she's talking to a baby.

"Where have ya been?" he asks me, ignoring her.

"Hey. Let's get out of here. Didn't you hear me? Why aren't you answering me, baby?"

Will looks at her out of the corner of his eye. "I was just lettin' you know this conversation was over."

She gasps. "Are you serious right now?"

"Why don't you run along?" He scoots his chair away from hers like she didn't just have her hand down his pants.

I laugh at his antics, par for the course for my cousin. If this chick thought she was going to call the shots with Will, she was wrong.

"Asshole," she mutters. She stands and walks away, leaving a trail of cheap perfume behind.

I accept a cold bottle of Sam Adams from Jordyn. She asks if I need anything else and I laugh, knowing exactly what she means. This girl can suck a dick like a porn star.

"I'll let you know," I tell her. She squeezes my shoulder before heading back to the bar.

"Who's Blondie?" I ask Will.

"I don't fucking know. I sat down. She sat down and grabbed my cock. I didn't really need her name for that, now did I?"

Will runs a hand through his short, brown hair, his eyes lit up in amusement. He smiles wide, his perfectly straight teeth shining.

"Where have you been, anyway? I expected you to show up an hour ago."

"I had to drop off some stuff at Julia's."

"I've told ya I can do that anytime you need me to," he says with a smirk.

"She's not exactly the type of girl that someone sitting in a shitty bar, drinking Craft beer could handle. And all bullshit aside, if I ever find out you said something to her, I *will* break your face."

"Dude, when I went to get her car yesterday, she about fuckin' castrated me. She was wicked pissed. I could see it through her pretty little smile."

"That's Julia."

"How can something so small be so ferocious?"

My chest stills because I know exactly how that's possible. When you're left alone, your world ripped from under you, you start fighting.

Fighting to live.

Fighting to survive.

Fighting to protect what little you have left.

This I know all too well.

Chapter THREE

JULIA

THE WIND ZIPS by, sending a ripple of goosebumps beneath my thin jacket. The sun is setting behind us as we head up the walkway to our building. Everleigh jumps into a puddle, splashing water all over my shoes.

"Quit, Ever," I say, tugging on her hand. "I don't have on rubber boots like you."

"Sorry, Mommy," she says, wrinkling her nose at me.

She's too cute to be mad at.

I hold her hand tightly and ignore the catcalls from the idiots across the street. The step in front of our building has been fixed. I wince, hoping Crew didn't piss off the landlord.

Again.

I rip the late notice off the door and fumble with the lock, trying to get the key to twist so we can get inside. Ever squeezes my hand and I know she senses my uneasiness. This morning, before we left the house, she came into the bathroom for me to braid her hair. I'd been crying. I played it off as allergies and she didn't ask questions but I knew she didn't believe me. I hated lying to her, but I didn't want to tell her it was the anniversary of her daddy's death and I was missing him so much I could barely breathe.

The lock finally turns, so I push open the door and guide Everleigh inside. "Take your coat and backpack to your room, okay? I'll get something started for dinner."

"Okay, Mommy. Can I color a little while in my room?"

"Sure, baby girl. That's fine."

She dashes down the hallway. I kick off my wet shoes and head into the kitchen. I wish I had a glass of wine to help me relax, but that certainly wasn't in the budget. I can't think of the last time I had a couple of extra dollars to splurge on something that wasn't absolutely necessary.

I toss the landlord's note on the table, a reminder my rent is two days overdue. I'll have to call him tomorrow and let him know I'll pay him this week. I try not to think too much about it; late notices and overdue bills are a part of this new life I live as a single mother. And if I think about it too much today on top of everything else, I'll probably have a meltdown and I can't afford to break down at this point either.

I grab some ground beef out of the refrigerator and start to make spaghetti. Everleigh loves it, so I hope that she'll eat it. Her appetite hasn't been good lately and it worries me. She's so tiny to begin with. Our neighbor, Olivia, says she'll eat when she's hungry, but I'll feel better when she's eating again.

I try to keep my mind focused on the task at hand, but it's hard. I've struggled all day to keep busy, to immerse myself in whatever I was doing, playing mental games with myself so I don't think about the date.

The knob to the old gas stove falls off, landing in the middle of the pan. I just stare at it, wondering how in the hell I got *here*.

I snort, remembering *exactly* how I got *here* . . .

"I gotta go get Crew," Gage said, shaking my shoulders gently.

I opened my eyes, trying to pull my brain out of the dream I'd been having. "Crew? What? What time is it?"

"It's after 2. He called me from Southie. He got into a fight tonight and I need to go pick him up at the police station."

"You're kidding me."

"I wish I was, babe. I'll be back in a little bit."

I sat up, still half asleep. "Gage, Crew has to stop this. I know he's having a hard time right now, but he can't keep acting like this."

"I agree. I told him yesterday that it's time to grow up. I get he's pissed off. I know his entire life plan has changed over the last few months, but he's lucky he's not in a wheelchair." Gage sighed, the burden of worrying about his brother weighing him down. "He'll come around. He'll realize eventually he was just given a second chance at life. He's strong and he's smart. He just needs *a little bit of time to figure things out."*

"He's had time, Gage. He does this every time things get hard for him. With me, your mom, now wrestling. He can't just do what he wants and forget his actions have an effect on other people!"

He roughed his hand over his head. "He's my brother, Jules."

I knew he was gonna go and I knew I couldn't demand he didn't. It was Crew, after all. And as much as I wanted to slap the shit out of him, I loved him in my own way. But still, I tried. "I don't want you to go. The roads are bad." I looked into his eyes and, as usual, was putty in his hands.

"Babe." His voice was soft, his eyes clear as a bell. A ghost of a smile touched his lips.

I kissed him for what I thought was the last time that night.

But it proved to be the last time I'd kiss Gage for the rest of my life.

The ringing of my cell startles me. I clear my throat and feel my heart thumping wildly in my chest. I take a deep breath and pluck the knob out of the pan, placing it on a paper towel. I check the caller ID.

Crew.

I send it to voicemail and put a pot of water on to boil.

When the ringing starts again, I don't even look. I just let it ring because I know it's him and I can't handle dealing with him. Not today.

After Gage died, I tried to push Crew out of my life altogether. Seeing him, talking to him, looking into his eyes was like salt into a wound that was already seeping in so many ways. But in typical Crew fashion, he did what he wanted.

I had done everything short of a restraining order to convince him to stay away. No matter how much I yelled, cried, pleaded—he was unrelenting.

There is a part of me that appreciates his help. There's some peace in my shaky world just knowing that, frustratingly or not, he will be by sometime each week. That Ever and I aren't alone. As much as I roll my eyes and act all offended, a little part of me sighs in relief when he knocks on the door.

But he can never know this.

At the end of the day, it's his fault I'm a widow. He's the one that couldn't get his shit straight and got my husband, his brother, killed. He's the reason all of our lives were turned upside down and he doesn't deserve to have it skated over.

Even more, we both know there will be a point when he will walk away. If there's one thing Crew Gentry does, it's that. His calling card is walking away when things get hard or something else looks more interesting.

That weighs heavily on my mind. I want Ever to have a relationship with him; she loves him to pieces. But I'm *terrified* of the day he lets her down and I have to see her heart break. I know how painful that is.

"Hello?" His voice wrapped around me through the telephone, the deep timbre making me relax. I've needed to hear his voice for days, but haven't been able to get in touch with him.

"Crew! Finally! How are you?"

"Hey, Jules." I can hear his grin through the line. I flop back on my bed, ignoring my father shouting from the room below.

"How are you?" I ask again. "How's wrestling? How's Minnesota?"

The line gets muffled before he clears his throat. "It's good. Real good, actually. It's a different life here. So much going on all the time."

"I bet. I've missed you so much."

"I miss ya, too. How are things back there?"

"Good. School's good. I get through each day by thinking this is my last year and I can come be with you. And every day is a day closer to Christmas break and you coming home. Just three weeks now. I haven't seen you in so long."

The line goes quiet and a sinking feeling creeps through me. "I'm really excited to see you, Crew."

Crew blows out a breath. "Look, Jules. I know I was supposed to come home, but I don't think I can. There's so much going on up here and I wouldn't be able to stay home more than a few days, anyway . . ."

I grab a jar of pasta sauce and focus on dinner. I jump at the sound of someone banging on the door. I walk to the curtain and peek outside. I'm not at all surprised at what I see. Or whom.

His hands are stuck in the front pockets of his jeans, his Carhartt hanging open. A white thermal shirt is stretched down the length of his torso. His shoulders are hunched over as he scans the area, taking everything in.

With a heavy sigh, I twist the lock and open the door. "What?" I ask, one hand on my hip.

His face is solemn, his eyes hesitant. I know this day is as hard for him as it is for me, but it should be. He's the reason we are both miserable. But as much as I want to slam the door in his face, *I don't*.

"Can I come in?" He shoves his hands deeper into his pockets.

"Why?"

He looks at me and holds my gaze. I feel my throat burn. I roll my eyes, lest he see my moment of sympathy, and head to the kitchen. I leave the door open behind me. When I hear it close, I don't look back, not sure if he's followed me inside or took off. And I don't really know which I prefer.

I head to the stove and grab the pasta and strain it.

"You all right?"

I shrug but keep my back to him. "Am I supposed to be?"

A chair is pulled back and the coins in his pocket jingle as he sits down. "I just . . . I wanted to check on ya today."

"Well, I'm fine. Making dinner, as you can see."

"Didn't you see I called?"

"I did."

"Why didn't you answer?"

I set the spoon down and close my eyes for a minute. I've avoided this conversation like the plague all day, a situation I don't want to think about, never mind discuss. A situation I'm in because of *him*. And here he sits, not taking the hint, showing up at my house even though I'm obviously not taking his calls and forcing me to discuss it. *Fuck him.* "Because I don't really have anything to say to ya, Crew. Another year has gone by without Gage. Thank you for that."

He looks at the floor and suddenly I feel terrible. He closes his eyes, wincing as my words, filled with such poison, hit him full on. Any other day and he would've just spouted off something back. He would've smirked, said something cocky, and walked out. But today's not just any other day.

"Crew—"

"Nah, Jules. Don't apologize."

"I shouldn't have said that."

"I said not to apologize." He's watching me carefully, his eyes somber. He's apologized to me so many times and I've never accepted it. Now he won't accept mine. Not sure what to do, I turn back to the stove. I fiddle with the knob, trying to get it back in place while feeling his eyes on me.

"Remember when I talked him into surfing with me on the 4th of July that year?" His voice is soft and if I wasn't listening for it, I might not have even heard it. "And he swore a shark was circling his board?"

I nod. I remember that day. Gage was standing on his board, shouting at Crew to get out of the water. Crew just sat on his and laughed and then paddled to Gage and they floated in together. Later, we had a bonfire on the beach. We told stories over marshmallows until the sun nearly came back up again.

I feel wetness touch my eyes and I bat my eyelashes to try to keep the tears from falling.

"Damn it, Julia. I'm so sorry. If I could switch places with him, I would."

I turn to look at him and he's watching me, the same pain that's downright killing me inside is also written all over his face. It's enough to send the tears down my cheeks, hot against my skin.

We look at each other and something sweeps across his face. It's a look of resolution, I think, like he's just decided something. All I know is that for the first time since the funeral, he reaches for me.

He stands and takes the few steps to me. "Come here," he says and pulls me against him. My body stiffens momentarily, thrown off by the gesture as much as the physical contact. As my cheek hits his chest, I come to my senses.

"No," I breathe, trying to shove him away. "Don't touch me."

My voice betrays me and cracks. His shirt is a haze in front of me, the tears blurring everything together. I press both palms against his chest and push with everything I have. "Get back, Crew."

He doesn't say anything. Instead, he wraps both his arms around me and pulls me in so tightly that I can't get free.

"Crew!" I say as everything inside me erupts. I try to pull away, hitting him in the sides where my hands are pinned. "Stop it!"

It sounds more like a plea than a command, the words broken with my sobs. I need to get away. I know that. But it feels good to be comforted, to have someone to lean on. And I can't get away, anyway. That in itself feels good, to not have to think about whether I should or shouldn't let him be nice to me for once.

Crew has never broken the barrier between us since Gage's death and I'm not sure what's changed. It feels strange having his arms around me, but so familiar at the same time. I can't force myself to pull away, even though a voice inside me tells me to. My emotions are so mixed that I can't think straight.

I lay my head against the rough material of his jacket and give into the tears that have battled me all day. I try to keep it reigned in, trying to keep it from splitting me into two. I knew I'd have this moment eventually, but I thought it would be in the bath after Everleigh went to bed. Having this moment *with Crew* almost makes it worse.

We stand there, in the middle of my kitchen, and mourn together—the loss of someone we both loved. For a moment, I set aside blame and fault and what could've been and just allow myself to grieve with the only person alive that feels the pain I feel.

I allow him to hold me while I release the emotion in waves. He just holds me tight and doesn't say a word, rubbing my back with one of his calloused hands.

Finally, I sniffle back the tears and clear my throat, wiping my eyes with my hands before pulling away.

He opens his mouth to say something when Everleigh rushes into the room and throws herself at him. I take a step back and he bends down and hugs her, his eyes trained on me as she babbles on about her day. I use the opportunity to grab a tissue and dry my face before my daughter sees.

"Are you staying for dinner, Uncle Crew?" Ever asks, zipping Crew's jacket up and down. "Mommy is making spaghetti. She's a good spaghetti maker!"

I keep my face blank, not sure what I want. Half of me wants him to leave, to have to suffer the night alone. To give me the space I need to miss my husband.

The other half wants him to stay, to have another person sitting at the table. For a distraction for Ever . . . and maybe for me.

Crew kisses Everleigh on the head and stands, clearing his throat. The lines on his face deepen and he drops his gaze slowly to my daughter. "No, monkey. I'm going to head on out now."

"No . . . um . . . you know . . . if you want to stay for dinner, that's fine."

"Yay!" Everleigh cheers, doing a little dance.

A surprised look flickers across his face at my invitation. I've never invited him for dinner. I've never really even been nice to him in so long. I don't even know why I am now. Maybe my defenses are down.

Maybe time is starting to heal wounds.

I'm not sure but I don't have the mental wherewithal to think about it.

"Sit by me!" Ever says, tugging his hands towards the table. "Please! Maybe Mommy will make us some orange Kool-Aid. I only get that on special nights, but if you're here, it's like a special night! Right, Mommy?"

She looks at me and beams. I glance quickly to Crew and think I see him press something into Ever's palm.

He forces a swallow, his Adam's apple bobbing. Darkness passes

SACRIFICE

through his eyes and he gives me a hollow smile.

"I'm sorry, monkey. I can't stay tonight. Maybe some other time."

He reaches for the late notice on the table and sticks it in his pocket.

"Crew—" I begin, but he silences me with a look I can't quite read. He shakes his head and leaves as quickly as he came.

Chapter FOUR

CREW

I HAD TO *get out of there.*

My head is a fucking mess and I know, from experience, this isn't a problem liquor is going to solve. I'm not sure running will fix it either, but it seems like the healthier alternative.

Leaving them tonight was harder than normal. Typically, I just head out and do my shit. I manage to block them out and focus on whatever, *whoever,* is in front of me. But not tonight. Tonight carries so many memories, regrets, what-if's that it's almost unbearable. Just seeing that look in her eye, like I'm the thief that stole her world, just about broke me down.

I start down the sidewalk, tugging my hood over my head. I loosen my shoulders, twisting from side-to-side as my feet find a rhythm on the pavement.

A cold burst of air rattles my lungs. I pick an object in the distance and jog towards it.

I plow forward, waiting for the numbness I normally feel by this point settle over me. But it doesn't come. I run faster, the pace causing acid to pump through my veins. I relish it. The physical pain should block out everything else.

I focus on my breathing, *in, out,* and turn a corner towards the park. *'Another year has gone by without Gage. Thank you for that.'*

As much as I hate it, she's right. Gage flipping his car two years ago tonight on an icy bridge *was* my fucking fault. I've drank myself nearly to death over it, I've cried over it, I've tried to escape the guilt in every way possible. I've fucked whores, I've hit punching bags, I've ran so many miles that you could probably lap the whole fucking planet with my steps. But none of it changes anything.

I fucked up. My life is what it is because of me. No one else.

Losing Gage, especially the way we did, was a wake up call. A little too late, no doubt about it, but I realized that I had to change. Yeah, I could be pissed about losing everything that mattered to me: my girl to my brother, my mom to cancer, my career to a fucked up neck injury at the hands of a prick, and my brother because I couldn't keep my temper. I had to stop using these things as an excuse; I had to quit making things worse . . . and I needed to try to make things right with the one other person that was also affected by nearly every one of my mistakes.

I often wonder what her life would be like if she hadn't met me that day or if Gage would've gotten to her first. I wonder if she would be happier.

I exhale as I turn a corner. I'll never know the answers to those questions, but I do know that I need to try to make sure her life isn't completely fucked because of me. I owe that to her. To Gage. To Ever. To myself.

The steps come easier. My breathing regulates and I feel my body falling into rhythm. If only my mind would follow suit, everything would be golden.

But it won't.

The chill in the air reminds me of early summer in Minnesota. I think back to my days at the University there, back to the days when wrestling was my life.

Wake up, practice, hit a few classes, practice, then maybe find a girl to spend a couple of hours with. Repeat.

It was such a wild time in my life, so many things changed so quickly. I was a poor kid from Dorchester one minute, a collegiate champion the next. A kid destined to work the docks and then destined to be the 'next big thing' in Mixed Martial Arts.

It was surreal and exciting. I woke up in March of my freshman year and realized I had barely talked to anyone from Boston since I left the summer before. I hopped a plane and went home to more than I ever expected.

"Crew, look, I didn't mean for this to happen."

I stood in the doorway of Gage's bedroom, wondering what the fuck was going on.

My brother with my *girl.*

Her dark hair was spread across his lap, a smile on her face by Gage. I'd never felt so torn, furious and destroyed at the same time.

"I can't believe what I'm fucking seeing here." I took a step back to prevent myself from ripping my brother into shreds, thinking maybe there was a logical explanation. I hoped to God there was some sort of easy way to explain this off without it being what I thought, what I feared, it was.

"Her parents got shit-faced one night a couple of months ago and she called me in hysterics—"

"They didn't touch her, did they?" My stomach tightened immediately. I'd kill the crazy fuckers if they hurt her. I looked at Jules, sitting on his bed, her eyes wide. "Did they hurt you?"

"She was okay, more or less, but she had to get outta there," Gage said, watching me start to lose my shit.

"So what? You thought you'd fuck her to console her?" I bellowed.

"Crew . . ." Julia whimpered. She buried her face in her hands and my stomach sank right along with it.

"Come on, Crew," Gage sighed. "Don't even act like that."

I looked at him like he was fucking crazy. How in the hell could he have the nerve to tell me, 'Don't even act like that'? After seeing him with my girl? Fuck. That.

My anger rose, boiling white-hot, and I had to find an outlet. I slammed my fist through the door, the wood splintering around my knuckle. "Why in the fuck did no one bother to tell me this shit? Huh? Didn't any fucking one of you think maybe I'd like to know that you two were together?"

I paced a circle, not sure how I walked back into a world I didn't seem to even know. How so many things, so many important fucking things, were different. How my life as I remembered it wasn't even my life anymore.

"I did call you, Crew," Julia whispered, "but you didn't answer."

"I'm not that fucking hard to get a hold of."

"I called you all the time for months!" she cried. "You never answered and when you did, you had like 5 minutes to spend talking to me. I stopped bothering to call you months ago. Months, Crew. Did you even realize that? How was I even supposed to know you cared?"

Gage put his arms around her and I wanted to flip him across the fucking room. Brother or not, the sight of my girl touching someone else was more than I could take.

"What were we supposed to do? Just sit here and wait on you to bless us

with your presence? Should I have asked her dad to wait to beat the fuck out of her until you could take a second to answer your phone?" Gage asked.

"No!" I shouted, glaring at him. "I just—"

Gage stood from the bed, standing straight, getting the most of the three inches of height he had on me. "What did you want us to do?"

"Well, fucking my girl wasn't on the list, asshole."

"It's not like we decided to just be together. It just happened."

"What? You tripped and your cock fell inside her?"

"Crew!" Julia's mouth hung open in shock.

"It's not like we planned this," Gage sighed. "I brought her here that night and she was afraid to go home. For fuck's sake, Crew, she'd stayed here so many times before that—"

"With me!" I took a step towards him, my blood boiling.

"Crew! Stop this!" Julia said, springing off the bed. "Just stop! You two are brothers. I won't come between you. This is all my fault . . ."

"No, it isn't," Gage said. "We didn't plan on being together."

"You've said that already."

"Then let me fucking talk and I won't have to repeat myself. You've moved on. You jetted outta here and did your thing and didn't bother to call, send a fucking letter, let anyone know what was going on with you. But you expect her to be sitting here waiting on you to pop in?" He ran his hands through his hair. "I was going to tell you before you came home, but I didn't know you were coming."

"It was a surprise," I snorted. "Surprise fucking surprise. Joke's on me."

"She's going to move on, Crew. It's not fair to ask her not to. And if you don't like that it's with me, then I'll figure that out. You're my blood." His shoulders sagged. "But I love her. She needs someone to protect her, to give her the entire world. That girl deserves it and, by God, I want to try to give it to her."

I turn into a park and drop to the ground, busting out a set of Burpees.

The more I thought about it, the more I realized he was right. I couldn't give her those things. I didn't *want* to give her those things. Maybe I had at one point, but I didn't anymore. There were too many things going on in my life to think about settling down or worrying about someone else.

But I loved Julia. And when I got past the anger of seeing her with someone else, my fucking brother, I realized something else—he was the only one I wanted her with. I knew Gage. He was the only guy that would ever be close to being good enough for her. He'd be loyal to her, do everything he promised her. I knew this because he'd always done that for me.

Growing up in Dorchester, the streets were a hard place to be. With a mother working two jobs, Gage and I learned to scrap real quick. It was the survival of the fittest and we always had each other's back. He never failed to back me up, regardless of what mess I'd gotten myself in.

And I got myself in some messes.

At some point, fighting became an acquired taste, a way to feel alive. Fighting was something I was good at, something that got me credibility and respect on the streets. If Coach D'Amato hadn't broken up one of my fights in the parking lot of Shaw's Supermarket when I was fourteen and introduced me to wrestling, God knows what would've happened.

Gage was more of a peacekeeper by nature. He'd avoid situations that he knew would probably result in a fight and try to keep everyone happy. My brother could bang with the best of them—he had one of the best right hands I've ever seen, but fighting wasn't his go-to like it was mine. He'd fight if he had to, but he tried to keep us out of trouble.

But trouble was something that just found me.

And the stress of that probably helped kill my mother.

And it's what definitely killed by brother.

I sprint the last few yards home, feeling my lungs burn, my legs like lead. It's a beautiful distraction from the ache in my mind.

JULIA

I WRAP THE sweater tighter around my body and pick up the ink pen. I can hear the people milling about outside. Their music is up entirely too high for this time of night.

I go through the numbers one last time. I will pay the rent in the morning for the next month and the minimum due on my credit card. That will leave me with just enough to cover groceries for the next week if I am careful.

I write out the rent check and then watch everything go blurry behind a wall of tears.

I hate this feeling.

I despise having to worry how I am going to feed my child. I hate the balancing game of "What can I afford this week?" I hate the hope I have that Crew will be by with a little charity because I don't want to need it. I don't want to depend on anyone, least of all *him*.

SACRIFICE

The tears run freely down my face and I struggle to keep it from becoming a full-blown sob. I'm so tired. I'm exhausted in every way, in ways I didn't know existed a couple of years ago.

When I married Gage, we never had a lot, but he always made sure we had *enough*. He was smart and worked hard. I worked until I had Ever and then he didn't want me working, so he picked up a second job at night.

And then he died.

The loss of him was pure devastation on every level.

Not only did I lose my best friend and the best person I'd ever known, but my entire life changed, too. It took our savings and then some to bury him and even then it wasn't a burial I wanted him to have. He deserved so much more than I was able to give him. He gave me the world and I gave him a small stone headstone with a name and date on it. "Loving husband and father" is written in a canned script on his stone and, while this is true, it feels like such a slap in his face to have something so simple when he was so much more than that.

I think back to our house in Cambridge and the cozy little life we had. How I'd have dinner made and he'd come home every single day and kiss me like it was the first time he'd ever kissed me.

The music outside drifts through the kitchen door, the vulgar lyrics shaking me out of my memory. I look around the room. The paint is peeling above the sink and the wallpaper is drooping in the corner. Reality hits me like a tidal wave, swamping me with more despair than I've felt in a long time.

An envelope with blue writing catches my attention, having hidden itself beneath another piece of paper. I pull it out and find the phone bill.

I let my head fall forward after checking the due date.

Gas or groceries next week?

I rest my head on the edge of the table, letting my tears fall to the floor. I feel like I'm failing at everything. I work as hard as I can for what? To barely make it? If it was just me, that would be one thing. But it's not. I have Ever to take care of, to be a role model for. What am I showing her about life? That you just grin and bear it? Because I'm certainly not showing her how to conquer anything. I'm not showing her what a family feels like. I'm not giving her the traditions I wanted, the full, warm life I always dreamed my child would have. The life I didn't.

I'm tired of fighting it. It would feel so, so good to let go and just *fall*. To give up and cry, to throw in the proverbial towel. Because without

Gage, what's the use?

And then I see her in her little green Tinkerbell nightgown, clutching her tattered monkey in both arms. She's watching me fall apart, her eyes wide, her hair a mess.

"Mommy? You okay?"

I wipe my eyes, trying to rid them of any signs that I've been crying. I feel guilty for even allowing myself to think the things that crept into my mind. She's the best thing that's ever happened to me. Hard or not, I will keep fighting for her.

"Yeah, baby. Come here," I sniffle.

She walks to me and presses her face into my side. "Why are you sad?"

"I'm not. I'm just tired. Why are you awake?" I brush the hair off her forehead and she feels a touch warm.

"My belly hurts."

I look at the bills on the table again and sigh.

"Let's get you to bed and see how you feel in the morning, all right?"

"I wish Daddy was here," she says softly. "Or at least Uncle Crew."

All I can do is nod.

Chapter FIVE

JULIA

THE EARLY EVENING sun trickles through the curtains. I pull them open and bathe the living room in light. The sun always makes things seem better, but today was a good day anyway. Ever was voted Student of the Week and came home with a ton of stories from school. I found a new position that just opened at work. I'm in a prime position to apply for it and brought the papers home to look through. It would be more money and more benefits, two things I can definitely use.

"Mommy?" Ever asks from behind me. "Can we go to the park? Please?"

I start to say no, but I remember I have to work most of the rest of the week at night at Ficht's Diner. "You know what, baby girl? That's a good idea."

"Yay!" she squeals, jumping up and down.

"Go get your rubber boots on and a jacket."

I swipe the rent check I made out the night before off the kitchen table and meet my daughter by the front door after getting ready. We head outside and head towards the park.

"Look at that red bird!" Ever says, pointing in the tree above. "Mrs. Bennett says that's a visitor from heaven! I bet it's Daddy or Butterscotch!"

I laugh. "It might be. Or it might be a sign of spring. It's a good thing either way, right?"

She ignores me, craning her head to watch the bird as we turn the corner.

My good mood is suddenly soured at the sight of a dark blue Ford F-150 truck parked next to the business office of our apartment complex.

I growl under my breath and pick up my pace, trying not to drag Ever behind me. The closer we get, the angrier I become.

We are nearly there when Crew walks out. His head is down, his hands stuck into the pockets of his jeans. A gray thermal shirt is hanging loose and a burgundy hat with a golden "M" sits low on his head.

"Uncle Crew!" Ever squeals, dropping my hand and running to him.

His head jerks up. He glances up at me and grimaces, then looks back to my daughter. He bends down on one knee as she leaps into his arms, a grin tugging at his lips as she buries her head into his chest.

"Fancy seeing you here," I say, unamused, as I reach them.

"Yeah," he says, his tone equally cool. "Imagine finding you here."

"Seriously, Crew. What are you doing?"

Ever looks between us, grabbing Crew's hand.

"What do you think I'm doing here?"

"I'm bringing the rent by now, so it better not be what I think."

"No sense. It's paid."

"Ugh. You didn't have to do that. Just . . . go back in and get it. I'll take my check in there."

Ever tugs on her uncle's hand, but looks at me. "What's wrong, Mommy?"

Crew picks her up and sits her on his shoulders. Ever looks down at me from her perch, her little blue eyes sparkling.

"Mommy's being hard-headed, Ever. No worries." His eyes never leave mine, his face blank.

"Damn it, Crew," I whisper low enough that only he can hear.

"No, she's not," Ever says, "she's taking me to the park. Will you come with us?"

"Uncle Crew doesn't want to come to the park. He has things to do, baby girl." I reach for her. "Come on. Let's go."

"No," she pouts, pulling away from me. "I want Uncle Crew to come, too. Don't be a hard head, Mommy."

"Ever—" I warn, but Crew cuts me off.

"Ah, monkey. I shouldn't have said that." He watches me, his eyes twinkling now, too. Mischief has always made him happy. "Mommy's just trying to make sure I have things to occupy my time."

I glare at him and he laughs.

"Like what?" Everleigh asks, confused.

"Like not giving me papers that she finds."

"Like the one on the door?"

I groan, praying my daughter keeps her mouth shut.

Crew nods his head slowly, a shit-eating grin sliding across his face. "What do you know about a note on the door, Ever?"

"Mommy got a note on the door yesterday. And she said she couldn't let you see it. I heard her."

"Everleigh, be quiet."

"Did she now?" Crew lifts my daughter off his shoulders and cradles her in his arms.

"Tell ya what, monkey. I'll give you a dollar every time you tell me you see one of those little notes on the door. Okay?"

"Okay," she says. She looks up at him with so much adoration it almost slays me.

"Crew . . ."

He looks up as I say his name. We watch each other, feeling each other out. I want to argue with him, make him go get his money so I can pay my own rent. But I can't, partly because there's something in his eye that makes the words not come out of my mouth. And partly because, as much as I hate to admit it, it will take a huge burden off me.

I sigh and look towards the sky.

"Can we go to the park now?" Ever asks.

I look down at her. She looks so small laying there in Crew's arms. Only yesterday, it seems, she was a baby.

"Come on." I reach for her.

Crew twists her up to his shoulders in one smooth movement. His grin reminds me of the Crew I used to know a long time ago.

"Wanna ride on my shoulders, monkey?"

Ever cheers, raising her arms over her head in victory.

"You don't have to do this." I take a step away from him. I'm not sure what he's doing. Crew doesn't go places with us.

I don't let him.

He doesn't want to.

"I believe I was invited by my niece to go to the park. If you don't want to come, go home," he shrugs and starts off down the sidewalk.

I watch them walk away, my daughter's giggles flowing through the air like a pretty song. It warms my heart. But the sight of Crew with her doesn't.

The closer they get will just cause her to get hurt more in the end. He's in a prime position to make her life better or destroy her and I can't control the way it falls.

I force my feet to move and follow them down the sidewalk and into the park. Crew squats down and lets Ever climb off. She makes a beeline to an open swing and pushes off, pumping her little legs as her hair flies behind her. Crew leans against a tree nearby and watches.

I take a deep breath and stand next to him. The corner of his lips twitch as he waits for me to break the ice.

He can wait all day.

I cross my arms over my chest and ignore him.

He chuckles and pushes away from the tree, standing straight. He isn't as tall as Gage, but still a number of inches taller than me.

"If you don't wanna be here, I'll bring her home." He doesn't look at me when he speaks, just watches Ever play.

"Of course I want to be here. I can't understand why you want to be though."

He lets his teeth graze over his bottom lip. He turns to face me. His eyes are narrowed and I can tell he's thinking about how to reply.

"It's time I man up."

I bite back a laugh. "Really? You just woke up this morning and thought, 'Ah, I think I'll take my niece to the park today?'"

"Something like that."

"We've made it without you coming to the park with us for a long time. Feel free to leave."

He turns to me and I take a step back. I've seen this look a number of times and I know by the way his eyes have darkened, he's itching for an argument.

"Why do you act like this, Jules?"

"Like what?"

"Like a bitch."

I gasp, not used to hearing him talk like that to me. "Crew!"

"Well," he says, spreading his arms out to his sides, "tell me how else to explain it."

"Like a mother protecting her child!"

"Protecting her from what?"

"*You.*"

"From *me?* You're fucking kidding me, right?"

I shrug and look back to the playground. Ever is now digging in the sandbox with a little girl her age. The sand is wet and getting stuck in her hair. She's giggling and building a sandcastle; I'll be picking sand out of the washer for a week.

"You do realize that everything I do is to protect her, right?" His tone demands attention. Without thinking, my eyes are drawn back to him. He's watching me, his face passive, but his eyes on fire. "My life would be a lot easier if I just worked and fucked and drank a little."

I glare at him to cover the touch of hurt his words cause. I know we weigh him down and that's embarrassing, even though I don't ask him to help us. "Yeah, well, that's really worked out for you so far."

His mouth drops, then clenches. "What I do isn't for you, *Jules*. It's for Gage, for Ever."

He may as well have filled my veins with poison because my breath is stolen. I know he's right but hearing it come from his mouth, that nothing he does is for *me,* is like ripping open an old wound. Although I've tried to convince myself otherwise, he's never done anything *for me*. There's no denying it now.

"Noted," I say with as much detachment as I can.

I turn away from him as Ever grabs my hand. She's covered in sand and the shimmer in her eye from earlier is gone. "I'm ready to go, Mommy. I'm sleepy."

I take her hand and start to the entrance of the park, trying to focus on the next few things I need to do so I don't think about what Crew has just said. I've never mattered to anyone but Gage. I don't know why I thought that Crew's assistance might have been to help me, but it clearly isn't. I don't know why it makes a difference, but it does.

"Will you carry me?" Ever walks slowly, her boots full of sand.

Suddenly, she's swept up into a pair of gray thermal-covered arms. She nuzzles into Crew's chest and he kisses the top of her head.

He looks at me, his brows furrowed. "I didn't mean that," he says roughly. He turns without a beat and starts towards my house and doesn't look back.

Chapter SIX

JULIA

THE HUM OF the copier a few cubicles down is soothing in a weird way. It's been going non-stop this morning and it drowns out the chatter between the people behind the cubicle walls surrounding me. I like it. My fingers fly over the keys on my computer, my mind blissfully unaware of the distractions that usually drive me a little crazy.

I work solidly for the first part of the day. When I look back up, it's lunchtime. I pull out my lunch bag from beneath my desk and retrieve the peanut butter and jelly sandwich, an apple, and a bottle of water.

"What I do isn't for you, Jules."

Crew's voice from yesterday barrels through my mind, knocking the wind out of me. It stings as badly today as it did when he said it, like a punch below the belt.

Suddenly, I'm not hungry. I gather my lunch and put it back in my bag. I hear my officemates. They're discussing their lunch at a fancy restaurant downtown, trying to decide what to have. The merits between the clam chowder and the bacon cheeseburger are weighed with a seriousness that astounds me. When I hear one of the women discuss fitting into her new Dior dress, I remember why I wouldn't go to lunch with them even if I could afford it.

I glance down at the brown dress that I wear on an every-other-week rotation and my I-wear-them-with-everything-brown heels. I brush a stray hair out of my eyes, feeling unkempt, even though I know I'm totally presentable.

I start back to work, but the speaker on my phone buzzes. "Ms. Gentry? I have Calhoun Elementary on the line for you."

The line rings. "Hello?"

"Mrs. Gentry?"

"Yes."

"This is the school nurse. Everleigh was sent to the office not feeling well. She has a slight fever and I think you should come pick her up."

I rub my forehead with my fingertips. She seemed to be feeling better this morning. She slept the whole way home from the park last night and then practically through her bath. I was hoping we'd turned a corner when she woke up bright-eyed.

"I'll be there as soon as I can."

JULIA

RAIN ROLLS ON my windshield and my wipers can barely keep up. I take a quick glance at Everleigh in the backseat. Her little head rests in a seemingly uncomfortable position, fast asleep. Her lips are pursed together like they do when she's asleep. It reminds me of when she was little and used to take a pacifier. She'd continue to suck long after it had fallen out of her mouth.

I wish I could take her home and tuck her into bed. I need a cup of coffee and some time to process everything the doctor said.

My hands tremble as I hold the steering wheel. I flip up the heat, but down deep, I know I'm not shaking because I'm cold.

I take another quick glance at her before pulling up to the curb beside Olivia's. I grab the umbrella off the floorboard and get out. The rain pelts the canvas of the shield so loudly that I wonder if there isn't ice mixed in with it. I reach in and unbuckle Ever and try to zip her coat back up. I maneuver her over my shoulder as best I can and whisk her to the front porch.

Luckily, Olivia sees us coming through the open curtain and lets us in right away.

"Get in here. It's pouring," she says, holding the door open. I rush past her and close the umbrella, shivering. She takes it from me and helps get Ever's coat and boots off. "Just lay her on the sofa."

I place Ever on the couch and she snuggles into the pillows. Olivia grabs a blanket out of the closet and I tuck it in around her.

I kiss her forehead and stand back up, looking into the hazel eyes of my neighbor. She wipes a hand through her brown hair and smiles hesitantly at me, clearly concerned.

"Want a cup of coffee, sweetheart?"

My stomach recoils, threatening to expel the cereal I had for breakfast, the only thing I've eaten today.

"Not really."

She gives me a motherly look and I know I'm going to get a cup anyway. She's not going to let me out of here without talking. I know she's worried about what the doctor said because Ever is like a grandchild to Olivia. They bonded on our first day in the neighborhood. She showed up with a basket of cleaning supplies and asked how she could help. I told her we'd be fine. She smiled, talked with Ever a little bit, and then started helping me unpack. She's been around every day since.

"I just . . ." My voice trails off as I watch my beautiful daughter sleeping peacefully. I don't know what to say and I certainly don't want to voice my deepest fears in front of Everleigh.

She crooks her finger for me to follow. We enter the kitchen and she pours me a cup of coffee. "I want to know what the doctor said."

I try to take a sip, but I can't get anything past the lump in my throat. My hands shake. Olivia watches me closely before taking the cup and placing it back on the counter.

"They said they aren't really sure what's going on with her. There's a little lump in her belly, where she's been complaining about it hurting. They said it could be nothing and that I shouldn't worry about it just yet, but we have to go back in the morning for some tests."

"What are they looking for?"

"I'm not sure, really. They just said to bring her to the Children's Hospital tomorrow morning. They named off a slew of things but then said it could be nothing, too." I sniffle and fight back the fear that's threatening to take over. "I'm so scared, Olivia. What if they find something? What if something is really wrong with her? What if—"

She pulls me in for a hug, holding me to her tightly for a long time. The warmth of her arms, the feeling of her caring about us, relieves me just a bit.

The rain is pounding on the windows and the sky is getting dark. I pull back and look at her crinkled face.

"I know it's hard, but try not to make yourself sick over this," she says, pulling away.

"I'm trying. But you know how it is . . ." The mere thought of something happening to my little girl is more than I can take. I know they said not to worry and I know it's probably nothing, but I can't *not* worry.

"I do. When my son was born, they thought something was wrong with him. Scariest time of my life, bar none. But look at him now. He's a healthy man with a beautiful wife and daughter. Things aren't always as bad as they seem, Julia."

"I hope not. She's all I have."

Olivia gives me a sad smile and instead of making me feel better, I feel worse.

"How did Ever react?" she asks.

"She doesn't really know anything. She knows she's not feeling good and we're going to have more tests. She just thinks she has the flu or something, I think. No sense in worrying her."

"Smart. I think we just keep her in the dark for as long as possible. I'm still betting it's nothing. You've had your share of grief. Surely you wouldn't be given something else to fight through. That just wouldn't be fair."

"No kidding," I sigh. "I need to go get ready. I missed a half a day at the office today and I'll miss all day tomorrow. I'm going to need these shifts at Ficht's. I'll pick her up when I get off."

I give Olivia a smile and make my way to the door. I stop by the sofa and press my lips against Everleigh's forehead. My lips linger against her skin and I say a silent prayer.

Dear God, I need you to fix this. She's my baby girl. I'm so scared. Just . . . fix this, please.

Chapter SEVEN

JULIA

"I SHOULDN'T HAVE asked Uncle Crew for crayons." Ever's voice is a little more than a whisper and I have to bend closer to her to even hear it. Her eyes flutter shut, her hands pressing against the hospital gown that's way too big for her little frame.

I brush a lock of hair out of her eyes. "Why's that, baby girl?"

She doesn't answer for a second and I think she's fallen asleep.

"Because I should've asked for red slippers."

"You just got a pair of Tinkerbell house slippers for Christmas."

She nods, her head barely moving against the bed. "Yeah, but I need ones like Dorothy in *The Wizard of Oz*. I could click them together and go home."

"We'll be out of here soon. Just try to rest."

"Can't you just pick me up and take me home?" She flutters her lids open. Her eyes are a grayish blue, not the sparkling ones I'm used to seeing. They begin to glisten with unshed tears. It terrifies me. It guts me. I can't stand to see her cry. "You're my mommy anyway. They can't say no. Take me home, *please*."

"We're just waiting on the doctor to come in and tell us we can go. I'm sorry, baby girl. We can't leave yet but we will soon."

She seems to believe me and closes her eyes again, drifting off to sleep. I watch her for a minute before collapsing back into the stiff vinyl chair. It's entirely uncomfortable and the springs are starting to make my back ache.

We've been here all day. We arrived before seven this morning. They carted Ever off right away and the poor thing has undergone test after test, including a biopsy that I wasn't prepared for. A *biopsy* seems so much . . . scarier . . . than saying *test*.

I glance at the wall and it's almost seven in the evening.

Twelve long hours.

It's too much for me and I was just waiting. I can't imagine how she feels.

My leg is bouncing, my hands folding and unfolding on my lap. I need to get back to work, try to pick up some extra shifts at some point this week to make up for being gone so much already. I bury my head in my hands

I need to walk or talk to someone. I haven't talked to anyone besides the hospital staff and Mrs. Ficht to tell her I wouldn't be in for my shift today. But I have no one to call, nowhere to go. Olivia is volunteering at the nursing home and Crew's the only other person that would be remotely interested in what's going on. But who knows where he is or what he's doing.

I release a sigh and try to settle back into the chair. Just as I find a semi-comfortable spot, the door creaks open.

A nurse that I haven't seen before and Dr. Perkins come in. The nurse smiles in a pacifying way. I don't know whether to believe it to be real or that she feels sorry for me. It seems to say, *'I'm going to smile really nice so the bomb we drop doesn't sting quite as bad.'*

"Hi, Julia," Dr. Perkins says. "This is Macie. She just came on duty."

We exchange hellos. She does that smiley thing again and it makes me nervous.

"I want to talk to you a minute in my office. Macie needs to take Everleigh's vitals, so she'll stay with her while we're gone. Is that all right?"

An overwhelming sensation, a swell from deep inside my body, rises unexpectedly and I think I'm going to pass out. I don't know if it's what he said or the way he said it, but I'm almost certain this won't be all right at all.

Chapter EIGHT

CREW

I SWALLOW THE last bite of the hamburger I made for dinner. I hate cooking, but years of watching my diet to make weight for wrestling, coupled with the four years at University of Minnesota studying sports nutrition, had a way of creating habits. You can't eat shit and stay fit.

It's been raining and the gray skies are fucking with my head. I feel myself slipping into a depression. I struggle to stay focused on the things ahead of me and the very few things that make me happy.

I think back to the park with Ever. She ran immediately to the swings, leaving Jules and me behind.

"Come on, Gage! Let's do something else. I brought a ball!"

Gage looked at me, pumping his legs back and forth, going as high as he could. "Nah."

"Come on," I begged, looking around for someone else to play with. Gage would play on the swings all day. They bored me. "I'm going to look for something else to do."

"Ya gotta stay here, Crew. We have to stay together."

I head into the bathroom and look at myself in the mirror. My body is lean and looks strong. It feels strong. It looks and feels like it's capable of doing what I'm sure I was born to do—fight.

I miss wrestling. Fighting is in my blood, wrapped tightly into my DNA. To be told I could never wrestle again was like a bomb being dropped on my life.

"Crew, if you continue wrestling, if you forgo our warnings, you could very well end up paralyzed. That's a best case scenario. Your spinal column simply cannot handle another blow like you just sustained. You're lucky you're young or you wouldn't be walking out of here this time."

The recovery wasn't as bad as they said it was going to be. Besides a shooting pain here and there across the top portion of my back, I didn't feel that injured. Physically, anyway. Mentally, I was devastated. Emotionally, I was destroyed.

Wrestling had been my life and fighting was my future. A contract with the North American Fighting League, or NAFL, was dangled in front of me and then ripped away after my injury. Wrestling had given me all the hope in the world. It was my Golden Ticket, my way out. It had taken absofuckinglutely everything that mattered to me away, too.

When I took the job on the docks, the doctors said that I shouldn't. That loading and lifting would strain my neck and back, but I really didn't give a fuck. All I knew then was I couldn't do what I loved. I just needed a paycheck until I checked out. Fuck it.

Week after week, month after month, I didn't feel like I was deteriorating. Not once. While that's a good thing, it's also a bad one. It makes me wonder, seriously fucking consider, that I could've still fought. That the doctors were wrong. That I gave up my dreams for nothing.

My hand is on the knob to the shower when my phone buzzes in my pocket. I take it out and look at the screen.

"Hey, Jordyn."

"Hi. "

"What's up?"

"Where are you?"

"Why?"

I hear her tap her tongue off the roof of her mouth and I grin. I know that sound.

"Well, I figured you were getting off work and I happen to be in your neighborhood. I was gonna stop by."

"People don't just *stop by*. Is that a nice way of saying you need fucked?"

Jordyn and I have a very *friendly* relationship. Neither of us are looking for anything serious and we both like to fuck. It works. It's refreshingly uncomplicated.

"Well, when you put it so eloquently . . ." she says, a door closing in the background. "I'm coming up the walkway now."

I end the call and head towards the door. When I open it, she's standing there, looking at her phone. She glances up at me, smiles and walks in, her fingers still flying across the screen.

I grab the phone out of her hand before she knows what happens.

"Hey!" she says, reaching for it. I hold it up where she can't reach it. The screen says "Elijah." I laugh, recognizing the guy's name from the bar. I type out a quick text while she watches, one hand on her hip.

Elijah—I'm about to get fucked. I'll message you later.

"Give me my phone, asshole." Her voice has a hint of a laugh and I know she's not really pissed. Not that I give a damn if she is.

I drop her phone into her purse and toss it unceremoniously to the floor. She looks hot as fuck in a white top that shows off her chest and a pair of black yoga pants.

I back her against the wall and grab her face in my hands. My body is charged, lit up. This wasn't the release I thought I was going to get tonight, but it's sure as fuck better than push-ups. Not to mention, I'm fucking horny as hell. She's not mine and I don't want her to be, but knowing that she was messaging another guy when she walked in here gives me something to prove. A reason to up my game, show her what's up.

I kiss her roughly, my lips pressing firmly against hers. She grabs the back of my head and works her fingers through my hair. I bite down on her bottom lip, making her half yelp and half moan. The sound goes straight to my cock.

I put one hand under her ass and lift her. She wraps her legs around my waist and I carry her into the dining area. She moans against my lips, my tongue invading her mouth, taking ownership of it.

The table still has my breakfast dishes on it. I swipe them off to the other side and sit her on the tabletop. I take a step back and catch my breath.

"Take your shirt off," I order.

She grabs the hemline and wastes little time removing the fabric, leaving her full breasts on display in a black lacy bra. The round tops of her tits makes my dick rock fucking solid.

I slip a condom out of my wallet and unbutton my pants. She lays back, her eyes wild, the scent of her vanilla perfume everywhere. I roll the condom over myself and then grab the waistband of her pants and yank them off her body, her shoes hitting the floor first.

SACRIFICE

My fingertips dig into her hips as I scoot her to the end of the table, guiding myself towards her opening. The initial contact has her panting, her back arched, waiting for the next move.

I slide into her with one thrust, her pussy so wet for me that it makes my cock throb. I groan as she constricts around my length. I pause when I hit the back, slide out, and then push inside her as far as it'll go.

She moans again, her voice filling the room as I fill her. I slide in and out, driving into her harder with each push. I take one hand and pull down the lace covering her tits and watch them spring free. I palm one, squeezing it as I continue to bounce in and out of her sweet little pussy.

She yells my name, arching her back, tossing her head back and forth.

The table is rocking, the dishes clamoring on the other side. One plate slips off the end and smashes onto the floor. The destruction just amplifies the animalistic feeling in the room.

I press down on her stomach, preventing her from lifting off the table. I slam into her, the angle allowing me to get even deeper inside.

She begins to moan and I know that means she's getting close. I rub her nipple a few times before returning my hand to her hip. I drive into her over and over, watching her tits rock on top of her creamy white skin.

Her phone begins to ring from her purse in the hallway. Knowing it's probably Elijah or some other fucker from the bar, I decide to tattoo my fucking name in the back of her pussy.

"Crew!" she yells as I slam into her, holding her down. "Fuck!"

Her muscles tighten and pulse around me as she shouts nonsense. I find my release at the same time, holding her still, my hands holding her down.

She lies back lifelessly onto the table. Our jagged breaths fill the air, the smell of sex overpowering her perfume.

I scoop her back up with one arm and kiss her mouth hard. She moans against my lips and I know she can barely move.

I love it.

I pull out and head to the bathroom, removing the condom and tossing it in the trash. She comes in behind me with her clothes in her hand. She puts them back on and runs her fingers through her hair.

"How'd that feel?" I ask.

"Like I got fucked." She smiles before leaving me standing in the bathroom alone. I hear her rummaging around in the hallway. "See ya, Crew," she calls out before the door opens and shuts.

And that's why I like her.

I jump in the shower, letting the hot water do its thing. I soap up and just finish rinsing when I hear the phone ring. I slide the curtain open and see Julia's name on the screen.

My gut twists. There's something about her calling that makes me uneasy, because she never calls me. *Never.* I flip the water off and wrap a towel around me quickly.

"Hello?" I ask, wiping the fog off the mirror.

The line is silent.

"Jules? You there?"

I think I hear her crying, but I can't be sure.

"Julia? What's going on?"

"Crew . . ." Her voice, barely above a whisper, drifts quietly through the phone.

I can hear it in her voice. Something is very fucking wrong.

Chapter NINE

JULIA

I CLICK THE phone off and literally drop it onto the coffee table. It lands with a thud that sounds like it's in another world. I sit with my arms on my knees and try to remember what the doctors said. I struggle to remember his words.

I feel like I should be reacting to this, but I can't. I feel like the tears are there but they won't come.

My breath comes out staggered. I hear the air going in and out of my mouth, the only noise in the room, and it sounds like I'm shivering. I look to my hands and see them shaking.

"Mrs. Gentry, your daughter has cancer."

I squeeze my eyes shut as the room begins to spin. *Round and round and round.* I raise a hand and touch the top of my head. It feels light, like I've been hit over the head with a board.

I think I'm going to be sick.

There's a knock at the door, but it sounds so far away. I'm not even sure, really, if it's my door. I hear it louder and I know I need to answer it, but I don't. I just sit with my eyes shut and rock back and forth.

I hear Crew calling my name. I vaguely remember calling him.

How long ago was that?

The door bursts open so loudly that it breaks through the haze. I open my eyes and see Crew storm into the room. His eyes are wild, his forehead marred with frustration. He spots me and then scans the room. "Where's Ever?"

My throat feels lined with gauze, thick, and I make myself swallow just so I can speak. But I still can't. Words are impossible now; nothing that I would have to say is anything I want to ever mutter.

Crew takes off through the house, calling Ever's name. I squeeze my eyes shut again, listening to him say it.

What if a time comes when he doesn't have to say it anymore?

I feel my stomach roll, twisting and knotting, churning with bile at the thought.

No! I won't think that way! This is a mistake!

I take a deep breath like I was taught to do when I was pregnant. I fill my lungs with air and blow it out, the air coming out in rickety spurts. The breathing is supposed to calm you, keep you from panicking.

It doesn't work.

"What the fuck, Jules? What's going on?"

He stands next to the sofa, the vein in his temple pulsing. He's looking at me like I'm ready to jump off a cliff.

Maybe I am.

I can't answer his question because I don't know. I don't know what the last couple of days have been about. I know my little girl had a fever and an upset stomach and I took her to the doctor. I know they told me not to worry. I know the bomb that was dropped on my lap today was more than I ever imagined.

It's more than I can take.

I can't comprehend it. I can't believe it. They have to be wrong. They *are* wrong. My beautiful baby girl isn't sick.

She isn't. She can't be.

He moves quickly around the furniture and is in front of me before I can process it. "Jules? Where's Ever?"

"She's . . ." I start, but I can't finish it. As soon as I say something, the dialogue is open and I'll have to tell him all of it. If I can just keep quiet, maybe it won't be real.

"Damn it, Julia." He grabs me, his large hands covering my shoulders completely, and shakes me. "Fucking talk to me!"

I hear the panic start to take over his voice. I want to save him from the panic he's going to feel when I speak. But I can't save anyone right now.

I've never been able to save anyone . . .

SACRIFICE

"She's with Olivia." I feel my bottom lip quiver but I can't stop it as much as I try. My teeth begin to chatter as Crew's hands leave my shoulders.

A shiver tears through me and, for the first time, I feel like I can cry. But the tears still don't come. I will them to, try to blink my eyes and force them over my lids. If I could just cry, I could feel something. I just feel so . . . *numb*. And with the numbness comes a sense of not being able to process what's going on, not being alert enough to make the quick decisions that need to be made.

That *have* to be made.

Life or death decisions.

I know I need to wake up and get out of this fog. I also know that when I do, I can never come back *here*. To this place where I feel a bit protected, a bit cushioned by the haze around me. It's like I'm sitting in a cage of lions and have this bubble around me that has to be popped. As soon as it does, I'm going to be eaten alive.

"She's all right, right?" He kneels in front of me, his hands now on my knees. "Jules? I need you to say something. You're freaking me out here. What in the hell is going on?"

"I don't know what to say."

"You better find the words pretty fucking quick. You never call me and now I'm here and I can't find Ever and you won't talk." He narrows his eyes and I know he's about at his wits end. "Fucking *now*, Jules." His tone is soft, but there's no denying the command.

"We went to the doctor today. She . . ."

And I can't say it. I can't say the words.

I watch his face fall, every muscle dropping in slow motion.

Everything feels like I'm watching it from another vantage point, an out-of-body experience. I see his pupils dilate. I can see the fabric of his shirt bounce with his increased heartbeat. I see the stubble dotting his face move as he clenches his jaw.

He's trying to stay calm. His hands are squeezing my knees and I think it's starting to hurt, but I'm not sure.

"Julia, you're gonna *have* to tell me what's going on."

The sob that I've needed to release, but now needs to stay away so I can speak, creeps up my throat like a thief. I open my mouth and it robs me of words. I take in a shaky breath and feel the tears start to trickle down my cheeks. They scald my skin, leaving trails of hot liquid down my face.

"She . . ." I look from his hands on my legs to his face. "She has cancer."

Crew shudders. His jaw drops, his skin pales. His eyes go wide and he shakes his head. The look on his face is pure disbelief. "She what?"

I only nod, unable to say the words again. I won't. I watch him absorb them, wrestle with the idea I've just tossed onto him in much the same way it was forced onto me earlier. Like a serpent tossed into a room with you. *'Here you go. Deal with this. Good luck. We'll be right outside if you need us.'*

"My God, Jules." He rocks back on his heels and takes off his hat. He smoothes his hands down his face, his mouth falling open as his fingers drag across it. "I . . ."

"We just got home from the hospital a little while ago."

"Is she going to be all right?"

"She has to be," I say, my voice shaking.

"My God." He bows his head before standing. "What do we do now?"

"I don't know. The final lab results aren't in yet, so they haven't put together a treatment plan. They won't do that until they know exactly what they're working with."

"What will they do? Chemo? Fuck, Jules. Can they do that on a little kid? She's a *baby*."

I choke back a sob. He's right. She is a baby. She's just a little baby girl that doesn't deserve this. I want to scream, to tell the universe to mess with someone else for once. I want to wrap my daughter in my arms and run away from this mess. I want to hide her from the ugliness touching her. I want to protect her like a mother should.

"They mentioned that," I say quietly. "They said if it hasn't spread, they might just try to remove it in one piece. We have to wait and see."

"When will they know?"

"On Monday."

His eyes go wide. "We have to wait all weekend? Shouldn't they be doing something now?"

My phone rings and we both jump. He grabs it off the table where I dropped it earlier and hands it to me. I answer without even looking at the screen. "Hello?"

"Everleigh woke up and wants to come home. I told her I'd call—"

"I'll come and get her."

"No, sweetheart. I'll bring her over. You've had a mess of a day."

A lump forms in my throat as I hear her disconnect the call. "That was Olivia," I say to Crew, who's watching me like a hawk. "She's bringing Ever home."

He stands and paces a circle. He pulls his hat over his head and then removes it again. I stand, too, and watch him, feeling completely defeated.

Crew is to the door before I can register the sound of someone knocking. I hear his voice and Olivia's, then the sound of the door closing again. He walks through the room, my daughter lying in his arms. He has her pulled to his chest, her black hair sprawled across his left shoulder.

He presses his lips together and looks at me. I walk to them and touch Ever's cheek. Her eyes are closed but she smiles.

"I'm so sleepy, Mommy."

"Come here and I'll put you to bed." I start to take her out of Crew's arms, but he doesn't relent.

He gives me a sad smile. He squeezes the blanket wrapped around Everleigh.

He clears his throat and says gently, "I'll lay her down. Wash your face and get something to eat."

He takes Ever to her room and I let myself cry again. I want to chase them in there and squeeze my daughter; every minute seems so precious right now. I know as much as I want to, I can't go in there bawling. She's finally resting and needs her strength.

I take a deep breath and remind myself that I don't know anything for sure. The doctor's could be wrong, just like Crew says they were wrong about his injury. And I can't let Everleigh see me like this. It'll scare her and I'm scared enough for both of us. I am her mother, her safe place. I have to be strong for her, carry us both through this.

Somehow.

The bathroom is bright when I flip the light on. I look in the mirror. My eyes are puffy, the whites now a pinkish red. There are bags beneath them and I know they'll only get worse. There's no way I'll be resting anytime soon.

I splash some cool water on my skin and pat it dry with a towel.

"Mrs. Gentry, your daughter's urine tests show very high levels of chemicals called HVA and VMA. The early MRI results also showed a tumor in her abdominal region."

"What does that mean?"

"That means when we take that, coupled with the biopsy results, I'm sorry to tell you that things don't look good. Mrs. Gentry, your daughter has cancer."

My legs go weak, my knees buckling beneath me. I grab the counter and force air into my lungs. I can hear the air wheeze and tremble as it enters and leaves my chest. I scoot back until my legs touch the stool and I collapse onto it, letting it hold me up.

I can't do this. I can't break down.

I hold a breath and blow it slowly.

Panicking won't get us anywhere. I have to get my head on straight. I have to think.

I take a deep breath and rise. I grab an elastic hair tie.

Get yourself together. Keep moving. Sitting is only going to give you time to overthink. You know nothing for sure at this point.

I pile my hair on top of my head and secure it. I rinse my face again, the cool water calming my startled skin. I just need to figure out how to deal with this.

Please, Gage. Help me. You'd know what to do. Tell me. What do I do?

A few minutes later, I pad down the hall to Ever's room. I'm sure Crew's ready to go. I wonder if it was the right thing to do to call him and just heave this onto him. I know he'd want to know, but my reasoning for calling him was more about me than about him. I needed him and that makes me feel guilty.

I peek my head around the corner and stifle a gasp.

Crew is stretched out on Ever's little bed. His feet are hanging off the end, his neck crammed in an awkward angle against the headboard. Ever and her monkey are tucked against his side, her head nestled in the crook of his arm, his cheek is pressed against the top of her head. She has her hand clutched around something yellow.

I cover my mouth with my hand and shut the door softly behind me. I shuffle across the hall to my room and close the door.

I throw myself on my bed and cry myself to sleep.

Chapter TEN

CREW

THE ENGINE OF my truck roars as I gun it through traffic and pull into a spot in the back of the parking lot. It is dark, the sky blacker than normal. Shenanigan's sign is only half-lit and I feel its pain; I feel like I'm only half-conscious right now.

The shock is just starting to wear off.

I woke up around two a.m. in Everleigh's bed. My back was hurting so damn bad but I almost didn't want to get up. I lay there a long time, watching her little chest rise and fall, wondering where in that beautiful little girl the sickness was. She looked so perfect, so beautiful, so *not sick*. It was so hard to believe.

Maybe she's not . . .

I spent the day trying to wrap my brain around what Jules said. My entire body aches, feels like it's been through a war. It has, I guess. A war of emotions. Disbelief, sadness, numbness, and now a blip of anger are beginning to form in the pit of my stomach. It's raw, my spirit bruised, and that only adds to the rage simmering right beneath the surface.

I get out and slam the door behind me, hearing the hinges creak as the door whips closed. There's a couple of guys milling around near the side door to the kitchen, the one I usually come out of when I stay late with Jordyn when she closes. They're dressed all gangster with their baggy jeans and long shirts. They look at me out of the corner of their eyes and

I know I haven't seen them around before.

I walk in the bar and Jordyn gives me a smile. I don't return it. I don't have it in me.

"What's wrong with you?" she calls from behind the bar.

"Bring me a beer."

I don't look her way as I head to the corner table. The place isn't very busy and I'm kind of disappointed. I wanted to blend into the scenery, not have to talk to anyone.

Will is sitting at the table alone, his arms stretched across the neighboring chair, watching television. He looks up and sees me and starts to speak, but stops.

I pull back a chair and sit down.

"What the fuck is wrong with you?" he asks, sitting up. He wraps his hands around the bottle in front of him.

I laugh angrily. Before I can respond, a bottle is plopped in front of me.

"You all right?" Jordyn asks.

"I just asked him that." Will takes a sip, eyeing me carefully.

"I'm fine."

"You're the moodiest son-of-a-bitch I've ever met," she says.

"You don't mind that when you're getting the cock."

"Whatever." She takes off, leaving Will and I alone. I glance over my shoulder and spot Adam and Dane at the bar. They nod but seem to sense my mood and don't get up.

I take a long pull of my beer.

"Is something actually wrong or are you just being an asshole for fun?" Will asks.

"I wish."

"So?"

I lean back and rest my hands on the table. I consider whether to tell him or not. I think about all the things we've been through together. He was a part of so much craziness with Gage and I back in the day. Finally, I say, "Everleigh has cancer."

The sound of that being said out loud is just mind-blowing. It obliterates a piece of the numbing sensation I've felt since finding out. It chips away a chunk of the possibility that maybe it's not real.

Will's eyes grow wide. "What?"

"Yeah."

"Aw, fuck. Man, I'm sorry. I don't know what to say."

"What is there to say?"

He clears his throat and I can see him trying to come to terms with the news. "How's Julia?"

"How do you fuckin' think she is?"

"Dude, just askin.'"

I rub my forehead. I want to rip something in half, make something fucking *feel* what I'm feeling. It's a sensation I haven't felt in a while. It's the same feeling I used to get as I stood on the mat and watched the guy across from me bounce up and down to psyche me out or, more likely, talk himself into actually walking across the mat. It's the same overwhelming urge I'd get when some asshole would run his suck in the neighborhood and Gage wasn't around to talk sense to anyone.

The problem with this is that I *like* this feeling. It's one feeling I know what to do with, how to manipulate. I just don't have anything to be on the receiving end of my rage tonight.

I take another drink. I try to talk sense to myself, remind myself that going ape-shit crazy isn't going to fix jack shit.

"Really, is there anything I can do to help? Shit, you guys have been through more than one family should have to take."

"Do you think if there was something we could do that I wouldn't have already fucking done it?" I grit my teeth, feeling my jaw pulse. "She's all the family I have, Will," I say, washing over the fact that we are, by blood, distant cousins. It's some sort of strange coincidence that our fathers were cousins, but Will's family are not people I've ever known more than acquaintances. "I'll do whatever I have to do to make her okay. *She has to be okay.*"

"Maybe it's something they can just take care of? Can they just, I don't know, kill it? Get it out of her or something?"

"I don't know. Jules is taking her Monday, I think."

"You *think?*"

"Yeah." I spin the bottle between my fingers, watching the liquid slosh inside. "I left last night before we could discuss the rest."

"You didn't call her today?"

"I stayed late. I stayed with Ever for a long time and just let Jules have some time to herself. By the time I left, she was asleep and I didn't want to wake her. Today, I . . ." I shrug again. "I called but I guess Ever was there or something because she didn't seem to want to discuss it."

"Yeah, well, that's understandable."

"I guess. But damn it, Will! I know shit happens in life, but this isn't fucking fair. I was so busted up when I got hurt. I remember thinking, *hell, I remember thinking yesterday!*, how unfair it was. That I should've been fighting." I bite back a laugh. "But that's fucking nothing. This, what's happening to Ever, *this* is unfair."

"I'm sorry, Crew. Really."

I shrug and turn my sights on the television. I don't want to think about this if I can help it. I've mulled it over a million ways and I feel so fucking helpless.

"Now for the news that's dominated the Mixed Martial Arts headlines today," the announcer on the television says. "Raul Reyes defeated Antonio Pampas in the NAFL's Fight 106 last night. The winner of that fight was slated to take on Hunter Davidson in just three months in Boston. It was announced today, Bruce, that Reyes has pulled out of that fight already."

"Yes, Mike, it's a pretty shocking revelation that's shaken the MMA community. Davidson's camp is thirsty, wanting to keep their guy fighting while he's hot. They know the best contenders in his weight class are Reyes and Pampas. With Reyes dropping out, Davidson has effectively cleaned out the division. There's nobody left to challenge him."

"That's true, Bruce. It's yet to be seen what the Davidson camp will do. They've released a statement saying Davidson has nothing to prove against Pampas, since he lost. There's just no one else without going up a weight class."

"Absolutely. He's gone through his opponents like a hot knife to butter. The only time he's been stopped, even as an amateur, was in his last collegiate bout. This is definitely problematic for the Davidson camp."

"Well, we'll have to hang tight and see what they do. We'll be right back after a commercial break."

A highlight reel of Davidson's victories flashes in time with their music. He's flexing, doing back flips off the top of the cage, acting like a complete dumbass.

I turn to look across the table and Will's eyeing me warily. My blood is boiling hot, burning my veins as it pumps through my tension-filled body.

"Is the world trying to piss me off?"

Will leans back, giving me space.

"Why can't that motherfucker die? Why can't he be sick? He's a fucking disease to everyone that's ever fucking met him!" I seethe.

Any attempt at responding by Will is stopped by Adam. He gives me a tight smile, sensing my less-than-stellar mood, and talks to Will. I ignore them both, not in the mood to discuss stupid shit. I hear Adam talking about some chick he's banging and it incenses me. He's worried about some piece of pussy and my five-year-old niece is fighting for her life.

Fuck this.

I scoot back from the table, knocking over the drink menu. I turn down the hall and into the restroom. I kick at a closed stall door. It swings open, letting me know I'm alone.

I growl into the air, the numbness completely fucking gone. I feel the pain, every fucking ounce of it, rip through me like fire through ice.

I smash the paper towel box on the wall until it hangs by one screw. I hit it again and it falls to the floor. I fill the air with a string of profanities, trying to quell the fury ripping me to shreds. I kick the box across the floor, watching it burst open as it hits the opposing wall. I watch it spin in a circle before resting.

My chest heaves, air rushing into my lungs, and I hope when I blow it out, I'll feel a bit calmer.

No luck.

Still infuriated, I burst back through the door, not any more leveled than when I went in.

I look down the hallway towards the front. The chimes ring as the two punks from outside walk in. They're nodding their heads, the ass end of their jeans dragging the ground.

They walk to the bar, the one on the right setting down a brown paper bag. They glance around, talking to one another in whispers. Jordyn talks to them a minute, but doesn't approach the bar the same way she normally does.

The air has changed. The vibe in the room is completely different. I can hear a tick of a bomb that doesn't exist.

Something's off.

Dane and Adam are sitting at a table by the door. As I start towards the bar, they catch my eye, sensing the same thing I am. They start to stand and I motion with my eyes for them to sit back down. "How ya doin'?" I level up to the bar beside one of the guys. He tries to brush me off, his eyes on Jordyn.

"I've seen you on the television," I say. "You're a rapper, aren't you? What's your name? Quarter or something?"

He ignores me and whispers something to his buddy. I act like I lose my balance and fall against the bar, bumping him enough to make him hit the brown bag. He turns to face me, scowling, and the bag opens enough so the nickel-plating inside catches the light.

Pistol. Just like I thought.

I find Jordyn watching us from the well. I shoot her a look and realization washes over her face. I nod subtly and she backs away, fear written all over her.

"Get lost, you little drunk ass bitch." The guy next to me pops his shoulder, trying to toss me off of him like he's gonna intimidate me. I want to laugh so damn bad, but I don't.

Not yet.

"Ah, I love that one song you sing," I murmur, watching them both. Quickly, I scan the area around me. I spot a heavy beer mug to my right and I drag it to me.

"GDFR" by Flo Rida begins to play across the speakers and I chuckle at the irony.

It's going down for real, all right.

The paper bag crinkles as his hand begins to draw the pistol out. His eyes are still fixed on Jordyn.

"Get the money outta the register," his friend barks in an accent I can't place.

The guy beside me removes the gun from the bag. He turns it toward me.

I raise the beer mug and smash it against his wrist. The sound of bones crunching rips through the room. The gun slams against the bar, skids across it and topples over the change collector, clanking against the floor.

He screams like a little girl and tries to pull back. His hand is limp, the bones that normally hold it straight now disjointed.

My left arm flies up under his chin. I take a fist full of his sweatshirt and jerk him across my body. His green sneakers pass by my eyes as he flies a good five feet in the air, slamming through a pub table against the other wall. The weight of his body causes the table to disintegrate and he crashes through it, napkin dispensers and advertisements caving in on top of him.

Movement from his friend catches my attention. His eyes are wide, badass gangster to scared-shitless little boy in an instant. He's moving backwards slowly, glancing around for an exit.

The mug still in my hand, I sit it down. I watch my next opponent back against a stool. As his legs touch the fabric, his eyes go even wider, realizing that there is no escape. Not tonight. Not without being royally fucked up, anyway.

I pull back like I'm gonna punch him in the face and he does what every guy does that's watched too much fighting on TV. He hunkers to his right. Instead of punching him, I yank him towards me. His face is met with my elbow. It slams against him, driving his nose into this skull. I feel the bones cave and splinter under the force.

His head knocks to the side, whole teeth and pieces of others fly from his mouth, rattling down the bar like someone just rolled dice.

I release his shirt, his eyes about ready to bulge out of his head. He stumbles against the stool. His hands are shaking as they grasp at his already-swelling and bloodied mouth.

My senses come back in full force, the silence in the room deafening. I can smell the fear on the guy across from me, the panic in the air as the patrons scattered about watch with bated breath. I've been in this position dozens of times and there's nothing like it.

I do a quick scan of the room. Jordyn is standing in the doorway to the kitchen with her hand over her mouth. Various people are standing around, mouths open. Will is still sitting in his chair, calmly sipping his beer. Our eyes meet and he chuckles, completely amused.

"Yahtzee," Will says, breaking the silence. I shake my head and he laughs, standing up. He walks over to the first guy, who's lifting his head, trying to make sense of what's going on. In one swift movement, Will's boot meets his face. His head falls back against the floor. Will looks at me and shrugs. "Just needed to be sure."

I turn back to the Toothless Wonder. His arms are still out to his sides, the same position they were in after I hit him. He starts to fall forward. I hook my arms under his and catch him before he completely lands against me.

"Was it worth it?" I ask, holding him up. He gurgles his answer, blood trickling down the side of his face. "You came in my fucking bar and scared my favorite bartender. That was a fuck-up." His eyes grow wider, the gurgling picking up pace. I grin. "I think you need to learn a lesson."

He starts to yell but it never has a chance to escape his lips. The top of my head drives into his skull *once, twice, three times,* before I let him go. He melts to the floor.

The bar goes wild. People start shouting and clapping. Jordyn collapses against the wall. I just stand in the middle of the chaos and try to get the adrenaline coursing through my veins to slow down.

Will grabs my shoulder and laughs. "That was more entertainment that I expected to get tonight."

I laugh.

"You'd probably have managed even if I hadn't jumped in. But I couldn't risk it. Wouldn't want you to look like a pussy in front of your fan club," he laughs, nodding to Adam and Dane.

"You're such a fuck-up, Will."

He roars with laughter and heads over to Adam and Dane. They have a cell phone aimed at the guy on the floor.

"Dude! You just got knocked the fuck out by Crew Fucking Gentry! You're gonna be famous," Adam exclaims.

Dane laughs. "I can't believe it. We finally got to see him fight. He's better than I even thought!"

"That was epic. I've never seen anything like that before," Adam says and turns to look at me with a look of amazement on his face. "You're the man!"

Chapter ELEVEN

JULIA

I LINE UP the paint pots across the paper towel that lays down the center of the kitchen table. The top of the table is still a bit sticky from this morning's pancakes, but I don't really care. My mind is too preoccupied to worry, for once, about spilled syrup.

Tomorrow is the day of reckoning. It will make me or break me.

Dear God, please let it be okay.

In a number of hours, which I refuse to count because that will only increase my panic. I have to take Everleigh back to the hospital to get the finalized results from her tests.

I know our lives will change forever once the sun comes up.

I think the worst is not knowing exactly what we're fighting. The possibilities are endless. I caught myself trying to Google things last night, but that only made it worse. I didn't even understand the majority of what I read and what I did read, I wish I hadn't.

A cold chill lazily drifts through my body and I shudder, remembering some of the pictures and language that was used. None of that should be used in the same breath as a child.

My child.

I unscrew the lids and listen to her singing "Sugar" by Maroon 5 in her bedroom. It both breaks and heals my heart. I keep holding on to some thread of hope that's she not really sick. That it's a mistake. My grandma used to say that God would never give you more in a day than you can handle. If that's true, this diagnosis can't be right. Because I can't handle it. Not my baby girl.

I listen to her sing and I know that she's dancing in that goofy way, like me, around her bedroom. I know her smile, the way her right cheek has a hint of a dimple, better than the back of my hand. I'm sure the sparkle in her little eyes is shining and I don't want to dim that. Not now and not ever.

That's why I still haven't told her.

Even though she's just five, the word *cancer* would scare her. I don't want her to worry or be afraid of what's to come. I know the feeling of being little like that and worrying about things that are way bigger than you are. I want her to have something I never did: the feeling of safety, of being loved, of knowing she has someone that will make it all okay one way or the other.

Because, after all, this whole thing might be a mistake.

I set a piece of paper and a watercolor brush by her chair and mine and call for her. She comes in, a wide smile and black circles under her eyes. My heart pulls in my chest. I try to focus on the good, on the grin, but I can't help but see the bad.

"Are we painting?" She climbs up in her seat and brushes her hair off her shoulders.

"I thought maybe it would be fun. We haven't painted in a while."

"I love to paint," she says, dipping her brush into the tub of yellow. She swirls it around on the page. "At school, Mrs. Yeryar painted a tree. And we all put our thumbs in paint and put them on the tree like leaves. You know what I mean?"

I nod, watching her rinse the brush off in the cup of water I placed between us.

"It's really cool. It's like a rainbow tree! Mrs. Yeryar says it's our class family tree. It's very pretty."

"I bet it is."

She sets the paper aside and gets out a fresh sheet. Carefully, she draws a brown line in the middle of the page and then thickens it. Her tongue sticks out the side of her mouth in concentration while she drags her brush out to the sides.

She drops it and dips her thumb into the yellow jar. She presses it very lightly against the paper. I hand her a tissue and she wipes off her thumb, appreciating her work. "Now your turn, Mommy."

SACRIFICE

I dip my thumb into the red paint and press it against the paper on the other side.

Ever studies the paper. She grabs her brush and dips it in the blue paint. Her eyes are narrowed in total concentration as she draws a blue swirl at the top of the page.

"That's Daddy," she says. "I made him a cloud so he's high in the sky and can watch us."

My heart can't take it.

I stand up and kiss the top of her head. I take the sheet and lay it by the stove to dry. My chest has a complete hole gaping in the center of it, like my entire soul is bleeding out. Everyone I've loved in my life have left me or been taken away from me. My daughter should be an exception to the rule.

"I'm going to paint a monkey," Ever says, a laugh in her voice. "That's what Uncle Crew calls me. Maybe I'll give this to him!"

"That would be nice."

Crew.

I haven't seen him since I left him laying in Ever's bed on Friday night. He called yesterday, but Ever was standing next to me and I didn't want to answer his questions in front of her. I was also a little embarrassed about having broken down in front of him and needed a little space between us again.

He hasn't called again or came by.

This is exactly why I have to handle this on my own. Crew's Crew. I know this. He might be here today and gone tomorrow . . .

I know I can't lean on him, but damn it if it didn't feel good to be able to lean on him a little. Every day for the past two years has felt like I'm in a war against the world on my own. The war just escalated to nuclear level. If I let Crew in, it'll set up Ever . . . and I . . . up for a let-down later.

"Where's Uncle Crew?"

Exactly.

"He's probably working, baby girl."

She paints away, her knees tucked up under her. "I bet he misses me."

A knock on the door saves me from having to respond. I walk to it and peek out the window. Hands in his pockets, jacket open, Crew's twisting a toothpick around his lips.

I open the door and step to the side. He walks in without a word or a glance in my direction.

"Uncle Crew!" Ever squeals and runs to him. He picks her up and hugs her tight, looking at me finally with curious eyes.

"How are ya, monkey?" He sounds like he hasn't slept much. His voice is gravelly, even for him. His knuckle is sliced and a little swollen. He catches me looking at it and glares. I glare right back. He better not be coming by here because he's in trouble or because he's leaving town. I swear to God I'll never forgive him. Screw family, screw blood. If he's done or is doing something stupid, that's it. I'm done even entertaining the idea that he can be a part of our lives.

"I'm good! Come see my painting! I painted something for you." She kicks her legs and he lets her down. Ever takes his hand and leads him to the table. He takes the toothpick out of his mouth and sticks it in his pocket.

"That looks like a monkey," he says, sitting at a chair.

"It does, I know! And here's my sunshine." She shoves her yellow painting in his face. He takes it and smiles. "And my tree!" Everleigh look around the kitchen. "Mommy! Where's my tree?"

I snatch it off the counter and hand it to her, crossing my arms in front of me. I hate the feeling of relief I had when I opened the door and saw him. I also hate the start of concern I felt when I saw his hand. These are dangerous things to feel. I need to find the anger I normally have towards him. Anger is easier. Anger is doable.

"This is our family tree. That's me and that's Mommy. And that," she says, pointing to the blue blob at the top, "is Daddy."

Crew laughs, his smile soft as he watches Ever and her excitement.

"Here!" She pushes the green paint towards him. "You put on a green leaf."

"Ah, well, I . . ." He twists in his chair, clearly uncomfortable. "I think it's perfect the way it is."

"No, it isn't. I want you on there, too! *Please!*"

He takes off his jacket and looks to me with pleading eyes. I shrug, not about to help him by getting him out of it. Do I want him on our family tree? Nope. But he can figure it out for himself.

Instead, he takes his thumb and adds a print in bright green to the sheet.

"Yay!" Ever squeals, bringing the sheet back to me. "Will you dry it?"

I nod and take it from her. She runs back to Crew and jumps on his lap. She takes something discreetly from his palm and shoves it in her pocket.

"How ya feeling today?" he asks.

"Ah, good, I guess." She wrinkles her nose. "I had a nightmare last night."

My ears hone in; this is news to me.

"Oh, yeah? What was it about?"

She shrugs and traces the gray lettering on Crew's shirt. "I woke up scared. I had a dream that I woke up and no one was here. Mrs. Bennett was even gone. It was just me and the kid across the street."

"Well, that's crazy, so you know it's not real. There's no way that mommy of yours will ever leave you."

He glances at me and smiles and I can't help but grin back.

"But Daddy left me," she points out.

Crew's smile fades quickly. "Not because he wanted to, monkey. Your daddy loved you more than anyone ever loved anyone."

"I know," she whispers.

"Tell you what," Crew says. "Tomorrow I'll bring you something to help with your bad dreams, okay?"

"You will?"

"I will." He tickles her and she wriggles in his arms, giggling. The sound is beautiful and I close my eyes and just listen. It's interrupted by someone at the door. I walk over and answer it.

"Hi, Julia." Olivia is standing on the porch, holding the hand of her granddaughter, Rory. She looks in the house and sees our visitor. "Hi, Crew."

"Hey."

"I was just checking on you," Olivia says. "I'm running to the grocery and wondered if you need anything."

"Ever! We are going to get ice cream! Do you want to go?" Rory bounces up and down.

Ever dances around me. "Yes! Mommy, can I? Please?"

"Ever, why don't you—"

"It's fine, if she wants to go," Olivia says. "It might do her some good to get out and get some sunshine."

"I don't know." I'm not thrilled at the idea of not being with her today. I want to tuck her against my side and breathe in every second with her. I want to remember every minute of this day and not waste a single moment with her.

"Mommy, please," Everleigh begs. "I never get to see Rory. *Please.*"

"Let her go." Crew's voice is low, his eyes as quiet as his voice. "It'll do you both some good."

He exchanges a look with Olivia and I lean against the counter and sigh. I know it's not right to deny her a fun day because I want to be selfish and keep her with me. She loves Rory and getting ice cream is a big deal for Ever. We don't get to do that very often. Even so, I'm irritated that Crew feels the need to butt into the decision. But at the same time, it comforts me in a strange way.

"Okay, get your jacket," I say with a tight smile.

Ever scampers to her room for her coat and is gone before I know it. I'm left in the kitchen with Crew.

He stretches his long legs out and kicks one boot on top of the other. He looks at me like he doesn't know what to say, so I do the honors.

"You don't have to stay now. Ever's gone." I watch him uncertainly, waiting for him to move.

I expect him to.

I want him to.

But he doesn't.

"How are ya, Jules?"

I feel my body sag with relief that he isn't leaving. It's an unconscious reaction, but one I don't miss. "Okay."

"Can I do anything?"

"Make her better . . ." My voice breaks on the last word and it's like it hits him in the chest. His shoulders drop, the corners of his mouth sliding towards the floor.

He doesn't say anything for a while, just stares at a spot on the wall. I gaze out the window wondering if I just grabbed Ever and took off, if I could outrun my problems.

"She goes in tomorrow, right?" he asks after awhile, his voice as raw.

"Yeah. I have to take her up first thing in the morning."

"Do you want me to come by and take you?"

"No. That's nice of you to offer, but we'll manage."

"I don't mind. I have sick days I can use."

I snort. "That's more than I have."

"You don't have any paid sick days?"

"No. I talked to Human Resources and explained that I don't know what's going to happen. If I miss three more days in the next month they *can* fire me."

His forehead pulls in and he tilts his head. I know he's getting pissed, but there's nothing he can do about this no matter how caveman he goes.

"They did say," I continued, "they won't fire me. They'll leave me on payroll so I have insurance and things, but I won't get paid when I'm not there. I'm just gonna pick up extra shifts at Ficht's, I guess. I don't know. *I just don't know.*"

I feel sick to my stomach. I don't know how I'm going to swing all of this. I was barely making it before, but now . . . There's so much coming at me that I'm dizzy. I just have to prioritize and getting through this week with Everleigh and seeing what we're facing, that has to come first. I'll figure out the rest later.

"You know all you have to do is ask me for help. Tell me what you need."

I roll my eyes. "I'm not asking you to help me."

"Why?"

"Really, Crew?"

"Yeah, fucking really. Why is it so damn wrong for you to ask me for help? Would you rather worry about every little fucking thing than take a little help from me? Am I that bad?"

His face is twisted in a mixture of anger and hurt. He takes a step backwards, like he needs space between us. I see the cut on his knuckle again.

"What happened to your hand?"

"Nothing for you to worry about."

"Fair enough."

We watch each other, a million things being said between our gazes. I know he won't say them out loud, just like I won't. No need to taint the air with more venom. At least I can count on him for that.

"You don't need a ride tomorrow?"

I shake my head. "No. We have to be there early, anyway."

"Will ya at least call me and tell me what they say? It's at Children's, right?"

I nod.

He heads for the door and a bubble of panic twists through me. His hand is on the knob when I say his name.

He turns to face me, the toothpick back in his mouth. He takes it out and says, "Yeah?"

My mouth goes dry. I don't know what I want to say. I don't even know why I called to him. My mind is churning like a storm and I can't seem to anchor in the middle of it.

"Thanks for coming by," I say finally, giving him a true smile for the first time in years.

He nods and gives me a crooked grin, the toothpick going back between his lips. "Let me know if you need anything."

And he's gone.

Chapter TWELVE

CREW

I HATE FUCKING traffic. I honestly believe I was supposed to be born on a farm somewhere in the middle of Illinois or something. I hate the rush to get shit done, the battle to make a left hand turn before getting smashed in the side by some cocksucker in a hybrid.

I pull into the hospital parking garage, pay the attendant, and make my way to an open spot. I find one and pull in as my phone starts to ring.

"Yeah?" I ask, cutting the engine.

"Where the fuck are you?"

I hear the guys shouting in the background, the sound of the cranes squealing in the distance. "At the hospital."

"Ah, so you aren't coming in today?" Will asks.

I grab the bag from the passenger's seat and get out and lock up. "No, I called the boss. I just think . . . you know . . . I should . . ."

"Yeah, I feel ya. Probably a good call. But I wanted to tell ya something."

I can hear a bite of excitement in his voice and that worries me. Will gets excited over stupid shit and I'm not in the mood to hear about how round the chick's tits were the night before.

"I was online this morning and someone uploaded your fight from the bar onto The MMA Forum," Will says. "Dude! You should see yourself. Fuckin' beast!"

"What the hell you talking about?" "The fight Friday night. Remember? Shenanigans? Yahtzee?"

"Someone recorded it and uploaded it?"

"Yeah. Had to be Adam or Dane, I guess. But that's not the point. The point is you look awesome. It's being shared everywhere. That video is going *viral*."

"Why? It's a bar fight," I say blandly. "There are bar fights every day."

He laughs wildly. "That was no bar fight, bro. That was a wicked pissah of a fight! And," he says, pausing for effect, "it's called 'Crew Gentry—The Only Guy To Beat Hunter Davidson.'"

While I'm mildly amused by this, it's not something I really need to happen right now. "Call Adam and tell him to take that shit down."

"Why in the *fuck* would I do that? It's you in all your glory!"

"*Because*," I say, "I barely got out of that with self defense with the police. I don't need it to look like I was showing off or something."

"But—"

"I gotta go, Will. Get it removed. I'll call ya later."

CREW

THE DOOR TO the room number given to me by the nurse is cracked open. I knock once before pushing it slowly. The room is bathed in light from the wall of windows. The television is playing some kid's cartoon and if you didn't see the hospital bed in the middle, you'd think it was a playroom or something.

Julia is sitting in a chair by the bed, flipping through a magazine. Everleigh is lying against a pile of pillows bigger than her in the bed, her monkey tucked to her side. Julia sees me and sets the magazine down.

"Hey," I say quietly, not wanting to wake Ever.

"Hey." She has dark circles under her eyes. Her hair is pulled back and her face seems dull in the sunlight. By every indication, she's a mess but I can't help but think how beautiful she is. She always is. She always has been. There's something beautiful and calming that just follows her, even if she doesn't feel either way.

I place the bag on the floor and lean against the wall. "How long you been here?"

She glances at the clock. "Four hours."

"Any news?"

"She had the last two tests. We're just waiting on the doctor to come in now."

Ever's eyes begin to flutter. I hope I haven't woken her, but I am glad she's awake anyway. I want to see her. Hear her. Get some reassurance that she's *still here*.

"Uncle Crew." I can hear the exhaustion in her little voice.

I pick up the bag and walk over to her, kissing her on the head. "How are ya?"

"I don't want to be here."

"I know. But we have to make you better."

"What they do to me doesn't make me better. It hurts. A lot."

I close my eyes for a second, trying to keep my cool. My first reaction is to kill anyone that hurts her, but I know in this case, they're hurting her to keep something else from killing her. It's a double-edged sword.

"They're doing what they have to do to get you a hundred percent again. You know that, right?"

She shrugs.

"I brought you something." I dig in the bag and pull out a little box. I hand it to her. She opens it and holds it in the air.

"What is it?" she asks, watching it twirl in the air.

"It's a dream catcher. You put it in your room and when you go to sleep, it filters your dreams. It only lets the good ones in."

"Where did you get this?"

"That one was mine when I was a little boy. My grandma bought one for your daddy and one for me. We had bad dreams, too. But that thing works and I don't need it now. So I thought you should have it."

"You still have that?" Julia asks. She's watching it move as Ever twists it around. "I thought you'd have lost it by now."

"Of course I do. It's magic," I say, tossing her a wink. "I wish I still had Gage's."

She smiles sadly at me. She starts to say something, but the door opens.

"Mrs. Gentry?"

Julia stands and walks around the foot of the bed. "Hello, Dr. Perkins."

I can see a bead of sweat glisten on her forehead, her lips a thin line.

"There are some things I'd like to talk to you about and I'd like to do it in my office." He glances at me. "Are you Everleigh's father?"

"I—" I start, but Julia cuts me off.

"No. He isn't. This is my brother-in-law."

I grimace, the sound of her making it clear I am not a part of her immediate family making me feel like a piece of shit. I extend my hand to the doctor anyway. "Crew Gentry. I'm Everleigh's uncle."

He shakes it firmly. "Dr. Perkins. I'm the pediatric oncologist. If you wouldn't mind staying here with Everleigh, I'd like to take Mrs. Gentry for a few minutes."

Julia looks at me, waiting for me to respond. She's chewing her bottom lip and I want to pull it from between her teeth. I have no idea what's going to be said, but I know it will be all right. It has to be.

"Yeah, absolutely. Me and the monkey here will watch some . . ."

"Doc McStuffins!" she says.

"Doc it is."

"We'll be back shortly. If you'll want to be apprised of her condition at any time, we'll need you and Mrs. Gentry to sign some forms." The doctor looks to Julia and she hesitates before nodding with a sigh. "I'll send a nurse in with them in a little bit for the file."

He turns to leave and motions for Julia to follow. She glances at me over her shoulder, her gaze full of trepidation, those dark brown orbs full of fear. It kills me.

"I'll be here when you get back," I say quietly.

Her eyes go cloudy, tears lapping across, and I'm ripped apart. I want to hold her, to make her know this will be okay. I want to rip every line out of Ever and toss them both over my shoulder and run away from all this bullshit.

But I can't. And the inability to do any of those things eats me from the inside out.

I take a deep breath and turn to face Everleigh. She's watching me curiously. I take the seat previously occupied by Julia and look at her over my shoulder. "What are we doing in here today, monkey?"

"I want to go home."

"I know. I do, too." I look around conspiratorially. "Think I could smuggle you outta here?"

"I do," she giggles. "Please! Take me home."

I tap my chin. "But if I do that, your mommy will wonder where you are. And she'll probably panic when she can't find you. Then she'll come after me and, I'll tell ya a secret . . . she scares me."

"She does not scare you!" she says, giggling. She settles back into her pillows, resting her face so it's facing me. "But she would worry. She worries a lot."

"That's what makes her special."

"You think my mommy is special?"

I laugh. "Where'd you think *you* got your specialness from?"

She smiles, but her eyelids are getting heavy. "Read me a story, Uncle Crew."

That's one request I'm not prepared for. "I don't have a book."

"Make one up," her voice is drifting off, sleep coming soon. "Or Google one."

I chuckle, not even able to believe she knows what Google is.

"I like princess stories," she says softly, her eyes now closed.

I summon my storytelling abilities in a child-approved form. "There was once a beautiful princess. She was nice and friendly and had the most beautiful face in the whole world. She met a prince that was roaming the world, looking for his kingdom."

I pause, thinking she's asleep.

"Was he lost?" she whispers.

"Yeah. He was lost, monkey." I sigh. "He found the beautiful princess and she loved him and he loved her. But he thought he found his kingdom somewhere far away. And he went to find it."

"Did he find it?" she asks.

"He did for a little while. And then he realized that it wasn't his kingdom at all. It was dressed up like his kingdom, but it was a trick. He rushed back to the princess, but she's not there anymore."

"She left?"

"Well, she's there. But she's been invited to a kingdom with another prince."

"Do they fight?"

I smile. "No, they don't. The first prince realizes that if he were a true prince, he wouldn't have left her for the shiny kingdom. He would've taken her with him. So he leaves her with her new prince because he really loves her. Not more than he does, but in a different way."

I glance out the window and feel the sunshine coming in. "The other prince loves her in a way that's better for the princess."

"I think that means they both love her a lot," Ever says, her breathing evening out. "Do they live happily-ever-after?"

I lie to her. "Yeah, monkey. They do."

Chapter THIRTEEN

JULIA

EVER'S ASLEEP IN my arms. I hoist her on my shoulder and fiddle with the key in the lock. I see a note stuck to the door, flapping in the wind. It's from the water department and I know it's a disconnect notice because I didn't get them paid last week. Once you've been late a number of times, they just go straight to threatening to disconnect you.

I heave a breath and push the door open.

One thing at a time.

I kick the door shut and carry a sleeping Everleigh into her room. I lay her on her bed and remove her coat and shoes. I kiss her cheek and tuck her in. She's out of it, completely exhausted from all of the tests today. Her arm is getting a bruise where the I.V. went in and it makes me sick.

Her hand reaches out instinctively for her monkey. She pulls it close to her chest as I watch it rise and fall, her breathing even. I just wish I could pause time and stay right here, my sweet baby girl sleeping peacefully and me watching her. I can look at her and pretend like everything's okay. I can close my eyes and try to pretend like I didn't have such horrifying conversations today. I've always said I wanted to stop time to keep her from growing up, but now it's even more than that.

What if she doesn't get the chance to grow up anyway . . .

I stifle a moan, placing my hand over my mouth.

SACRIFICE

This can't be happening.

The front door rattles and I don't want it to wake her. She needs to rest. With a final glance, I leave her room and head to the door. I pop it open to see Crew standing there, shoving something in his pocket. The notice is missing from the door, but I don't bring it up. Maybe it's flown off.

Keep telling yourself that.

He has a fast food bag in his hand and I realize I haven't eaten all day. The smell makes me nauseous.

I step to the side and let him in. He heads straight for the kitchen, but doesn't sit.

"Where is she?" He places the bag on the table.

"Asleep. She passed out as soon as I got her to the car."

I see his Adam's apple bob and his eyes find mine. They're dark and brewing. I see him hesitate, trying to get the courage to ask the question I know is coming.

"What did they say?"

I wouldn't talk to him about it in front of Everleigh. I know I'm going to have to explain it to her, but I'm not sure how to do that. How do I tell her that she's going to have to get one poison pushed into her body in hopes that it kills a poison already residing there? That she's going to be so sick, experience so many hateful, painful things, all in hopes that that it will ultimately save her life? The doctor gave me suggestions and reading material and even volunteered to help, but I told him I'd take care of it. I don't want to do it, but I want it done with more love and less sterility as possible.

I take a look at Crew and gather the tiny morsels of strength I have left. "It's not good."

His face falls. He grabs the back of a chair, his knuckles turning white.

"I don't remember all the fancy words they used, so I'm just going to tell you how I understood it." I fumble through my purse and pull out a stack of pamphlets and paperwork and drop them on the counter. "I haven't had time to read all this, but they said I should."

Crew pulls his ringing phone out of his jacket pocket. He doesn't even look at the face; he turns it off and slips it back inside.

It feels like I'm watching this conversation from another dimension. I hear the words coming out of my mouth, but it doesn't feel like I'm saying them. My entire body feels so vacant. *Numb.* I remember this feeling vaguely from right after Gage died. People would talk to me and

I wouldn't hear them, they'd sit beside me and I wouldn't even notice. They'd cry on my shoulder and I'd just pat their back and then they'd leave, wiping their tears.

"Basically the tumor has already started to spread, which means the cancer isn't located in only one spot. That's bad for a couple of reasons, one of which is that they can't just go in and remove it."

He dips his head. I hear him take a deep breath and release it. I know he's processing what I'm saying but I just go on, ready to get the words out and leave them in the air. He can do with them whatever he wants. I don't even know what to do with them right now.

My daughter has cancer.

My hand trembles as I pick up a pamphlet. "Dr. Perkins said that it's an aggressive form, so the treatment needs to start right away. There's a plan in this folder if you want to read it. I just . . ." My sight gets blurry, Crew's face muddled through the tears clouding my vision.

"Jules . . ."

I wipe my face with the back of my hand. "But here's the thing . . . there's a new therapy out right now. It's been very effective in kids under six. They want to get Ever in the testing group."

"Where will that be done?"

"In Boston."

"So that's in addition to the chemo?"

"I'm honestly not sure, Crew. There's so much information. I just feel like I'm drowning in terms and dates and definitions right now. I should have taken notes or something."

"Is it leukemia?"

"No. It's called neuroblastoma. I don't know if that's better or worse . . ." My voice cracks, the events of the day finally starting to catch up with me. "I feel so stupid, Crew. I don't even know what they said after the word 'cancer.' I must've sat there with a stupid look on my face!"

I start to cry, but he doesn't come toward me. He just pulls his eyebrows in together and watches me like I might throw something at him.

"I'm failing her at every turn. I should've taken her in earlier. I should've—"

"What you should do is shut up," he says, standing tall. "You're rambling right now and that isn't going to help. None of this is your fault, do you hear me?" He takes a few steps in my direction, his head dipped. "Not your fault."

"I'm scared. No, I'm *terrified*. I don't know how to deal with this."

SACRIFICE

"I know, Jules. But let's try to focus on what we *can* do," he says, his voice full of more conviction than his eyes. "So this trial will help?"

"This trial is our saving grace, I think. I keep repeating what Dr. Perkins said; the trial will be more like a nuclear bomb instead of a drawn out war. That's how he explained it." I move to the table and sit down, my legs feeling weak. "I'm so scared, Crew. Their faces when they explained the diagnosis . . ." I shiver and Crew reaches out and places a hand on my shoulder. I gaze at the wall, the wallpaper peeling away. "This trial is the only thing holding me together right now. The only thing giving me hope. The doctors really think this will work and will work quickly. Or that's how I took it anyway. Maybe I wanted to take it that way, I don't know."

"So when does that start?"

"They're just waiting on the insurance to approve it and then the doctor in charge of that will basically take over Ever's care. Dr. Perkins assured me that they're the best of the best. In the meantime, we go back for some blood work and another scan tomorrow. We start the treatment after that."

"So, they seem optimistic?"

"They do." I wipe at the tears with the hem of my shirt. "They had a panel of doctors go over her results today and they seem very confident that we have a good 'game plan.' The therapy is what they talked about the most."

"Are you going to need help getting to the hospital or anything? I can't miss too much work, but Will is on a different shift than me. I know he'd jump in if you need him."

"I'll figure it out." I look at his pocket, knowing my water notice is in there. I feel like such a burden to him. I wish more than ever that Gage was here . . . for all of us. "I'll take care of my water bill this week, too."

"Stop it." His tone gives little room for argument. "I've got it."

"No, Crew. I'll pay it this week." I don't want to argue about this. Honestly, I don't want to give two thoughts to the damn water bill right now. I don't even have the money to pay for it, but I've figured these things out before. Maybe Mr. Ficht will give me a small loan.

"Damn it, Jules. You have enough to fucking worry about. Stop fighting things that you don't have to fight."

"These things are my fight. They aren't yours."

"How can you fucking say that to me?" Even he blanches a little at the level of his voice. He shakes his head, his voice quieter. "How can you act like this isn't my fight? Huh? Fucking explain that to me, Julia."

I swallow hard and try to remember why. Everything is blurring together. "We aren't your responsibility, Crew. I don't want your pity. I don't want to burden you with my problems."

"*Pity?* Is that what you think this is? You think you aren't *my* responsibility?"

"We aren't, Crew," I all but whisper. "I'm your brother's widow, the mother of your niece. You have no obligation to us." I look him in the eye and force a swallow past the lump in my throat. "And I can't have you be a part of our life and leave us, too. Especially not now."

"What are you even talking about?"

"You walk away when everything gets hard. You walked away from me once. You walked away from your mom when she was sick. You walked away from your responsibilities and good judgments and look where that got Gage. I just . . . I can't count on you, Crew. I can't. This isn't my heart or water bill on the line. This is very seriously *our lives* in the balance now. You have a way of barreling into people's lives and taking over and then just going and not caring how it affects them. And right now, I have to be completely focused on Ever and not worrying about when you'll leave. You'd crush her if you left her now, more than normal."

"You're saying you think I don't care about you two?" He looks at me in disgust and my heart drops.

"I know you care about Ever. I'm not saying that, I'm just saying that I have to protect her from you in case you take off. Her life is so unstable already."

"Protect her from me? Damn, Jules. Give me a little credit here, won't ya?"

"Crew, I'm sorry. I just . . . I'm overwhelmed right now. I'm just so *completely* overwhelmed right now."

"Don't you know I care about you, too?"

"I'm recalling a conversation from the park where you made it very clear you don't do anything for me. And that's fine. But I have a lot on my plate right now that I need to deal with. Things just got really serious here and I . . ." I hiccup back a sob.

His chin dips and he swears under his breath. "Jules, I didn't mean that. I was just pissed."

"It doesn't change the truth behind it."

"There is no fucking truth behind it," he says defiantly, taking a step towards me. "You've always been something to me. Don't you see that?"

"Yeah, sure. I saw how much of 'something' I was to you the day you came home after months of being in Minnesota and you just walked away. Again."

"You have no idea what you're talking about."

"You know what? That doesn't even matter. We haven't talked about it in years; there's no reason to talk about it now." I hear Ever cough in her room and my breath catches in my throat. "Especially now," I whisper.

He watches me intently, his eyes searching my soul.

"Call me if you need anything. *When* you need something, I should say." He walks to the door and opens it but stops one last time. "But just consider for one fucking second that me leaving you and going back to Minnesota was me telling you how much I cared about you. And *that*, Julia, has never fucking changed."

I watch the door shut behind him.

Chapter FOURTEEN

CREW

THE CHAINS BOUNCE with each hit.

I drive my fists into the heavy bag suspended to the ceiling of my garage from every angle. I rip into it, knuckles kissing the leather, making the bag pop with every strike.

"Ah!" I growl, glancing my elbow across the stiff leather. The sweat from my skin causes my arm to slide across the bag, leaving a glistening trail behind.

I stop, out of breath, and glance at the clock. I've been at this for a solid hour.

I heave air into my lungs and feel the lactic acid in my arms and thighs. I need my brain to concentrate on that and not on what Julia had to say.

"It's not good."

"Fuck!" I yell, throwing another combination. My anger surges once again and I take it out on the bag. Throwing another jab, cross, hook, I feel a burning sensation in the top of my back.

I stand still, watching the bag spin. My chest feels tight as I try to locate the source of the pain.

I've never really felt this before. I've pulled every muscle, ripped every muscle, in my body a number of times. But this isn't that. It feels eerily reminiscent of my last fight at Minnesota, only much, much, *much* less.

"Son-of-a-bitch," I mutter, grabbing a towel off a chair in the corner. I dry my face and then throw it across my neck. "*Son-of-a-fucking-bitch.*"

I try to tell myself that it's probably a pull on something from work. That I've never had anything hurt like that before, so the odds that it's nothing serious are good. Maybe something just strained when I hit the bag.

Yeah, that's probably it.

I head inside to grab a bottle of water. I ran three miles as soon as I got home. But when I was done, I was as pissed as I was when I started, so I decided to hit the bag instead. No matter how many times I threw, I couldn't diminish any of the anger.

"Knock, knock, motherfucker." The door swings open and Will waltzes in.

"I need to lock the fucking door."

He just laughs, but I hear the hesitancy in it. "What's happening?"

I down the rest of the water and toss the bottle in the trash.

"Well?" he asks, leaning against the wall.

"Well what?"

"Dude, come on." He shakes his head and walks into the living room. I follow him and sit on the couch while he takes a seat in the chair he always uses. "How are things with Ever?"

"I don't wanna talk about it."

And I don't. I don't want to discuss this shit. It seems asinine you'd ever have to discuss this shit. A kid getting cancer. How the fuck does this even happen?

"Fair enough."

"There's nothing fair about it."

He twists his head back and forth, considering my statement. "True. So, moving along, I was going to ask what you were doing tonight, but I'll skip over that."

"Smart move."

He laughs again and I know it's for my benefit. He's trying to make me relax, settle down. Gage had words to pacify people; Will has his laugh.

"What are you here for, anyway?" I ask.

The asshole smirk leaves his face and he looks somber. "I was just checking on you."

I blow out a breath and look to the ceiling.

"I feel like I should do something," he says seriously. "I mean, I don't really know Julia, but Gage was my friend. And you, I'd go to war with you, man. We're blood. A small percentage, maybe, but blood anyway. I just don't know what to say or do."

"So what's going on in Will's world today?" I ask, changing the topic. I doubt it'll take my mind off of Ever, but if anything can, it'll be Will's escapades.

His eyes widen at the opportunity to say something stupid. "I banged this chick last night. Tightest pussy I've ever felt. Ever. Fact as fuck."

"That's saying something," I laugh.

"No shit."

"You seeing her again?"

He shrugs like he's never thought about it.

I roll my eyes and flip on the television.

"This isn't really my world, more your world, but your fight video has exploded over the weekend. I wanted to call you this afternoon, but I knew you were busy."

"Pull it up."

He grins and reaches in his pocket. In a minute, his phone is in front of my face with YouTube open. I make out the interior of Shenanigan's. The video starts playing. I'm jerking the first guy through the air. The camera is on me and then hits the guy just as he lands in the middle of the table.

I've seen myself in a number of videos before, but it's always been wrestling bouts that I've had to watch to see where I lacked or where I fucked up. I've never seen myself in a street fight. Now I know why people don't fuck with me after they see this.

The camera gets closer as my elbow strikes the second guy across his mouth. You can hear muffled voices whispering back and forth as his teeth go bouncing down the bar.

"Did you see that?" Will asks, pointing at the screen.

"It was even better first hand."

"That thing is everywhere. Literally on every MMA forum, social media, the whole thing, man. I know you're dealing with serious shit right now, but you're kinda fucking famous again. Google yourself."

"It'll just bring up Minnesota shit," I say, starting to hand his phone back to him. I do not need a reminder of what used to be, what could've been. I'm acutely aware.

"Nah, it won't." He takes the phone away from me and pulls something up. He hands it back. A ton of search results come back, but instead of the University of Minnesota after the top results, it says, "Crew Gentry:

This Guy Beat Hunter Davidson."

"You're a legend," Will says. "But that hip toss shit was a little sloppy."

"What the fuck do you know about anything?" I laugh.

"Dude. I watch Ronda Rousey videos."

"Oh, I bet you do."

"I do. It's my way of multi-tasking. Porn and fighting in one."

"Shut the fuck up," I laugh. "She'd kick your ass."

"It'd be a real hard fight when I'd throw myself to the mat and say, 'Mount me, baby.'"

I laugh, handing him his phone back.

Will shrugs. "So, what are we gonna do tonight? Want to head to Shenanigans?"

"I'm gonna grab a shower and then probably just try to go to bed. It's been a long day."

He stands and stretches his arms over his head. "All right. I'm outta here then." He walks to the door and pulls it open. "If you need me, call me. Otherwise, I'll probably be with this little redhead I met a little while ago."

"Do I know her?"

"Nope. But she's totally my type," he grins.

"Doesn't having a pussy make them your type?"

"You know my type: a little bit of sugar, a little bit of spice, and a hint of whore."

"Have fun," I say, shaking my head.

He laughs and closes the door behind him.

Chapter FIFTEEN

JULIA

I LOATHE WAITING rooms.

They're inhumane boxes of random people expecting bad news. You just eye each other but try not to make actual eye contact. You hear each other on the phone, crying, talking but try to act like you don't hear any of it. You are all in there for some serious reason, maybe even life or death, and you have to maintain some sort of composure because if you totally break down, there are a bunch of strangers there that 'won't' be watching or hearing it.

I dig a notepad from my purse and try to keep my mind from going into a spiral.

I need to control what I can.

A theme of my life is feeling out of control, like the world spins and I'm always trying to catch up. I've battled that for a long time by taking care of the things that I *can*. Sometimes it's having the laundry done or the kitchen clean before bed, but those things allow me to feel a bit like I have some sort of say in my life. Like Olivia said last night, I have to control what I can and let the other things go.

"Just think about it, Julia."

"Olivia, I can't do that to you. You do so much for us. I can't move in with you!"

"Yes, you can. You need to realize how hard things are going to be and *you're going to need help."*

"I know, but I—"

"It's okay to take help. Especially now. You aren't going to be able to work as much as you did and by living here, we can share the bills. I can take some of that responsibility off of you."

"I don't know . . ."

"I do. You can't do this on your own."

It felt like I was giving up, admitting defeat. But when I realized how many shifts of work I was going to miss and how much attention Ever was going to need, I realized I had to get real. Crew was right. I had to pick and choose my battles and cancer had already chosen me. War had been declared and I had to put all my resources towards it, even if that meant giving up a little pride.

I start making lists of hours I might be able to go into the office and hours I might be able to swing at Ficht's based on the "cycles" the doctors have laid out. She'll do a one week on and two weeks off rotation until we get her into the new therapy. While we want to hit it hard, we also need her body to stay strong and not completely wear down from the treatment.

I grab a sip of the water bottle next to me and then start another list. This list covers things I need to get rid of before we move. I try to look at it objectively and not get as emotional about it as I did when I did this very same thing after Gage died and we moved into the apartment.

They're just things. Things can be replaced.

It doesn't make it any easier. Some of these *things* are the last reminders of a life before things went bad in ways I'd never considered.

My purse shakes on the floor beside me, my phone ringing inside. I grab it and look at the screen. The number seems vaguely familiar and I think it's Mr. Ficht.

"Hello?"

"Julia?"

I cup my hand over my forehead and squeeze my eyes tight. I consider just hanging up before anything else is said. I don't know why she's calling, but I know she's going to want something. Although I normally have very little to offer her, I have even less now.

"Julia? It's your Ma."

"Yeah?"

She snorts. "Well, don't act so damn excited to hear from me."

For a half a second, I wish for a normal relationship with my mother.

I wish I could ask her to come sit with me, talk to me, distract me . . . maybe bring me a coffee that hasn't sat in the pot all day.

"You still there?" She sounds annoyed and instead of making me angry, it just depresses me. It makes me feel lonelier.

"Yeah, I'm here."

"I need a favor."

I look around the room as a doctor in a white lab coat comes in. He glances around, a blank look on his face, and makes eye contact with me for just a second. It causes my heart to nearly stop beating.

He announces, "Parker," and a family that's been crying all day stands and follows him out. I can't help the relief that washes over me and I feel guilty for being happy that it was them and not me.

"Julia! I need a favor," she repeats with an exaggerated sigh.

"I'm kinda busy."

"Aren't we all."

God, if you let this be okay, I promise to never complain about being busy again. I won't complain about laundry or dishes or having to work two jobs. I get it now. I swear. All that matters is that Everleigh gets well. Please. If this is a lesson, I've got it loud and clear.

"It's just 'til next weekend," she rambles. "Your daddy is going to Atlantic City with some buddies and we need just a few dollars to get there."

"I—"

"I promise we'll give it back to you . . ." She goes on, her smoker's voice crackling at the end of every word.

The door opens again and my eyes find Crew's immediately. He watches me nervously as he makes his way over.

A wave of relief washes through me and I can't focus on anything my mom's saying. All I can do is watch Crew walk across the room towards me. I didn't know he was coming. I didn't expect him to come, but I can't deny the gratefulness I feel seeing him.

"Julia! Are you even paying attention to me?"

"Yes, Ma. I hear you. But I don't have it. I'm sorry."

"We'll pay you back. He's gonna gamble a bit while he's there and you know how good he is at Hold 'Em."

"I just don't have the money, Ma. I'm kinda going through a lot right now—"

The phone is snatched out of my hands in an instant. I gasp and whip my head to face him.

SACRIFICE

"Don't you ever call her and ask her for anything again, do you hear me?" Crew's eyes are burning holes into mine as he holds the phone to his ear. Heads turn to face us from around the room and I feel my cheeks heat.

I hear her spout off before Crew speaks again. "I don't give a shit. Call her again and *I'll* be knockin' the fuckin' door down to *your* house." He listens for a minute and laughs, a growl emitting from the bottom of his throat. "Send him over. 1112 Culver Street. It'd make my fuckin' day."

He pulls the phone back and looks at the screen. The call was ended. He hands it to me, the vein in his temple throbbing.

"She calls you again, you tell me," he orders. The blues of his eyes are rolling and clouding like a storm.

"It's my ma, Crew."

"She's not your ma, Jules. She's never done one decent thing for you."

"What brings you by?" I ask, hoping he'll let it go.

"I work the night shift tonight, so I wanted to drop by now and see how things were going."

"They're just doing a final set of tests and then they're going to get everything set up for the first round of chemo. I think it starts on Monday." I sigh, the weight of the world on my shoulders. "We should be able to go home tonight."

He nods and I know he's thinking. He glares at the onlookers until they look away. Finally he says, "I got a call today."

"Who from?"

"The office manager of your apartment. They said I could either come by next week and pick up the security deposit I made for you when you moved in or they could mail it to me." He looks at me out of the corner of his eye. "Since you're moving and all."

I sag.

"Where ya goin'?" His tone is too calm. I know there's a burst of anger floating right behind the words.

I was going to tell him about the move, but I hadn't gotten around to it. It was a last minute decision and, quite frankly, he's not on the top of my priority list.

"You were right," I say, sadly. "I have to stop fighting *everything*. I have no idea what I'm facing right now but I was struggling to make it before all this happened." I hate admitting this out loud, to *him*, of all people. "I'm so far behind as it is and things are going to get worse. I just have to consolidate everything and try not to drown. So, we're moving in with Olivia."

He doesn't say anything, but I know he's trying to keep himself in check. He cracks his knuckles, his elbows on his denim-covered legs. His vision is focused on something across the room as he listens to me.

"She volunteered last night and I . . . I don't want to. It feels like I'm losing every battle in my life, Crew. But what can I do? I can barely afford to survive at this point and the best I'm gonna be able to do is work at Ficht's and the office when I can just so they keep me employed and I—"

"Stop."

"What?"

"Stop rambling."

"Rambling? If you don't want to hear what I have to say, don't ask!"

His jaw pulses as he studies me. He searches my face and starts to bring a hand up, but drops it back to his lap. "You're moving in with me."

"What?"

I know my mouth is sitting agape, but I can't help it. I can't believe he just said that. Of all the reactions I might have anticipated, that was not one of them.

"You and Ever are moving in with me," he repeats. "Jules, I'm done playing games with ya. You two aren't moving in with some neighbor lady when I'm here. No fucking way."

"She's not just *some neighbor.*' Olivia has been a blessing to me."

"She's good to ya. I know. But we are family."

I scoff. "No, you and Everleigh are family. *We*," I say, motioning between us, "are not."

"Semantics." His gaze narrows. "Look, if it makes you feel better, then fine. Let me do this for *my* family. Let me do this for Everleigh and Gage. Let me do what's right by them, Julia. All it'll do is help you out in the long run."

"Crew . . ." I start to argue with him, but there's something about the way he's looking at me that makes me want to hear him out.

"I've pretty much done wrong by everyone in my life. I know this. I know you don't trust me and you have every right not to." The shadows across his face darken, his voice lowers. "But give me a chance to make some things right. Give me a chance to do something I'm proud of, for once." He smiles to himself. "Give me a chance to man up."

My heart twists in my chest. I've not heard Crew talk like this in a long time. I'm reminded back many years ago, before he left to wrestle. Everyone would come up to him to hear about his fights and exploits around town. But late at night we'd lay in bed and he'd tell me different stories. They would be stripped down, without the fanfare, and sometimes he'd question whether he should've done it or not. I could see that he wasn't *just* the bad boy everyone thought. I spent a lot of time wondering why he acted out like he did when he was so clearly *more* down deep.

I thought this Crew was long gone.

"You and me, we don't have anybody else," he says. His eyes soften and he smiles sadly. "I'm not asking ya to be nice to me. I'm not asking ya to trust me. I'm not asking ya to like me or to not give me shit."

His smile brightens a bit and I can't help but grin back.

"Good. Because that'll never happen anyway," I laugh.

"I'm also not asking ya to move in with me. I'm telling ya that's what's gonna happen."

Maybe it's because he seems so genuine. Maybe it's because I'm exhausted. Or maybe the antiseptic odor of the hospital has demolished too many of my brain cells. But whatever the reason, I don't argue. But I don't agree, either.

It's probably another mistake on my part, but it can just be chalked up with the rest of them.

Chapter SIXTEEN

JULIA

THE AFTERNOON LIGHT pours in the windows. The bank is bustling, patrons going in and out, men sitting behind large desks laughing loudly from the offices lining the walls.

I drag my phone out of my purse and send a text to Olivia. I hate being away from Ever, but I have to do this and I need to know she's okay. Her response is immediate:

> Olivia: *She's coloring and watching cartoons. Everything's fine.*

If only.

My hands shake as a man announces my name from a door way. I drop the phone into my bag and stand, smoothing my shirt. I try to smile back at him, but I'm sure it's a grimace.

I follow him through the door and down a long hallway. Each step gives me another moment to re-think my decision. I fight the urge to run from the building and jump in my car. I want to leave, I *desperately* want to leave. But I know the solution to a few of my problems is here and I have to go through with this.

I sign a book while he unlocks a large, steel door. Once inside, I sign another book and show him my ID.

"Once you're finished, just press this button," he says, pointing at the wall, "and someone will escort you out."

SACRIFICE

I nod and thank him. He leaves, letting the door shut tightly behind him.

The room is large with steel boxes lining three of the four walls. I've only been in this room once and today I'm just here to re-do why I was here the first time.

It smells cold and I shiver, probably more from nerves than from the actual temperature. Letting the stagnant air fill my lungs, I walk around the table in the center of the room and find box 7285.

Slipping the key out of my pocket, I unlock the box and pull the drawer out. My hands are trembling, the box shaking, as I remove it from the wall. I sit it on the table behind me and take a step back.

I've never really looked inside.

Gage got the safety deposit box soon after we were married. I know our marriage license is in here, as well as a few things of his mother's that he didn't want to get lost. But that's all I know. When I was here the one time before, I just dropped my wedding ring inside and left.

I pull out a chair and sit. I look around the room and wonder if someone is watching me. I'm sure they're taping this and it feels like I'm being spied on, like someone is privy to such an intimate moment. I want to flip them the bird and have a little meltdown for all of them to see. Strangely, it seems like a cathartic option at the moment.

I don't want to do this, but I don't see another choice. Crew was right when he said I have to stop fighting everything. Everleigh is my only priority right now. And as much as this is going to rip me in half, I know Gage would understand. He always said we'd do anything we had to in order to make sure Ever had a better life than we did.

He'd understand.

The lump in my throat that seems to be permanently lodged there starts to burn as my hands make their way to the sides of the box. A baggie is laid on top and I remove it. I open the top and let the contents fall to the table.

A locket that belonged to Gage's mom reflects the lights above. A couple of old coins roll around before spinning and stopping. There are two old Polaroid-style pictures of Gage and Crew from when they were kids. In one, they are at the beach, probably seven or eight years old, Crew giving Gage bunny ears. In the other, it appears to be Christmas morning and they're both asleep in the middle of a wrapping-paper mess. They're adorable, all tousled hair and sweet little faces. They remind me of Everleigh and I press a gentle kiss against them before sitting them aside.

I pull out a couple of concert tickets. Beneath that is a picture from our very first date. My eyes water heavily at the sight of us. I'm looking at him through the corner of my eye and he's smiling at the camera, his hand protectively around my waist.

I spot my ring and start to reach for it when I see an envelope. My breath hitches in my throat when I see "To Jules" written in Gage's handwriting on the front.

A cold chill tears through me. My mouth hanging open, a shiver racing down my spine, I pull the envelope out of box and run my finger along the writing. A single tear lazily drops down my cheek.

The envelope is dry from sitting inside the box for God knows how long. Carefully, I turn it over and open the unsealed back. A single piece of paper is folded inside. I remove it, my heart pounding, and unfold it slowly.

Dear Jules,

I ran by here today to drop off a few things and I decided to jot down a note to you. I've been thinking about my ma a lot. Probably because baseball season is starting and she would've been all over the Red Sox this year. They're gonna be good, I think. Anyway, I've been thinking about something she said to me once. She said that when my dad left her when she was pregnant with Crew, the worst part about it was not knowing what to do. He had taken care of everything and then just took off and she had no idea how to even deal. It made me think—if something happened to me, would you know what to do? I try to protect you from everything and make your life as easy as I can. And I hope to hell you never have to live without me, but things happen, you know? What won't happen is me leaving you willingly. You're my world.

But if something does happen, I want you to remember a few things. First of all, always remember I love you. Always. And if we have children, remind them that I love them, too. I haven't met them yet, but I can imagine seeing a little me and you. Also, make sure they're Sox fans.

SACRIFICE

Don't be scared. I know that's easier said than done, but don't be. You are so much stronger than you even know. Your strength inspires me every day. You'll figure things out.

There's a picture in here of Crew and I. We're at the beach and the bastard is giving me those stupid bunny ears. That picture was taken one morning when we decided to go swimming at the beach with Will and another kid whose name I don't remember. Later that day, Crew and I bought lunch. He wanted another ice cream and I wouldn't give him the money for it because we needed it to get home. He got really mad at me and wouldn't speak to me all day. Typical, I know.

Anyway, I'm out swimming in the ocean with Will and the other kid when I start to get pulled under and out. I remember seeing the light through the water above me, my chest burning, needing oxygen. I'd come up but not even long enough to yell for help. I was just being tossed around like a ball. Finally, I come up long enough to see Will and the other guy, but they're standing on the beach. They're pointing towards me but neither are coming my way. And I know I'm done. My arms and legs are getting tired, my head feels heavy, my chest is burning. I'm choking on the saltwater. And then I feel something grab my leg. I remember thinking that at least death by shark will be faster than drowning. And then an arm wraps around my waist and pulls me up. I get to the top of the water and my little brother is shaking me, telling me to 'man up' of all things.

He helps me back to shore and I puke up a gallon of seawater, but I'm okay. Crew probably saved my life that day.

I'm telling this to you for a reason, babe. I know you and Crew don't always see eye-to-eye and I know you don't think much of him sometimes. I know he's hurt you and he can be an unpredictable prick. But I also know this—he's never let me down when I've needed him. He'll be there for you. He has some growing up to do,

I know, but he'll do what needs to be done. If there's anyone in the world I trust to take care of you, it's my brother.

Have a happy life. I want you to enjoy things and smile and laugh. I don't want you to try to do everything on your own, like I know you try to do. I don't want you to be miserable or hold back and feel guilty for living. I want you to promise me that you'll live with no regrets. That you'll do what you have to do to have a good life. Don't feel bad for any decisions or choices you have to make. I know your heart and your soul. I'll support you 100% (unless you make our theoretical children Yankee's fans).

I have to get back to work. I hope I've just wasted twenty minutes writing this and I show it to you some day when we're eighty and we laugh at how dumb I am. I'm making cheesecake tonight. I hope you like it.

Love,
Gage

I press the paper to my chest and fix my gaze on the wall of boxes in front of me. It feels like he's in the room with me and I don't want to lose the moment. I want to hold on to this feeling of being safe and loved, to the memories, for as long as possible.

I hear the paper crackle in my hands and I pull it away from my body, realizing that I've been squeezing it too hard. I read it again, hearing his voice inside my head, and I know what I have to do.

JULIA

"DON'T FEEL BAD for any choices or decisions you have to make."

My palms are sweaty and I wipe them on my jeans. An old country song is playing through the speakers as I pass the lines of yard equipment on the floor of the shop. A long glass counter lines the side wall, guns lined up neatly against the wall behind it.

An old man is sitting at the end, drinking a cup of coffee. He pays me no attention and continues to work his crossword puzzle.

I tuck a strand of hair behind my ear and look for someone else to help me. The shop is empty.

"Excuse me?" I ask, my voice wobbling.

He glances up but doesn't say anything.

"Can you help me?"

He stands up and sets his pencil down. "What can I do for ya, Miss?"

"I have this," I say, making my way to the counter. I place my wedding ring on the glass, the clinking sound seeming so much louder than it probably is.

"Is this yours?"

I nod, batting back the tightness in my throat.

"Where'd ya get it?"

"It was my wedding ring."

I almost can't do it. A surge of panic hits me hard and I straighten my back and look him in the eye, hoping I appear more confident than I feel.

"You want to pawn it or sell it?" He sets the ring down and braces himself against the counter. He seems curious, but I don't want to discuss anything with him. I want to get this over with.

"Well, there's no way I'm going to be able to buy it back, so sell it, I guess." My voice breaks a little on the final word and I clench my teeth. This has to be done. I need the money.

"If you sell it, it's mine. You realize that, right?"

I nod again, not trusting myself to speak. I try to force the ball of tears in the back of my throat to dissolve.

He sighs. "I can give you $500."

I feel all hope drain from my body like an open sieve. Pawning my wedding ring, the most precious thing I own, is my last resort to keeping us afloat. $500 isn't going to get me far.

But it's ahead of where you are now.

"Can I ask you something?" He takes his glasses off and sets them down. "Why are you pawning this? Did you get divorced?"

"My, um . . ." I watch the hands of a clock tick between two guns behind his head. I can hear the second hand tick softly; it's almost hypnotic. "Um, my husband passed away and I need the cash."

"For a vacation or something?" His forehead is wrinkled, his eyes narrowed.

I snort at the insinuation.

I wish.

I try to smile politely, frustrated that it's taking so long and irritated that he would think I would sell my *wedding ring* to him for a *vacation*. I want to shout at him, lecture him on the ridiculousness of the question, but I don't want to draw this process out any longer than necessary. Every question makes the pain of this process amplify even more.

"No, sir. My daughter has been diagnosed with cancer and I'm broke." My words come out clipped, yet I feel my bottom lip quiver.

He watches me for a moment and then picks up his glasses. He puts them on, bends down, and grabs a form from under the desk. "Fill this out, honey. I'll be right back."

I answer the questions and get out my driver's license, trying to keep my mind blank and *not* focused on what I'm doing. I don't want to think about it. I know the ring is setting off to my right and I have half a notion to pick it up and run out the door.

The man comes back and takes the paper. He notes a few things and slides my license back. I pop it into my wallet and watch him expectantly. The walls are closing in and I can't breathe.

He hands me eight $100 bills.

"You told me $500," I say, looking up to him.

"Take it."

"Sir . . ." I can't say anything else. I can feel the heat in my chest, the burn in my throat, and I know the ever-present lump is going to interrupt any words I try to say.

"My wife and I will pray for your daughter. I hope she gets well, honey."

I can only nod and smile, the tears streaming down my face. I allow myself one final glance at the token of love Gage placed on my ring finger one beautiful August day and turn and walk out.

Chapter SEVENTEEN

CREW

I TAP MY foot against the plank and it gives a little. As usual, the landlord fixed it but half-assed. It's a good thing they're moving because I have a little inkling that he and I would be going toe-to-toe if they were here much longer.

I move the toothpick around my mouth and watch the street. I'm not sure where she's at and if Olivia knows, she's not telling. She did let me see Ever. She was sleeping in her bed. She seemed a little pale but it was good to just see her laying there. The dreamcatcher I gave her was hanging in the window and I hope to hell it works for her. She is living a real life nightmare, whether she knows it or not. Her dreams should be her safe place.

Jules' little blue Toyota rumbles up the street and pulls up to the curb. She looks up before turning her back for a minute and then getting out of the car. She makes her way up the sidewalk.

As she gets nearer, I notice her eyes are swollen. Her steps quicken.

"Hey," she says, sniffling.

"Hey."

"Is everything okay? Olivia didn't call."

"Everything's fine. Ever's asleep."

I see the relief settle across her. She balances her bag on her shoulder.

"Where ya been?" I ask.

"I had a few errands to run."

"Like?"

"What are you? My keeper?" she bites out. I know I've hit a nerve but I'm not sure why. All it does is make me more determined to figure it out.

I eye her, warn her to tread carefully. "Maybe."

"Go away, Crew." She rolls her eyes and starts up the stairs.

I rise, peering down at her. Something has happened and she's not telling me. Again. This shit's gonna stop.

"Where were you, Jules?" My tone is harsher than I even intended, but fuck it. I'm done playing with her.

"I was *trying* to pay my water bill," she says, her hand on her hip. "If I don't get it paid before I move out, they'll hold the security deposit and I could use that money right now. But, it was already paid." She glares at me.

"Where'd you get the money to pay it?" A hundred scenarios go through my head and I'm not comfortable with any of them. She doesn't have the money to pay for anything. Where is she getting it?

My jaw ticks while I wait for an answer.

"None of your business." She starts to go by me, but I block her path.

I reach out and grab her arm. I spin her to face me. "It *is* my fucking business. Where did you get the fucking money?"

Her eyes fill with tears and I'm thrown off balance. I don't know what's going on. If someone has hurt her or manipulated her, I'll decimate them into a million fucking tiny, microscopic pieces.

"I sold my wedding ring," she whispers.

"Why in the hell did you do that?"

"I just . . ." Her chest heaves. "I need the money . . ."

The tears flow instantly, pouring down her face. I pull her into me and wrap my arms around her. She buries her head in my chest and pounds on me with both fists, sobbing into my shirt. I hold her tighter and just let her use me as a punching bag.

She winds both fists in my shirt and cries like I've never seen her cry before. It kills me. I feel so fucking helpless, so unable to fix this like I want to. I can't fix the root of the problem—I can't fix Ever. God knows I'd give her my fucking heart if it'd help.

As I hold Jules to me and feel her misery, her struggle, her heartbreak, I know what I *can* help. And I'm going to do it whether she likes it or not.

Man the fuck up.

She pulls away and wipes the clumped hair out of her beautiful face.

"I'm sorry," she whispers, clearing her throat.

I give her a second to get herself together before I speak. "I'm going to say this one time, Jules. And it's not open for discussion."

She doesn't argue with me, but tries to change the topic. "I thought you worked tonight."

"I took the night off to move you in with me. Like we agreed at the hospital earlier."

"About that . . ."

"Yeah, about that." I tip her chin up so I can see into her eyes. "I appreciate you wanting to take care of your life. I know it makes you feel vulnerable to need someone. I remember what it was like with your parents, remember?"

She smiles sadly.

"I also know what I did to you, so I get it. I get all your stupid reasons for not wanting me to be involved. And, logically speaking, you're probably right. But I'm not logical and I'm not letting this shit happen anymore. You selling your ring was bullshit, Jules."

"I'm so behind, Crew. And I don't know when I'm going to be able to catch up. I need money just to survive: food, gas to the hospital . . ."

I drop her chin. "This is the way this is going to happen from here on out. Listen carefully, take notes if you gotta, but by God, pay attention. You are moving in with me. I'm taking care of you and Everleigh, at least until she's better. Once that happens, and it *will* happen, Jules, then if you want to leave, we'll discuss. But I'm drawing a fucking line in the sand right now and it'd do ya some good not to cross it."

"You can't afford to take care of us."

"Julia. Stop."

She sighs and looks down. Like Everleigh, she's pale. Her cheeks are hollowed, her lips ragged. It's so fucking sad.

"Right now, your job is to worry about that little girl we love. My job is to figure out the rest. I'm done pretending like you're Superwoman."

"But it's okay for you to pretend to be Superman?"

"Yeah. Feel free to call me that if you want."

She starts to smile but catches herself. I can tell she's worrying about something and I know we'll stand here all fucking day before she just comes out and says it unless I push. So I push.

"What's wrong? Why are you looking like that?"

"You won't leave us?" she asks softly.

"No." It's the simplest, most honest answer I can give her. I don't know how in the hell I'm going to pull this off, but I will. I have to.

She looks at me again. For the first time in a long time, I see a bit of hope. "I just don't know if it's the right thing. I mean, what will Ever think? Will it confuse her? And Gage . . ."

"I tell you what," I say and start to the house. I'm not playing twenty questions with her. I don't have the fucking answers to everything. I just know this is what's gotta be done. "You can call the cops and have them remove me or you can get your ass in here and help pack your shit."

Chapter EIGHTEEN

JULIA

MY MIND RACES and I'm unable to slow it down. It could be the pot of coffee I've drank, the lack of sleep last night, or the mere fact that today is a day I never thought I'd be facing. The day I'm moving in with Crew Gentry.

Granted it's for Everleigh and granted it's probably not going to change much between us, but it's still nerve-wracking. This isn't what I want to happen . . . not by a long shot. I'd much rather be living in this apartment than with him, but I don't have a choice. And when the options are considered, I know I'm going to need help and Ever is going to be happier with him than Olivia. So I'm doing what must be done.

Lord help us all.

I take a quick glance around the apartment. Everything I own is stuck in one box or another and lined against the wall of the living room. Crew has furniture and I can't afford to put ours in storage. Olivia's nephew is going to come and get what I don't take. She helped me get packed up last night and even brought coffee over earlier this morning. She's the only thing I'll miss from here. This place never felt like home.

A quick knock beats off the door and it pushes open. Crew's head pops around the corner. He grins and comes in and closes the door behind him.

I see the hesitancy in his eyes, the careful way he's looking at me. He gazes slowly around the room and takes in the boxes. When he turns back to me, he seems more assured.

"You ready?" he asks.

I take a deep breath. "Yeah, I think so. I've already filled my car up with stuff. This is all that's left."

"What about your furniture? Do you want to take any of it?"

I shake my head. "No. We just need a bed and a dresser. If your spare room has that, we'll manage."

I try to focus on the good. That we will have a place to stay. That having Crew, Ever's favorite person, around will be good for her. That I won't have to worry about bills. If I don't focus on that, I start to panic, thinking that this is going to end in another tragic mess. That I know better.

That if I had a different option, I'd take it. But I don't.

He smiles and his full lips part. The sunshine comes in through the windows making him seem younger. His grin soothes me a little and I appreciate having the edge taken off my nerves.

Even though I'm scared to, I appreciate *him*.

"Yeah, it does. Will is going to be by in a minute. If you and Ever want to go ahead—"

"Uncle Crew!" Ever squeals as she bursts through the door, Olivia following close behind. She heads straight for her uncle, just not as quickly as normal. She's tired, her little body's been ran through the gamut the last few days.

Crew picks her up and holds her with one arm. "Heya, monkey. Ready to go home with me?"

"I am! I'm so happy we are going home with you! I made sure Mommy packed our family painting. Can we hang that at your house?"

He grins. "It's your house now, too. You can hang whatever you want." She cheers and he looks back to me. "You two can head on over. I'll unpack your car when I get there. Just go on in and make yourself comfortable."

I reach for Ever and she climbs into my arms. She's lighter than she was even a week ago. "We'll see you soon."

I could easily be overwhelmed with this situation emotionally. It's the start of a new chapter in our lives. I have no idea what the future holds, only that I now officially have became dependent on my brother-in-law. I just try to keep everything in a box in my head. Ever's cancer in this box. The things I have to do in order to be able to deal with the cancer in this one. Everything else in this one. It's the only way I can manage. I can't get caught up in how I feel about everything because I think my emotions cross the entire spectrum. From the anger and devastation of Ever's diagnosis to the embarrassment of needing Crew in such a blatant way to the exhaustion of dealing with everything, I nearly can't deal.

"I guess we will see you soon," I say to Olivia.

She wipes a tear from the corner of her eye. "You girls are like my family," she says, pulling us into a hug. "You call me, Julia, if you need anything. I don't care what time it is or what you need. You call me."

"I will."

"She will," Ever says happily, "because I will need to see you and Rory a lot. I love you."

Olivia laughs through a sniffle and pats her hair. "And I love you, little girl." She looks back to me. "Did you call the school?"

"Yeah, they're going to send her schoolwork home and we'll do it. They're really nice about everything. As long as she's where she needs to be by the start of next year, everything should be fine."

Blowing out a breath, I look over my shoulder. "See ya at your house then?"

He nods, a stormy look brewing over his face. I hope he isn't having second thoughts because I'm absolutely confident that'll be the final straw.

CREW

I WATCH JULIA walk out. Everleigh waves at me over her shoulder. I wave back and her little eyes light up. It pulls at the knot in my stomach.

I hope this is the right thing. I hope I don't somehow mess up their lives more by forcing myself in it, because messing shit up is what I do. I can work. I can play cards. I can work on trucks. But I *can't* do people.

Dealing with other people hasn't worked out well for me in life, hence the reason I keep most people at arm's length. It's safer for everyone. Otherwise, I'll do something careless and hurt them, like I did Ma and Gage. Intentional or not, that's what happens.

"Crew, I wanted to say something to you."

I jump at the sound of her voice. I'd forgotten Olivia was still there. "Yeah, what's that?"

"I didn't know your brother, obviously, and I don't know you that well. But I wanted to thank you for taking care of those girls. I know you've been watching over her for a while and I know she argues with you about it . . ."

"Yeah, well . . ." My voice sounds rough and I turn my back to her, pretending to look at the boxes. "Jules was my brother's wife. I don't really have a choice."

My words are met with silence. I wait for her to say something, but she doesn't. I turn around to see her leaning against the wall. "You do have a choice. And I can see when you look at her, and at Everleigh, that you care about them. And not just because they were your brother's wife and daughter."

"Those are some pretty big observations," I say brusquely. I don't know what the hell her point is, but she can shut the fuck up right about now.

"I'm sorry." She pulls the door open, but doesn't step out. "I've heard stories about your brother. I just want to say that your mother must have done things right to raise sons like the two of you. You're a good man."

Let's hope.

Chapter NINETEEN

CREW

"KNOCK, KNOCK, MOTHERFUCKER."

I look up and see Will coming through the door. He closes it behind him and then gazes at the pile of boxes stacked up around the room.

"Is your OCD killing ya yet?" he laughs, knocking the top of one of the boxes with his knuckle.

I pump out another twenty push-ups and stand. He's disappeared, but I hear him in the refrigerator milling around.

"You do realize you're gonna have to feed them, right?" he shouts from around the corner. He reappears, twisting the top off a beer. "You have, like, no food."

"No shit, Sherlock."

"I still can't believe they are gonna live here."

"Yeah, about that. You're gonna have to at least start actually knocking if you drop by."

Will sighs dramatically. "This is gonna fucking blow."

I head to the kitchen, letting my shoulder bump his as I walk by. I grab a bottle of water and down half of it.

I hope he's wrong.

Last night was a little awkward.

The sheets from the guest bed are heaped in the middle of the floor. She's re-making the bed, the room smelling like Lysol.

"What are you doing?" I ask, leaning against the doorframe.

"Making the bed."

"Those sheets were clean."

She smiles sheepishly. "I know. I'm sure. I just . . . I thought maybe Ever would be more comfortable on sheets of ours?"

"You know, I'm not a dirtball, Jules. Lysol-ing the mattress wasn't really necessary."

"I know. I'm sure. I mean, I know you aren't dirty." She forces a nervous a laugh and gathers the sheets. "I'll put these in the washer."

She walks by me and, a few minutes later, I find her washing down the kitchen counters.

I kept telling myself that it was just because it was their first night here, but I still had a raw feeling in the pit of my stomach. It was like I was some fucking stranger she was forced to live with. She seemed to not trust anything about the situation, my cleanliness or my temperament.

Our interaction was anything but comfortable. I honestly thought she was expecting me to laugh and tell her I was only kidding about the whole thing. No matter what I did, I couldn't get her to relax. Even Ever's enthusiasm about living with me didn't seem to take her edge off. I know she's worried about what sort of sign this gives Ever, but I think she's overreacting.

It was early when they went to bed in the spare room and I didn't see them before I left for work this morning. I left Ever a piece of taffy hidden under her coloring book on the table.

"Where are they now?" Will asks, looking around.

"I sent them to the grocery store. I told them I'd go, but Julia started telling me what Everleigh liked. It just seemed easier to give her the money and let her buy the shit."

"You're more of a man than me," he says, shrugging.

"What the fuck is that supposed to mean?"

"You are taking on a whole family, man. That's a lot of responsibility." He presses his lips together. "You just gave a chick cash and sent her on her way. That's—"

"If you don't understand this, then just get the fuck out."

He holds his hands in front of him. "Relax. I'm just saying that what you're doing is . . . a good thing. Not something a lot of guys in their twenties are gonna do."

I'm ready to tear into him when my phone rings. I cast him a look before heading into the living room. The phone is buzzing on the coffee table.

"Yeah?" I ask, knowing it's Jordyn.

"Hey, Crew. There's a guy in here looking for you."

"Where? The bar?"

"Yeah. He says he's from the news station Boston 15 and wants to talk to you about your fight in here last week."

"Tell him to fuck off."

The line gets grainy and when she comes back on, her voice is quieter. "Crew, I think this is important. He has a suit on in the middle of the fucking bar. This isn't a suit-wearing establishment."

"He's probably some old fucker that wants to talk about fighting. This Davidson fight has everyone all riled up and my name in the news now over that stupid bar fight has made people yap. I have nothing to say to him, J."

"All right," she sighs and I hang up.

Hanging my head, I try to not let myself go *there*, to the place of what might have been. Back to the time when I got calls from scouts and agents, all wanting a piece of the soon-to-be-famous Crew Gentry.

I thought I'd finally made peace with the way things went for me, tried to look at it like fate. Maybe I wasn't supposed to be in the NAFL, wasn't meant to have a huge contract. Normally I can go on about my day and not think about it, but with all the shit happening right now with Davidson and that fucking bar fight, it's been harder not to. Just thinking back to when those things were discussed, when they seemed like such a reality, makes me so damn bitter I can barely function.

And I don't have time for that now.

I know it's gonna be hard to ignore for the next few months with Hunter's next fight in Boston. Shit like our ties, the location, the history makes people want to speculate. I'm not sure what guys like this fucking reporter want me to say. *"Yeah, assholes, I know what happened. I know who he is now and I'm keenly fucking aware of what I could've been, too. Yup, still workin' the dock. Fighting in bars. Go fuck yourself."*

My gaze lands on a box with Ever's monkey on it. Will's right. My OCD would normally be going ballistic about the state of the mess of my house. But for some reason, it isn't. Actually, *I kind of like it*. And that has me worried more than anything. I noticed it last night after they went to bed. Something about seeing their things laying around made me feel calm, even though I knew they were there because of something tragic. I couldn't shake it. I went to bed with a gnawing sensation in my gut.

I growl under my breath as I turn around.

Will is watching me, arms crossed in front of him. "Sometimes I don't even know if I know you."

"What's that supposed to mean?"

"I was kidding. What's going on with you, man?"

I look at him blankly. I don't know where he's going with this, but he better get there fast. I walk over to the couch and sit down.

"This," he says, motioning to the room, "none of this bothers you?" He smirks and walks across the room. He steps exaggeratedly over two boxes and plops in his chair.

"Not really."

"Huh. That's strange. The Crew I know got pissed at me one time for leaving a fucking shoe in the middle of the room."

I close my eyes for a minute and consider my next words. Maybe I shouldn't project them into the room, and maybe I should never say them out loud. But I do.

"I kind of like it, actually." I open my eyes and look at him. Guilt overcomes me and I know I should've kept my mouth shut.

Fucker smirks harder.

"I shouldn't for so many motherfucking reasons. I know that and I know I'm going to hell."

"Man, you were going to hell way before you just said that!"

I shake my head, knowing he's right. But still . . .

"You're doing the right thing. You don't think if Gage was here, he'd *make* you do this?"

"If Gage was fucking here, I wouldn't *have* to do this."

"Not the fucking point," he says, leaning towards me. "You don't *have* to do this now."

I glare at him, but it only encourages him for some reason.

"Gage would expect you to take care of them. Hell, I'm kinda thinking if I didn't support this decision, your brother might throw a lightning bolt at me. That's how sure of this I am."

"Not the fucking point," I say, giving his words back to him. "I shouldn't *like* this. They aren't *my* family. She's not *my* wife, Ever's not *my* kid. They're my *brother's family*." I put my head in my hands. "Julia was right. This was a bad idea. There's just too much history between us. All of this makes my brain start thinking about things that could've . . . I just . . . damn it!"

SACRIFICE

Silence surrounds us. The more I talk, the guiltier I feel. Yet, having it off my chest and into the universe seems to lessen the burden in some strange way. But it's still wrong. Even Will in all his douchebag glory probably sees how wrong this is.

"Gage loved them," he says, slicing through the silence. "They were the world to him."

I look up and open my mouth but he cuts me off.

"Let's say you have a puppy," Will starts, the trademark smirk on his face. "And you love this puppy more than anything. It's the best puppy in the world. It's been your puppy from the time you were a little boy."

"Then it would be a dog. I don't see the point in your little analogy here."

"Shut the hell up and listen. Let's say you were going on a vacation or dying or something. Would you leave that puppy to me?"

"No."

"Exactly. Because I'd forget to feed the motherfucker and it'd die. Right?"

I laugh, starting to feel exasperated.

"Right?" he asks again.

"Right."

"Okay. So let's think of Jules and Ever as Gage's puppies. He'd want someone to take care of them and feed and water them."

I nod cautiously.

"But he'd also want someone to love them—"

"Thin ice, Will," I interrupt, my heartbeat picking up. I don't need connections made that aren't already linked.

I *need* him to shut the fuck up.

Will rolls his eyes. "Interrupt me all you want, but it doesn't change the fact that I'm right. Gage wouldn't want them to scrape along and be miserable. He'd want them to be happy and smile and be safe *and* loved, man."

"But it shouldn't be by *me*. The fact that you are even saying this is a million ways of fucked up."

"I'm saying what's written all over *your* face. I'm saying what I've known since *you* pussed out and went back to college and left her to fall in love with your brother."

"Will . . ." I warn, but I can see in his face that he's going to press the issue. His usual happy-go-lucky persona doesn't leave room to talk about shit that matters, but I can see that side of him isn't present tonight. I have the Will that thinks he knows things he doesn't. I have the "I-invented-the-Internet" Will Gentry.

"Just listen to me. I don't know why you left her behind. I don't know why she hooked up with Gage and I don't know why that was fine with you. And honestly, I don't give two fucks. It matters not to me. But things have changed and I didn't just walk in the front door and meet you today."

I bury my head in my hands, the conversation starting to make me sick.

"Gage trusted *you*," Will says, his voice without the edge from earlier. "You two had each other's backs from day one. Don't you think he'd want you to have it now?"

"I do!" I say, my voice rising with frustration. "I'm doing everything I can to take care of *his* family! I've moved his wife and kid in with me! What more can I fucking do?"

Will watches me, his eyes narrowed. "Do you think when Gage married Jules the fact that you dated her first was wiped from his brain? Because I assure you it wasn't. I fucking guarantee you it wasn't, man. He knew you loved her."

"I still don't see your fucking point and you better make it crystal clear quick."

"He trusted you, Crew. Only fucking you. And I think if he could pick anyone in the world to take care of her, *make her happy*, it'd be *you*. So you feeling guilty and having a conscious for the first time in your damn life is kinda dumb. If you're going to become some philosophical badass, pick another topic because this one's stupid."

I burst up and take a deep breath.

"I don't want to talk about this. This isn't what I was saying." I don't look at him. What he's just spewed is blasphemy. It's fucking craziness and I don't even want to think about it. I don't want to consider it. It's not the way things are fucking done.

The phone rings, cutting through the tension. I see it's Julia and I grab it off the table, grateful for the interruption. "Hey."

"Crew," she says, her voice choking back tears.

"Jules? What's wrong?" The hairs on the back of my neck stand. "Where are you?"

"We are on our way home. I just got a call from Dr. Perkins' office." She pauses and I hear a slight gasp. "The therapy has been denied."

"What?" I shout.

"Yeah," she says, her voice trembling. "I shouldn't have called you, but I just..."

"Why?"

"Insurance denied it. Said that the medicine would be covered, but all the other things would not." Her voice wobbles and I know she's trying hard to control it. "So they denied us unless I can get fifty thousand dollars."

Adrenaline surges through my veins, the top of my head feeling light as the energy courses through my body. *Motherfucker!*

"I'll be back in a few minutes. I just..."

"We'll figure it out," I say through gritted teeth. "We'll figure this out."

"We can't come up with that kind of money, Crew. We can't get a loan, we can't pawn or borrow that kind of money." Her voice cracks again and the sound resonates in my chest. I hear Ever in the background, singing, and I can't handle it.

"I'll figure it out. I swear to God, I will figure this out." I look at Will and he has turned the television on, watching SportsCenter. "Hey, Jules?"

"Yeah?"

"I might not be here when you get here. It's important. But I'll be back, okay?"

"Okay."

"I promise you, I'll be back tonight."

I end the call, scroll through my contacts, and press SEND.

"Get your ass up and let's go," I bark. Will's on his feet in a flash, tossing me a curious look.

"Shenanigans."

"Hey, Jordyn. Is that guy in the suit still there?"

She laughs. "Yeah. He's sitting at the end of the bar watching the door. He ordered a *mojito*. What guy drinks that?"

"Pour him another. I'll be there in twenty."

Chapter TWENTY

CREW

THE GRAVEL CRUNCHES behind me as Will jogs to catch up. The streetlights are on, casting a weird glow over the parking lot. I park in the back next to Jordyn, the lot fuller than usual for a weekday night.

"You gonna tell me why we're here? I've got the feeling we aren't getting a beer."

I twist the toothpick around in my mouth. I've went over this meeting a hundred times in my head on the way over. I'm not sure what they even want. I just know I need it to go a certain way, to plant a seed that with a little luck will grow just in time.

"I'm meeting with a reporter," I say.

"For?"

"Watch and learn."

"Watch and learn," he mutters, stepping back as I open the door to Shenanigans. The chimes going off and we enter. Jordyn looks up and smiles.

The bar is pretty full, but the atmosphere is calm. Too calm. There's no music going and the televisions are even on mute. Just the sound of someone playing pool cracks through the air.

Jordyn nods her head to the end of the bar where two men, completely out of character for this place, are sitting. One is in a large sweatshirt, a bag sitting at his feet. The other is sipping a drink, a suit jacket thrown over the back of the stool.

Will's hand clasps my shoulder. "You need me?"

"Nah, just stick around 'til this is over. Grab a drink and tell J to add it to my tab."

The two guys at the end look bored. I size them up as I approach. The guy in the hoodie is surfing around on his phone, the other guy scribbling in a notepad.

I know everyone's watching me as I walk through; I can feel their eyes heavy on my skin. There's no threat, just curious patrons wondering if they'll get to see some action tonight. And they will, I hope, just not the kind they're thinking.

"Hey."

Both men's heads snap up. The guy in the suit's eyes widen and he struggles to get off the stool. "Crew Gentry?"

"I heard you wanted to talk to me."

He nods exaggeratedly and extends a hand. "I do. Thank you for coming. I'm Brett Wiskin. This is Chuck Stells."

I shake Brett's hand. "What can I do for ya?"

He glances around the room. "Let's move over to the corner for a little privacy."

Brett and Chuck load up their shit and we make our way to the corner table where Will and I usually sit. I try to block out everything but what's in front of me at the moment. My mind naturally wants to process everyone in this room, take inventory of who is where. That's not to mention the fact that I'm purposefully blocking out Julia and Ever. I can't get distracted . . . for all of our sakes.

They get their stuff situated around the table and I begin to get impatient. I grab the salt shaker and tap it lightly on the tabletop, hoping to kick them into action.

"So, Crew, are you here often?" Brett asks finally, running a hand through his journalist-hair. I've seen my share of these sportscasters and they're all the same. Guys that talk because they can't walk.

I set the shaker down. "This isn't a date. Cut the shit and tell me what you want."

He seems a little taken aback, but recovers quickly. "First of all, this conversation is completely off the record."

I nod.

"I saw a little video online this past week. If I'm not mistaken, that video was shot inside this bar."

I wait for him to continue. I'm still not sure what he's after and I don't want to play my hand too soon.

"It's created quite a splash in the online community."

"Has it really?" I ask, sounding purposefully disinterested.

"I'm sure you've seen it around."

I shrug. "I'm not much of an 'online community' type of guy."

Brett considers my statement and glances at Chuck. He's fumbling with a camera, oblivious, it seems, to the entire conversation. That surprises me . . . the camera guys are usually the smart ones, just not good-looking enough to be in *front* of the camera.

"Well, it was pretty impressive. Want to walk us through what happened?"

"I stopped a couple of bums from robbing a bar. Not much to walk you through."

"You're being quite humble, Crew. You threw those guys around like rag dolls. That wasn't a bar fight. That was like something we'd see on TV." A slow smile crosses his lips. "While we were sitting at the bar, a handful of people came in and asked the bartender if you were here."

I raise my eyebrows and wait. *This is why I'm here.*

"You still fight?" Chuck asks, sitting the camera on the table.

Yahtzee.

"Only for fun," I smirk.

"So no sanctioned events?" Brett asks. "I'm telling you, it looks like you haven't missed a beat since Minnesota. If you're telling me you haven't been training, I'm surprised."

I lean forward, resting my elbows on the table. "Athletes train for an *event*, Brett." I say, boring my eyes into his. "Guys like me, we train to *live*. So have I been training? Yeah. *I train for fucking life.*"

My table mates watch me like I'm crazy. The fear in their eyes makes my dick hard. I love the feeling of intimidating someone, of controlling the situation.

I push out the realization that if I don't control this one, other, more important ones, are gonna be outta reach.

"Your background is wrestling," Chuck points out. "But you clearly know how to throw a punch. Ever think about joining the NAFL now?"

"Nah, not really."

"There's a lot of talk about you coming in. You fought at the 185-lb weight class in college," Chuck remarks. "That's an exciting division right now. There's a lot of speculation about how things will go down in there."

"So I've heard," I say. I try to appear bored, like I don't give a fuck, but it's all I can do not to just blurt out what I need to happen.

Stay calm, Crew.

"Since you're so disconnected from things nowadays," Brett says, "I'll catch you up on a few things. There was supposed to be a big fight in Boston in a couple of months. A middleweight named Reyes was supposed to take on the man of the hour, the undefeated Hunter Davidson."

I chuckle. "Undefeated? Nah, I believe I'm 1–0 against him."

Brett's eyes light up and he shuffles in his seat. "That was a long time ago . . ."

I know he's fucking with me, wanting me to go crazy. But he's just laid his hand wide open and I'm seeing fucking spades.

"Pretty sure I had no problem handling him," I laugh through semi-gritted teeth.

"There's a camp of people," Chuck says, watching me carefully, "that don't appreciate his showmanship."

"You mean people don't like the fact that he's a cocksucker? Go figure."

Chuck laughs. "Apparently. And those people have proposed the idea of you taking Reyes' place. Taking on Hunter Davidson right here in Boston." He plays with his camera, a grin on his face. "I'd say that's crazy, tossing a guy in the cage that hasn't fought in years. A guy whose last fight ended with a stretcher."

Chuck's eyes glimmer. He's much better at this game than Brett.

"But I saw your fight," he continues. "So I'm solidly in that camp. I'd love to see it happen."

I wrap my hands around the sides of my chair, squeezing it to release some frustration. I know I have to stay calm, make this seem like all their idea. I gotta come across as indifferent, confident. I can't blow this now.

"I follow MMA a little bit and Davidson's career is on the right path. I'm pretty fucking sure his people aren't going to want to put him back on the mat with a guy that has already proven he can kick his ass. I've got that punk's number and beating him in front of the world would destroy his career; they aren't stupid."

"So, hypothetically speaking of course, you'd be willing to fight Davidson again?"

"If Davidson wants to ruin his career, I'm more than happy to do that for him."

I push back from the table, my hands shaking from the adrenaline.

"Is that all you guys have to discuss?"

"It is," Brett says excitedly. "Can we snap a picture real quick?"

I stand and Brett walks around the table. Chuck snaps a couple of pics and then shakes my hand.

"Where can we get a hold of you?" Brett asks. I jot down my number on a napkin and hand it to him.

"All right, guys. I'm outta here." I nod and turn to leave. Will is sitting at the bar, talking to Jordyn. He grins and I turn back around.

"Hey, Brett?"

"Yeah?"

"Make that conversation on the record."

Chapter TWENTY-ONE

CREW

I'VE REPLAYED THE conversation a million ways on my way home. My head is pounding, the back of my neck aching like it does when adrenaline wears off. It's almost like a hangover. I'm hoping some clarity will come; a moment when I'll feel like something I'm fucking doing is the right thing.

How would I even know what that feels like if it did?

I unlock the door and start inside but stop mid-way.

My house usually doesn't smell like much of anything. Maybe cologne from the morning or bleach if I've cleaned, but that's it. It's always just like I've left it. But tonight, the house smells different. A mixture of spices and warmth hits me hard and throws me a little off balance.

I shut the door softly, still feeling skewed. It's my house, but I don't know who's up or what they're doing. It doesn't feel like I'm walking into my house, but walking into a home.

I toss my keys on the kitchen counter and make my way towards a light in the living room. I round the corner and see Julia sitting on the couch, hunched over a box. She looks up and her eyes meet mine.

Her beautiful face is marred with the misery she's under. She has bags under her eyes, her forehead lined with tension. It adds to the weight I'm carrying on my shoulders.

"Hey," I say quietly. "I didn't think you'd be up. It's late."

She half-smiles. "I'm trying to get some of this mess cleaned up."

"Don't worry about it," I say, sitting in the chair Will always uses. I try to ease her worries with a smile, but it doesn't work.

"I know you hate a mess, Crew. I feel bad still having boxes lying around."

"It's been a couple of days, Jules. Relax."

"Relax? What's that again?"

I feel like an asshole. Of course she can't relax.

Neither can I.

"Is everything okay? You were gone a while."

I consider how much to tell her, but I don't want to get her hopes up. I don't know if this is gonna work, it's a long shot anyway. I'm not putting any eggs into this basket and I don't really want her doing that either.

"Yeah. Everything is fine. I had to meet up with a few guys about a side job."

As soon as I say it, I know it was the wrong thing.

Her shoulders slump. "I'll see if I can get some shifts this weekend at Ficht's. I—"

"No, you won't," I cut her off. "That's not exactly what I meant. Just . . . don't worry about it, all right? Your job is to focus on Ever. My job is to focus on the rest."

I see her throat bob and her hands begin to shake. "I'm scared, Crew."

I grab the armrests of the chair so I won't stand and grab *her*. "I know. But we'll figure it out. Somehow, we'll figure it out. *I promise you.*"

"Without the therapy, I don't know what the odds are. They just said we'd talk about it on Monday when we go in for day one of the chemo, but this was the winning shot . . ."

"I promise you, we *will* figure this out. *I* will figure this out. I don't want you worrying about it now. There's a chance she won't even need the therapy, okay?"

She tries to grin, but I know she doesn't believe me. Hell, I don't even really believe me. I don't know how this is going to play out, other than I have to do whatever I have to do to get this baby healthy.

"Let's stay positive and not fall apart until we hear the doctor out, okay?"

"Just . . ." She looks scared all of a sudden. "Just please don't leave us, Crew."

The English language becomes as foreign to me as Arabic. I cannot speak. I know down deep she's not kidding. She's been left or turned away by everyone, but I'll be damned if I'll fall into that pattern again.

She clears her throat and pulls out a blue bowl that I recognize. She holds it up and smiles. "This was your mom's. Do you remember?"

"Yeah. I remember her using that to make pancakes sometimes."

"It was one of the things Gage didn't want to get rid of. He said the same thing, that she used to make pancakes with it."

"We didn't get many home cooked meals. Pancakes were her specialty," I laugh.

"She tried to make Gage pancakes the day before she died, but she was so weak," Julia says and then stops abruptly. "I'm sorry."

I've never talked about her or what happened between us with anyone. When I didn't come back when Gage called and said she was dying, no one brought it up again. I flew home once she passed, went to the funeral, and then headed back to Minnesota again. Gage never questioned me on it; I think he always knew why I acted how I did. Gage got me in ways that no one else did. No one else ever will.

"Nah, it's okay," I say.

"Why didn't you come back?"

The million dollar fucking question is now laid grandly at my feet.

I look at her blankly, hoping she'll apologize again and change the topic. Instead, her big, brown eyes fill with expectancy. She actually waits for a damn answer.

My instincts say to get the fuck out of here. Stand up, walk to the door, and go. My heart says otherwise. Its beats are telling me I've done that to her more times than I should've and I can't do it to her again.

"I don't know," I mutter, giving her another chance to change topics.

"Yes, you do."

I release a ragged breath and try to look at her, but pull my gaze to the wall instead. I can't look into those eyes. I know she's hoping for some beautifully fucked up answer, something that makes some motherfucking sense and will make her think I'm not some kind of bastard. The truth isn't that kind.

"I'm the asshole you think I am."

"Crew," she says. She doesn't continue until I look at her again. "Why didn't you come home?"

"What does it matter?"

"It just *does*."

I think about the hundred reasons, the way they interconnect like a spider web, each reason weaving into the next. I don't even know where to start.

"I was a disappointment to her." I sound like a pussy. I know I do.

"You were not."

"Nah, I was. Remember when I came home?" I cough, trying to decide whether to bring up that she was with Gage then. Choosing not to, I continue, "I was only here for a night. Before I left, she and I talked."

"And?"

"She was in the kitchen, drinking her tea, and I kissed her on the cheek. I was so fucking pissed off for obvious reasons. I was just going to walk out, but she asked me to sit down. So I did. She just watched me for a while like she did when I was a kid."

My hands shake at the memory of realizing I had lost every-fucking-thing. College had been a blast: parties, girls, wrestling. But I had started to get the feeling that everything was superficial. The girls, the invites, the friends . . . that all came with winning. What would happen if I lost? Nothing felt real, anymore. Nobody knew who I really was, me included.

I woke up one morning and realized that I'd not talked to my mom in months. That I had no fucking clue what was going on with Gage. That I hadn't said anything substantial to Jules in more days than I could remember. The chick lying next to me that morning looked so different from her and I remember how it rolled my stomach, her blonde hair sprawled across my chest. For some reason, everything hit me at once. I needed to find that scrap of whatever it was that made me *me*. I needed a second chance to make things right with everyone. So I bought a ticket with some money loaned to me by my coach and flew home to surprise everyone.

Surprise, fucking, surprise.

"Ma asked me if I was happy. I smarted something off and she shushed me and asked me again. I yelled, you know, how could I be happy walking in to the mess I did? That everyone in my life had changed and I knew nothing about it. That I meant nothing to any of you."

I remember her face, all lined with years of hard work and little else. How her eyes looked like mine and Gage's, but colorless in a way, a film on them from days without a smile. I felt like shit for leaving her behind and basically ignoring her, but feeling that in front of her made me angry.

"Ma told me she thought I'd lost my way. That I'd gotten too big at school and had forgotten who I was. That I'd let the glory or whatever dumb word you wanna use get to my head. That she and Gage missed me. That she wanted me to remember that."

SACRIFICE

I stand, embarrassed for saying this out loud, embarrassed for having done this at all. But at the same time, it is freeing.

"She said she wanted me to not get tied up in the rich man's game. To be a simple man. To find a woman to love, a job I didn't hate, and enjoy the nice things in life. And by nice things she didn't mean cars and watches."

I chuckle and look at Julia. "That was it for me. You were in the other room with Gage. When she said that, I got pissed. I don't remember what I said to her, exactly, but it had something to do with her not understanding who I was. That she liked Gage better than me and was rubbing it in my face that I lost you." I shrug, as if that would explain things. "I kissed her again and left. And then a few months later when Gage called and said I needed to come home . . ."

I stop talking. I don't know what to say.

"Were you going to come?"

"I was young," I say, sadly. "I didn't really think it was that serious. I don't know, maybe I was just butt-hurt. But I should've gotten on a plane that night. I should've been here. But I didn't and I wasn't."

"Were you going to come?" she whispers again, hopefully this time.

"No."

She looks shocked, her mouth dropping open. It's what I expect.

"I'm not Gage, Jules. I didn't know how to deal with everything . . ." I sit down again and take a deep breath. "I called her the night before she died. Did Gage tell you that?"

Her eyebrows sink together as she shakes her head.

"I did. I still don't think I really thought she'd die, but we talked. Not one of those 'say everything you wanna say' talks, but we did have a conversation. I just . . . I know I didn't handle that right. I've not handled a lot of things right . . ."

The current in the room shifts and I know she feels it. She just looks at me.

"I'm sorry, Jules."

"For what?" she breathes.

"I've not handled things right with you either."

"Crew—"

"No, hear me out. I told you I wasn't going to Minnesota and then basically just left you. I shouldn't have been surprised that you moved on."

"It wasn't like that."

"It doesn't matter."

127

"No, it does," she says, sitting the bowl down. "I didn't just hook up with Gage as soon as you left, Crew."

I roll my head, my neck now throbbing. Regardless of what she says, this doesn't matter. It's done. And I don't even think I want to hear it.

"When you left, yeah, I was devastated. But even then, I knew I couldn't expect you to walk away from a scholarship like that. I wasn't stupid. I just went to school and got through each day and hoped you'd come back. Then one night . . ."

She presses her lips together. She gives her head a little shake, her ebony hair swishing across her shoulders.

"One night, things got bad at home. My parents had been drinking, as usual, but they started fighting. Bad. I locked my bedroom door at one point because things were getting crazy. Things started busting around the house and before I knew it, my dad was banging on my door.

"I finally open it, afraid he was going to bust it down," she says weakly, "and he barges in. He was yelling, asking me something but I couldn't understand him through the slur. My mom was behind him, yelling her own slew of things, and I was trying to make sense of it. I just couldn't, Crew. I didn't know what they were even talking about. I tried to appease them, to just say yes or no, depending . . ." She swallows hard. Her eyes refuse to meet mine. "He grabbed me across the throat and slammed me against a wall . . ."

"He did fucking what?" I roar, leaping out of my chair. "How in the fuck did I not know this? That's not what you guys said then!"

"You didn't answer your phone," she whispers, her face to the floor. "And then, I'm sure Gage gave you an easier explanation so you wouldn't go crazy."

I groan, knowing I should never have left her with them. I wish I could punch myself, tear myself apart for what I've done. I've regretted it a million times, second-guessed my decision a million times, but it was worse than I ever fucking dreamed.

"Were you okay?"

"Yeah. Mostly. He screamed at me and eventually got sidetracked by my mother yelling and I slipped out the door. I ran down to the gas station. I didn't even have shoes on," she laughs sadly. "The lady at the counter let me use the phone . . . I didn't even know who to call."

"I'm so fucking sorry," I choke out. Fury and guilt choke me, drown me in their depths.

"I finally called Gage. I didn't know anyone else that would come."

SACRIFICE

"Jules—"

"Don't worry about it, Crew. That was a long time ago."

"Damn it, Jules. Damn it! I . . ." I run my hands across my face, scrubbing at them for some feeling. I feel so many things I'm practically numb. "Ah!"

"Everything worked out. Gage came and took me home with him." She smiles to herself. "I had to beg him, literally beg him, not to kill my father."

"He should've," I bite out. "He should've sliced his fucking throat."

Julia leans back on the sofa, her arms across her stomach. "That's how things started with Gage and I anyway. I was afraid to go home, so I stayed with him and your ma for a while."

I don't give a shit about that right now. I'm glad Gage went and got her. God knows what might've happened if he didn't. I'm just pissed he didn't kill her cocksucker father.

"I never should've left you. I should've fought for you," I say, my voice so low I don't even know if she heard me.

"You couldn't. You weren't in a good place, Crew. Things happen for a reason."

"Fuck that. I could've and I should've. I've never fought for anything good, anything honorable. I should've done that for you."

I watch her watching me and think about the weird way things have happened. She and I are together now, but not together, all because of the baby she had with my brother.

Fucking life.

"I want you to know something," I say, hoping this is the right thing to do. "I came home that day because I missed you."

A small gasp escapes her throat as she struggles to sit up.

"I walked in and saw the two of you sitting there, your head lying in his lap while you watched TV." I shake my head, the pit of acid that comes with the image hitting me yet again. "I stood there for a couple of minutes and watched you both. I was ready to grab Gage by the back of the head and beat the fuck out of him. Then I heard you giggle."

I fix my gaze against a wall, remembering the way it sounded like it just happened. So carefree, so happy, so safe. Three things I knew I'd probably never be able to give her. I was irresponsible, unpredictable . . . even to myself. She didn't deserve me. What could I even offer her but one fuck-up after another?

"You and Gage deserved each other. You are the best people I've ever known."

I see her irises blur with tears and I smile. "Don't cry."

"Crew . . ." She wipes her face with her fingertips. "I had no idea you came home because of me. I thought you'd forgotten about me. Gage and I . . . we never expected anything to happen. It just . . . did."

"It should've. You two being together was the world actually working for once. I fucked up your lives time and time again. Gage did us both a favor by saving you from me."

"I found something the other day. A letter from Gage."

"Where?"

"At the bank." She closes her eyes and I'm not sure if she's going to continue. "I went to get my ring and when I found it, I also found a letter he'd written to me."

"What did it say?" I feel my heartbeat pick up, wondering what my brother said.

She laughed sadly. "He told me if anything ever happened, he wanted me to trust you."

"Me?"

"Yeah. I'll show it to you sometime. But for now, I want to just keep it, if that's okay?"

I nod, trying to figure out why in the hell Gage would say that.

"He said he loved you, Crew. And that you always had his back and that you would have mine."

A pinch pierces the back of my neck and I grab it, rubbing it down. Julia makes a face.

"What's the matter?"

"Nothing." I roll my shoulders, trying to loosen the pull.

"Are you hurt?"

I laugh. There's no fucking way I'm telling her that. "No," I lie.

She cocks her head to the side. "Maybe you should stop doing push-ups all the time and lifting weights and stuff. I bet that would help."

"Not likely," I say, twisting side-to-side. I figure I may as well test the waters. "I might be fighting again."

"What?" she shrieks. "Oh my God. You aren't. You can't, Crew."

I shrug. "Maybe. It might be fun."

"If you fight again, I'll send you to meet your brother," she says, only half joking. She rises from the couch and yawns. "I think I'll head to bed. We have a long week coming up." She starts to leave the room but stops. "Crew? Can I ask you something?"

"Sure."

"I need to tell Ever this weekend what's going to happen to her. I . . . um . . . I don't know how to do that. Will you help me?"

"Of course."

"Thank you." She heads down the hallway again, the back of her tattered blue shirt hanging behind her.

"Hey, Jules?"

"Yeah?"

"You can sleep in my bed, if ya want. I'll take the couch."

"You don't have to do that, Crew."

"I know. But you're gonna need a good night's rest while you can get it."

She smiles softly. "I can't. I've taken so much from you already."

"You've given me more than you've ever taken, Jules," I whisper. "And, by the way, I didn't answer you earlier."

"About what?"

"I'll never leave you again."

Her cheeks flush. She dips her head, a small grin gracing her lips, and slides through the door to the guest room.

Chapter TWENTY-TWO

JULIA

DARKNESS ENVELOPS ME as I step inside the bedroom. It's cool and calm. Ever's sweet, rhythmic breathing is the only sound besides the wild thumping of my heart.

I close the door and lean against it, my back flat to the wood. I take a few controlled breaths and try to make sense of what just happened. My mind is spinning, already replaying the conversation from just a few minutes before.

I have no idea what just happened.

Everything I thought I knew was just pulled out from under me. I have no idea where I'm standing, except that I'm on shaky ground. Never in a million years did I think Crew came back for me.

I close my eyes and remember hearing his voice call Gage's name through the house that day. I remember feeling like I was going to come out of my skin when he walked in the room.

I hadn't seen him in months. I hadn't heard from him in weeks. Even then, the conversations were short. Impersonal. I didn't think he cared anymore. And when I looked up at him, his eyes were locked away. They only served to strengthen my conclusion that he had grown away from me, found a more exciting life in Minnesota.

But was I wrong?

I let my head hang forward, hoping the rush of blood to my brain would help me think.

Did I do something wrong? Should I have waited on him?

Was I wrong for being with Gage?

Everleigh's breathing shifts and she rolls to her side. Her pink lips pucker in her sleep. *And I know.*

Regardless of why Crew left or why he came back, regardless of when and how I got with Gage, it wasn't wrong. That little girl proves it. She's the tie that binds us together, even under these terrible circumstances. She's what bonded Gage and I together, solidified our marriage. A marriage that I am absolutely certain would stand the test of time if he was still here.

But he's not.

She's also what kept me going after losing him. And now, she's the reason that Crew and I are able talk without killing one another.

I scoot Ever over and climb in the bed. She snuggles against me, resting her monkey on my chest. I squeeze her tight.

This may be one of the last normal nights we have in a long time.

The moon shines through the blinds, casting shadows through the room. Ever's dream catcher is hanging on the window, right where she and Crew put it the night we got here.

I watch the shadows dance on the walls and feel a sense of peace start to wash over me. It's soothing and I feel settled in a way I haven't in a very long time. The quietness of the room, so unlike the apartment, is a simple pleasure I didn't even realize how much I'd missed.

I force my eyes shut, but Gage's eyes don't come for me like they usually do. Instead, I see Crew's face from moments before.

Did I misjudge him this entire time?

No. I know I haven't. He's irresponsible. He's a hedonist.

The dream catcher twists as the vent beneath it turns on. I watch it spin. Crew and Ever placed it carefully so it would pull the most light from the streetlamp outside. He's so careful with her, so tender. He's sacrificed so much of his life to help her.

To help me.

I hear Ever moan. Her hand shifts under the blankets and holds her stomach. She moans again and the sound shakes me to the core.

I make sure she's settled and then feel my worries take over.

"Mrs. Gentry, I'm sorry," Dr. Perkins says, his voice controlled. "The insurance has denied Everleigh's admission into the therapy program. We've filed an appeal on her behalf, but we haven't heard back yet."

"What does this mean?"

A million thoughts fly through my head, making me dizzy. This can't be happening!

I toggle the phone in my hand. I shouldn't have answered it in the parking lot of the grocery store. I knew better. I should've let it go to voicemail and called him back.

I turn to smile at Ever in the backseat, safely buckled into her seatbelt in the parking lot of the grocery store. I whisper to stay put and then exit the car, leaning against the hood. "What do you mean she's been denied?"

"Unfortunately, this treatment isn't a standard procedure. Insurance companies are more hesitant to approve these things because they're very costly and unproven in the long run."

I can't breathe. I feel like my chest filled with cement. Things start spinning around me and I squeeze my temples with my free hand, trying to stay clearer minded than when I got the original diagnosis.

"So what does this mean?" I ask. "What do we do now?"

"We wait and see what they say. We'll talk about it more on Monday. I know this is not the news you wanted to hear. It's not the news I wanted to hear either and, honestly, not the news I expected to hear. Regardless, we will keep pushing on our end."

"What if she doesn't get in?"

"If she doesn't get in, we'll modify our game plan and go with Plan B. I don't want you to panic over this. I just want you to know where we stand so if you do have resources to fall back on, now would be the time."

I snort. Who has an extra $50,000 to 'fall back on'?

What if we can't get her into the therapy? What can I possibly do to get that much money?

I know there's nothing I can do. I don't have those types of resources. I can't even dream up a scheme, short of robbing a bank, to get half of that amount.

Crew walks down the hallway outside the door. I hear the floors squeak as he enters the bathroom. I listen to him run water and then the light switch flips off. The floors bend again with his weight and his bedroom door shuts softly down the hallway.

Just knowing he's close makes me feel a little better. I know it makes Ever feel better. She's mentioned a few times that she likes not hearing the neighbors fighting and her little face lights up so brightly when Crew walks in. Aside from making us feel a little safer, I pray that he can finally follow through on a promise and actually help me figure this out.

Chapter TWENTY-THREE

CREW

"GENTRY!"

I toss the bag on the dock and turn around. My boss gestures to me and yells, "Take your break!"

I walk across the shipyard. The weather is calm and warm, the last cold front ushered in warmer weather. It's a near-perfect day and I wish I could appreciate it. But I'm too torn up about Everleigh to enjoy anything.

I slept like shit the night before. Too many damn things on my mind. One thing bled into another and I watched the time switch on my clock and I turned off the alarm before it had a chance to ring.

My brain could've at least figured some shit out after being awake all night. But it didn't. Ever still has cancer. I still need to come up with a ton of fucking money. Julia probably still thinks I am a fuck-up.

When I rolled out of bed, the only thing different than the last few mornings was that Julia had made me coffee. She wasn't around and there was no note or anything, but the pot was full when I ventured into the kitchen.

Inside the small break room, I open my locker and grab a bottle of water. I take a drink, grateful to be alone for a few minutes. The cool water feels good as it trickles down my throat. I rummage around and find my phone and turn it on. One missed call. I press the voicemail button.

"*Hey, Crew. It's Brett from Boston 15. I wanted to let you know that I've* filed my report from our talk with the station and it'll air tonight at ten PM. I've penned a little column for the website and posted it this morning. Just letting you know in case you get any calls or want to check it out for yourself. Thanks again for meeting with us. I wish you all the luck in the future."

I look to the ceiling as my throat squeezes shut.

Holy shit.

I hope Brett took what I gave him and ran with it. *He bit, but did he bite hard enough?*

I can't ignore the touch of anxiety growing in my stomach. I need to make this happen, but I know for it to happen, I need the stars to align. I need the right people to see it, to share it, for it to hit the right nerve with the right people.

It's such a long shot it probably isn't even a shot at all. For all I know, Hunter Davidson already has another contender lined up.

It will take the stars aligning and the grace of God to even get this stupid idea off the ground. Stranger things have happened, of course. *But even if it does, how do I know I can even perform at that level?*

I throw the bottle against the back of my locker. It drops onto the floor, spilling liquid everywhere.

CREW

IT'S STRANGE HAVING clean towels in my bathroom cabinet. I always kept the laundry done, but never bothered to keep more than a couple of towels in the bathroom. I'd just use one and hang it on the back of the door. It's another change from living with Julia. Another change that doesn't bother me all that much.

I wrap a fresh towel snugly around my waist and use my hand to clear the moisture from the bathroom mirror. My reflection is peering back at me, calling me out on all the lies I've been telling myself.

That things will be okay. That I'll find a way out of this mess.

The lines around my mouth, the way my shoulders hang. . . . I don't know what the hell I'm doing. I'm trying to play hero and I haven't got the first fucking clue where to start. My only hope is a fucking pipe dream, one that I don't even know will work if it does fucking work.

The lights on my phone flash on the counter. I turned the sound off before I got in; the calls and texts were starting to go haywire. A text from

SACRIFICE

Brett was waiting for me after work with a link to his article. In his favor, and mine, he was as suggestive and dramatic as I'd hoped.

"By all accounts, Crew Gentry should be washed up. A star student of local legend Sal D'Amato and a wrestling standout at the University of Minnesota, Gentry hasn't been seen or heard since leaving the mat on a stretcher. That is, until last week.

Waves were made in the MMA community last week after a video popped up online showing Gentry in a fight. The images were grainy but nonetheless impressive. He was explosive and so reminiscent of the guy so many of us followed years ago. It made me wonder . . . what's Gentry up to these days?

When he agreed to meet me, I expected a shell of the person most of us in this community remember. I know the effects time and injury have on a man. And I vividly recall Gentry being carted away from Davidson at Iowa in the NCAA finals. The entire sports world waited to see if he'd survive the spinal cord injury and a collective sigh of relief was heard when we thought he was just paralyzed.

Crew Gentry walked up to me last night and whatever I thought he'd be; he was the exact opposite.

He's been working the docks for the past few years. He's strong, fit, and, more importantly, still has that twinkle in his eye.

I asked him about fighting again. He gave me a fighter's response and said he wouldn't turn down a fight. I pressed further, asking if he thought he could take Hunter Davidson again. He was more curious if Hunter Davidson could handle him again.

Before meeting Gentry, I would've thought it was crazy to even consider such a thing. But after seeing him, feeling his energy, my money's on Crew.

Calls and messages are starting to pour in. A good sign in one respect, meaning the article was getting shared and talked about. A bad sign in another because the attention was not from the right people and it was only adding to the fraying of my nerves.

I see Jordyn's number and pick it up. "What's up?"

"Hey, Crew. You home?"

"Yeah. Just got out of the shower."

"I'm like two streets over. Can I drop by?"

"Nah, you better not."

"Okay," she pouts. "You coming by the bar tonight?"

"Nope. Listen, things are kinda busy for me right now. So I won't be around much."

The line goes quiet for a moment. "Fine. You seeing someone else?"

"It's not like that."

"It never is," she sighs. "You know what? Don't worry about it. Just don't come chasing me when you're done with whoever it is."

"I don't even chase my fucking liquor, J."

"Whatever. Bye."

I end the call and look at myself again. It's a Friday night and I've just turned down free pussy and I'm not going to the bar.

Who the hell am I?

"Crew?" Julia's says from the other side of the door. Her voice is quiet, tired, but has that underlying edge of determination that it always does.

Hearing her voice saying my name reminds me of the man I was, the man I am, and the man I'm determined to become. She gives me a reason to want to do better.

"Yeah?"

"Dinner's ready, if you're hungry."

I shake my head at myself in the mirror.

She is a fighter. Take fucking notes.

Chapter TWENTY-FOUR

JULIA

THE MOMENTS TICK by, each breath advancing us forward to Monday morning.

I rinse the last breakfast plate before putting it into the dishwasher. Over my shoulder, I see Crew and Ever on the couch watching cartoons. In the middle of this hell I'm living in, a world of diagnosis, vitamins, antibiotics, unknowns, denials, and uncertainty, the scene in front of me gives me something to hold onto.

I've toyed all day with when to tell Ever what's going on. At first, I was going to wait until Sunday to tell her, figuring it would give her the least amount of time to worry about it. Then I thought maybe it'd be easier for her to know now and have all day today and tomorrow to ask us questions and get comfortable with the idea.

My stomach aches with dread. I'm sure an ulcer is forming. I can't eat. I can't sleep. I just go from motion-to-motion, looking at the clock. Even that is a source of anxiety. I don't want to see Monday get any closer; I don't want to witness such horrid things happening to my baby. Yet again, each day that passes is a day that she's not getting treatment. I just pray the doctor's know what they're doing.

"We need all our ducks in a row, Ms. Gentry. We need all the lab work back and time to call in a team to study it. This is what we do and we want your daughter to be as strong as possible when it's time for treatment. Trust us."

I trust no one.

I dry my hands on a dishtowel and gather my courage. "Crew? Can you come here for a minute?"

He looks up and pulls his eyebrows together. He pats Ever on the head and walks toward me. He stops a few steps away.

"I was thinking . . ." I know once we do this, there is no going back. It has to be done, but I'm terrified to do it. I don't want to see her scared. I don't want to see her cry.

"Maybe we should tell her tonight. Give her a couple of days to think about it? Ask questions? Before we have to show up and start everything."

"Yeah," he says gruffly. He nods, like he's still coming to terms with the idea and stands taller. He pulls me in to his chest and I let him. I need this bit of reassurance that I'm not going through this alone. Maybe it makes me weak to need him, but damn it, I do.

The warmth of his embrace, the hardness of his body, the scent of his skin that I remember begins to fill up that part of me that seems empty. The part of me that I rely on for strength.

Pulling back, he brushes a strand of hair out of my eyes. "Ready?"

"Now?" I ask. I wasn't prepared to do it later, let alone *now*.

"Let's do it now. Get it over with."

I nod because agreeing to this out loud is more than I can do. He turns and heads back into the living room. I follow. My throat is so dry, my chest stinging so badly that I'm not sure I'll be able to say anything.

"Hey, monkey. Your mommy and I want to talk to you for a second, okay?" Crew glances at me, waiting for me to sit. I lower myself beside Ever and he sits in the chair by the window.

Ever sits up and looks from Crew to me. "Okay. What do you want to talk about? Taking me to the park?"

"No, but maybe we can go tomorrow, okay?"

She seems pleased with the answer and looks at me.

"So, remember how we were at the doctor earlier this week? And they did all kinds of tests and things?" I ask.

Her eyes grow wide and she scoots back to the back of the couch. "Yes. It hurt."

Her words strangle me. I look at Crew pleadingly.

"Yeah, those things suck," he says, getting Ever's attention. "Before you were born, I got hurt. And I had to do all kinds of tests like that. It doesn't feel good."

"You did?" she asks. "I didn't know that."

"I did. So I know what it feels like."

Crew pauses, waiting for me to join in. I know he's letting me lead the conversation and I appreciate that. I just don't know what to say.

"Your doctors called, Everleigh. And you know how your belly hurts a lot?"

She nods and places a hand on her tummy.

"Inside your belly, there's a knot. We can't see it, but it's there."

She makes a face, her little nose wrinkled like a bunny. "A knot?" She rubs her stomach, trying to feel it.

"Kind of. And it's going to keep making you really sick if we don't get the knot to go away."

"Okay. How do I do that? I don't like my belly hurting."

Like a baseball player, up to bat with three balls and two strikes and only needing a base hit to win the World Series, I choke.

"Here's the thing, kiddo. We gotta give you some medicine that will get it to go away," Crew says, taking the reins.

"Like the pink bubble gum stuff?"

"No, Ever." Crew steeples his fingers and rests his chin on them. He studies her. "You're a smart little girl, aren't you?"

"I am! Mrs. Yeryar gives me a star on all my papers. And sometimes I get to be the Student Of The Day because I never have to move my slip to blue." She looks seriously at Crew. "Blue is bad. That means you weren't listening."

He smiles at her, but I can see his heart breaking right alongside mine. "I'm going to talk to you like a big girl because you are such a good listener. Can you listen like a big girl for me for just a minute?"

Her face is somber and she nods, sitting a little taller. She likes being responsible and I know she's going to listen to everything he has to say. I'm not sure, under the circumstances, if that's a good idea. But I don't really know what is at this point.

"In our bodies, we have things called cells. They are like little bubbles of information. Sometimes, and no one knows why, some of those little bubbles get the wrong information. They don't listen."

"I bet they move their slips all the way to black!" she laughs.

"They probably do," he smiles sadly. "These little black-slip cells form little groups and as the group gets bigger, it makes you sick. And it can make you very, very sick if the doctors don't get them to listen."

"Is that what's wrong with me?"

Her innocence destroys me. I have to look away, unable to make eye contact with either of them. This conversation is just as painful as losing Gage because, in a way, I'm losing Ever, too. I'm losing the purity of my baby girl. I'll never be able to look in her eyes and see the untainted joy of a child again. She'll have this looming over her head; she'll always fear something is wrong. Cancer not only seeps into your body, it melts in your consciousness. As much as we try to keep things normal, our version of normal will be forever changed.

"It is," Crew replies, his voice raw. "And we are going to have to give you some medicine at the hospital. You'll be there for a few days and it's gonna be yucky. But, I promise, it's better than letting more cells turn their slips to black."

She reaches out and grabs my thigh. She wiggles herself closer to me and picks up my arms and lays it over her shoulders. I pull her in close and kiss the top of her head. I start to speak, but she cuts me off.

"Uncle Crew, I don't want more yucky medicine."

"I know, monkey. But your mommy and I will make sure everything is okay."

He glances at me and I look at the ceiling. The tears are building, threatening to break the levee, and I can't cry in front of her. I can't let her see that I'm scared as shit . . . that I don't necessarily believe that everything is going to be okay. I don't want her to even suspect that I feel utterly helpless right now, unable to provide her with the damn therapy that will save her life. I don't want her to worry about the banks denying me for every loan I've tried to take, every tear-filled phone call I've made this morning, pleading with the insurance and the hospital while Crew took her to the grocery store for milk.

I am her mother! I am the one that's supposed to protect her from the world. And I'm letting her down.

A sob starts to escape and I swallow it down. If I'm going to fail her at everything, at least I can be strong while I do it.

"How long will it take?" she asks.

"We don't know, sweetheart. We'll have to see."

She gazes into the distance and I know she's thinking about what we've told her. Crew catches my eye and we wait for her to say something, give her time to process the information.

"Is it like the flu?" she asks finally. "Like I'll get sick to my belly? My throat will hurt?"

"Kind of. What you have is called cancer," Crew says tentatively.

Everleigh stiffens. "Cancer? Megan's mommy has cancer! She was very sick. Megan cried on recess. She thought she would never see her again!" She whirls around to face me, a look of horror on her face. "She said she lost all of her hair. Will I lose my hair, Mommy?"

She runs her hands through her long, black hair. When I don't respond, she looks to Crew.

He looks baffled for a second before a slow smile graces his lips. "Honestly, Ever? Maybe. But you never know." He pauses for a minute. "You know how we call all candy on a stick a lollipop? But there are all kinds of lollipops, right? Some have gum inside, some chocolate, some are red? That's like cancer, monkey. We say 'cancer,' but there are all different kinds and every one does something kinda different."

"Will it fall out in the bathroom? That's what Megan said happened to her mommy. She said she would get out of the shower and a bunch of her hair would be in the bottom. That would be so scary." Her bottom lip trembles as she looks between us.

She doesn't understand. In her little mind, that's all she can control. Her hair. Something so basic and something we take for granted is the one thing she's focusing on.

"Did you know I used to be a fighter?" Crew asks her.

She shakes her head, tilting her head to the side. She's obviously as confused as I am by his line of questioning.

"Well, I was. I used to fight a lot. And you know what we would do before we fought?"

She shakes her head again.

"We would shave our hair off."

She blanches. "Why? Why would you do that?"

"Because," he says exaggeratedly, "when you go into a fight and you have no hair, that tells the guy you're fighting that you're serious. That you came ready to win. It gives you power because it was your choice to shave your head. He can't do that to you."

Her little eyes light up and I hold my breath.

"So that's what we should do. Cancer wants to fight us? We show it that we came ready for battle." He tilts his head down, looking at her like they're discussing strategy. Maybe they are.

"We have to shave our heads?" She seems to consider what he's saying. "Am I going to die, Uncle Crew?"

I gasp, my stomach falling to the floor. Crew, too, looks shocked at the question but recovers quicker than me.

"No. You won't. I promise you. We are going to fight this together."

He looks up at me, his eyes crystal clear. "The three of us are going to beat cancer. It's going to take a lot of work and it's not gonna be fun. But if we show it we are serious, we'll win."

"Are you sure?" she asks, watching him closely.

Crew laughs, but I know it's for her benefit. "Sure I'm sure. Have you seen me?" He pulls the edge of his sleeve back and flexes his muscle, making Ever laugh. "I'm a monster." He reaches forward and tickles her. She twists around on my lap, her laughs rushing over me.

"Okay," she says simply, catching her breath. "Let's win!"

"That's my girl." His eyes blur with unshed tears.

"We have to be scary," she says, wiggling her fingers in front of her face like a monster.

"Let's do it." He bends so they're eye-to-eye. In a hushed voice he says, "Wanna shave our heads? Show it who's boss?"

She stills. I'm not sure what she's gonna say. I'm not sure I'm prepared for that either.

"You'll do it, too?" she asks, touching the top of his head.

"Of course. We are both fighting this thing. I'm not going into this fight letting it think it's gonna beat me from the start."

She stands and then turns to face me, sinking her back into Crew's front. "Will you shave yours, too, Mommy?"

"Ah," Crew laughs, picking her up. "Your mommy isn't much of a fighter. But she is awful pretty."

I laugh and wipe my eyes.

"She is pretty!" Ever says through her giggles.

Crew twists her around and sits her on his hip. They look at each other, a smile on both of their faces. He taps her nose. "Let's let mommy be the cheerleader. That'll be her job. We can't have her getting in the way as we do the dirty work."

"Okay."

"We need to give her a job so she doesn't feel left out though," he says, looking at me through the corner of his eye. "We'll let her do the shaving, okay?"

"And make us Kool-Aid?" Ever asks hopefully.

"And make us Kool-Aid," Crew laughs, pulling me into his other side.

"This is gonna be okay, girls," he says and squeezes me tight. I look up into his eyes and he mouths, "I promise."

Chapter TWENTY-FIVE

CREW

MY NEWLY-BUZZED SCALP feels smooth against my calloused hand. I hear Ever playing in the bathtub while Julia finishes sweeping up the mess.

I grab a bottle of whiskey out of the cabinet and pull the cork. I take one gulp, letting the liquor burn down my throat and pool into a fire of acid in my stomach. One more mouthful slides smoothly down and adds to the mix.

That was the hardest thing I've ever done in my life.

Her eyes were wide as Julia braided her long locks so we could cut it off. Jules' hands shook and she kept looking at me, like she wanted some assurance that this was the right thing.

Fuck if I knew. But it seemed better to do it here than to watch it fall out. Ever, Jules, hell even I needed to feel some power in this situation. Everything is out of our control. How powerless would she feel if she had to watch her hair fall out strand by strand? This was the one thing I figure we can control. This was one thing we can take hold of and not let cancer do to us.

Ever gasped when she saw herself in the mirror. Jules and I held our breath, waiting for her response. She ran her hand over her head.

"I look like Caillou, Mommy," she whispered, referring to a cartoon character she likes. "I look like him, but a girl."

"You're much prettier than Caillou."

"Will it grow back?" Her voice cracked as she touched her head again.

"It will."

"This will make me stronger, right, Uncle Crew?"

"Yeah. Look at how powerful you look. I wouldn't mess with you."

Ever *giggles and turns around.* "Okay! I'll believe you. But it better grow back!"

The bathroom door creaks open and Jules comes into the kitchen. She tosses the hair into the garbage. When she looks at me, her face is paler than I've seen it.

"Fuck," I mutter and grab a hold of her. I pull her into me. She wraps her arms around my waist and I rest my chin on her head. "That had to be done. You know that, right?"

She doesn't say anything, just sniffles. "I don't know if I can do this, Crew."

"You have to do this." I rub her back and she squeezes me tighter. "You know I have to work this week, right? I'll try to come by the hospital after work, but I can't afford to take time off."

"I know," she whispers.

"If you need anything, you tell me and I'll figure it out." I sigh. "I hate that you'll be there alone. Do you have anyone that can sit with you?"

She shakes her head against me. "Olivia will be by sometimes, but she's got her own stuff to do and Rory to watch." She pauses and takes a deep breath. "I haven't told my parents."

"Don't."

"I don't want to deal with them, Crew. But it is their granddaughter."

"Think long and hard before you say anything to them. You know they'll just make it harder on you in the long run."

We stand in the middle of the kitchen holding each other. Every now and then, we hear Ever giggle or sing some song about sugar.

"I'm working on a few things this week to come up with the money."

"It's too much," she says, pulling back. "How do we come up with that kind of money? I just . . . I'm her mother, Crew! And she's not going to get what she needs because I just failed her!"

Tears rocket down her skin and I pull her into me again. "Shut the fuck up, Jules." I know I sound harsh, but I'm on the verge of breaking myself. "You've never failed at a damn thing in your life. Take care of her. I'll take care of the money."

"How?" she cries.

SACRIFICE

"I haven't figured it out yet. But I will."

Jules sniffles and pulls back again. She wipes her eyes with the end of her shirt. "Thank you."

I turn my back to her and grab the liquor again. I down another mouthful for good measure.

"Really, Crew," she sniffles. "You've put yourself in the middle of this mess and you could've just walked away from us."

"Stop."

"No. I want you to hear me," she says, grabbing a hold of my waist and turning me to face her. "I spent a lot of years not being very nice to you. I . . ."

"Jules, stop. I deserved it all."

She studies me. "I thought you did. But I don't think I understood everything the right way. Had I known . . ."

"You don't get it," I say, dropping my chin so we are eye-to-eye. "You were pissed because I walked away from you. But I did it on purpose. You see, I *did* understand. I knew that you being with me, especially then, would fuck you all up. Fuck, I didn't know if I was coming or going, Jules. You deserved someone that would love you without the fucking chaos that always finds me. You deserved someone that would do right by you, give you babies, come home every night from a 9–5. Someone to treat you like a princess."

"So you didn't want me?"

I laugh because she just doesn't get it. "When I walked in there and saw you with Gage, I realized something. That was the way it needed to be. I didn't deserve you; I couldn't give you the things you needed. But Gage could. And he was the only guy I wouldn't kick the shit out of for touching you because I knew he'd treat you right."

I shrug and turn away again.

"Crew?"

"Yeah?"

"Did you love me?"

I smile and look over my shoulder. I start to explain something that's been burning in the back of my mind for a long time. I open my mouth, but I can't find the words.

Not here. Not now. Not like this.

Instead, I turn, touch the side of her face and look into her eyes. I hope she can see what I feel in them. I hope she can see that I've loved her since the day I fucking saw her. I hope she can see that I will love her 'til the day I die.

Chapter TWENTY-SIX

CREW

"YOU WANT SOMETHING to eat?" I glance at Ever, lying on the couch. She has her Tinkerbell blanket wrapped tightly around her and is staring blankly at the television.

"No," she says, her voice shallow.

"You sure? I can make ya something. Maybe an ice cream sundae?" I try to think of things a little girl might like. She hasn't been eating and is starting to wither away to nothing. "With bananas and sprinkles?"

She doesn't answer me, just gazes at the screen but I'm not sure if she's even watching it.

"My belly hurts real bad," she says finally, squeezing her eyes shut. "Real bad, Uncle Crew."

I clutch the armrests of the chair I'm sitting in by the window. I don't know what to do. Jules went to see Mrs. Ficht about her schedule, or lack thereof. She was also going to pick up a heating blanket for Ever at the store. She gets so cold and shakes like a leaf. I don't know if the blanket will help, but it's worth a try.

"Make me better, Uncle Crew."

"Ah, Ever," I say, trying to keep my voice from shaking. I'm supposed to be the man, the stability, the *unshakable* one. But fuck me if hearing those words come out of her little lips doesn't fucking shake me to the ground. "I'm trying. I promise you, I'm trying."

SACRIFICE

"I think I just need a new body," she whispers, opening her eyes. The pain in the dark irises is palpable. "I want to go back to the way I felt before. When I played with Rory and went to school and slept over at Mrs. Bennett's house. But I don't want to move back to our other house. I want to live here."

"I can't get you a new body and I can't make things the way they were. But I can promise you that you won't have to move out of here until you and your mommy want to."

"I never want to. I like it here with you."

"I like you here with me, too."

She groans and her hands fly to her stomach. "It hurts so bad. It feels like a volcano." She pulls her knees to her chest and squeezes her eyes closed again.

I've never felt more useless, more fucking worthless, than I do right now. It's the most humbling experience I've ever had. I would literally do *anything* to make her better and there is *nothing* I can do.

Not one single motherfucking thing.

"Will you cuddle with me?" Her voice is so soft, I barely hear it over Doc McStuffins or whatever her name is. "Please hold me."

I stand and go to her, sitting at her feet. I lift her up and gently sit her on my lap, pulling her Tinkerbell blanket over her. I tuck it in around her little frame as she lays her head on my chest.

"This feels better," she whispers.

"I'm glad."

She lies quietly for a long time and I think she's dozed off when she speaks again. "I have to go to the doctor tomorrow."

"You do. They're gonna start making you better."

"I know it's going to hurt."

I squeeze her even tighter. I can't refute it and I don't want to lie to her.

"Will you come see me?" she asks.

"I will. And I'll bring you taffy."

"Bring me two pieces."

"I'll bring you four."

Ever yawns and pulls her legs up against her. "When I'm better, will you take me to the beach?"

"I will. And we can go to the park every day."

"You'll take me every day?"

"Every day."

"And to a baseball game?"

I laugh. "Baseball? Since when do you like baseball?"

"I think my daddy liked baseball."

"He did. He liked the Red Sox. But I think you should like the Yankees."

"Do you like the Yankees? Because if you do, I'll like them both."

I chuckle, knowing if Gage was listening, he'd be having a fit.

"I'm sleepy."

"Go to sleep then."

"Will you hold me while I sleep?"

I smile. "If you want me to."

"I do."

"Then I will."

She snuggles against me and I hold her as she falls asleep. For the next couple of hours, I pray to a God I don't quite believe in.

Chapter TWENTY-SEVEN

JULIA

I'M GRATEFUL THAT Ever's hospital room is at least a little appealing. The bright yellow walls and swirly designs seem playful and fun. Still, it's a *hospital room*.

My daughter's hospital room.

They've tried to make it as comfortable as possible for the both of us. What they can't make comfortable, however, is the gnawing feeling in my stomach. *That* is what they can't fix . . . until they fix Ever, anyway. I'm not even sure if that'll go away completely once she's better.

Do you ever relax after a diagnosis like this? Can you ever go back to that blissful, cancer-free life?

I look up at the clock. It's right at noon. My stomach growls, but it's more from anxiety than hunger, although I haven't eaten in a few days, really.

I can't get the sight of Ever being rolled back for the port procedure out of my mind. The port is a semi-permanent I.V. line that the doctors will use to give her medicine. It's supposed to make things easier and more comfortable for her. They said it shouldn't take long but it seems like it's already taken too long.

I'm gonna have to get used to this. This is going to be the way it is for a while.

I'm sitting in a chair that reclines, situated next to where Ever's bed is parked when it's in here. There's also a couch that turns into a makeshift bed. I'll be spending at least the next six nights there because I won't leave her. Not for a second.

I dig through my large bag and find my phone. I promised Mrs. Ficht I would call her back today and let her know I was okay. As I start to press the numbers, it vibrates in my hand.

Crew: You okay?

Me: They're putting in the port now.

Crew: I'll come by tonight.

Me: It's okay.

Crew: I wish I was there now. I'm fucking sick.

Me: I'll text you when I know something. Just waiting now. Guess I better get used to it.

Crew: I'm on break so I gotta get back. If you need something, call the dock. I put the number in your bag.

Curious, I sort through my bag again and find a baggie. I hold it in the air and see a folded up piece of paper, a couple of granola bars, and a couple of twenty dollar bills.

Me: I just found it. You didn't have to do this.

Crew: See you tonight.

I press the bag against my chest. It feels odd to have someone thinking of me, but good at the same time. I fight off the anxiety that always rises when I consider Crew walking away again. I really don't think he'll leave us, at least not until Ever is better. Something's changed in Crew.

I dial Mrs. Ficht and smile when I hear her voice.

"Hello?"

"Hi, Valerie."

"Oh, Julia. I'm so glad to hear your voice, sweetheart. How are you? How's Everleigh?"

SACRIFICE

"I'm waiting on her to get out of surgery. They're putting in her port now. They were wheeling her out when you called. I'm sorry I didn't return your call sooner."

"Don't apologize. I understand and I don't want to keep you. I just wanted to let you know that we are having a benefit for you at the park on Sunday. If you can come, that would be great. And if you can't, that is no problem. There were a bunch of customers here that wanted to help out."

My bottom lip quivers at the sentiment. I deliver these people coffee and pie and they care about my daughter?

"Thank you," I whisper. "Is there anything I can do to help?"

She laughs. "No. We were going to set up an account for people to donate at one of the banks. Would that be okay?"

"Yes," I barely choke out.

"It's the least we can do, Julia. If you need anything else, please call me. Promise?"

"Yes."

I wipe the tears away but they're quickly replaced.

"I've gotta go get the pies out of the oven for the dinner crowd. If you need anything, anything at all, you call me."

"I will. And thank you."

"Take care of yourself and that little girl. We're all praying for her."

JULIA

I NEED TO relax. I know this. But it's impossible to do that in this situation to begin with, let alone while sitting in the hospital. The staff is constantly coming in. Every time the door opens, my heart races. I fear the worst every time a nurse or a doctor comes in. I feel like I'm on a roller coaster; every time I get to the bottom and begin to breathe easy, I'm shot back to the top of the tracks again.

I flip off the television and stretch my legs on the sofa. The late afternoon sun is warm and it feels good on my skin.

Ever is fast asleep in her bed, still a little woozy from the procedure. She wakes up and then dozes back off again, which the nurse says is normal and encouraged. We want her to get as much rest as possible today before the chemo starts tomorrow.

Dr. Perkins comes in, his white lab coat open and a chart in his hand.

He does a quick assessment of the room before setting his sights on me.

"How are we doing?" he asks, his voice warm.

"As good as we can be, I guess."

He sits in the chair by the bed and does a quick once-over of Ever. Then he turns to me.

"Everything went great today," he says assuredly. "She's a trooper."

I try to smile back. My chest tightens as the anticipation of what he's about to say builds. I've come to learn that every time I see him, it's going to be bad or good. It's like getting your check at work and seeing if you've gotten a bonus or not.

"She told us in recovery about how she's a fighter. That cancer was going to be scared of her because she cut her hair."

A small grin finally touches my face. "That's what we told her."

"That was smart. We're going to need to keep building her up as we go through this process." He sets the chart down and rests his elbows on his knees. "We'll be starting the chemo tomorrow. We'll use the port we installed today to give her the medicine. I wish I knew what to tell you to expect, but it really depends on the person."

"Will she be sick?"

"Probably. We'll just have to wait and see. Remember, this is a marathon, not a sprint. You have to think of this as war and we fight one battle at a time."

He's right, but I want that magic pill that will make this all better in one swoop.

"As far as the therapy goes that we discussed earlier . . ." His voice trails off. "I've personally appealed to the head of the trial and reviewed the appeal paperwork to the insurance company. I'm doing everything I can to get her in there. I want you to know that."

I'm afraid to ask, but I must know. "What happens if we can't? What then?"

"We have a panel of experts that have reviewed her case and we have a plan in place to treat her. The therapy is the best path, I won't lie to you. We have a big fight on our hands, Julia. But there are lots of kids that don't get approved and there are other options of treatment available."

"They just aren't as effective," I whisper.

He nods slowly. "There are a couple of new trials taking place in New Mexico. I'm researching them, as well as putting out my feelers to my peers around the country."

"I don't get it. Don't lots of kids get neuroblastoma?"

"They do. But Everleigh's seems to be pretty aggressive so I want to fight it as hard as possible. Also, this is the medical world. New things happen daily. I won't let a stone go unturned. I promise you that."

I sigh and close my eyes, feeling the sun hit my face. I wish I could open them and be home with Gage and Ever in our little house in Cambridge.

Dr. Perkins' voice cuts into my thoughts. "I don't want you to get down. This is a team effort and we are going to need you to be strong."

Team effort.

I smile, recalling Crew's explanation to Everleigh.

"We need you to take care of yourself. Make sure you eat and get rest. It's imperative that you stay strong for your little girl." He stands and straightens his jacket. "If you need anything, alert the nurses. Otherwise, I'll see you in the morning."

"Thank you."

He stands and before he gets to the door, it swings open. A red-headed nurse I remember from another visit comes in.

She's small, maybe five foot, with a creamy white complexion and bright green eyes. Her smile is wide and friendly.

"Hi," she says. "I'm Macie. I don't know if you remember me or not."

"I do," I smile. "I'm Julia. This is Ever."

"She's a cutie," she says, looking at my baby girl. "Can I get you anything? Water? A Coke? Something to eat?" She flips through the file in her hand and makes a few notes.

"No. I'm fine. Thank you."

She turns her attention back to me, leaning against the end of the bed. "Tell me about you."

I shrug, not sure why she's asking. "About me?"

She laughs easily, her red ponytail swishing around. "We are going to be seeing a lot of each other for a while. It just makes things easier if we have something to talk about, right?"

"I guess . . ." I don't like the idea of getting to know the staff here. I don't want to be here enough to know them. I want to pretend like they don't exist.

"Well," she says, "I'll go first. I like the color purple, the Boston Red Sox, and Sex on the Beach—both in real life and the drink," she laughs.

Her laugh is light and friendly and I find myself wondering what it would be like to drink wine and watch a movie with her. She seems like someone I'd like outside of the hospital.

"Okay, fair enough. I like to cook, watch movies, and the color purple, too."

"One thing in common. That's a start!" She moves around Ever's bed and presses a button to stop the beeping it started to make. "Are you married?"

I shake my head. "My husband is deceased."

"I'm sorry."

"It's okay. What about you?"

She shrugs carelessly and I wish for a split second I knew what that felt like. "I'm just having fun. Seeing a couple of guys semi-regularly but nothing serious." She glances at her watch. "Okay. I have to give some meds in just a few minutes. It was nice talking to you, Julia."

"It was nice talking to you, too, Macie."

She smiles and heads out, leaving me with a bit happier spirits than when she arrived.

Chapter TWENTY-EIGHT

CREW

I SLIDE INTO the cab of my truck and toss my bag in beside me. Before starting the engine, I turn on my phone to see if Julia has texted me. Every time I check it, I have a shit ton of missed calls and voice mails from people that have seen the interview on the news or the web somewhere. It would be completely entertaining if the circumstances were different. I'd be eating this up, but there's too much attached to it now.

I scroll through six messages before I find Jules' name.

> *Julia: Port is in. She's sleepy but doing well. She's asking for you and I told her you'd try to be by tonight.*

I start to respond when it vibrates in my hand. I don't know the number.

"Hello?"

"Is this Crew Gentry?"

"Yeah. Who is this?"

"Good evening, Crew. This is Don Wetzel with the NAFL."

My mouth goes dry. I remember this guy. He's the guy that I talked to my senior year at Minnesota. He's the one that approached me about joining their organization.

It fucking worked. It. Fucking. Worked.

"You don't happen to remember me, do you?" he asks.

"Yeah," I say and clear my throat. "What can I do for you?"

He chuckles. "I'm pretty sure you know why I'm calling."

"Humor me."

"Very well. We had a fight lined up in a little less than three months for your old buddy Hunter Davidson. You might know a little something about that."

It's my turn to laugh, but I'm not about to show my hand too early. "Maybe."

"Well, it seems a certain bar fight and interview have put you back in the spotlight."

"So I've heard."

He pauses. "How's your health these days?"

"I'm workin' the docks. What's that tell you?"

"Look, Crew. I almost didn't call you about this . . ." He sighs into the line and my heartbeat quickens. "Davidson's opponent dropped out, which I know you know. Your little . . . demonstration . . . last week and the discussion with the television station has fueled Davidson's camp. I'm just going to be honest with you here. Davidson's making himself known as a helluva fighter. He's ending his fights in dramatic fashion. With Reyes dropping out, he'd have to fight either Patterson or Hickman and he'd have to go to all the way up to 205 to do that."

"They'd destroy him," I interject.

"Possibly. But this is a business decision and everyone is chattering about you, Mr. Gentry. Davidson's camp is looking at this as a big PR move. They can clear up his record and they think he'll end you in a very flamboyant way. I'm not going to lie to you."

"Cut to the chase, Wetzel." I drum my fingertips on the steering wheel, my knee bouncing up and down.

"I'm calling to offer you a fight."

I hold the phone away from my face and blow out a breath. I give myself five seconds to get myself together before putting it back to my ear.

" . . . you'd fight on July 13th. That's not far off, especially if you haven't been training. I don't want to throw you in there to be fed to the wolves—"

"What kind of money we talking?"

He laughs. "So you're interested?"

"For the right price, yeah."

"I'll come to Boston tomorrow. Meet me at our office on Peiffer Street tomorrow at one. Can you do that?"

SACRIFICE

"I'll be there."

CREW

I LOOK OUT across the field and I don't even know how I got here. I hung up with Wetzel and just drove.

I step out of my truck and shut the door behind me. My boots sink into the lawn as I make my way across the grass. The sun is warm as it prepares to set in the west, birds chirping in the trees strategically planted around me. I'm on auto-pilot, drawn to my destination like a magnet.

My stomach churns, my chest hot as choices roll through my mind. I know, ultimately, I don't *have* a choice. I gotta do what I gotta do to get the money. I just feel so fucking overwhelmed, like my life is flashing before my eyes. Everything is rolling, compounding, and I have no one to talk about anything with. All I have is Will, but he doesn't know anything more than I do about anything. I need someone logical, someone level-headed.

I need my brother.

I spot the gray headstone in front of me. I've only been here once since the burial. I didn't stay long. Seeing his name carved into the cold stone, his life defined by two dates, was more than I could take. It was fucking brutal.

I notice the purple flowers Julia has put in the urns on either side of the stone. They're weathered and fraying. They stand there and do their job and take all the abuse the world throws at them. That's me these days. Fuck it if life wasn't easier when I just ran away from everything. *Why can't I do that this time?*

"Hey," I say gruffly.

I glance around, but no one else is here. I kick at a rock and shake my head, feeling like a damn fool. But I can't help it. I just need to be *here*.

"I don't know what the fuck I'm doing, Gage," I laugh. A red bird chirps overhead and watches me.

I release a breath and feel my energy leave my body with it. "I'm in over my head here, brother. I really fuckin' am. I don't know what I'm doing."

My voice starts to crack. The words start pouring out. "Am I doin' the right thing? I'm trying to take care of your girls. I've moved them in with me, I've told Jules not to worry about anything but Ever. I'm doing everything I can, Gage, but I feel like none of it is enough. None of it is what you'd do. I just keep making fucking decisions and it solves nothing. Just gets me to another fucking problem.

"I'm gonna take this fight tomorrow. Between you, me, and this headstone here, I'm worried. I mean, I gotta do it. I don't see any other way to get the money. But what if it doesn't work? What if I manage to swing this fight and then I don't win? Then what? We both can't abandon them!" I groan into the air, frustration boiling over. "Damn it! There has to be another solution and I just don't fucking know what it is!"

I place both hands on the tombstone and bow my head. "I love them, too, you know. I don't know if that's right, either, but I do. And if you were here, I'd stay away but you aren't and I'm trying to do the right thing and I can't help but love them." I laugh. "I bet that little confession has you turning over right now, huh?"

The bird chirps again and I watch it jump from branch to branch. "I don't even know why I'm here. I guess I just wanted you to know I'm trying. As long as I live, I'll protect them and do everything I have to in order to make sure their lives are better than ours were. But if you have any genius ideas about how to fix this shit, feel free to impart your knowledge."

I nod and take a couple of steps backwards. "I won't let you down, Gage. I'm manning the fuck up."

The little bird calls out and I look up. It leaps off the branch and flies across the graveyard and out of sight.

With a final glance at the stone, I head back to my truck. I know what needs to be done. I just have to work out the details.

Chapter TWENTY-NINE

CREW

"MR. GENTRY?"

My head snaps to the brunette behind the large mahogany desk. I run my hands down my jeans.

"Mr. Wetzel's ready for you."

She nods towards a door to her left. I stand and walk across the room and knock on it.

"Come in," a man's voice says from the other side.

I pause just a second before opening it.

After my discussion with Gage last night, I headed to the hospital. Ever was having a bad night, sicker than fuck. Julia was a nervous wreck and I stayed late, trying to be the calm in the storm for them both. As I sat there and watched my niece heave into a bucket and Julia pour her heart and soul into caring for her daughter, it drove reality home.

Life is about choices and I had made mine.

It was time to stop worrying about it.

Don't talk about it. Be about it.

Don Wetzel is sitting behind a desk. His hair is a bit grayer than I remember, otherwise he's the same. A little shady but very smooth. He smiles widely and stretches his hand towards me. "Good to see you again, Crew."

I shake his hand and then take a seat across from him.

"How are you?" he asks.

"Good."

He studies me for a minute. "You look good. Strong."

"Yeah. I'm no worse for the wear," I say nonchalantly.

He seems satisfied with that. He rolls his chair around and grabs a file before turning to face me again. He sets the file down and clasps his hands on top of it. He watches me with narrowed eyes. "You're sure you want to do this? There's little time to prepare and Davidson's hot right now."

"Absolutely." I keep my features steady, confident. I don't want to say too much, just let him do the talking. Saying too much can get ya in trouble; you can't regret things you never say.

"What about your injury?"

"I'll sign a medical waiver," I state. "It's not your problem."

"Fair enough," he shrugs and opens the file. "We are prepared to offer you $30,000. Not bad for one day."

"Thirty grand? You're kidding me. You expect me to take a fight for thirty fucking grand?"

"Crew, I hate to say this, but you're a nobody."

What the fuck did he just say?

"I'm a nobody that happens to be the only guy to beat your boy. In my book, and in a lot of people's books out there, that makes me a somebody."

He chuckles in a self-absorbed kind of way. "First of all, he's not my boy—"

"This is bullshit," I say, leaning forward. "The fans are demanding this. Davidson himself wants this fight. Don't think I'm going to go out there and do all of you a favor, because that's what this will be, Wetzel, for thirty fucking grand."

"We don't really care what Davidson wants. We care what's going to make us money. And this fight will pull in some viewers but the NAFL isn't going to give some guy off the street, even with a vendetta like yours, a six-figure payout, Crew. It's just not going to happen."

My mind races, scrambling to come up with a solution. I need more fucking money. I need to make this happen.

I feel Don's eyes on me as I plot.

Think!

"I'm just gonna be blunt here, okay?" I say. "The truth is you think Davidson's gonna kill me. So you're gonna throw me a bone to get in there, let him win, so he can move on."

SACRIFICE

He shrugs. "That's what the odds say. And the NAFL isn't going to pay a guy much more than that to lose."

I laugh angrily. "You're so sure I'm gonna lose, huh? Well how about this? Make it all or nothing."

"What do you mean?"

I lean even closer, my heart thumping in my chest. "If I lose, you pay me *nothing*. If I win, you pay me one hundred grand."

He laughs. "Are you serious?"

"Does it look like I'm joking?"

Don leans back in his chair and looks at me like I'm off my rocker. "I think I can make that work. But are you absolutely certain you want to do that? Have you given this much thought?"

"Make it happen."

He leans forward and pushes a file across the desk. "Here are the contracts. You want to take these by an attorney or some sort of counsel before you sign? It'd be the smart thing to do."

"Give me a pen."

Don takes the papers and changes the contract amounts to reflect the new agreement. He hands them back with a pen. I quickly sign my name by the red tabs and close the file. My signature is a little wavier than usual, but there's so much damn adrenaline pumping through me right now that it's amazing I can even hold a pen.

"Done."

"I hope you know what you're doing," he says.

"Again, not your problem," I mutter.

He blows out a breath, running a hand through his salt and pepper hair. "Okay. Let's get Davidson's camp on the line and get this show on the road." He presses a few buttons on his phone and the sound of a line ringing echoes around the room.

"Killian."

"Killian. Don Wetzel."

"How'd it go with Gentry?"

"I got him right here. We just signed a contract."

"Hunter! Come here!" Killian shouts.

Don watches me shrewdly, looking for signs of me backing out. Not fucking happening.

"I have Hunter right here," Killian says.

"Mr. Davidson, I have Mr. Gentry here with me. We've just signed a deal. The two of you will be fighting on July 13th."

Davidson laughs and the sound of his voice sends a chill up my spine. I hate this motherfucker more than I've ever hated anyone. Even his laugh is cocky. I recall the things he's said about me over the years, the excuses he's made as to why he lost to me, the insinuations that I'd never have made it in the NAFL.

I want to end him.

Again.

"Hey, Crew. You ready to get your ass whipped?"

"Good luck with that," I laugh.

He cackles maniacally. "I'm gonna end you, motherfucker."

"No, *motherfucker*. I'm going to beat you. *Again*."

"I've waited for this day for a long time. You'll be lucky if I don't kill you. Fuck, I almost killed you last time and you were in your prime," he laughs. "Better be ready, fool."

"You've got a $100 mouth and a $5 ass. I'm gonna humiliate you in front of the world just like I did last time."

"Okay, gentleman," Don says, winking at me, "that's enough for now. Just getting us all on the same page. Good luck to you both."

"We'll talk soon," Killian says and Don ends the call.

Shit just got fuckin' real.

Chapter THIRTY

CREW

I POP MY keys on the counter. I have so much shit to do, I don't even know where to start.

I glance at the clock as I dig through a kitchen drawer and it's nearly seven already. I pull out a notebook and ink pen and sit on the sofa. I gotta get a plan in place and I gotta do it now.

Getting through the rest of the work day after the meeting with Wetzel was almost impossible. I had to stay a couple of extra hours to make up for the time I was gone. Unloading the ships gave me time to roll everything around in my head and by the time I left work, I had a weird sense of focus. I've never felt anything like it before. I wouldn't say it was clarity because there are still pieces of this mess I don't know. But for once in my life, I know, without a shadow of a doubt, this is absolutely what I am supposed to be doing. Even not knowing how this was going to end for *me*, I knew how it'd end for *Everleigh*, and that was with a chance at a future.

I lean against the cushions and give myself just a minute to breathe. Looking around the room, I realize how empty it feels without them here. I see their stuff strewn around, but that just makes me miss them more. With a sigh, I pull out my phone and dial Jules.

"Hey," she says when she picks up, her voice sweet but tired.

"Hey. How are you?"

"I'm okay. Ever's sleeping now, so I'm trying to get a few minutes myself. It's been a long day."

"Did I wake you?"

"No. It's fine. It's nice to hear your voice."

I smile, wishing I was with her. "I was gonna come by tonight, but I, uh, I had a few things come up today. I had to work late and now I'm planning this side job I've taken on."

"Oh, Crew," she says, "I feel so bad."

"Don't. I volunteered for all of this. Remember that."

She doesn't say anything, so I fill the void.

"You guys should be home this weekend, right?"

She yawns. "That's the plan. If everything goes okay and she tolerates the treatment with no complications, we should be out of here sometime after Friday."

"How is she? I know you said she had a rough day."

"She did. She was pretty sick, but from what the doctor's said, her side effects are pretty minor. I can't imagine them worse though. It's just the most awful thing I've ever seen."

I stand up and pace the room. "Maybe I could come by for an hour or so . . ." I immediately start trying to figure out how to swing everything. I feel so damn torn. I need to be *there* and I need to be *here* . . . all for the same goal.

"We're both going to sleep, so there's no sense in you coming by, really. The doctors told me to take care of myself because Ever needs me to be strong." She takes a long pause. "I need you to take care of yourself, Crew. I need you to be strong for me."

And that's all it takes to re-focus me.

CREW

I CIRCLE THE table, phone to my ear. On the fifth ring, a cheery voice answers, "Blackrock Gym."

"Hey, is Sal in by any chance?" I ask.

"Yeah, I think he's still here. Who's calling?"

"Crew Gentry."

"Hold on just a second."

Instead of putting me on hold, she lays the phone down. I hear the usual gym sounds trickle through the line. The sound of leather hitting leather, notes of music, sounds of people yelling all filter through the phone. I didn't know how badly I actually missed it 'til now. A yearning to jump through the line and join in the mayhem flitters through me. I know what the gym smells like, what the light looks like coming in through the glass doors.

The line is ringing again before it picks up. An old voice answers, "D'Amato."

"Hey, Sal. It's Crew Gentry."

"Well, what do ya know," he drawls out. "What's goin' on, kid? How ya been?"

"Good. I'm good. Just callin' to see if you have any openings around there?"

"What for?" he asks blatantly. I can hear the skepticism in his voice.

Since picking me up behind Shaw's, Sal followed my career through high school. He trained me on the side nearly every night after my high school practices were done. He was one of the few people that believed that I could fight at a collegiate level. Without him, I never would've gotten the chance.

He's from the old school. When you train with Sal, he pushes you. He has expectations and doesn't cut anyone any slack. When you're on Team D'Amato, he takes care of you. Which I know is either gonna hurt me or help me right now.

"Well, I've got myself a fight lined up and I need a trainer."

"You what?" he barks. "What the hell ya doing, Gentry? You get cleared by the doc?"

I rub my forehead. I knew this would be a sticking point with him and I'm not sure if there's a way around it. *Fuck!*

"That doesn't matter."

"The hell it doesn't!"

There's a long, tension-filled pause.

"What are ya into, Crew?"

I blow out a long breath. "I have a re-match with Davidson on July 13th. I need a trainer."

"I heard that part the first time. You have a fight. My question is why?" I know he's taking off his glasses and shaking his head. I've seen it a million times. "Why would you go put yourself in that situation? You're not an idiot, Gentry. You have nothing to prove against that piece of shit. I sure as hell heard those docs tell you that if you fight again, it'd probably fucking kill you. Don't be fucking stupid, kid."

"I need the money."

"Ah, fuck," Sal says, probably thinking I'm into something no good.

"It's not like that," I say.

"It never is, kid. It never is."

"My niece has cancer, Coach. I need about fifty fucking thousand dollars so she can get the treatment she needs."

I hear him sigh and the squeak of a chair.

"I'm doing this with or without you," I say, my voice steady. "It would give me better odds to have you in my corner. But if you don't want to do it, no worries. I'll do it myself."

He clicks his tongue against the roof of his mouth like he does when he's thinking. I wait him out. This can go either way.

"I wish I could talk ya outta this. But if you're hell bent on doing it—"

"I am."

"Well," he sighs, "be here tomorrow night at six. I'll have the puke cans ready for ya. You better be ready to work."

Chapter Thirty-One

JULIA

I WATCH THE poison roll into my daughter's veins. It's asinine. We are pumping her full of chemicals that are essentially toxic to her system. I know it's for her own good, it just seems crazy. This entire situation is just mind-numbing.

Everleigh is watching cartoons. She's tolerating things so much better today. She's tired. You can actually see the fatigue on her face, but she's not as sick. We slept more last night than I expected. I'm getting as used to this little makeshift bed as I'll ever get.

She squeezes her monkey to her chest and points at the television, the I.V. lines and monitors weighing her little arm down. "Look, Mommy!" she laughs. Her voice creaks like her throat is dry.

"Do you need a drink of water?"

She shakes her head. "No. My belly will get sick."

The light glances off her head, the absence of dark locks catching my breath in my throat. I think I'm more affected by the loss of her hair than she is.

She hasn't said much about it. I've caught her running her hand over her head and picking up a brush and then setting it back down, but she doesn't seem upset about it. I've tried to talk to her about it and she just changes the subject. Maybe she's just had so much thrown her way that she hasn't had time to really consider it. I just know that seeing her without her little ponytail kills me every time I see her.

"Knock, knock." The door pushes open and Will pops his head around the corner. I haven't seen him since he took my car for tires; it seems like a year ago. He smiles broadly and enters the room, a bag in his right hand. "How are ya, ladies?"

Ever watches him carefully. She doesn't really know Will that much, even though he was around a lot when Gage was alive. I, on the other hand, had the *pleasure* of growing up with him and the Gentry boys. Will was always their sidekick, the gray to Gage's white and Crew's black.

Will Gentry is a goofball but a genuinely good guy. I don't know much about him anymore. I know that's partly because I've pushed everyone away since Gage died.

I've pushed everyone away.

It was a conscious decision, yet looking at things from this perspective; maybe I was wrong to do that. I recall Will bringing by a pizza one night shortly after Gage's funeral. I thanked him and told him that I would be fine. To go on about his life and let us be. He came around a couple of times after that, but then stopped unless Crew sent him over to do something.

Crew was the only one that didn't stop no matter how ugly I acted.

The fog that has sat so heavy on a part of my life lifts. Shutting everyone out was wrong. Segregating as much as I could from those I loved before, being too afraid of being hurt again, was wrong. Letting them come around would've given them the opportunity to hurt me, to hurt Ever, but it also would've given them the opportunity to help us. Not in a selfish way, with money or things, but just as friends. We had known each other forever and I'd denied them the right to be my friend and to honor Gage.

I feel embarrassed. After all the things I've said to them, done to them, the ways I've made Crew and Will feel over the past couple of years despite knowing them most of my life, here they are. Showing up at the hospital. Taking care of us.

I feel ridiculous.

I look up and see Will's face blanche for a split second as he takes in Everleigh lying on the bed. "How are you, Ever?"

She shrugs. "Okay, I guess. I want to go home."

"I bet you do," he says. "But at least you don't have to hear that grumpy uncle of yours."

"I miss Uncle Crew," she says sadly.

"Well," Will says teasingly, "he sent you something today."

"He did?" She tries to sit up a little but the wires restrict her movement.

"He did. He said to tell you he wants to be here with you, but he has to work today. But he will come as soon as he can."

"Tell him I miss him. And tell him I love him."

Will's face softens and a small grin touches his lips. "I will." He fishes through a bag and pulls out a box of Laffy Taffy. "He said you really like this."

"She's never had that," I say.

Everleigh giggles and exchanges a look with Will. He hands her the box and she sets it by her side. "Uncle Crew always gives me these," she tells me.

This is news to me.

Will rustles through the bag again and pulls out a pair of red glittery house slippers. "He said you should close your eyes and pretend you're at the park. Click them four times and he said he'll meet you there. He'll be waiting by the swings."

Four times . . .

Tears dot my eyes at the randomness, but maybe not quite randomness, of the number. I'm not a little girl needing rescued from my parents, but I do need a knight all the same.

Will's smiling at me. He reaches across the end of the bed and hands me an envelope and a box of coconut macaroons. "These are for you."

"He didn't have to send me anything," I say, my cheeks flushing. I'm slightly embarrassed, but more than a bit touched, at Crew's gesture. It adds to the feeling of guilt I have over the way I've treated him. "How did he even remember I liked these cookies?"

"I don't think he's forgotten anything about you," he grins. He puts both hands on the end of the bed and peers at Ever. "So, Miss Everleigh. How ya feeling?"

"Icky."

"I bet. You'll be home before you know it."

"Do you know where I live now?" she asks.

"I heard you are keeping that uncle of yours company."

"We are! We stay in his extra room. He comes home from work and Mommy has dinner made. And you know what? I don't have to always wear a sweatshirt in there. Our apartment was always cold but Uncle Crew's is warm. I like it there."

I squeeze the envelope in my hand and try not to cry. I forget sometimes how aware of things she really is. I wonder how much she understands about what is going on with her. And me. And Crew.

Although I'm not even sure what is going on with Crew and I. I only know that when I look at him now, I don't hate him. How could I? But not hating him scares me.

I will always love Gage; it isn't that. More than anything, I don't want Everleigh to get the wrong impression by us living there. I don't want her to ever forget Gage or to think that somehow he wasn't the most important man in the world to us. Because he absolutely was. I will love Gage Gentry until the day I die. But we were parted by death, not by choice.

"I'm pretty sure Crew likes you there, too. He called me last night, crying like a little baby."

"He did?" Ever giggles.

"He did," Will sighs dramatically. "He was pouting like a little girl."

"Uncle Crew is not a little girl!"

"No, but he can sure act like one," Will winks. He grabs her blanket-covered leg and shakes it a little, making her laugh. He then turns to me and sits beside me on the couch. "How are *you* doing?"

"Hanging in there."

"Yeah?"

"Yeah."

Will watches me intently. He's extremely handsome, a mix of ruggedness and playfulness that women find endearing. He's silly most of the time, cocky and simple, but I've seen him serious a few times before. It always kind of throws me off to see him this way without his grin and jokes.

I wonder how much better I'd know him if Gage was around. How many more times I'd fix brownies for a Red Sox game while they sat around and discussed batting averages.

"Thanks for bringing this stuff by."

He shrugs likes it's no big deal.

"What? Were you just in the neighborhood?" I laugh.

"Nah, I was really on the other side of Boston. So it was kind of a pain in the a—" He looks up to Ever who's engrossed in another episode of television.

"She's heard it before."

"I bet. Especially now that you're staying with Crew." He says it in a way that I know he's leading me, but I stay quiet. Will runs his hands through his hair. "He won't be by tonight, I don't think."

My shoulders sag. As much as I hate to admit it, I've been hoping to see him. I miss him. "That's all right."

SACRIFICE

"Jules, if he could be here, he would. It's killing him not to be here. Believe me when I say that. He's just . . . working on getting everything figured out financially, you know?" he says with a quick glance to Ever. "Just give him some time. Everything he's doing is for the two of you."

"The diner I work at part-time is having a benefit for us this Sunday. They said they put together a fund for us, too. I've got a few more calls in for loans now and the doctors are appealing. I don't know what else to do."

The corner of his lips turns up and he places one hand on my knee. "There are no guarantees, but I think Crew has some things worked out."

"I know he took on a side job."

Will laughs and stands up, an awkward smile on his face. "He did. And it's gonna be a *hard-hitting* three months."

I put my head in my hands. "I hate he's doing this. I hate he's halting his life because of this."

"Hey," Will says, patting me on the head until I look up. "Crew is right where he wants to be, all right? Don't feel sorry for that mother—" He catches himself and shakes his head.

"I know. But that doesn't make it any easier to accept. So many lives are changing . . ." I look up to my daughter again and she's licking a piece of taffy, her tongue darting out tentatively. I hope it doesn't make her sick.

"They are. But that's how things go, right? Things change." He looks me right in the eye. "When you love someone, you're willing to make sacrifices for them. And what Crew's doing right now . . ." A dark cloud flashes across his face before he shrugs and grins again.

I eye him warily, not sure where he's going with this.

"Did I say something wrong?" he laughs. When I fail to laugh in return, he says, "I've been around from the beginning, Jules. Just remember that."

That's true. He's been around since the first day I met the Gentry boys. And he's known Crew longer than I have, which seems funny because I can't remember a time in my life, really, that didn't include him in one form or another. Will has seen every change in my relationship with both Gage and Crew. If anyone understands the complexities of the situation, it's him.

The door opens and Macie walks in, her eyes on a chart. "Hey, ladies," she says cheerfully before looking up. Once she does, her face falls. "Oh. I'm sorry . . ."

Will jumps to his feet, looking directly at Macie. "What are you doing here?"

"Working," she says flatly. "What are you doing here?"

"Visiting friends."

I look between them, not sure what's going on. "You two know each other?"

"Yes," Will says at the same time Macie says, "Kinda."

I laugh. "Okay then."

"I'll come back in a bit," Macie says, giving Will a tiny, flirty smile and walks out.

"That was interesting," I mutter, looking at him.

"Fact as fuck," he mutters under his breath. "You have no idea."

He flashes me a trademark Will grin, says a few things to Ever, and is out the door before I know it. My daughter goes back to her cartoon and I open the envelope.

There's a gift card to a local eatery and a note.

Jules,

I know you won't leave her, but you gotta eat. Order stuff and have it delivered. I mean it. I won't be able to get by there much this week, but I can't wait to see you guys when you get home. It isn't the same without you two here.

Tell Ever to keep fighting. Make me proud.

Call me if you need anything.

Crew

I look up at Everleigh. She's trying to put on her new slippers, the cords getting wrapped around her arms preventing her from getting them situated. I stand and help her get them on her feet.

"I love these," she says, admiring the sparkle woven into the red fabric. "They remind me of Dorothy's." She watches them catch the light before looking at me again. "Since we live with Uncle Crew now and he loves us, are we his family?"

"We were his family anyway, Ever. Remember? Uncle Crew and Daddy were brothers."

"But he's my daddy now, too, right?"

"Oh, Ever. No. No, he isn't. You only have one daddy."

She twists her head and peers up at me. "My friend Kenley, she has two daddies. They live in different houses. She used to kinda think it was weird, but her second daddy is really nice to her and her mommy. So now she thinks she's lucky because she has two and most kids have one."

"That's a nice way for Kenley to see things," I say, figuring her parents are divorced. I tickle the inside of her arm, causing her to squirm. I hope this conversation is over.

"Well, that's like me, Mommy. My first daddy lives in heaven and my second daddy lives with us now. See what I mean?"

"But it's different for Kenley," I say in a rush. My hand is shaking as I untangle the wires on the side of her bed.

"How?"

"Kenley's mommy probably fell in love and got remarried, so now she has a daddy and a step-father. I didn't get remarried, baby girl. You have a daddy and an Uncle Crew."

"You're silly, Mommy. Uncle Crew loves you and me." She rolls her eyes in a six-year-old kind of way and turns her attention back to her cartoons, leaving me speechless.

I sit down again and roll around what she just said in my head.

Does Crew love me?

I shake my head, totally unsure.

He's nice to me. He's twisting his life around for us. But would he do that if it was me and not Ever?

The note he sent with Will is sitting beside me and I pick it up. It's such a sweet gesture, something I'm sure not many people get from Crew. I smile to myself, thinking back to all the sweet things he's been doing.

This is the Crew I loved a long time ago. The Crew that would do anything for me. The Crew that was fiercely loyal to those he loved.

I'm not sure how he feels about me. Hell, I'm not sure how I feel about him. But I do know that he won't leave us this time. I feel it.

Chapter
THIRTY-TWO

CREW

"FASTER! FASTER! YOU better work, Gentry!"

My chest explodes as I sit up with a medicine ball. I clench my teeth and growl into the air, moving faster on Sal's instructions.

"Give it to me, Crew! Come on! 5. 4. 3. 2. Work! And 1. Done."

The stopwatch clicks and I drop the ball off to the side, forcing air into my overworked lungs. My daily runs have nothing on Sal D'Amato's workouts. Hands on my knees, my t-shirt soaked with sweat, I heave in precious oxygen while my coach watches.

The gym is closed for business, the lights in the front of the building on Seventh Street off. Will sits on a heavy bag on the floor, watching me kill myself. It's like old times, except for the elephant sitting on my shoulders in the form of a beautiful little girl with neuroblastoma.

Sal leans back against the boxing ring set up in the middle of the room. The way he holds himself commands respect. Even if you didn't know that he was an Olympic-qualifying wrestler back in the day or that he started one of the very first MMA gyms in Boston, you could tell he was *someone* just by looking at him.

In his old age, he's still in shape. He wears tracksuits around the gym during the day, training some of the best fighters from around the country. I've considered so many times how my life would've ended up differently had he not seen me fight behind that supermarket. And how it would have been different if he hadn't taken me on as a charity case, maybe even as a foster kid in some ways.

"Well, you're not in as bad shape as I thought," he says, crossing his arms over his chest. "But still, for the time we have to work with, we have our work cut out for us."

I bow my head and stand, rolling my shoulder. "I'll do whatever I have to do."

"Are you sure you want to do this, Crew? I've seen Davidson fight. He's—"

"I'm sure," I say, cutting him off. The decision's been made. Now the work must be done.

"What are you gonna tell me about that injury?"

I shrug. "Nothin' to tell."

"You think I'm some kinda fuckin' idiot?" he asks. "I've been around this shit longer than you've been alive, Gentry. Not to mention that I know you like a fuckin' book. Don't lie to me."

My gaze turns icy. I owe my life in some ways to Sal D'Amato, but I'm not going to sacrifice someone else's to save my own.

"What do you know about this?" he asks, turning to Will. "How bad is it?"

"Hey," Will says, putting both hands in front of him, "I don't know jack shit."

Sal laughs loudly. "Ain't that the truth."

Will feigns shock, his mouth dropping open. "I'm offended."

"Good," Sal laughs, turning his sights back to me. "I get why you want to do this, Gentry. But have you thought it through? I mean, really thought it through and what it might mean for you? I was there when you were carried off that fuckin' mat, boy. I don't want to see that again."

"You won't."

"You sure about that? I need to be absolutely certain that you've thought this through in an unemotional way. That you've made a clear choice."

I laugh angrily. "I don't have a fucking choice."

"You always have a choice."

"Not in the real world. Out there," I say, motioning through the doors behind me, "there aren't choices, Sal. There are things to be done and this is one of them."

He throws his head back and sighs. After a few seconds, he stands straight again. His shoulders are square, his eyes steel. "All right then. Be here every night at six sharp. I mean sharp, Gentry."

"Yes, sir."

"You still remember how to use that degree, right?" he asks, referring to my degree in Nutritional Science that I've never used. "I want you eating clean. Lots of protein. Keep yourself hydrated. No cigarettes. No drugs. No beer."

"Woah! Wait up," Will says, getting to his feet. "No beer?"

"Shut up, Will," Sal says, "And your job is to babysit this guy and make sure he does what I just said."

"Yes, sir," Will says meekly.

I start to laugh, but the seriousness in Sal's tone stops me.

"We gotta cram a year's worth of work into a couple of months. If I think you aren't 100% in, I'm out. Got me?"

"Yes, sir," I reply.

"All right. Get outta here. Get some sleep and be back in here tomorrow."

I shake his hand, grab my bag by the front door, and head out. Will grasps my shoulder once we're in the dimly lit parking lot.

"You look good, man," he says.

My entire body aches already. I know it's only a taste of what's to come and it's gonna hurt like a motherfucker. But I like it. I like the pain. I like the punishment. I like knowing with every blast of discomfort that comes from my muscles, I'm one step closer to Everleigh getting the medicine she needs. Because as much as I look forward to decimating Davidson, I could've lived my life without seeing him again. But I can't live my life without Everleigh.

"So, I was gonna ask you if you want to go to Shenanigan's, but I'm guessing that's a no," he laughs.

"Yeah. Not happening for a while." I open the door to my truck and toss my bag inside.

"Guess I'll have to go find Macie." He grins and wiggles his eyebrows.

"Macie?"

"Fuck me, Crew. This one," he blows out a whistle. "This one is different than every woman I've ever fucking met."

"She's nice?" I ask, climbing in the cab.

"I'm not fucking her personality, man. What the fuck?"

He seems offended I even asked. I laugh and start the engine. "How'd my girls seem today?" As soon as the words are out of my mouth, I regret it.

"Your girls?" He taunts.

"Not what I meant."

"That's totally what you meant. And we've already been over how they were today. Ever liked the girly shit you sent over. Jules almost cried when I gave her the envelope." He shrugs. "I don't know what else you want me to say. That Jules smelled like flowers?"

"You get that close to her and I'll plant you into the asphalt."

He backs away chuckling. "I gotta go. See ya at work tomorrow."

"Later, man."

I pull onto the street, the rush hour long gone. The moon is bright and it seems like I'm following it as I take turn after turn towards my house. The sky is dark except for the big silver ball. It looks lonely up there, hanging by itself.

The driveway is vacant when I park the truck. I cut the engine and just sit, staring at the front of my house. There are no lights on. There will be no smells from dinner, no giggles from a little girl watching some crazy cartoon with singing animals. I won't have to step over any toys or get a suspicious eye from a beautiful, dark-headed woman wondering why I'm late and what I'm up to.

Those are all the things I told myself I'd never enjoy.

Those are all the ways in which I lied to myself.

Chapter THIRTY-THREE

CREW

THE KITCHEN IS a complete disaster. Dishes and utensils are sitting everywhere, syrup sticking most of it together. I reach across my ma's blue bowl, pancake batter dripping down the side and onto the counter, and grab a banana. I need a quick bite to eat before I head to the gym.

Julia and Ever are in the living room getting situated. They got home yesterday afternoon. I was nervous as hell, only seeing them a couple of times while they were at the hospital. I didn't know what to expect. I'd talked to Jules on the phone every day multiple times, but I'd only been able to see them three times over the week they were there. Between work and training, by the time I'd call Jules, she'd say they were sleeping. I hate it. I want to be there for them. I missed them when they were there, worried like fucking crazy. But I have to do what has to be done . . . which is also why I haven't told Julia what I'm up to. I know it'll add to her worries and that's the last thing I want. I know I'll have to tell her at some point, but the right time hasn't popped up.

"Hey," Jules says, coming around the corner. Her hair is pulled back, a bit of shine back in her eyes. Everleigh tolerated the first round of treatment better than they expected and it's brought a little life back to Jules. Yesterday when they got home and got situated, she made dinner. I offered to get takeout, but she wanted to eat "real food." We ate and watched a movie; Jules and Ever both fell asleep on the sofa. I carried them both to bed.

"Hey," I say, smiling at her.

"Your pancakes were good." She brushes passed me and pours a glass of orange juice. "I'll get this cleaned up."

I love the way she looks in my kitchen. Probably too much.

"I'll get it when I get back. You relax."

"When you get back?" She looks alarmed. "Where are you going? I thought you'd be here with . . ." She looks down, embarrassment staining her cheeks.

I reach out and touch the side of her face. As soon as my hand makes contact with her skin, her head whips up. I start to take my hand away, worried I've overstepped my bounds, when she surprises the fuck out of me. As I pull it back, she wraps her little hand around my wrist and puts it back against her cheek. Her eyes are wide as she leans into my touch. Ever-so-carefully, I place my other hand against the other side of her face. I feel her breath hitch, her heartbeat pulsing.

"Hey," I whisper. I force a swallow, her eyes going to my throat. I want, *need* to kiss her, to wrap her up and never let her go. But I don't. "I have to work today."

"But it's Sunday."

"I know," I say, rubbing her skin with the pads of my thumbs. "And I'm sorry. But I have to do it."

Her face falls and I pull my hands away. She tears her eyes away from mine. "I know. I'm sorry. I know you're doing this for Ever and I—"

"No," I say softly, "I'm doing this for *us*. For Ever. For you," I grin. "And for me because I can't live without either one of you."

Her eyes go wide and a breath catches in her throat. I know saying it out loud, cut and fucking dry, is probably a bit much, but I can't help it.

"Maybe I shouldn't have said that," I say.

"I love that you did."

Things are starting to get complicated and, for both our sakes, I need to keep them simple.

"I'll be back later." I grab a bottle of water off the counter and start to leave.

"Crew?" she calls, her voice shaky.

I turn to look at her.

"I've missed you."

The swell of warmth hits me from head to toe. "I've missed you, too."

Chapter THIRTY-FOUR

JULIA

I CINCH A pair of sweatpants around my waist. I have lost a few pounds in the past couple of weeks. My appetite has been non-existent with everything going on. I've been able to eat a little this week since being back at Crew's—or home, for all intents and purposes—but not enough to make up for the days of eating nothing.

I settle into the sofa and try to doze off but sleep doesn't come. I'm too tired to actually sleep, which seems crazy, but I know it's true. With the interruptions and buzzers and monitors going off all week, plus the stress of everything, I'm past the point of needing rest. I need solutions.

Ever has done well in her first week of treatment, but the therapy still eludes us. She was denied again this week by the board and the insurance. The doctors are being very cautious as to what they say to me . . .

I squeeze my eyes shut and try not to let my mind reel. A counselor came in and talked to me, explained the stages of emotions I might and might not feel. I've accepted the fact that she is sick; seeing her lay in the hospital bed for a week helped that hit home. Now I'm just angry about the whole thing.

Why my daughter? Haven't I had enough pain in my life?

I'm trying to stay calm for Ever's sake, trying to keep my head on my shoulders. But it's getting hard. I've never been a particularly violent person, but I'd cut the throats of the people that denied Ever the therapy without a second thought. I'm sure those people have the money if their children get sick.

Bastards.

I know the doctors are doing everything they can and Ever seems to be handling everything really well. They said that's a good sign, to be not panicking over the therapy yet. They'll explore other options . . . and I'll pray for a miracle and try to keep myself sane by controlling the little things, the things I can control. It gives me some sense of being anchored, of not spiraling out of control, while I figure out the big things.

I fixed Crew dinner earlier tonight, just as I had all week. I'd been too exhausted to stay up the first few days we'd been home, so I wrapped it up and left it in the microwave to heat up. I figure it's the very least I can do for all he's doing for us. This second job he's taken on is keeping him from getting home 'til late every night. I'm not sure what he's doing, but he's getting banged up a bit. It's really wearing him down. And I hate that. I hate seeing him work himself to death but, at the same time, I've never seen something so beautiful. A man doing absolutely everything he possibly can to help a child he loves.

This whole situation has changed me. I've heard cancer changes people, but I never could've dreamed how without going through it like we are. Old grudges and hurt feelings don't matter. Worries about what other people think seem silly when death is facing you head on. All that matters is that you're right with your life and are as happy as you can be. Life goes on, even when you're dealing with cancer. The world doesn't stop. Feelings, life, relationships . . . none of that stops because you have to deal with the illness.

And that's partially why I called my parents today. It had been weighing on my conscious. I am their daughter and Ever their only grandchild. Maybe my parents are assholes most of the time, but they are my parents.

I didn't tell Crew I called them because I know he'd be angry. It wasn't a lengthy conversation, anyway, and I'm not sure my ma was sober enough to even realize what I was saying. But it was off my chest and I could cross that off my mind.

Sitting up at the sound of the door opening and shutting, I see the light in the kitchen bounce off the walls of the hallway. His bag drops to the floor and I hear his shoes hit the tile before he comes around the corner.

I haven't been up when he's gotten home from work this week, so I'm surprised to see him in gym shorts and no shirt. Before I can ask him about it, he spots me on the sofa.

"Hey. What are you doin' up?" he asks.

"Can't sleep."

"Ever okay?" He looks alarmed and glances down the hallway.

"She's staying with Olivia."

He raises his eyebrows and I know the feeling. I'm not thrilled she stayed there, either.

"She came by and Ever wanted to go with her," I shrug helplessly. "She was feeling good and cried when I told her she couldn't go. I can't keep her from having fun, living her life, can I? Olivia is like a grandma to her." Suddenly, I feel like I made the wrong decision. I start to stand. "Maybe I shouldn't have let her go."

"No, you did the right thing," he says, walking across the room. "She's safe with her." He sits down beside me and I notice a big bruise on the side of his thigh.

"What happened?" I ask, pulling back the leg of his gray shorts to get a better look.

"Got hit at work. It's fine. Just a bruise."

"You look like you just got home from the gym," I point out, my curiosity peaked.

He laughs. "Well, I did get a workout in tonight. That's for sure." And by his tone, I know he's done talking about it. I can't question him on it; it's not my place. Even if he went to the gym after work, there's no harm in that. God knows he's giving every other hour of his life to us. "You staying up for a while?"

I yawn and shrug. "I don't know if I can sleep. I tried to while I waited on you to get home . . ."

"You waited on me?" he asks cheekily.

I shrug again, my cheeks heating. *Maybe I shouldn't have said that.*

"Let me grab a shower and a bite to eat. Then maybe we can watch a movie or something?" His gaze is heavy, his voice controlled. The combination makes my stomach flutter.

I can only nod.

He smiles in return and heads to the shower. He disappears down the hallway and I take a deep breath. The smell of his skin, his sweat, is thick in the air. It is overwhelming in the very best way, in total contrast to the overwhelming odor of antiseptic and disease at the hospital.

Crew's in and out of the shower in a flash. I hear the microwave kick on in the kitchen and before I know it, he's walking back in the room. He has on a pair of black sweatpants and is carrying the plate of food I left him.

He's shirtless and his body takes my breath away. He's lean and toned beyond belief. His ab muscles ripple with every step, his shoulders rigid and strong. His arms are cut without flexing.

I spy the tattoos I know exist. There's an "M" for Minnesota on his right shoulder and "Ma" written in script over his heart. "Gage" is on his right forearm in block letters and I know "GENTRY" is written boldly across his back. It was his first tattoo.

He sits the plate on the table in front of us and collapses back onto the couch, wincing.

"You all right?" I ask, watching him move his right shoulder around.

"Yeah. Just a little sore, that's all."

My hands itch to touch his skin and a thread of guilt starts to spool in my stomach. I'm pushed and pulled, guilty for feeling and needing to feel . . . human again. A feeling of something other than sadness, responsibility, helplessness. For just a moment, I want to be a twenty-something girl without all the baggage I tote everywhere. I feel guilty for that, too.

I pull my gaze away.

"You okay?" he asks softly.

I laugh shakily because the hell if I know. Even if I am okay this second, the way my life goes, I may not be in the next. My life is a series of unpredictable events aimed at wearing me down.

"What does it matter?" I ask, more to myself than him.

He tips my chin gently so I'm looking straight at him. "It matters. It always matters to me."

"When did you start being so nice anyway?" My heart pounds, sending red-hot blood bursting through my veins. His fingertip sears my chin, yet when he lets his hand fall, I crave its return.

I am immobilized by the weight of his stare, held in place by his gaze. I can't look away. I don't want to look away, although I know I should.

"When you let me."

I tuck a strand of hair behind my ear.

"You're the strongest person I know," he says simply. "You just take everything thrown at you and keep on going."

I laugh at the ridiculousness of what he's saying. "Yeah. I'm strong all right."

"You are, Jules. The strongest people aren't the ones that walk around, flexing their shit. The strongest people are the ones that fight the battles no one sees. You amaze me."

"What I do is survive. There's nothing amazing about it."

"You sell yourself short."

We sit in a comfortable silence. He's dazed off, his focus on something far away. "Do you remember the day we met?"

"Um . . ." Whatever I expected him to say, this wasn't it. "Yeah. Of course. Why?"

"We saw you and your friends walking around that morning. I think it was actually Gage that saw you first. He wanted to go talk to you, but I sort of nipped that in the bud. I said, '*See the one in the black swim suit? She's mine.*'"

My mouth falls open. I had no idea.

"I wanted you from the minute I saw you. I needed you to be my girl. And by some fucking miracle, I got ya."

I can't help the smile that spreads across my face as I allow myself to remember the good times we had together. How protective he was of me. How intimidating he was to other people, but to me, he was softer. Considerate. At least until he left.

"Do you wonder what things would've been like if Gage would've gotten to you first? If we never would've been together?"

The way he says it makes my heart clench, makes my lungs struggle for air. I have thought about it, many times in fact. But for some reason now, *today, lately,* I don't want to. I don't want to have not had those moments with him. Those moments made me a part of who I am. Maybe it didn't end well, maybe it wasn't supposed to be between us forever, I don't know, but I wouldn't give those moments up for anything.

"You ended up with him anyway, so in a sense, it wouldn't make any damn difference." He smiles softly. "But those years we spent together, Jules, they're the only good part of my entire fucking life."

The honesty in his face, the way he looks at me, leaves me breathless. All the sides I've seen of him over my life, this is not one I've seen many. Maybe ever, really.

"I don't know what to say."

"You don't have to say anything." He fumbles with the drawstring to his pants, winding it around his finger. "There are days lately that I wake up and can't believe I'm in this position. My whole life seems like it's been flipped around so many times, given to me on a platter, or ripped out from under me. I just go through my life and wait for the next fight."

His eyes are the bluest I've ever seen, crystal clear. "It's taken Ever to get sick for me to realize the truth behind what my ma said to me. I've fought for so much dumb shit, Jules. But I've never fought for anything that I've really wanted. My priorities have been all over the fucking place, but never where they should've been."

"Look at what you're doing for us now. Now *you're* selling yourself short."

"Nah, I'm just being honest," he laughs.

"Do you remember the letter I told you about? That I found from Gage?"

He nods slowly.

"In that letter, he told me that if there was one person in the world that could help me, that *would* help me, if anything happened to him . . . it was *you*. He told me to trust *you*, Crew. That you never failed him when he needed you and that you wouldn't fail me either."

"Is that why you're letting me help you now? Because Gage said it was okay?"

"What do you mean?"

"I know things between us are complicated as fuck. I get that. But I need to know something, Jules." He twists around, facing me. His features are blank, braced, and I'm terrified for what he's about to say.

"What am I to you?"

"What is that supposed to mean?"

"You know what I mean. Am I the brother of your husband, the guy he told you to let take care of you? Or am I something else to you, too?"

"Crew . . ."

"It won't change anything," he says assuredly. "Because the way I feel won't change. The way I felt has *never* changed. But I gotta know. I gotta know, Jules."

I look to the floor, my hands shaking on my lap.

"I'm just going to lay this out there," he says, his voice rough. "You're a hell of a lot more to me than my brother's wife. When I look at you, I have to fight the way I've always felt about you. I have to remind myself that we aren't kids and you aren't mine. *That I let you go.*"

"What I'm doing now for you," he continues, his voice strained, "is because we're family. But it's also because *I love you*. And Everleigh. And I wouldn't be having this conversation with you if Gage was here because you were his and I halfway don't feel right even saying this now. But shit's about to get fucking real with what I've got going on. I need to focus to make it happen and maybe a little reassurance, I don't know, that things . . ."

He jumps to his feet and starts to head to the front door.

"Crew!" I call out, my voice trembling. He stops mid-step and turns to look at me. "I don't know how we got *here*. The past few years are so convoluted," I say, trying to find the right words but knowing I'll come up short. "I've pushed you away. I've downright been awful to you. Things between us have changed so many times and here we are . . ."

He faces me head on, his eyes pleading with me to continue.

"I keep thinking, 'What if,' but it doesn't matter. What I've learned over the past years is that today is all you have. And that's been reinforced these past few weeks. This moment is all that's promised to any of us and you can't live in the past . . ."

He takes the distance between us in just a couple of steps. He kneels in front of me so we are face-to-face. "What am I to you?" he asks again, his voice soft.

"You . . ."

"What am I to you?"

"You're the first boy I ever loved," I whisper, a nervous laugh to my voice.

"What about now?"

I know what he is to me. I've buried it, ignored it, fought it, and pretended like it didn't exist. Maybe it didn't for a time in my life, but that was then.

And *this* . . . this beautiful man in front of me, this man I may have pegged wrong for so many years out of fear or frustration, I'm not sure . . . is my *now*. I don't understand it, I don't know how or if it'll work out, I don't know if it's the right thing to do. But what I do know is that I do, in fact, love him. I'm not sure what that means or how he'll respond or if it even matters, but if I'm being honest, I do. And he deserves to know that. I deserve to know that.

"You're the first boy I ever loved," I breathe. "And the man I love now—"

I don't get to finish the sentence before his lips are on mine. It is a mixture of tenderness and ferocity that leaves me breathless.

Chapter Thirty-Five

CREW

I REGRET A lot of the things I've done, but I'm one hundred percent sure I'll never regret *this*.

Her lips are soft against mine, sweeter than I even remembered. She tenses for a split second and then relaxes into me, wrapping her arms around my neck. Her lips move with mine and it's pure fucking heaven. I don't want to break the kiss, but I do. I have to.

I rest my forehead against hers, listening to her ragged breaths. I'm sure mine sound the same, but I can't hear it because I'm concentrating on remembering everything about this moment. Her sounds, her smell, the feel of her in my arms. My body trembles with excitement. I have to talk myself down from just letting myself go and losing myself in the moment with her.

When I pull back, I have no idea what she's gonna say. I know she wasn't expecting that, but she said she loves me. Whether that was a mistake or not, the kiss we just shared wasn't.

With more apprehension than I've felt in my life, I rock back onto my heels and peer up at her. I study her face, looking for any sign that I've pushed her too far. I'll apologize if I did, but I won't really be sorry. How could I?

Her eyes are wide, her gorgeous lips parted. I run my thumb against them, stroking her bottom lip. She presses them together and against the pad of my finger and I let it linger for a moment longer than I anticipated.

She returns the grin on my face, her cheeks turning pink.

"Even if you're pissed about that, it was worth it."

She turns another shade of pink and grabs my face in her hands. Her touch lights up every cell in my body, warmth flooding through me like wildfire. She bends forward and kisses me, her lips moving with mine like they'd been there a million times before. Like they belong there.

Jules pulls back and I can see the same feeling running through me alive in her eyes. It's the first time in years I've seen the gold flecks sparkle in the dark irises. "Crew . . ." she whispers, her voice needy. "I . . ."

"I'm giving you a choice, Jules," I say, my voice wavering a little as I try to stay composed. "If this goes any further, then that's it . . . you're mine."

"Okay," she whispers.

"Be sure about this. I'm going to think about you every minute of every day. I will be jealous over everything you do. There will be no turning back."

"No turning back." She wraps her arms around me again, her mouth finding mine.

I stiffen for a split second in a moment of shock. This woman is all I've ever wanted. This woman is the bane of my existence and the reason I live, all wrapped in one beautiful package. Not having her is the reason I've wanted to die, yet it was a choice I made because I loved her so damn much. To have her back in my arms was something I never dreamed would actually happen, something that I never thought should happen. But things change and here we are.

I stand and pick her up with me, her legs finding my waist and wrapping around it. Our kiss never breaks. Each moment that passes, the energy between us grows. I can feel her fingers begin to grip my shoulders, her lips moving more frantically against mine.

This isn't gonna happen like this. No fucking way.

I head down the hallway and kick open the door. I lay her gently on my bed and she falls back against the white comforter. Her dark hair is splayed against the light sheets, her white t-shirt raised up, showing the bottom of her stomach. I can't take my eyes of her.

"Crew?" she asks, her voice trembling.

"Come here, love." I motion for her to sit up as I kneel at the side of the bed. She bends forward, our eye contact never breaking. My lips find hers, my arms trembling with anticipation as I grab the side of the bed on either side of her.

This is what I've wanted my entire life. Her, in my bed, in my home. *Mine.*

I lay a trail of kisses across her cheek and down her neck. Her skin is soft, her scent overtaking all of my senses. I almost feel high.

Her chest moves unevenly with ragged breaths, her heartbeat pounding against my fingertips as they trail down her skin and to the hem of her shirt. I drag it quickly over her head and toss it off to the side.

My own breathing is shaky as I take in the most beautiful thing I've ever seen sitting on the edge of my bed. Her skin is creamy against the dark lace covering her breasts. Her skin is hot to the touch as I press her chest against mine and wrap my arms around her back. I unfasten her bra and toss it away.

I cup her breasts, bigger, rounder, more perfect than I remember. She exhales at the contact, a soft moan escaping her swollen lips. The sound goes straight to my cock.

I slide my sweatpants down my legs. I kick them out of the way, blood pounding over my eardrums.

She lays back and begins to work her sweatpants down. Her hands are shaking when I brush them out of the way. My eyes on hers, I drag her pants slowly over her hips and off her body, and discard them onto the floor.

Just looking at her, I'm ready to fucking explode. My body shivers at the sight of the only girl I've ever loved lying naked in front of me.

The air is thick, sex lingering in the air, the sound of our breathing heavy.

I kneel again in front of her and her panting increases. I position myself between her legs and lick, with one lazy movement, through her pussy. As my tongue lands on her clit, a muffled moan hits my ears. The taste of her is sweeter than I even remembered and I lick through her one more time, not able to get enough.

Her hand runs over my head, her fingertips scratching against my scalp as her legs shake under me. I raise her thighs over my arms and work my mouth against her opening. She moans, tilting her pelvis up to allow me more access. I suck her swollen bud into my mouth, her pleasure obvious as her voice breaks through the silence.

"Crew!" she moans, her fingernails digging into my back.

I lick harder, using my tongue to stroke firm circles around her clit. She tastes so fucking good that it's hard not to come from this alone.

"I'm going to come if you don't stop." Her voice is broken with gasps, her tone heavy with lust.

Not wanting to end this yet, I drag my tongue up her belly. She shivers as I make my way up her body, pausing at her breasts. I work her nipples in my mouth, rolling them around my tongue. Her back arches, her eyes flutter closed, as she exhales my name.

I kiss her for every kiss we've missed. I kiss her to remind her that I am not going anywhere. I kiss her to let her know I love her and that she's inarguably my girl.

I roll my body onto hers and brush my cock against her opening. She's so wet that I stifle a moan of my own. I want to bury myself in her and find myself again.

"I love you," I whisper into her mouth. I kiss her once more and then pull back and look into her beautiful brown eyes. "I've never stopped loving you and I've dreamed of this for so damn long."

Her hands find the small of my back and press gently. "I love you, Crew."

"Oh, Jules," I whisper, kissing her again. I wrap my arm under her and hold her in place. My cock is throbbing against her opening. I press firmly, her wetness allowing me to enter her tight little body. She stretches as I fill her and moans into my mouth. Her eyes fly open and I feel her muscles contracting around my length.

"Crew," she tries to yell, but I capture her words with my tongue. I want every part of me inside every part of her. I want to own every part of her, mark every part of her body as mine.

Her body pulses around my cock, tighter than anything I've ever felt. Her body feels like it was made just for me. "Look at me, Jules."

I pull nearly out and push back in with one swift movement, her eyes fluttering shut before opening, her gaze holding mine.

Her fingernails find my skin, digging into it, sending waves of lust through my body. She moans in pleasure, her legs now wrapped around my waist. I continue to stroke her, lapping up the pure fucking bliss of feeling her come apart around me so quickly. I love making her feel like this.

"I love you," she pants, the riot in her body seeming to calm a bit.

"I love you, too." I pick up speed, feeling the aftershocks of her orgasm, and find a rhythm that promises to push me over the edge. She squeezes herself around me again, tightening her pussy. I have no control. Not when I'm buried inside the girl of my dreams, her perfect tits pressed

SACRIFICE

against my chest, her mouth making love to mine, my hands wrapped in her silky hair.

I am no match for her. I've waited too long for this.

I press again and bury myself against the back of her body. I empty myself into her, feeling her entire body pulsing around me.

If there is such a thing as heaven, this is it.

Chapter THIRTY-SIX

JULIA

I CAN SENSE light. I can feel the warmth on my face, but I can't open my eyes.

Rolling onto my side, my hand drops to the sheets. They're softer than I remember. Something's not making sense.

I drag my eyes open just as the door opens. Crew walks in, a green towel wrapped around his face, water droplets speckling his chiseled body.

I pull the covers over my body, which is still naked. He smirks, knowing good and well I'm uncomfortable.

"How are ya, Sleeping Beauty?" he asks, standing at the foot of the bed, his hands on his trim hips. He hasn't shaved and the dusting of stubble across his face only makes him that much sexier.

I stretch, my muscles complaining. My body is worn out from the previous night's exertion.

I forgot what it's like to be with Crew.

My body is a wreck, but my mind is strangely clear. And calm.

"You slept straight through the night," he says, turning his back towards me and rifling through a dresser drawer. He pulls out a pair of black gym shorts and a gray t-shirt and lays them on the bed. "I think I used up the last bit of energy you had last night."

I tighten the sheets around me. I wait for the feelings of guilt or disgust to sweep through me, but they don't come. I don't feel dirty or impulsive or careless lying in Crew's bed.

It feels right.

And that in itself makes me question my sanity.

"What time is it?" I ask, trying to give myself a minute to figure this out.

"A little after eight. I gotta, uh, head to work in a little bit."

"Ever should be back around ten. I better get up and get a shower," I say, watching him pull his shirt on over his body. It's a sight to behold. "You're wearing *that* to work? Gym shorts and a t-shirt?"

"Yeah." He sits on the edge of the bed and puts on his socks and sneakers.

"What are you doing, exactly?"

He doesn't say anything. A feeling of unease creeps through my spine. "Crew?"

His shoulders shrug before he stands and faces the bed. "I'm fighting."

He says it like it's the most natural thing in the world. Like he's informing me he's going to the gas station or the grocery store.

"You're what?" I ask in disbelief. "Crew? What are you doing?"

"I'm fighting. I told you."

It all starts to make sense. I thought he was kidding when he mentioned it before. What man in their right mind would fight once they've been hurt and warned of the possible ramifications for doing it again? But the bruises, the workout clothes, the late nights . . . it all makes sense.

"Crew, you can't."

"I have to, Jules. I have a fight lined up and I'll make the money we need."

"What are you talking about?"

He sighs. "I got a fight with Hunter Davidson. I fight on July 13th. If I win, I'll get $100,000. For Ever."

I can't believe what he's saying. He's not joking.

The room starts spinning. I squeeze my temples and try to separate this mess in my mind.

"You can't," I breathe out. "What if something goes wrong? What if you get hurt? What if . . ." I can't say it. I can't say the ultimate possibility. I can't even fathom losing him now.

"What if I don't?"

"Then we'll figure it out!" I cry. My hands shake and I lay them on my lap. My thoughts start to separate, boil down to the basics, and I realize the fundamental problem with this whole thing. Is it selfish? Probably.

But still.

"I can't lose you, too," I whisper, tears filling my eyes.

"Hey," he says, walking over to the side of the bed. He sits on the edge and kisses me gently. "What did I tell you last night?"

I can't speak, so he answers himself. "That I'll never walk away from you again."

"But—"

"No buts, Jules. I'm going to be fine. This is the first time in my life that I'm fighting for something real, for something that matters. I'm doing this."

"What if something happens to you?"

"I'm never leaving you."

I don't trust him and not because it's him this time. But because I've heard that before and been left even though they didn't want to leave me. Sometimes it isn't your choice, sometimes fate has different plans. And Crew fighting seems to be taunting fate and its devilish ways. How would I make it? How would Ever take it?

Ever . . .

"Crew, about last night . . ." My throat starts to burn. I don't know how to navigate whatever this is between us now. When he said he won't walk away, I'm not sure what that means. I'm also not sure what's best for Ever right now.

"Last night was the best night I've ever had," he says simply.

His reply makes me grin.

"Why do I get the feeling I'm not gonna like where your head is at today?"

I shrug, tugging the blanket back up around me again. "I don't know what all, if anything, this changes between us."

"It changes everything," he says matter-of-factly.

"How?"

"What do you mean, 'How?'"

"I don't know how to do this, whatever this even is. I don't want Ever confused, I don't want her having to deal with anything else in her little life."

"Let's get a couple of things straight. This," he says, motioning between us, "is you and me together. It's you and me tackling this fucking world as a team. This," he says, pointing at himself, "is me not giving two fucks what you say about it. I gave you the option to stop last night and you didn't take it. Now you deal with me."

SACRIFICE

His lips part into a small grin, but I know he's not joking. I'm semi-relieved that he's not.

"I can see how you want things to move slowly for Everleigh and that's fine. I get it. She's dealing with enough changes right now."

"But just so you know," he says, leaning in and kissing me again before standing up, "you and I aren't up for negotiation. You'll have to make it work." He winks before heading to the door. "I'll be back this afternoon sometime. You gonna be okay?"

"I don't like you fighting, Crew. I really don't like this. I want to know exactly what's going on. I want the details. I want to know everything."

"Later," he says, turning the handle. "It's really nothing for you to worry about."

"How can you say that?"

He shrugs. "I just did."

Chapter THIRTY-SEVEN

CREW

MY SWEAT STREAKS the canvas of the ring. My opponent, Victor, is sitting across from me, catching his breath, too. We've been training for hours and the one thing I've found out is this: my cardio isn't what I thought it was. I forgot how long five minutes can feel.

Victor groans as he stands and slips between the ropes. He disappears into the locker room. He's young, mid-twenties. His forte is striking and he's damn good at it. I'm sure he thought what every striker thinks when they told him he was going in with a wrestler. Regardless, he left the ring having taken more blows than me.

My entire body aches. Sal's game plan for this fight is quick and hard—there's no time to baby my body into peak performance. I gotta get it as good as I can in just a quarter of the time it normally takes to prepare for a fight. It's not much, but all I got to work with.

Sal comes up beside me and rests his hands on the top rope. "Not bad today, kid. Your body still has muscle memory, thank God."

"As many years as I did this, it better."

"I need ya to head to the camp tomorrow."

I dip my head. Camp is an hour outside of the city, an acre of country that the gym owns. Most training-style camps are held there exclusively. There's even a small dormitory set up so you don't even have to leave. It's the perfect place to get in shape. No phones, trails to run, wood to chop,

SACRIFICE

bales of hay to toss. Sal is very old school with his methods, but they work.

"Be there around noon. We'll be there 'til dark at least." He shakes his head. "I wish we had more time."

"Me fucking too."

"Well, you're the idiot that took this fight."

My head whips around to face him. "Say what?"

"I have no idea what you're thinking, Gentry. That shoulder of yours is shit. You know it and I know it. This is a suicide mission and I have to wonder if I've not lost my fucking marbles helping you do it."

I scramble to my feet. "Look, you took this on just like I did." I glare at him, asking him to challenge me.

"So you're gonna risk everything? What if something happens to you out there, Gentry? Huh? What then? Have you thought about that?"

"Yeah, I have."

"And you're gonna risk it all?"

"I'll sacrifice everything I am. I'll do whatever it takes for them." My body shakes with anger. "Now you can shut the fuck up and help me or not. Just let me know because I'm not gonna spend the next couple of months worrying about it."

He places one hand on my shoulder. "All right, kid. We won't discuss it again."

"Good."

"Just promise me one thing."

"What's that?"

"You'll stay focused. Eyes on the prize. Keep your head clear."

"I will."

"No, I mean it, Crew. No distractions."

CREW

I PULL THE shirt over my head and glance down at my bed. The pillows are in place, the bed made. I smile, knowing a few hours before, I had Julia right there. I breathe in deeply, trying to catch a trace of her scent. It's a unique smell, her body mixed with the vanilla body lotion she wears. It creates an overwhelming sensation of lust, mixed with something I only know as love, and I gotta get the hell out of here or I'll spend all day here thinking back to last night.

Making my way down the hall and into the kitchen, I stop in the doorway and watch her. She's on her tiptoes, reaching for something in the top of the cabinet. She's too cute as she struggles to grasp the box just beyond her reach.

"Want me to get that?" I walk up behind her so that my chest is touching her back. I rise up slowly, aligning our bodies. The box becomes irrelevant, my brain only registering how close she is to me. How good she smells. How amazing she feels.

"Crew," she breathes, looking at me over her shoulder. "Not here. Ever's just in the bathtub."

I laugh and step back. "Not here what? I was just getting you this." I sidestep her and grab the box off the shelf. She whips it out of my hand and shakes her head.

"You don't play fair."

"Me? Nah, I don't play at all. I fight to win."

Her eyes narrow. "Speaking of fighting . . ."

"Jules . . ."

"Crew."

"I'd rather fight with you than love anyone else," I grin.

"What's going on? *Really.*"

I study her face, hoping I'll see some chink in her armor. I know I'm going to have to discuss this with her sooner or later, but later always sounds better.

I sigh and lean against the counter. "I fight in a few weeks. I got a one fight contract with the NAFL. It'll give us enough money for the therapy."

Her face falls. "I got the mail today. I got denied the last loan I tried to take out."

I grab her and pull her into me. "It's fine. I got this taken care of. Just give me a little more time. Don't get down about this yet. Ever's doing fine so far. We just need to hold on a little longer."

"I don't want you to fight."

I chuckle. "That sounds familiar."

"I've never liked you fighting, Crew. But especially now."

"You're afraid I'll get hurt? Because I won't. I haven't fought in a while, but I've been working the docks. That's not pussy work."

She lays her head against my chest. "I know. I just don't want anything to happen to you."

"Stop that. Nothing is gonna happen to me."

"But what if it does? Not only will I lose you, but so will Ever. It just seems like such a risky idea. I know why you're doing it and I can't argue it, although I want to. The selfish part of me, the mom part of me, can't say no to that. But Crew . . ."

I kiss the top of her head. "I've made two decisions. I'm fighting and you're mine. So you don't need to worry your pretty little head about either one of them."

She wraps her arms around my waist and pulls me closer, then pushes me away just as quickly.

"What?"

"We can't do this," she hisses.

"Oh, Jules, we've already done *this*. I warned you."

"No, Crew. *This.*" She takes a few steps back.

I hate the distance. Although it's a couple of steps at best, it feels like a fucking mile compared to her being up against me and in my arms.

"*This*," I reply, looking at the empty space between us, "is fucking stupid."

"I told you I don't want Everleigh to be suspicious. How would I ever explain this to her?"

My eyes instinctively roll. "Oh, I don't know. That I've loved you my entire life?"

"Crew . . ."

"What do you want me to say?"

She turns her back to me and it amplifies my frustration. *I fucking warned her! Less than twenty-four hours and she's already done with me? Not happening.*

"Look, I told you I'd give you space for this. And I will. But I'm telling you right now—"

"Are you arguing?" Her voice is small, yet it makes both of us jump. Our heads whip to the doorway to see Everleigh standing, purple towel wrapped around her, bald head shining, watching us.

Julia retreats from me, leaving me standing on my own. She goes to Ever and picks her up. "No, sweetheart. We aren't arguing."

"Good," she says. She looks at me. "Families don't argue."

I laugh. "Sometimes they do, monkey. But we weren't arguing."

She twists her face, like she's considering I'm lying to her. It makes me laugh.

"What? You think I'm kiddin' ya?"

"Well, Mommy and I argued a little."

"We did?" Jules looks at Ever, obviously confused. "When did we argue?"

"When you said Crew wasn't my daddy."

My jaw drops. I'm abso-fucking-lutely certain I heard that wrong. I had to have.

She's watching me carefully while Jules watches her. "Are you?" she asks me. Her little eyes are wide, full of some emotion I can't pinpoint. They're bright, completely clear, and they remind me of her dad. And that isn't me.

I plaster on a smile. "No, monkey. I'm not your daddy."

Her bottom lip trembles and it breaks my heart. "But I don't have a daddy."

"Oh, baby, you do," Jules says, her eyes filling with tears. "He's just in heaven."

"I know that. I know my daddy is in heaven right now. But I don't have a daddy here." She looks back to me. "Daddy's protect the babies and the mommies. Daddy's make sure there is food and they make sure everyone is happy. I learned that in school. We were talking about animals, but it's the same thing."

"Well—" Julia starts, but Ever cuts her off.

"But that's what you do," she says, ignoring her mother. "And I know you love me and my mommy. So why aren't you my daddy? You don't want to be my daddy?"

Julia gasps and I feel her gaze on me. But I don't look at her. I just watch Ever.

I love this little girl with everything I am. I'd give anything for her, sacrifice it all to make sure she's better off than I ever was. I will protect her and make sure she has food and that she's happy. I twist my gaze to Julia. And I will do all those things for her, too.

I reach my arms out and Ever falls into them. I hold her in front of me. "Your daddy was my brother."

"I know."

"And he loved you more than anything in this entire world. Do you know that?"

"Yes."

Julia is leaned against the wall, one hand over her heart. I know this is the bottom line for her. It's important to her that Gage is always remembered by Everleigh, but hell, it's important to me, too.

"I never want to take the place of him, Ever. Being someone's daddy is a special thing. But I tell you what . . ." I look at Julia and her eyes grow wide. "I tell you what," I repeat, looking back at Ever, "I promise you that I will always do all of those things for you. I'll do any daddy thing you need me to and I'll always protect you and make sure you have food."

I hoist her over to my hip and touch her nose. "And I'll always love you. And your Mommy, too."

Ever's head tilts to the side. "Told you," she says to Julia.

Julia laughs, her eyes filling with tears. "You did," she says, trying not to sound choked up but failing.

"So can I call you Daddy?" The hope in her voice breaks me in two. This little girl can call me whatever she wants, although I'm nowhere good enough to have that title.

"If that makes you happy, monkey, I'd like that, I think."

She wraps her arms around my neck and buries her head in my shoulder. "I love you," she says, her little voice all muffled.

I rub her little head with my hand, my eyes glued to the woman standing before me. "I love you, too."

Chapter Thirty-Eight

CREW

"GET OFF YOUR back!" Sal shouts. "Damn it, Crew! Get off your fucking back."

I try to burst through my sparring partner, using my legs to kick him off. I roll onto the top of my back and shove off, sending Victor tumbling to the other side of the ring.

"That's it. You gotta stay off your back, damn it. If you let Davidson get you on the mat, you're gonna have a helluva fight on your hands."

I hear him, but I'm not listening. I'm more concerned at the fucking moment with the fire burning through my upper back. It's hot. It's intense. And it hurts like a bitch.

"Gentry! You listening to me?"

"Yeah," I say, trying to hide the pain from my voice. "Just taking a second."

He releases a breath. "All right. Good workout tonight, boys. Tomorrow at six."

"See ya tomorrow, Coach," Victor says. "Later, Crew."

I lift my hand a bit, barely off the mat, and feel the canvas dip as they both hop out of the ring. I open my eyes, sparkles dancing through my vision, flames dancing through my body.

Holy fuck.

The canvas dips again and Will bends beside me. "Hey. You all right?"

I groan. "Yeah."

"You're a liar, too. What happened?"

I struggle to sit up, the pain ripping through me as I move.

"What happened, man?" Will steps back as I stumble to my feet.

"Nothing. I'm fine."

"You rolled up on your shoulder . . ."

"No shit."

I amble out of the ring and Will grabs my bag. We head into the parking lot, the warm air wrapping around my body, taking the chill of the pain out of it.

"Crew, man, if you've hurt your spine again . . ."

"Will," I warn, turning to face him, "shut the fuck up. What's hurt and what's not hurt is none of your business. I don't want you saying a word about it. Got it?"

He tosses my bag in my truck and watches me climb in. "Okay. This is your call. I'm team . . . What are we called?"

I think a second. "Team Believe." I turn the engine on. "Believe I don't fucking kill myself."

"Not funny, man."

I laugh anyway. "I'm heading home. Want to come by and drink the beer that's left in my fridge? It's not that fancy Craft shit you drink, but it's free beer."

"Free beer is free beer. I'll follow ya."

I close the door and head home, fighting to ignore the pain that is starting to lessen a bit across the back of my shoulders. Team Believe. Although I was joking when I said it, I like it. I like the word believe. It's what I'm doing now in every aspect of my life—believing I won't get fired for being so tired at work. Believing I'm doing the right thing in this mess I'm in the middle of. Believing that I won't fuck it up worse than it already is somehow. Believing that I will figure out a way to win this fight with Davidson.

I pull into my driveway, Will on my tail. There's a red beat up car parked along the curb and I don't recognize it.

I get out of the truck and meet Will on the lawn.

"Who's that?" he ask, jabbing a thumb over his shoulder.

"Don't know."

We walk to the front and up the steps, a strange quietness moving between us. I twist the handle and go inside, the light on in the living room. I hear voices, more voices than there should be.

Standing next to my television are Jules' parents.

"What the fuck are they doing here?" I scowl. "You have about two seconds to explain this."

"Crew," Julia says, jumping off the sofa. She runs to me and I pull her in close. She falls into my side like it's the most natural thing to do. Any other time, I'd relish the moment. But right now, there are two assholes staring at me that I want to deal with.

"Crew, my man," her father extends his hand. I let it hang in the air. They smell like stale cigarette smoke, the odor permeating the air around them.

Harry and Greta are almost unrecognizable; the years have not been good to them. They're unkempt, their hair practically uncombed. They look dope sick, like they're desperate for their next hit of whatever they're on. I wonder vaguely if Julia realizes they've moved on from alcohol.

"Why are you here?" I ask.

Will walks to the other side of Jules. "Where's Ever?" he whispers.

"Bedroom. Asleep," she whispers back.

"Join her," I growl.

"Crew, wait—"

"No. There'll be no waiting, Jules. Unless they came here to tell you how sorry they were for fucking up your life, there'll be no waiting."

"We came to see our daughter. Apparently, our granddaughter is sick and we wanted to see her, too."

"And they wanted me to sign a car loan for them," Julia says softly. I can hear the sadness in her voice, the feeling of being letdown by her parents yet a-fucking-gain.

"You had the audacity to walk in here, knowing your granddaughter has cancer, and ask her to sign a car loan for you?" I can't believe it, even from them.

Harry puffs out his chest. "I gotta do a lot of runnin' back and forth between here and Baltimore. I need a car that will make it. Why do you fuckin' care?"

"I bet you do. Runnin' a lot of dope between the cities now, are ya?"

"That's none of your business," he says, his voice sloppy.

I look down at Jules. "How did they know you were here?"

"Because she called me," Greta says. "She told me what's going on. I didn't think you'd want us to know. You never wanted her around us. You took her away from us!"

I take Julia's hands off my waist and gently nudge her towards the

SACRIFICE

hallway. "Go in Ever's room and stay there. Okay?"

"Crew . . ."

"Jules, I'm not playing."

With a last, tear-filled glance at the people that brought her into the world, she heads off down the hall. I wait until I hear the door gently close before I speak.

"You two worthless pieces of shit aren't to contact either of them ever again. Do you hear me?"

Harry steps to me, pointing his finger at my face. "You can't tell me if or when I'm going to see my daughter and grandkid. You're nothing to her. You're not her husband and even if you were, I'm her father!"

I laugh angrily. "You're gonna want to get that finger outta my face before I fucking remove it from your body."

High as a kite, Harry steps another step towards me. "You think you can do that, big boy?"

Greta grabs his arm and shoves him toward the front door. "Harry, let's go," she says, seeing the wickedness behind my expression. "Come on." She leads him to the front and out onto the porch.

Harry shakes her off and turns to face Will and me again. "I'll be back here again whenever I damn well feel like it."

I turn sideways to set myself up to throw a punch at his face when Will steps between us.

"Harry, trust me on this, you need to shut your suck." Will looks at me over his shoulder and winks. "Now, as a totally unbiased opinion here, *Harry*, you're a complete fucking douchebag that needs his ass whipped in a royal fashion. You've needed that for years now, you cocksucker. And Crew, as much as I'd like to see you give out the beatin' I know you're capable of, you need to *not* go to jail for obvious reasons. But I can."

Will shoots a right to Harry's face, busting his nose. He staggers back, already off balance from whatever drug he's taken this morning.

Greta screeches, catching Harry as he falls against the column on the porch.

Will pops a left-right-left into Harry's face again and he's too slow, too out of it to even defend himself.

"You're an animal," Greta breathes out in disbelief. She wraps her arm around Harry and practically drags him to the car while he holds his nose. "I'm calling the police!"

"That's fact as fuck. But you better think that cop-calling bullshit through," Will says.

There are little droplets of blood dotting the ground from the porch to the car. It's better than the pieces of flesh like would've happened if Will hadn't stepped in the way.

We watch them drive off as fast as their car will go, the tailpipe rattling the whole way down the street.

Will shakes his hand again. "Man, that fucking hurt."

"Suck it up, pussy," I say, working my shoulders in a circle to alleviate some of my own discomfort.

Will starts to comment on it but stops himself. "Can I get some ice?"

I laugh. "No. You want to be a fighter, you gotta deal with the pain." I wince at the last word as a burst of it sends chills down my body.

"I don't want to be a fighter. I want to keep you from going to prison. If you touched him—"

"I'd have killed him."

"Exactly."

The door cracks behind me and Will looks over my shoulder. He smiles before turning his eyes back on me. "I'm going to head out. I've had enough excitement for the day."

"Thanks, Will."

"No problem. See ya, Jules."

"Bye, Will."

I turn and she's standing wide-eyed. "Do I want to know?"

"Nope," I say, pulling her into me and forgetting, for just one minute, the world outside of she and I exist.

Chapter THIRTY-NINE

JULIA

"WHAT'S GOING ON?" I ask.

Crew comes into the kitchen after work, followed by Olivia. She's grinning ear-to-ear.

"Crew called me this morning and asked if I could sit with Everleigh this evening."

"Why?" I look between them, not understanding. "Did I forget something? Did something happen?"

Crew chuckles. "I want to take you somewhere. Just the two of us."

A small flutter begins in my belly, reminding me of a time long ago. I feel almost giddy that he wants to take me somewhere. He looks tired and worn down. His hair has started to grow back, a couple of days' worth of stubble dotting his face. He's incredibly handsome, the boy I fell in love with years before grew up into one fine man.

Even so, I hate the idea of leaving Everleigh.

"Do you think we should?"

He nods, biting his lip. "We are."

"But what if—" I start.

"Julia, I'm here. She's been fine today. You said so yourself when I called earlier."

"You set me up!" I look between them and they laugh. "Crew!"

"Take it easy on him," Olivia laughs. "He wants to do something nice for you and it's exactly what you need right now."

"When did you get on Team Crew?"

She grins at him and then looks back to me. "I never said I wasn't." She turns on her heels and heads to the living room. I hear my daughter squeal when she sees Olivia. I hope it helps her spirits. She was so sick last night, throwing up and complaining of stomach pains and a headache. It was a long night. I called the doctor and they said it was normal, but if she seemed at risk for dehydration or got a fever to bring her right in.

I feel Crew's gaze resting on me and I know this isn't a battle I'm going to win.

"Just an hour or so, okay?" I ask carefully. I don't want to offend him, but I can almost not bear leaving her.

He kisses the top of my head, smelling all dirty from work. "Yeah. I'm gonna grab a quick shower and then we'll go."

"Where are we going?" I ask.

"For a little drive."

"Don't you have to train tonight?"

"Night off." He winces a little as he rolls his shoulder. "Gotta rest the body a little bit."

"Should I change?" I look down at my jeans, a rip tearing through one knee, and my Boston Red Sox shirt.

"If you're gonna be seen out with me, that shirt's gonna have to go."

I roll my eyes. "The shirt goes or I don't."

He growls playfully. "Fine, but it's a good thing you're pretty."

JULIA

I GLANCE AT my phone again. I'm worried Olivia will call or text and I won't hear it. I thought Crew was going to have to pick me up and carry me out the door. It feels so unfair, so hedonistic, to leave Ever when she's sick, even though she told me to leave so she could play Candy Land with Olivia.

Crew's hand grabs my thigh and gives it a little shake. "She's fine. She's having fun."

"I know," I say through gritted teeth. "I just feel bad . . ."

"For what? Recharging your battery for an hour? You feel bad about that?"

"Yeah." I rest my head against the back of the seat and let the early evening sun warm my face.

He turns the radio down. "You're dumb."

"Thanks."

"No, I mean it this time," he laughs. "You can't feel bad about leaving Ever with the only person besides the two of us she loves. She's going to have a good game of Candy Land while we go out and get an ice cream."

I look at him and he grins.

"We're going for ice cream?"

He nods and pulls into Castle Island. "I thought it would be a nice thing to do. Grab a cone, sit by the water, have a few minutes together. Just the two of us."

My heart fills. This is exactly what I need.

He parks his truck and we climb out. He meets me at the front and grabs my hand immediately, like it's the way we always do. I like it. I like all of it. As we walk through the entrance and over to the ice cream stand, I like every bit of this evening.

Our hands, clasped together, swing gently between us. His thumb strokes my knuckles and each swipe sends a warm sensation through me. I love the way I feel safe. I adore the way I feel important to him. I love looking up to him and seeing him looking at me through the corner of his eye and the grin that tickles the corner of his mouth.

"What?" I ask, a grin tugging at my lips, too.

"Just wondering how I've stooped so low to be seen with a girl wearing a Red Sox shirt."

I bump him with my shoulder and he feigns like it hurt. He covers his shoulder with his other hand and sours his face. "Ouch. I was kidding."

I shake my head. The ice cream stand is in front of us, the menu hanging off the front just like I remembered.

"What do you want?" he asks. "You still like the coconut flavor?"

"I haven't had the coconut ice cream here since the summer you left."

A look flitters across his face. "Really?"

"Gage and I never came here. Not for ice cream."

He nods and looks away. "What do you want then?"

"Coconut."

He orders me a cone and himself a chocolate one while I do a quick check of my phone. I'm relieved to see the screen blank. He hands me my cone and we walk away, licking our treats. "Want to go sit by the water?"

"Yeah. Let's do that."

His hand finds mine again and our fingers interlock. We walk leisurely down to the beach and sit close together on the sand. It's warmer than it has been, but the breeze still makes it a little chilly. The waves roll in easily, lapping against the shore.

"I think the first time I ever saw you, you were right over there," he says, pointing to an area near an outcropping of rocks. "You were with your friends and laughing. You looked so beautiful, like you didn't have a care in the world. There were guys walking past you, checking you out, and you seemed oblivious."

"I was," I said, thinking back to that day.

"You know, if I could go back to that day, I'd change everything."

He holds his cone in both of his hands in front of him, his elbows resting against his knees.

"If I could go back to that day, I'd tell you I loved you right off. It might scare you, but you'd know that I was serious. And I'd get a job and save money and get us a house together as soon as I graduated high school."

He takes off his Golden Gophers hat and puts it on my head, grinning. "I'd move you in with me and away from your parents and take care of you for every day of the rest of our lives. I wouldn't go to Minnesota, I wouldn't worry about being famous. I'd give all of that up just to have you."

My cheeks ache from smiling, his words something I never thought he'd ever think. It's the exact thing I'd wished had happened more times than I could count, but never in my wildest dreams did I think he'd wish for that, too.

He leans to me and kisses me sweetly on the lips. "I wanted to bring you here tonight to tell you that. To tell you if I could take you back here on that day we met, I'd change everything I've ever done for you."

"Oh, Crew," I say, cupping the side of his face.

"I don't expect you to say anything," he says. "I know things are more complicated for you than they are for me. Just know I loved you then and I love you now. As a matter of fact, you're the only person I've ever loved and the only person I'll ever love."

"I love you, too," I whisper, kissing him.

He rests his forehead against mine. "Whatever happens with everything, just know that. Know I love you and that I never loved anyone else. It's important to me that you know that. Things are going to get really serious with this fight and I want to be able to rest assured that you know that. Okay?"

"About the fight—"

"No. There's nothing to discuss."

We watch the waves lap at the beach, the seagulls squawking in the air.

"I'd do anything for you and Everleigh," he says, almost to himself. "Whatever happens the night of the fight, I want you to know that I made that decision. I'm not going into it thinking it's gonna be roses."

"What are you telling me?"

He shrugs. "Nothing in particular. I just want you to know that I've considered every angle. I don't want you to ever think you didn't argue enough for me to not fight or try to think another way out of this money thing. This wasn't your choice." A small smile graces his lips. "This has given me a purpose in life. A way to give my life back the meaning it lost when I lost you."

"Crew . . ."

"No, it's true. This is my second chance at so many things, to right some of the wrongs, to put some good into the world . . . to love you the right way."

He presses a kiss against my lips, stealing my breath. He starts to say something else when my phone buzzes beside me. I snatch it off the ground, my heart leaping in my chest.

"Hello?"

"I'm sorry to have to call you, Julia," Olivia says, "but I think you need to come home. Ever's not well."

Chapter FORTY

JULIA

MY CHEST IS warm and not just because Everleigh is curled up on my lap, her face buried into me, sleeping. The peaceful rise and fall of her chest, the way her little lips dip together like she's kissing, the way her little eyelids flutter with her breathing, warm my heart. When she's sleeping, everything else goes away. The pain from her face, the fear in her eyes, diminishes just a bit. I don't get that relief often anymore; I know she never does. I hope her dreams are as peaceful as they sometimes seem.

Last week we were home and, until the last couple of days, it was bliss.

Ever demanded special "daddy time" with Crew. It was my first instinct to object, to panic, but the look on both of their faces when they came into the kitchen and told me they were going to the park stopped me.

They walked out the door, her hand tucked safely inside his, my heart completely melting. Regardless if it worried me if it was right or wrong to allow her to call him daddy, it made her happy. The smile hadn't left her face all morning, something of a miracle these days.

After a few tears, a mixture of happy and sad, quietly in the bathroom, I felt my first true moment of peace. Some normalcy, although nothing normal at all, seemed to be back.

I went to the grocery store, something I normally hate because it's just a big battle of "what can I afford?," but really didn't mind. Crew sent me a couple of pics of Ever on the swings, a smile so wide on her face that I couldn't help but beam in the middle of the produce department. On the way home, I called Human Resources and updated them on what was going on with Everleigh.

And then Crew and I went to Castle Island and all hell broke loose.

We rushed her to the ER and they admitted her. Luckily, it was something they were able to control with fluids and more antibiotics, although she never seemed to regain the energy she had before she got so sick.

This was the first time she really, really looked as sick as they said she was. She looked almost . . . lifeless. And there's no pamphlet, no television show, no pictures, no lectures from doctors or nurses that can ever prepare you for that. To see your normally vibrant daughter without hair, puking into a bucket, trying to cry but having no tears, trying to talk but having no voice, trying to smile but having no energy or color in her cheeks . . . it's soul crushing. Hell cannot be worse.

I am sitting in the yellow room at the hospital, in the middle of another round of chemo. A round that is devastating my baby girl in every way. It's such a contrast to the first round, her little face swollen, pain in her tummy that's so bad she can barely even cry. It's hell on earth. Pure, absolute, living hell.

It makes no sense logically to think she has to be so *abused* to get *better*. It's even harder to explain to *her*. Looking into her little face, telling her I can't take her home, I can't make it stop, is nothing short of devastating. I wouldn't wish this on my worst enemy.

Ever stirs and stretches. I stand and climb into her bed, careful not to disturb her cords. She shivers and I cover her with a blanket, wishing I could do something. That's the hardest part, not being able to use your hands to fix it, to make it better. It's beyond difficult to put your trust in people and poison.

I hear my phone ring and I glance at the clock. I grab it off the bedside table. I know it's Crew on his lunch break. He calls every day.

"Hey," I whisper, trying not to wake Ever.

"Hey, love. What's goin' on over there?"

I smile at the term of endearment he's started using for me. I sigh and climb back out of bed and curl up on the couch beneath the window. "She's still in a lot of pain. They gave her more meds an hour ago or so and she's sleeping now."

"I wish I could be there," he says and I know he means it. He managed to swing by last night after training. I'm not sure how he keeps going.

I'm in awe of him.

"Me, too. I miss you."

I know he's smiling. I know he's slightly shaking his head, maybe even running a hand across his scalp.

"I miss you both."

There's a long pause. I imagine his face, his full lips, his gorgeous eyes. I miss him so much. He's quickly become the light in my life, my lifeline in this disaster.

"Do you need anything? Will gets off early today. I can send him by."

"All I need is you. So if that can't happen . . ." I'm only teasing, but I know he took it wrong. "Crew, I didn't mean that like that."

"I know. I need you, too." He shifts the phone, the line going fuzzy. "I gotta train tonight and Sal wants to talk about the media bullshit for the fight."

"What's that mean?"

"There will have to be a couple interviews and shit to drive sales. This is a pay-per-view event. So we have to do a few things for them to get people to wanna buy it."

This is all new to me. I don't know a lot about fighting, I don't know a lot about this fight Crew has taken on; I just haven't had time to really deal with it. Crew doesn't want to discuss it when I do bring it up. I feel like in some ways, we are living in two separate worlds in order to live in the same one half the time. It's frustrating and isolating.

"I see. Well, do what you have to do."

"I miss you," he says softly. "If this wasn't the only way out of this mess, I'd never leave your side. You know that, right?"

"And if this wasn't the only way out of this mess, I'd never let you leave my side. You know that, right?"

"I hope so." He clears his throat. "My break is about over. I'll call you later, okay?"

"Crew?"

"Yeah?"

"Thank you."

"For what, love?"

I shrug. "For everything. For proving me wrong about you. For not giving up on me. For fighting for us, in every sense of the word."

"Always."

Chapter FORTY-ONE

CREW

"GET YOUR HEAD outta there, boy!"

I jerk my head out of Victor's hold, drive around him, dodging a punch, and throw him to the mat. My neck's still giving me problems but it isn't hurting as bad as it was. I'm icing it a lot and alternating it with a heating pad and lots of ibuprofen. I just need it to hold up a little while longer then it can go to shit for all I care. I can deal with the pain for the rest of my life as long as it gets me through those rounds.

"Stop!" Sal walks into the ring. "That's good. Your foot work has gotten a lot better. I like it."

I roll to my back and my lungs struggle to breathe. It's been a long night. I glance over at the corner and see Will watching, his hands draped over the bottom rope.

"You can go, Victor. Thanks for staying late," Sal says, dismissing him.

Victor tips his chin to Coach, shakes my hand, and bounces off into the locker room. My hand hits the mats with a thud.

"The NAFL wants to meet with us next week for a press day. We don't have long 'til show time and they really want to start drumming up the hype."

"Drumming up the hype? Fuck that," Will says, climbing over the rope and into the ring. "I think we—"

"Will," Sal cuts him off, "there is no *'we.'*"

"What the hell does that mean?" Will looks offended. "You gave me a job. I'm like a trainer now, too."

"The hell you are."

"You gave him a job?"

"Yeah," Will says proudly. "I'm a part of Team Believe. My job is to keep your ass in line."

"Team Believe?" Sal asks. "What the fuck is that?"

"Us," I groan, shaking out a cramp in my leg.

Sal puts a hand on his hip. "Do I wanna know?"

I shrug. "That's up to you. Anyway, the media?"

"Yeah. The NAFL wants to hype the shit out of this."

"The hype surrounding this fight is in-fucking-sane already," Will says. "You should see the boards online. This is all they're talking about."

"What are they saying?" I ask, rolling onto my stomach and then sitting back on my knees. My side aches a little from a blow from Victor.

"Doesn't matter what they're saying," Sal says. "Don't worry about that. You worry about you and the work in front of you. Hear me?"

"I hear ya. But I wanna know what they're saying."

"I said it doesn't matter," Sal glares. "No distractions, Gentry. What a bunch of wanna-be assholes sitting on a couch somewhere that can't fight their way outta a wet paper bag think doesn't mean jack shit to you or this fight. All we care about is that they want to watch it."

"Frankly," I say, standing up. "I don't even care if they wanna watch it. I just wanna get paid."

He looks at me and I know he knows what I'm implying.

"Let's just cut the shit. You and I both know that I don't have some career in this. This is a one and done for me."

Sal turns his back to me for a minute. When he faces me again, his eyes are blazing. "Then you better make it worth your while." He crosses the ropes and heads towards his office in the corner of the building.

"I want Brett from Boston 15 to get in on this somehow!" I shout.

"Be here tomorrow at six!" he replies without even turning around.

Will and I stand in the center of the ring, the lights hanging from the ceiling shining directly on us.

"What did ya mean by that?" he asks, jamming his hands in his pockets.

I grab the back of my shoulder with the opposite hand, wincing as the pain starts to wear through the adrenaline. "I always wondered if the doctor's were wrong, that I could've gone ahead and fought. And now I know. I've got one fight left in me, Will. That's it."

"You hurt?"

I laugh angrily. "What difference does it make?"

I climb out of the ring and grab my bag off the floor. Will follows me outside, the cool air slapping us in the face.

"What are they saying online?" I ask as we walk across the parking lot.

"You sure you wanna know?"

"I wouldn't have asked if I didn't want to know."

He stands back as I open the door to my truck and toss my bag inside. "They're saying you're the man to dethrone that motherfucker. That you're his kryptonite. That you about fucking died and still beat him."

I love it. I love hearing this. It feeds that place inside me that needs fuel, that needs built up. The key to fighting is confidence. It's going into that ring and knowing you'll be the victor. This helps.

"Vegas odds only have him winning by a slight margin right now," he says. "Dude, you haven't fought in years! This is pretty crazy. They're dubbing it 'The California Kid vs The Comeback Kid.'"

I shut the door behind me and lean against the cab. "Are you serious?"

"As a heart attack."

"Let's hope they're right."

"I'm heading over for a beer. Don't forget tabs are due today. Did you pay yours?"

"I haven't paid it in a few weeks and I've been ignoring Jordyn's calls. I better swing by there and pay mine, too. I'd just send it with you but I have no idea how much it is."

"See ya there."

CREW

I HAVEN'T BEEN to Shenanigan's in a few weeks but it feels like home.

Everything's the same: same drooping green lights behind the bar, same people sitting on the same stools, the same salty smell.

Jordyn is working, talking up a couple of college-aged kids that come in every now and then. They're wearing Tap Out shirts, which lets me know they're not fighters. The only guys that wear those shirts are either endorsed or incompetent. By the look of the spare tire wrapping around their waists, it's the latter.

Will got here before me and is already sitting in the corner, sipping on his beer. I lean against the end of the bar and watch Jordyn purposefully ignore me.

"I just need my tab, J," I say. She pours a shot for an old guy that practically lives at the other end of the bar and then goes to the register. She sorts through the sheets and pulls one out. She brings it to me. "Forget how to smile? Or do you need my cock out for that?"

"Fuck you," she says.

I laugh and whip out enough money to cover the tab. "Keep the rest," I say, knocking my knuckle against the top.

I make my way through the building, stopping to chat briefly with a couple of regulars before getting to the back corner table. Will's watching the television.

"Hey," I say, pulling out my chair and sitting down.

"Hey. How'd it go with Jordyn?"

"Great. She's a little pissy, but nothing she won't get over."

"What is it with women and their pissy-ness?"

"What are ya talking about?"

"Macie," he says, almost in disgust. "I think I hate her."

I laugh. "If you think you hate her, you don't."

"How's that? I think I hate her. No, I hate her."

"No, you're pissed at her for not playing the game you play," I laugh. "Let me guess . . . she doesn't like being fucked and chucked and then called to fuck again later when you're bored?"

"Exactly!" he says, slamming his bottle on the table. "What's wrong with her?"

"Sounds like she's got class, which means it'll never work between you two. Move along, man."

He tips his beer back and finishes it. "Yeah. Fuck her. Who needs a chick with perfect tits, the best ass I've ever seen outta clothes, and a pussy that grips my dick like a vise? Not me. Not. Fucking. Me."

I laugh, grabbing a tooth pick out of my pocket and sticking it in my mouth. I want a beer pretty fucking bad and I gotta keep my mouth distracted.

A group of three girls appears at the mouth of the hallway leading to the bathrooms. They're obviously well on their way to being soused, giggling and trying to balance on their heels. They spot us sitting in the corner and head our way.

"Remember, you're with Jules now. You really need to do the right thing here," Will says, his eyes lighting up at the opportunity that seems to be presenting itself.

I watch them walk our way. Their perfume gets to our table way before they do.

"Hey, boys," the tallest blonde says. Her red lipstick is the color of cherries. "You guys need some company tonight?"

"He doesn't," Will says, nodding at me. "But I am kinda lonely."

The shorter blonde bends down, her tits in his face. "Ah, we can fix that, baby." She sits on his lap, wrapping her arm around his neck.

Will looks at me incredulously, but not about to argue it. The taller blonde sits in a chair on the other side of him. The brunette looks at me.

"You need some company, sexy?" she asks me.

"Nah, I'm good."

"Okay." She walks behind Will and massages his shoulders.

He looks at me like he's hit the jackpot and, for him, maybe he has. Maybe not.

His eyes go wide and he fidgets in his seat. His face pales, looking like he's seen a ghost.

I follow his line of sight to the front door. Two girls walk in and one is looking directly at Will. She stops mid-step and glares his way.

Will swallows, ignoring the three girls around him.

This is going to be interesting.

She nods to our table and says something to the girl with her. She looks our way and heads towards us. Every step they take our way, Will looks more nervous.

"Hey, Will," the redhead says brightly. There's a layer of irritation just beneath her words and I realize who this is.

"Hey, Macie," he says, gritting his teeth.

I can't help but laugh. Will flashes me a hateful look and I just laugh harder.

"Who are your friends?" she asks cheerfully.

"I . . . Uh . . . I—"

"I'm Wendy. This is Trista and that's Maggie." The blonde on his right flips her hair back off her shoulder. I settle back into my seat and watch the show.

"Nice to meet you," Macie says, glaring at Will. "I was going to call you tonight, but I can see you're busy."

"No, I'm not. Not really. I just . . ." He looks on either side of him and realizes just how bad this looks. I almost feel sorry for him because he didn't pursue these girls and nothing has happened. But Macie isn't going to believe that.

"No, I think you *really* are. Have fun."

She turns on her heel, her friend close behind. Will forces a swallow and watches her walk away. She sidles up to the guys at the end of the bar in the Tap Out shirts. She glances at Will over her shoulder and chats them up. One of them touches her shoulder and Will bristles.

The three girls around him are absorbed in their own conversation, a mix of slurred words and giggles. They're oblivious to what's going on.

"The universe hates me," he mutters, his eyes glued to Macie. "What are the fucking odds she shows up here?"

"You asked them to sit down," I point out. "A few minutes ago and your mind wasn't on *her*." I tip my head towards the bar.

He scowls.

"You wanna come home with us? You can come, too." Wendy looks me up and down and licks her lips.

"Nah," Will says, downing what's left of his beer. "I'm good."

"Suit yourself," Wendy says. "Let's go. Our DD is here."

The girls get up and stumble out the door. I'm not sure Will even notices.

"You just let three easy pieces of ass walk out without you. I'm shocked," I point out.

He doesn't respond. I'm not sure he even hears me.

I watch his face completely fall. Macie is looking over her shoulder at Will. She tosses him a wink and places her hand in Tap Out's. Together, they walk out of the bar.

"Fuck her." He leans on the table, his eyes blazing. "I seriously liked that girl and look at what she did."

"She walked in here and saw you with three chicks."

"Fuck you, too."

"You fucked yourself."

He laughs. "There's a lot of fuckin' going on here tonight and none of it feels good."

"That's true. And on that note, I'm going home."

He doesn't respond, his fingers flying over his phone.

"I think you just got a taste of your own medicine," I laugh.

"I'm fucking allergic to it."

Chapter FORTY-TWO

JULIA

IT'S A BEAUTIFUL day. The park is buzzing with people, the smell of grilled hamburgers and hot dogs filling the air. The trees are blooming and laughter floats through the breeze. An auctioneer is standing at a table near the picnic area, drumming up bid for items generously donated by the community for Everleigh.

"This is unbelievable," I whisper to Crew. We walk through the events going on to raise money for my daughter in awe. I don't know most of these people. Some are patrons of the restaurant that I recognize, but most are faces I can't place.

I asked Mrs. Ficht what I can do to assist, but she brushed me off. She told us to relax and try to enjoy the day. I love her heart, but there's no way I can enjoy the day. Not with my daughter in a hospital bed across the city, sick as hell.

"I wonder how she is?" I look up at Crew.

His eyes reflect everything I know are in mine. He grabs my hand and squeezes it tight. "She's sleeping. I just called Olivia. She said she'll call if anything happens. But she's gonna be fine and the fresh air will do you some good."

"I shouldn't be here," I say, batting tears back. I feel extremely guilty looking at gold balloons tied to everything that will stand still, creating a festive feeling in the park. Kids are laughing and running and I have an iced tea in my free hand while my daughter is sick or sleeping. Fighting for her life either way.

I drop Crew's hand and turn towards the harbor. I need space. I need air. I need to keep myself together.

The water is peaceful, rolling gently towards the shore. A couple and their two children are playing by the water. They seem like the perfect little family, the dad tossing a little red football to his son while the mother and daughter hold hands and dip their toes in the water. They must get out a little too far for the husband's liking because he stops and says something and they walk towards him laughing.

Pangs of jealousy hit me head on.

Why can't I have that? What did I do so wrong in my damn life that I can't have even a bit of that?

Crew's arms come around my waist, his front pressing against my back. He just holds me, rocking me gently back and forth. The connection helps me relax and the tears to scatter across my cheeks.

"Everything's gonna be okay," he whispers.

I nod but don't say anything. I'm afraid to say anything out loud. Just when I start to believe it, something sets us back.

Crew's phone rings and we both jump, my throat squeezing shut. I grab mine out of my pocket, afraid I've missed a call.

"It's Sal. Let me take this, okay?"

Relief washes over me like the waves on the shore. He walks away and I turn back to see the little family on the beach coming towards me. I wipe my eyes, trying to not look like a complete mess.

The little boy rushes towards me, giggling.

"Ben! Get back here!" his mother shouts. The father races forward and scoops him up, making him laugh harder.

"Hello," the lady says as they approach.

"Hi."

"Are you okay, Miss?" the little girl asks, her eyes full of concern. She's a little older than Everleigh, but not by much.

"Yes, I am. Thank you."

"I'm sorry. Annie is at that stage where they haven't yet learned manners," the man laughs, rolling up his sleeves. "We're working on it."

"No worries," I say, smiling at Annie. "I have a daughter just about her age."

"You do?" she asks, her eyes lighting up. "Is she here? Can I play with her?"

SACRIFICE

I smile sadly. "No, she isn't. She's in the hospital." I look up to the woman, a confused look on her face. "I'm actually here for her benefit," I say motioning behind me. "I probably should get back."

I don't know why I'm telling these strangers this. I'm rambling. I know it but can't stop.

"What's the matter with her?" Annie asks.

I don't want to say something and scare the little girl. It's not my place. The woman smiles, seeming to understand, and takes her hand and the little boy's. "I hope she's okay. I'll pray for her," she says. She exchanges a look with her husband and leads the children away.

"If you don't mind my asking, what's the matter with your daughter?" he asks, tucking his sunglasses in the front of his shirt.

"She has neuroblastoma."

His face hardens, his eyebrows pulling together. "I'm sorry. Are you here alone? Do you need anything?"

I shake my head, feeling foolish. "No, no, I'm okay. My . . . Crew is right over there. We'll be going back to the hospital soon."

He glances at Crew. "Okay. We'll be thinking of your family. Nice to meet you."

I sit on the ground and watch the waves roll in. It just seems like yesterday when we would come to the beach and splash around happily. How times have changed.

"Ready?" Crew asks. He takes my hand and pulls me to my feet.

"Yeah. Everything all right?"

"Just a few promo things we have to do. He doesn't want to do them because he thinks they're distracting. But the NAFL is pushing hard, so he ran it by me."

"Okay. Let's get out of here. But I need to say goodbye to Mrs. Ficht first."

He guides me through the maze of people until we spot her. She's twirling pink cotton candy out of a machine, a bright smile on her face as always. She sees me coming and wipes off her hands. "Hey, sweetie," she says, pulling me in for a hug. "Are you enjoying yourself?"

"Yes. This was amazing. Thank you so much. We are going to get back to the hospital, though. I'm just worried sick and hate not being with her."

"Do not explain. I'm a mother, too." She releases me and looks at Crew. "Nice to meet you."

"Same here," he grins.

"Well, you be careful. Call me if you need anything."

"We will."

"We've gotten more donations than I thought," she says, a curious look on her face. "Do you happen to know anyone by the last name Alexander?"

I shake my head and look at Crew. He shrugs his shoulders.

"A man came over and gave me a check for five thousand dollars a few minutes ago. Cane Alexander, I think he said his name was. I've never seen him before."

I gasp. "Did you say five *thousand* dollars?"

She laughs in disbelief. "I don't know if the check will cash, but we'll put it in your account. Worth a try, anyway, right?"

"My God," I whisper, wondering who he is. "Thank you so much for everything." I hug her again. "I appreciate this so much."

"Go on. You get back to your little girl."

"Thank you again," I say, my voice breaking. "Thank you so much."

Chapter FORTY-THREE

CREW

THE ROOM ON the other side of the wall goes quiet. My stomach twists, reminiscent of the way it feels before a fight. Except there's no fight today. Not a physical one, anyway.

In just a few minutes, I have to walk around a thick, black curtain and take a seat a few feet away from Hunter. There'll be a mic in my face, a swarm of reporters staring at us, hoping to get some quote they can spin. A few reporters asked to meet with me privately before the start of the conference, but I denied them.

I don't want to be here.

This fight isn't some ploy to get famous or endorsements for me. I've seen the reporters come and go from Hunter's dressing room all afternoon and I know he's using that to his advantage. He has a whole team around him designed to build press. I look around the room. Sal is leaning against the wall, drinking coffee from a thin paper cup. Will is flipping through his phone. This team was designed to win one fight. That's all I need.

My stomach rumbles. I try to focus on what I'm doing and not on what I'm feeling. Because what I'm feeling is like a whore. Not because I'm fighting for money, fuck that, but because I've already been informed that the reason *why* I'm fighting will come up. Apparently the NAFL decided that it was a good marketing ploy and reporters will undoubtedly be asking me questions in regards to Everleigh.

I don't want my personal business out there like that. I don't want her name in the mouths of those vultures. I don't want what's precious to me to be tainted with the filth that I know is this industry. I don't want some asshole in a suit, some silver-spoon fed motherfucker with insurance no less, making money off of my niece's sickness.

My blood singes my veins. I stand up, needing air.

Will looks up from his phone. "Keep your head together."

"How in the fuck do I do that?" I kick my chair, sending it skidding across the room.

"Because," Will says, standing, too, "if you don't, those cocksuckers win *today*."

"They already win!" I roar. "I had to call Julia and listen to her cry today! I had to tell her it's going to be okay when she takes her sick kid home later on and I'm not there because I'm here, fucking using her situation, splashing her business all over the fucking media!"

"This situation blows. I get it. I do. But, man, look at it this way: maybe this will get people to donate. Maybe this will *help* them."

I pace a circle, untucking my black dress shirt. Fuck appearances.

"Just go out there and say what you want. Don't say what you don't want. But stay fucking calm. Hunter's gonna try to get under your skin. You know this. So be prepared."

I laugh and watch Sal toss his cup in the trash. "I want to break his face on any given day. How do I stay calm when he's across the table from me, asking me to fuck him up?"

Will laughs and shrugs. "Pretend you aren't you, I guess."

Sal walks towards me, his face stern. "You have a few weeks 'til the fight, Gentry. Your sidekick here is right. Davidson is going to try to work you up. That's why we're here, to some extent. You know that. Play with it, try to have some fun with it. Use this to your advantage."

"What if I just smash him in the face?"

"Then I'll jump across the men with pens and start throwing. I've got your back."

"Don't encourage him, Will," Sal barks.

"Be ready to bang," I wink at Will.

"If you don't fucking stop, Davidson won't have a chance to kick *both* your asses because I will," Sal says, popping open the door. "It's showtime."

CREW

I DIDN'T KNOW cameras still clicked.

I walk up the steps and onto the stage. A long table is set up along the edge, a podium separating the two sides. Journalists and members of the media are sitting in folding chairs facing the man standing at the podium. I take the last step and make eye contact with Hunter Davidson coming up the other side.

Suddenly, this room doesn't seem big enough for both of us.

He smirks, his surfer-boy blonde hair sticking up every which way.

I want to rip him apart right now. And he hasn't even said anything yet.

Sal and Will are sitting in the front row, facing the seat I pull out. Coach gives me a look, obviously noticing I'm ready to rock. He points to his head, mouthing, "Use it."

I grab a seat as Kyle French taps the mic. He's the face of the NAFL, a slightly overweight former fighter turned mouthpiece, a guy who, quite frankly, couldn't walk the fucking walk.

"On behalf of the NAFL, I want to thank you all for being here today. We are so excited about this card coming your way on July 13th."

The journalists' cameras click, the lights above us hot. The air is thick, the room filled to capacity.

"Not only are you getting the title fight between Deacon Love and Mario Brusci, you're going to get to see two old enemies go head-to-head in the form of Hunter Davidson and Crew Gentry. It's going to be an amazing night!"

Kyle glances at Hunter, then me, and then turns back to the crowd. "All right. Let's get down to business. This is gonna be one helluva fight! On this hand, we have Hunter who has been tearin' up everyone we've thrown at him since his debut. No one's made it through the second round against this animal. On this hand, we have Crew Gentry, a kid that owns the only blemish on Hunter's record."

"Tickets go on sale today for this card and I suggest you get them quick. This fight alone will be worth it," he says. "Now let's open the floor to your questions! Media, raise your hand and we'll send someone out with a mic."

I keep my eyes focused on the back wall and try not to buy into the chaos surrounding me. Hunter is pulling some antics on the other side because I see heads turning towards him and laughter erupts.

Focus.

"Bob from The Gazette. Kyle, this fight is replacing the one that was supposed to happen between Davidson and Reyes. What made the NAFL decide to replace Reyes with Gentry?"

I look at Kyle. He's shifting from one foot to another like he's jacked the fuck up. "Well, to be honest, there wasn't anyone left in this division that would be an interesting fight. Davidson's pretty much cleaned out this division and his camp didn't want to wait the nine, ten months to see him fight again. When Gentry resurfaced," he grins, "well, there's not an empty seat in the house tonight."

Laughter ensues.

"Lowell from Boston MMA. Davidson, this is for you. We know the last time you met with Gentry, he took you to the final minute of the fight. And he beat you. Granted, you are both in much different places right now, but what's your prediction of this fight?"

Davidson's laughter fills the room. It's like nails down a chalkboard.

"Yeah, I'd say we are in a different place right now. I'm a professional fighter, the champ no less, and he's making $18 an hour on the docks." I don't know what he does, but the crowd laughs again. "Seriously, none of my opponents have taken me outta round two. I think it's safe to say this fight will be ended fast and hard."

"Oni from One Division. Gentry, your last fight that we know of took place against Davidson and concurrently ended your career. Now you're back. What makes you think you can walk back into the fighting world and be competitive?"

Oni gives the mic back and stands with his little notepad and watches me. He has on his requisite MMA shirt and smarmy smile. I laugh because no matter what I say, a guy like this won't get it.

I lean towards the mic attached to the table in front of me. "Once a fighter, always a fighter."

The journalists all begin chattering, cameras clicking again, and I lean back and watch.

"Jerry from Meosho Tribune. Gentry, word going around is that you're fighting so your niece can get a medical procedure. Is that true? If so, are you prepared to actually fight or are you just doing it for a paycheck."

"Let me cut in here real quick," Kyle says, glancing at me. "Crew's contract is an all or nothing deal, which means if he doesn't win, he gets nothing. He only gets paid if he wins. So I'm pretty sure it's safe to say the kid is ready to fight. It'd be pointless otherwise."

"It's pointless anyway," Davidson chuckles through his mic.

I start to scoot my chair back when Sal shakes his head and points again to his temple.

Breathe.

"The rumors are partially true," I say, feeling a hundred set of eyes on me. "My niece is sick and I will pay for her treatment with my winnings. But I can't say I'm not chomping at the bit to knock this guy out."

"So, you're predicting a knockout?" Jerry asks, pulling the mic back in front of him. "Can we quote you on that?"

I shrug. "Quote what you want. I'm telling you I'll win this fight."

"Lisa with Sports One. Gentry, what can you tell us about your niece? How serious is it?"

"I want to keep the focus on the fight, on me and Davidson. Whatever happens after the fight, what I do with my earnings, is none of anyone's concern."

"You seem very sure of yourself," she replies.

"I'm just sure of what I know."

"Don with Qurom. Davidson, does what your opponent is fighting for make any difference to you?"

"You know," Davidson says, "the charitable side of me almost just paid the tab. But I got to thinking about it and the fighter side of me couldn't pass up the opportunity to kick this guy's ass."

"Frank with The Tribe. Davidson, what are you looking forward to most about this fight? You've already been quoted as saying you think it's going to be 'fun.' Is that what you're excited about? Or is it clearing your record? Maybe giving the fans something they've been demanding for the past few months?"

"Frank, I'm ready for all of it. Getting in the ring is like home to me. The people in this organization, the fans, they've all been great to me and just slipping inside the cage is the only place I want to be. Getting to humiliate this guy in the process is the cherry on top."

"Do you worry that maybe getting in the ring with the one guy that's beat you is a bad idea?" Jerry asks him. "Have you considered what'll happen to your career if he beats you again?"

Davidson laughs loudly. "Uh, no. I haven't. Let's be real."

"I like that question, Jerry," I say, causing the room to erupt.

"Do you think you have the key to stopping him?" Someone shouts from across the room.

"I think the past speaks for itself," I say into the mic. "I have nothing to prove. I'm just going to go out there and do what I know how to do: beat him."

"I've waited for this day for years," Davidson says, turning in his chair. Kyle steps back so we are looking directly at each other. It doesn't get by me that three large men step onto the stage discreetly, there to keep us from ripping into each other right here. "You might have gotten one over on me in our younger years, but I'll guarantee you I will destroy you. It's gonna hurt, brother, hurt like a bitch." He leans towards me and away from the mic. With a lowered voice and a glimmer in his eye, he says, "You'll be in the ground before your niece."

I'm off the chair in a flash, sending it barreling backwards into the table. I lunge at Hunter, blood soaring past my eardrums so loudly that I'm oblivious to the commotion my actions have caused below. He stands and I'm twisting to throw my first punch when I'm grabbed from behind and pulled backwards.

I fight against the security, ripping my arms out of their grasps. I struggle forward, needing to feel his blood on me, when I'm hit with another set of arms around my waist.

"Cool it, Gentry," one of them whispers in my ear.

"Fuck you," I bite out, trying to get away.

Davidson is being led off the stage across from me peacefully. He glances over his shoulder and smiles.

"I'm gonna fucking kill him," I say, shrugging the guys off me. They let go as Davidson disappears and guide me off the stage.

I hear Kyle tap the mic, settling down the chaos in the chairs below. "Well, if that doesn't get your blood pumping for this fight, I don't know what will!"

Chapter FORTY-FOUR

CREW

THE NURSE SIDESTEPS one of the many boxes containing medical supplies that seems to have taken over my house. Boxes of gauze, tubing, anti-bacterial gel, medical tape, and God knows what else are stacked all over.

She stands next to me and adjusts the straps on her duffle bag hanging off her shoulder. She hands Julia a card. "I've taken some blood and her vitals. I'm guessing the doctor's office will call you in the morning once they get the results." She smiles sympathetically. "I'm surprised they let her come home yesterday if she was this bad."

"She wasn't. She seemed better yesterday," Jules said, her voice defeated. "She was sick, but today she . . ."

"She had some color to her last night," I say, pulling Jules into my side. "She ate a little bit. She's just gone downhill all day. You could just see her getting weaker."

There's nothing that will bring you to your knees faster as a man than a sick little girl. You're supposed to be the man of the family, the protector, the one to make everything okay. Nothing will make you feel more obsolete, worthless, and impotent than watching her look at you and know there's not a damn thing you can do.

It's heartbreaking. It's maddening. It's infuriating.

"This happens," the nurse says, turning to me. "Just let her rest tonight. Try to get her to take a drink when she wakes up. If anything happens overnight, take her to the hospital or call us on the 24-hour line and one of us will come by. Actually . . ." She rummages around in her bag and removes a pen. She takes the card from Julia and writes on it before handing it back. "That's my cell number. I just live a couple of miles from here and can swing by any time."

"That's sweet of you," Julia says, her voice barely above a whisper.

"I'm a nurse. It's what we do. I'll be thinking of her all night." She heads to the door and then pulls it open. "Have a good night."

"You, too," I say, closing it behind her. I take Julia's hand and lead her to the couch. I sit and pull her down beside me. She curls up, her head on my lap. I brush her hair away from her face.

"What are we gonna do?" she asks finally. She sounds exactly like she looks. Broken.

I have to fight the lump in my throat before I can speak. "We are going to take this one day at a time."

"What happens when the days run out?"

"Don't talk like that."

She stares off into space. I wonder what she's thinking about, but I don't ask. I let her have her thoughts. I just brush her hair and try to wrangle my own demons.

"I'm really scared," she whispers. "I'm really, really scared."

"I know." I bend and kiss her on the head.

"Nothing will ever be 'normal' again, you know? I mean, even if she—"

"When she," I correct.

She swallows. "When she gets well, things will never be the way they were before all of this."

She twists in my lap and faces me. She's so beautiful, more beautiful than the girl I loved before. I'd give anything to go back and do things differently, to know then what I know now. That people are more important than things. That sometimes the boring things are the best things. That nothing, *nothing*, is better than having someone to share your life with.

"If another person tells me to take care of myself," she says, "I'm going to cut someone."

"People worry about you."

"I wish they'd spend all of that energy worrying about me on my daughter! Who gives a shit if I've lost weight or had a hair cut?"

"I do," I whisper. "You're the one that keeps this whole thing together."

SACRIFICE

She smiles vaguely but I lose her to an empty space again. She gazes into thin air, in another time and place. I watch her face, her long eyelashes fluttering, her dark hair catching the moonlight coming through the windows. She looks at me again, her face solemn.

"I haven't let myself consider the worst case scenarios. But on days like today, I think I'm stupid for not. But I can't make myself go there..."

"There's no reason for you to go there."

"How do you know that? You can't promise me that."

"I can promise you that Ever isn't done fighting. I can promise you that she's going to get the therapy and that will—"

"You don't know that!"

"I do." I stare into her eyes, searching for her soul. "I promise you she'll get the treatment. Trust me."

"I'm afraid to trust anything." She yawns and snuggles down into my lap.

"Why don't you get some rest? I'll stay up and check on Ever."

She shakes her head, her locks falling into her face. "I can't sleep. I'm afraid if I doze off, I'll miss something. Every time she smiles, I try to commit it to memory. Every time she laughs, I try to record it in my brain. I've caught myself taking notes during the day, just so I remember the things she says. I just feel like I'm living in an hourglass and the sand is slipping."

A flurry of goose bumps ripples across my skin, a dream I had months before coming back in vivid color.

"Get your shit together, little brother. You've had enough time to fuck around and play games. It's time you man the fuck up. I'm not asking you to. I'm telling you to. I'm counting on you."

"I just go through my days," she continues, "like a crazed robot, programmed to keep track of everything she does. I don't remember who I am or what's going on with you or if we've paid the bills..."

I reach under her and pull her all the way onto my lap. She lies across me like a baby.

"I feel like I'm losing it, Crew. I'm feeling my hope slip. I'm so angry... bitter, even. I just feel so much fear."

I kiss her temple. "Feel me love you. Feel me here with you."

"I don't know what I would do without you," she whispers, grabbing both sides of my face. "I wish things were different. I wish Ever wasn't sick and you and I were here under different circumstances."

"One day," I say, feeling her thumbs brush against my cheeks. "One day Ever will be better and we'll take her to the beach. I'll show her how to surf. Then we'll come home and you can make dinner while she watches baseball with me. I just hope Gage didn't breed some Red Sox fandom in her."

Her eyes glisten, but she doesn't speak. She seems to have attached herself to my words, so I keep them coming.

"We'll eat and then I'll help you clean it up. We'll put her to bed and I'll read her a bedtime story. I hope we've moved on from princesses by then. Then we will crawl into our bed together and I'll hold you all night long."

"Oh, Crew . . ."

I kiss her gently on the lips. Her eyelashes flutter and her body relaxes a bit.

"We are in this together. For as long as I live, every battle you face is mine, too. And I promise you," I say, leaning in like I'm telling her a secret, "I'm one helluva fighter."

She giggles and it's music to my ears.

"Let's go to bed," I say, starting to lift up.

She sighs and I sit back down, rolling my eyes.

"She calls me Daddy. There's nothing wrong with us sleeping together." We've been over this nearly every night that she's been home since the night we were together. I don't see her point; she won't see mine.

"She calls you Daddy because you fill that role for her, not because we are married."

"Let's fix that then."

"Crew . . ."

I know by the look on her face I've pushed her and I feel like shit, in a way. But in a way, I don't. I'm not kidding. In my head, this was the way things were always supposed to have been. It's as natural as anything to me.

"You girls are mine, Jules. That will never change. As far as I'm concerned, she's my daughter. And you *are* mine, like it or not."

A hint of a smile appears on her face. She wraps her arms around my neck. "I am yours. And I love that you love her."

"Of course I do."

"I just want to give her time to get used to us being together before she wakes up and sees me in your bed."

"Or sees me touch you or me kiss you . . ."

"This is hard for me, too, Crew. You don't think I want you? You don't think I want your hands on me, that somehow they don't piece me back together? You think I like sneaking affection from you when she's not looking? Because I don't. I don't like this at all. But I'm trying to be a good mother and not disrupt her little life more than it already has been."

I stick out my bottom lip. She leans in and bites it gently. My hands wrap around her, slipping beneath her ass. "Let's go," I whisper. I grab her hand and stand up, leading her to my bedroom. I guide her in first and shut and lock the door behind me.

I close the distance between us with a couple of wide steps and am behind her before she knows it. I sweep the hair from her neck and she gasps a shaky breath.

I know exactly how she feels. Every time she touches me, every time I brush her skin with mine, it feels the same way. Like the very first time. It's always that way with her.

Leaning close, almost touching her neck with my face, I take a deep breath, breathing in her familiar scent. It's intoxicating and makes me so fucking hard that I almost can't stand the wait. I want to lick her, taste her, touch her, own every single fucking piece of her so badly that it makes my head spin.

She bends her neck, giving me more access. I lay a trail of kisses from beneath her ear gently down to the collar of her shirt. As I work my way back up, I raise her shirt and tug it over her head. I see her breast bounce, braless, and my hands go to them immediately. I pull her back against me, working her nipples with my fingertips, my tongue licking the silky skin right beneath her jawline.

She lets out a clip of air, her body melting into mine. I work my hips against her, letting her feel how hard she makes me with no effort.

I plant one single kiss on her cheek and turn her to face me.

Julia grabs the bottom of my shirt and draws it over my chest, tossing it to the side. She runs her hands over my body, caressing every ridge as she works her way down to the waistband of my pants.

I can't stand not having contact with her. I pull her into me, our bare chests against each other, and gaze into those deep brown eyes. "I love you," I say with reverence.

She starts to reply, but I capture the words with my mouth. Our lips work together, creating sparks that light up my body. Her hands run down my back, mine entwine in her hair as I walk her backwards to the bed.

Sitting on the edge, I grab her behind her thighs and pull her towards me. I breathe her in again, not able to get enough of her. Her skin has beads of sweat dotting in and I run my tongue across her stomach, tasting the saltiness. I push her pants over her hips and she steps out of them while cradling my face to her abdomen. Her body rises and falls with her hasty breaths and it turns me on even more.

I raise my hips and slide my pants down. They hit the floor and Jules moves them off to the side. She's on her knees in an instant, my cock in the palm of her hand. I go to stop her, my first instinct to make this all about her, but she pushes my hand away. She looks up at me through her long, thick lashes as her lips touch the head of my cock.

She strokes it up and down, her mouth licking the top like a piece of candy. Her tongue flicks out and swipes the bit of pre-cum from the tip.

I feel like I'm going to fucking explode.

She takes me into her mouth, pumping my length as she licks and sucks the top. I hiss out a breath and lean back, watching her make me feel no less than unbelievable.

She draws her tongue up the shaft, rising up enough so that her breasts brush my thighs, and I can't handle it. I'm going to burst in her mouth and that's not what I want.

I pull my dick back and out of her mouth. Before she can speak, my mouth is on hers. I can taste myself as her tongue licks into mine. I grab her hips and pick her up, sitting her on my lap facing me. She places one leg on either side of my hips, my cock sticking straight up against her belly. She palms it in one hand, pushing it against her body as her mouth works feverishly against mine. I can feel her wetness slide against me as she tries to work her clit against me.

I run both hands under her ass and lift her. She assists in positioning herself over my cock, but I grab her waist and hold her in place. I want to savor this and I can tell that if she has her way, I'll be losing myself sooner than later.

Holding her by the hips, I slide her slowly down onto me. Almost possessively, I control her descent until I'm completely buried inside her. She begins to moan, but I capture it with kisses. I work her hips in a circle, feeling her body clench as it moves around on my length. She tosses her head back and I lick her nipples, feeling them harden against my tongue.

Working my hands beneath her again, I work her up and down slowly, feeling her pussy work my cock. It pulses around me, encouraging it to expel itself into her. I lick her neck, nibbling at the spot just behind her ear that's always made her crazy. The little sounds that escape are the sexiest thing I've ever heard.

She wraps her arms around my neck and takes control. She pumps up and down harder, faster, gyrating in small circles at the bottom to hit her clit. She groans in what must be a mixture of pleasure and pain as the head of my cock massages the back of her body.

My mouth is on her, any skin exposed is fair play. I lick, kiss, nibble everywhere, my head starting to blow. My hands are on her ass, feeling it jiggle with every movement.

It's. Fucking. Perfect.

Her tits bounce in my face, my stubble razing across her skin. She reaches down and grabs one and brushes it against my face, letting the five o'clock shadow scratch the skin. I turn my face into it and suck the delicate skin.

I feel her body clench around me and I know she's getting ready to let go. She's breathing heavily, her eyes have that glossy look that comes right before she goes over the edge. A look I've remembered in my dreams more nights than I can count. A look that I plan on putting on her face every night for the rest of my life.

She begins to whimper and I can't hold it back any longer. My senses are overloaded: sight, sound, smell, taste, feel . . . everything is completely over-stimulated in the very best way.

My legs begin to shake as my orgasm builds. She works harder against my cock, slamming herself down, her tits bouncing against my face. I feel her muscles clamp down on me and I watch as a wave of pleasure washes across her face. Her long hair falls back, off her face, and she continues to grind herself against me.

And I let go.

I explode into her body, filling her with my orgasm. I pull her head down to mine and kiss her while we ride high.

Finally, I lean back and pull her on top of me. I kiss her forehead as she cuddles into my chest. She looks up and we lock eyes and I know she's thinking what I'm thinking: this is where we were both meant to be.

Chapter Forty-Five

CREW

THE BAG HITS the deck of the shipyard with a thud. I've tossed a hundred of these fuckers this morning. They're heavy but a good workout... as long as my neck doesn't scream with pain. I've been babying it as much as I can and it's been sore but not agonizing. I've gotten a few raised eyebrows from Sal, but that's been it.

I walk across the dock and pick up another one and toss it on the pile. I wipe a bead of sweat off my forehead with the end of my shirt. It's hot today, the sun beating down for the first real time this year. The humidity makes everything feel strangled. As if that's not bad enough, I have to deal with the rumors and speculation from all the fools I work with. Most of them didn't realize what was going on until the pre-fight conference aired. Walking into work the next morning, everything had changed. I hate it. Work was the one place where my life was normal. Shitty, maybe, but normal. Unaffected by everything else going on. The bullshit has even tainted my job now.

Everyone has a prediction. Everyone has a wager to make. Would I make it out of the first round? Would it end by decision or knockout? It's starting to piss me off.

I pick up another bag and tossed it on the pile when I hear my name being called.

"Yeah?" I shout back, my voice barely heard over the activity of the dock.

"You got a call!"

My stomach falls. I never get calls at work. With the feeling of lead in my stomach, I head into the office. Any other time, the coolness of the air would've been nice, but I don't even notice.

"I got a call," I tell the secretary, heaving in a breath.

"Yes. You can take it over there," she says, pointing to an empty desk next to the wall. "I'll transfer it over."

I walk to the phone and it lights up. I pick it up. "Hello?"

"Crew," she breathes and my heart skips a beat. Then two.

"Jules? What's wrong?"

"I called the ambulance to come get Ever a little while ago. We're at—"

"What? Why?"

"She was just so pale and I couldn't get her to wake up. The doctor's office called while I was trying to get her to do something and they asked me to bring her in. I told them what was going on and they said to just call 911."

"Is she okay?"

"I don't know," she cries. I hear the panic start to take over.

"Jules. Stay calm. I'm coming there."

"But you're at work."

"I'll be there in half an hour or so."

"I'm supposed to meet with Dr. Perkins in a little bit. So I might be there . . ." Her voice falls off and I know I'm losing her. This fucking thing is finally wearing her down.

I just need a couple more weeks . . .

"I'm on my way, love."

CREW

DR. PERKINS SITS back in his chair and places his glasses on his desk. He looks at us, waiting for us to react to what he's had to say.

"What do you suggest we do?" Julia asks. She reaches over and grabs my hand. I squeeze it.

"That's up to you. Your options are the ones I just gave you. You two can talk it out at home, if you want, but we are going to need to move pretty soon. I just don't think we are having a lot of luck with the chemotherapy, not as much as I'd hoped, anyway."

"She's signed up for the therapy, right?" I ask, looking from Julia to the doctor.

"Mr. Gentry, the insurance company denied Everleigh for that."

"I know," I say, confused, "but you said if we came up with the money that she could get in."

He nods. "Yes, that's true. But a substantial amount of that must be paid in advance. This isn't something you can sign a promissory note for."

"I understand that," I say, not appreciating his tone. "What I don't understand is why she isn't ready to go."

I look at Jules and she's watching the floor. "You did tell them we had the money, right?"

"We don't," she says.

"Yes, we do." I try to stay calm as I turn my attention back to the doctor. Getting charges for assault before my fight isn't gonna help anyone. "I will have the money, in full, on July 13th. Get her ready to go."

"Excuse me for asking, but how are you getting that kind of money that quickly?"

"You're excused." I'm not about to answer this motherfucker. I know his type: a know-it-all, holier-than-thou asshole that thinks he's better than us. If I tell him I'm fighting for the money, he'll automatically think it's a cock fight; it'll be handing him my sins while he sharpens his knife.

"Mrs. Gentry, I'll need to know your choice in a few days," he says softly.

Julia pulls her head up, her eyes wide. She searches my face, studies me for a long couple of minutes before turning back to the doctor. She takes a deep breath, a look of resolution falling across her face. She squares her shoulders.

"We will have the money on July 13th. Please get things ready."

Chapter FORTY-SIX

CREW

"SO, SAL'S GIVEN me an assignment," Will says, sipping a beer. The drink looks all too good and I have to fight the urge to drink one. "I'm supposed to figure out what music you want to come out to and what color trunks to order you. Apparent-fucking-ly, I'm your bitch."

"I've said that for years," I say, putting my feet up on the coffee table.

Will rolls his eyes and settles back into his chair by the window. "Funny. Real fuckin' funny."

The television is on, but I'm not watching it. None of it matters anymore. Nothing they say, nothing going on in the world, no home-runs or funny commentary really fucking matters.

I just got home from the hospital and Ever is still not well. The chemo is destroying her faster than it is the cancer. Today was her last day in the cycle, so she should come home tomorrow.

Home. Funny how this place just started feeling like a real home since the girls moved in. I loved being a bachelor, living in my own space, and now I just want their shit strung everywhere. I want pink globs in my shower from Ever's bubble bath. I want house slippers by the sofa, dishes in the sink, dark locks in the bathroom drain. I want all of it. I want all of those things that turn a house into a home.

"So?"

"Get me black trunks. Black shoes. Gold hand wraps. Get us black shirts with. . . . '*Believe*' on the front in gold writing. Put whatever you want on the back but don't make it fucking stupid. And no intro song on the speakers. Just the one I'll listen to in my headphones."

"What?" Will asks, sitting up. "Come on. That's the best part of the entire fucking event! I'll just pick something for you. Maybe a little Eminem or—"

"No song, Will."

"You seriously suck the fun out of everything. Lame."

"So, help a lame ass out. I don't want to talk about fighting tonight. I don't want to talk about anything that's gonna give me a headache. Entertain me."

"All right," he says and tips the rest of his beer back. He sets the empty bottle on the coffee table. "But I do want to point out that you are, indeed, lame. It's like I don't even know you anymore. You have responsibilities. *Morals. Considerations.*" He shivers, making me laugh.

"Who you fucking these days?" I ask.

"There's the Crew I know. I'm actually still banging Macie."

"Macie?"

"Yeah, I've fucked her for a few weeks now. She was in the bar the other night, remember?"

"Oh," I say, teasingly, "the one that walked out with the Tap-Out King. I do remember."

"I don't wanna go there, asshole."

I laugh. "You a little fuck foundered?"

"I just don't get it. The only one I'd ever think, 'Oh, I just kinda wanna fuck her' is the one that is like, 'Oh, I'll fuck you if I have time.' What. The. Hell?"

My chuckle turns into full-blown laughter. "She's giving you an economics lesson, Will. Supply and demand."

"This is so not funny," he says, smiling. I know he's telling me this to take my mind off of everything else and I appreciate it. "What do you do in this situation?"

I shrug. "Hell if I know. The only girl I ever felt that way about before is Jules."

"Well we know how messed up that has been, so maybe I need to get advice elsewhere."

"Probably so."

"How are things between you these days?" he asks carefully.

"Fine. Good. I mean, under the circumstances . . . You know, here we are, building this relationship together again. Some days it feels like we are seventeen again and things are like they should be, you know? And then reality hits and we look around and I know she feels guilty to be enjoying any part of her life when Ever's so sick." I blow out a breath. "I feel that, too, sometimes. But what do you do? Do you stop completely living? Do you stop feeling? Do you stop loving? Do you stop needing someone else?"

I run my hand across the top of my head, feeling the loss of hair driving home my point.

"So you two aren't *together*, together?"

"Oh, we're together. Don't get confused," I warn. His little innuendos were funny when she was married to Gage. Now? Not so much. "I'm just saying that if things were different in our lives right now, that maybe we would be a little farther along than we are. That's all."

"Before all this happened with Ever, she didn't even like you much."

I laugh. "That's true. So who knows . . ."

"Who knows." He rises from his seat, stretching his arms over his head. "I'm going to head out. I have this asshole friend that trains early and I think I'm going to head over there and figure out what to do about his trunks. Since I'm his bitch."

I stand and grab his shoulder. "I appreciate everything, Will. Seriously, all joking aside."

He eyes me, his face blank. "You kill that motherfucker in the ring and I'll consider it even. Okay?"

We shake hands. "Deal."

Chapter FORTY-SEVEN

JULIA

I TURN THE radio on and press through the saved stations. I turn it off. I glance into the rearview mirror and see Ever snuggled into her booster chair watching the world go by.

"How are you feeling, sweetheart?"

She turns her head and smiles at me through the mirror. "I'm okay."

"Do you hurt?"

"I always hurt a little. But it's not so bad now."

It's just another pin in my heart.

The nurses gave her a stronger dose of pain medicine before we left the hospital. Macie, our favorite nurse, seemed to push us through dismissal quicker than usual. I think she sensed our need to get out of there.

Macie has been a Godsend to us. We've formed a little friendship over the past few weeks. She's funny and smart and very no-nonsense. I'm not sure how she and Will met, but from our conversations and his name being brought up, I'm positive that there's something going on between them.

I really thought they'd keep her another day, but the doctor said she was stable enough to go home today.

When did "stable" become the preferred word to use to describe a child?

The thought makes me sick. I breathe deeply, warding off the puking sensation and the tears that feel like they're going to pour. Everything is hitting me at once and I don't know how much longer I can do this. I just want to sleep. I want to close my eyes and not have nightmares that wake me up in a cold sweat, just to see I've only been out a matter of minutes. Nightmares so bad that I don't want to risk going back to sleep again.

I want to have a normal conversation with my daughter. One where I'm not trying to absorb every little word, every nuance. I want to do all of the stupid little things that I normally hate but miss so badly, things like dishes and laundry and vacuuming. What I wouldn't give to have a day just to crank up the radio and clean because that's all that had to be done. I remember back to worrying about the water bills. I still do, but it seems so . . . trivial . . . at this point. I look back at Ever again and she's watching me. I wish I had realized earlier that nothing matters but us. Together. How many days did I let pass and not cherish them? How many days did I let pass and miss the entire point of the day? If I wake up tomorrow and she's not. . . .

No! Don't go there.

I fight back the tears springing to my eyes. I can cry tonight when she's sleeping and Crew is training. I can cry in the shower and blame my puffy eyes on the hot water. I can cry to myself and not add anymore stress on the two people in the world that I love and are fighting things of their own.

I can't even think about Crew fighting. I can't. I know it's coming up. I can feel him shifting. He won't talk a lot about it. He just tells me not to worry but I do. When I let myself think about it, usually late at night while I'm watching Ever sleep, I worry. I don't know how he's going to fight. I don't know why he thinks for sure he's going to win. I don't know much about the guy he's fighting or what it all entails; he keeps me protected from that. I'm grateful for that, in a way, but I also feel like there's so much more to what's going on than I know.

"Are you happy, Mommy?"

"Of course. I'm with you, aren't I?"

She doesn't look convinced. "I want you to be happy, Mommy. I want you to smile like you used to smile. It makes me happy to see you smile and you don't very often anymore."

"Oh, baby," I say, trying not to break down in the middle of traffic. "I am happy. I'm just worried a lot right now."

"About me?"

"I always worry about you. You're my baby."

Ever doesn't respond. She just traces something on the window of the car.

"Are you happy, baby girl?" I ask.

"Kinda." I hear her sigh. "I miss going to school. I miss staying all night with Mrs. Bennett. I miss having good dreams."

"You don't have good dreams?"

"No. I have bad ones. But don't tell Daddy that his dream catcher isn't working, okay? It would make him sad."

"It'll be our secret," I say softly.

"You know what does make me happy?"

"What's that?"

"Going home. I like having us in one spot. I like it when he comes in my room and thinks I'm asleep and kisses my forehead. He always whispers a little prayer and then tells me to fight. It makes me feel happy."

My willpower is nothing against her words. The tears begin and all I can do is make sure they don't come out in full-blown sobs.

"He says I'm a Gentry and Gentry's are fighters. We can beat anything. He makes me feel strong. I like that because I don't feel very strong."

I turn onto Crew's street, thankful we are so close. My vision is completely blurry and my heart is breaking.

"I'm really sick, aren't I?" she asks.

"You're sick, but you're going to get better. Remember the doctors telling us that you have to feel yucky before you can feel better again?"

I pull into the driveway and shut off the engine. I take a deep breath before unlatching my seatbelt and twisting around to see her.

"I hope so," she says. "But sometimes I think maybe I'm just going to see my other Daddy."

"Ever, no . . ." I feel my face twist as I gasp for breath. "Don't say that."

She's completely calm. Her little rosebud lips quip up in the corners. "If I do, it's okay, Mommy. I think Daddy misses me."

"Everleigh Nicole, stop that. You stop this right now." I jump out of the car and throw her door open. I start fiddling with her seatbelt, trying to get her out as fast as possible. I can't take it. I need to hold her. I need to reassure her.

"Mommy," she says. Her tone halts me. My eyes rise to meet hers. "Everything is going to be okay. I know it."

Chapter FORTY-EIGHT

CREW

"HE SAID FUCKING what?" I roar, stalking across the gym towards Will. "Repeat that."

"Crew—"

"Read it again!" I look at Will. "Now."

"'He's really put me in a spot, you know?' Davidson says, wrapping a towel around his neck," Will reads from the article on his phone. "'But at the end of the day, this is a business transaction for the both of us. Everyone gets into this business for their own reasons. His is just a little sadder than mine, I guess. But yeah, knowing his niece won't have the funds to get her treatment . . . that blows. But it's really not my problem and it isn't going to change my game plan. I'm going to end him fast and move on. I hope he has a Plan B because all this fight's gonna do is get him another bed in the hospital.'"

"I'm going to kill him."

"You're going to focus on the fucking fight and not what that punk says," Sal says firmly. "He's saying this shit to get in your head because he knows someone will fuck up and read this shit to you."

"I think this is good motivation," Will says.

"I'm this close from kicking you the fuck out of this gym," Sal tells him.

"I'm going to pretend like you didn't say that," Will grimaces.

Sal blows out a breath and heads to his office. "We have days! *Days* left 'til this fight!" He yells over his shoulder. "Don't lose your head now, Gentry."

I push open the doors and head into the late afternoon sun. I know Sal's right but it's hard to control everything at this point. Davidson running off at the mouth, thinking he has any right at all to even discuss Everleigh.

Fuck that motherfucker.

"I think Sal's wrong. I think you need to hear this bullshit," Will says, stopping by his car.

"I think he needs to die."

"I agree." He leans against the hood of the car. "You okay?"

"Just a few days left now." I see my reflection in the windshield. I look ready. I'm lean. I'm strong. I feel good, more or less. "I've gotta block the rest of this shit out. No more Davidson bullshit, okay?"

"Yeah. Okay. How's Ever?"

"Hanging in there. They switched up her medicine and she's having a hard time with it. The tumors are shrinking but not as quickly as they'd like. I don't understand all the numbers and shit, but what I gather is that the progression has kind of paused but hasn't started going the other way very much."

His face falls. "I'm sorry."

"Yeah, me too. They keep telling us that they'll keep trying different things. That you can never predict how someone will react to different formulas and shit."

"But this medicine you're getting with the money you win," he says, pausing to let that sink in, "it's supposed to help."

I smile, appreciating the sentiment. "Yeah. That's what they say. There are no long-term studies on it because it's a new thing. But they have kids sicker than Ever go through there that are currently cancer-free, kids that they'd basically written off."

"How's Julia?" he asks.

"She's hit the wall. She's just sick. I know sitting there day in and day out is rough and I hate that I can't be there to lessen that load. But I have to work and I have to train." I sigh. "Olivia and the lady from the restaurant try to come by and let her go eat or sleep and she just won't leave Everleigh anyway." I sigh. "I'm just over this shit, Will. I just am getting hit from every fucking angle."

"I don't envy you. At all. But I respect you. I can't imagine what would be going on if she didn't have you."

"Yeah, well, I just have a few days 'til the fight. I've intentionally not told her much about it. I just want them untainted by it all. They have so much going on and this fighting world is so dirty. When I go home, it's pure. It may not be happy because Ever's sick, but it's my little world. And I just want them to be . . ." I take a deep breath. "Look, Will. I don't know how to say this. But if things don't go the way we think they will and something happens to me—"

"Shut the fuck up."

"Let me finish."

"No. I know what you're going to say." He's pissed. His usual goofy smile is gone, his features completely changed. "And I'm not going to stand here and even entertain the fucking thought. You know this game. It's more mental than anything. So push that shit out of your head, Crew."

"I know, but what I want to say is that if something goes wrong, I need you to—"

"That goes without saying," he cuts in. "Just shut the fuck up and go home and tell those girls you live with that I said hi."

He jumps in his car and pulls out before I can say another word.

CREW

I SIT MY bag down and turn the corner. My girls are sitting on the couch, watching cartoons. Ever looks a little pale, but not as pale as Jules.

I walk across the room and kiss Ever on the cheek. I turn to Julia.

Fuck it.

I kiss her, too.

She might get pissed but I don't care. I only have a few days left before I fight and I'm not wasting any more time. I've been thinking of the things I'd say to my Ma or to Gage if I had another day with them. How I'd tell Ma that she was right. That I was sorry for causing her so much worry. I'd thank her for doing her best with me and apologize for making her life so much more complicated with my antics. I'd tell Gage thank you for always having my back, even when everyone else turned against me. I'd thank him for picking up the pieces of my life and just kind of holding them until I could find them again. I'd tell him that I respect him more than any other person I've ever met.

I'm not wasting anymore time with Jules. She can be angry. She can second guess it. But what can she say? I love her and I'm going to show her that, show Everleigh that, for as long as I have left.

"Crew!" she pulls back, eyes wide.

"What?" I'm not sorry and I won't be.

We have a standoff, eyeing each other, until it's broken by a burst of tiny giggles. We both turn to see Ever, her hand over her mouth, her eyes shining.

"What's so funny?" I ask, grinning.

"I wondered why you never kissed her," she said, her giggles growing louder. "She's so pretty. Boys always kiss pretty girls but you never kissed Mommy."

"Listen here," I say, picking her up. I sit in her spot and place her on my lap. I wrap one arm around Jules and pull her into my side. She looks up to me, a little color back to her cheeks. "Boys do kiss pretty girls. And your mommy and you are the prettiest girls I've ever seen. But here's the thing—no boy better ever put his lips on you. Hear me?"

"I don't want to kiss a boy!" she laughs.

"Damn right," I say, pulling her head to my chest. "You two are my girls. You aren't allowed to have any other boys' lips touching you or I'll kill them."

We sit quietly. Jules grabs the remote and turns the television off. I've got one of my girls beside me and one on my lap. Eventually their breathing evens out and I know they've both fallen asleep.

If I could stop time, I'd do it now.

Chapter FORTY-NINE

JULIA

HOSPITALS ARE SUCH a double-edged sword.

On one hand, they're a place of hope, a respite from a disease-filled world. A place where people work together, tirelessly, to heal your loved ones. On the other, they're a grim reminder that sickness exists. That with sickness is pain, sadness, frustration.

Ever has been taken out for testing and I'm alone in her room. Her monkey lies on the sofa next to me and I pick it up and press it against my chest. It smells like her, like strawberry bubblegum and that little note that's just Ever. It reminds me of when she was a baby, of Gage carrying her around on his shoulders, of going for snow cones on warm days, like today.

The door presses open and Dr. Perkins comes inside. I've been expecting him.

"Hi," I say, sitting the monkey on my lap.

"Hello." He walks around the bed and takes the seat next to Ever's bed. "How are you holding up?"

I laugh. "Let's just move the questioning along, shall we?"

He smiles. "Well, I just wanted to keep you up-to-date on what's going on. We've arranged for her to be transferred on July 15th for the therapy. She will be in the hands of Dr. Morrison over there. I can honestly say that it's the best place she can be. All of the arrangements have been made." He pauses. "Except payment. And I hate even saying this because it sounds so harsh and cold."

"Of course it does. Because it is."

"Mrs. Gentry, if I could have gotten her in there any sooner . . ."

"No, I know that. You've done everything you can. I believe that."

"This isn't my favorite part of the medical field. I want to heal people, not have to do that within the constraints of red tape."

"I understand. We will have the money to them on the 14th."

He leans back and studies me. I'm not sure what he's thinking or if it's a good thing or a bad thing.

"I don't know how you've managed to get the money and it's none of my business. But I want you to know that, quite possibly, you've just saved her life. As professionals, we normally keep guarded about a lot of things. We tell patients what they need to know and don't reveal a lot. This field is a lot of speculation, we try a lot of things and don't know whether they'll work or not. But I'm going to be frank with you, Mrs. Gentry. I've been worried about Ever."

His words hit me hard, causing my head to spin. I pick up the monkey and squeeze it to my chest.

"Whatever sacrifices you've made to get her into this therapy are worth it. I can't guarantee anything with that, either, but I do give you my word that it is her best chance. If it was my child and I was in your shoes, I would have sold my soul to the devil if I had to."

A sinking feeling takes over me as I realize, not for the first time but for the first *real* time, that maybe, *just maybe,* that's what Crew's done.

JULIA

EXHAUSTION WOULD BE a relief right now because I'm so far past it that I can't even remember what just being tired feels like. My entire *being* aches. My body can't rest on this hospital sofa and my mind can't zone out, either. Not that it could if we were home and not at the hospital, but my chances would be better.

In. Out. In. Out.

I watch her chest rise and fall, listen to her breath move softly through her lungs.

In. Out. In. Out.

SACRIFICE

My stomach rumbles. I glance at the clock and it's mid-afternoon. I think I'm hungry. I try to remember the last thing I've eaten, but can't recall it.

A banana at breakfast? No, that was yesterday.

Ever moves in her sleep and I jump up, untangling her cords. I don't want her pulling them out when she's sleeping.

We're supposed to be released again today. We're just waiting on the paperwork to be done. Sometimes I think that takes longer than anything. We know the procedure by this point. We know the instructions, know when to be back, know who to call, know what she's supposed to eat, drink, and take and when. It's routine, just like breathing at this point.

A loud knock hits the door, making me jump. Ever's eyes flutter open.

"Come in?" I say, more of a question than an offer. I'm not sure who it is or why they are so inconsiderate.

It opens swiftly and two men come in. One is a shorter, dark-haired man. The other is taller with blond hair shaped into a mohawk. They're smiling wide, like we are old friends, but I have no idea who in the hell they are or why they are here.

"Can I help you? You just woke my daughter up."

Ever tries to sit up. I grab her under the arm and help her get situated, keeping an eye on the two strange men that I'm sure I don't know.

"My apologies, Mrs. Gentry," the dark-headed one says. "My name is Jason Drake. I'm with the NAFL."

This makes no sense. "Crew isn't here."

The larger of the two men laughs and the shorter one shakes his head. "Oh, we know that, Mrs. Gentry."

"Then why in the world would you be here?"

"Please, relax. If you want us to leave, we'll be on our way. But I'd appreciate you hearing out what we have to say first."

The blond one crosses his arms in front of his large chest and smiles. I don't like him. He sets off something inside of me that tells me to keep my distance.

"Make it quick," I say.

"We are here because Mr. Davidson has generously offered a donation of his earnings from the fight this weekend to your daughter's care."

I take a step back. *Why didn't someone tell me this? Why didn't Crew mention this?*

"We would like to present you with a check for three thousand dollars on behalf of Team Davidson."

"Oh," I say, obviously caught off guard. "I . . . um . . . I had no idea. Thank you."

"You are so welcome."

"Why didn't Crew mention this?" I ask. Ever reaches for my hand and I squeeze it. I'm trying not to show that I'm thrown off for her sake, but she's so attentive, just like Gage was, that I know she reads through my facade.

"I'm not sure," Jason says. "We are contracted with Davidson, not Crew. I'm not really sure how much the NAFL communicates with your . . . well, whatever he may be to you."

"He's my daddy," Ever says quietly.

The smile on the blond's face grows wider.

"That's nice," Jason says, smiling half-heartedly at my daughter. He hands me a check for exactly three thousand dollars.

My hands shake as I look at it. "Thank you," I say, not sure what else to say. My cheeks heat under the gaze of the blond and I'm embarrassed, completely put on the spot. "I wish I would've known. I feel so unprepared."

"You had nothing to prepare for. It's just a kind gesture aimed at making your hardship a touch easier. An act of charity, if you will."

"Thank you. Please extend my gratitude to the Davidson team."

Jason laughs. "This is Mr. Davidson. You can tell him yourself."

My eyes grow wide as I realize just who this enormous man is. I feel like I've been played, like the wolf has gotten into the henhouse.

The check is burning in my palm and I want to tell him to take it back and get out of here. I know the awful things he's said to Crew. I know this is the guy that hurt him in Minnesota. I want to have Crew's back on this, to tell him to stick this up his ass.

Ever squeezes my hand again and I'm thrust back into reality. I have to stay calm. I can't do something stupid, especially considering the reason they're here. They're here to help Everleigh and, if I make a scene, it could make Crew lose his focus or the fight altogether.

I plaster on a fake smile. "Thank you, Mr. Davidson." I hate the sound of the words coming from my lips.

"You are welcome. It was really my *pleasure*."

The last word rolls suggestively off his lips. He makes my skin crawl. There's something very reptilian about him, something that makes me shiver. I just want them to leave. *Now.*

The door pushes open again and Macie walks through. She starts to smile but stops after seeing the men against the wall. She's our nurse nearly every time we are here and besides Crew and sometimes Will, there are never other men here. I know she's suspicious but I don't need her causing problems right now either.

"Is everything okay in here?" she asks, crossing her arms in front of her. She's clearly ready to flex her muscle and toss them out on their ass. I'd love that, but can't risk making them mad.

"Everything is fine," I mutter.

Her eyebrows are pulled in, obviously not believing me. "Okay. I need to take Miss Ever down for a test."

"That's fine."

Macie winks at Everleigh and gets the poles and bed rails up and ready to go. "You ready, my lady?"

"I am." Ever's voice is soft, but she's grinning at Macie, her cracked lips spread as far apart as she can. "I'll be back, Mommy."

"I'll be here, baby girl. I love you."

"Love you."

Macie wheels her out and casts me a final glance. I subtly shake my head and, before I know it, she's gone. Immediately, the walls seem to start closing in. I feel like a mouse trapped in a cage with a couple of large cats, ready to pounce on their prey.

I know I have the deer in the headlights look going on. I also know that won't do me any favors in the midst of characters like these.

Before I know what's happening, Hunter is beside me. He has his arm around my waist. His hands are huge, his fingers spread wide around my hip, the tips nearly touching my breasts.

I try to pull away, but he draws me even closer against his solid frame.

I gasp, my hands shoving against him. "Get away from me," I spit, sucking in a large gulp of air as I react to the violation. My senses are overtaken with the scent of a vomiting department store, expensive colognes mixed with douchbaggery. I push away as hard as I can, but his body is a brick wall.

He laughs a low, bellowing chuckle. I can feel his ribs moving beneath my hands.

"Does it make you nervous to be touched by a real man?" He begins to stroke my skin and my stomach threatens to expel the milkshake Macie brought me earlier.

"Let go of me," I say through gritted teeth. "Let go of me or I will scream."

"I can probably get you another three grand if you play nice." His hand drags slowly down my side and lands on my ass.

I turn to respond, to tell him exactly what he can do with his three grand, and his lips land on the side of my face. He presses them hard, barely missing my mouth.

My hand comes up and finds the side of *his*. The sound of my hand smacking his face zaps across the room. He howls with laughter and my blood pressure soars even higher.

I grasp at his fingers and try to remove them from my body, lifting his thick, meaty digits away from me. It's obvious that he lets me lift his middle finger and that only enrages me further. The fact that I can't make him stop, that I'm at his will, is both terrifying and infuriating.

With each second, the panic in my core starts to increase. I glance to Jason and he's amused.

Hunter squeezes my behind in his palm before finally releasing it. "Oh, that's tight," he says, his voice full of innuendo.

"Get out of here!" I shout, my body rocking with fury. "Leave! Now!"

"I'd like to see what else is tight on you, sweetheart." Davidson grins, acting like he didn't hear me. He leans forward and I take a step back. And then another. And another until my back is flat against the wall.

He looms over me, caging me in with his hands. I can feel his breath on my face, his aggression rolling off of him.

I glance around quickly for something to grab, for an alarm to push, but there's nothing. Just the bedside table with a coloring book and a foam cup.

"Get away from me," I growl, pressing myself against the wall and as far away from him as I can.

He doesn't flinch. He takes his right hand off the wall. I breathe in a small sigh of relief that's one second too soon.

In one lightening quick move, his right forearm is across my chest and his left hand is cupping me between my legs. I try to jerk forward, but am caught by the tree trunk he has for an arm.

"You asshole!" I all but scream, my throat constricting around my words.

He leans his face in close to mine. "Your body knows a real man when it sees it. Don't feel bad. It happens all the time."

I take advantage of him being so close and bang my forehead off of his nose. He isn't expecting it, but it doesn't exactly hurt him either. I can see a glimmer in his eye and I prepare myself to scream bloody murder.

SACRIFICE

He releases me and takes a couple of steps back, his hand wiping across his nose. He watches me, almost with a look of approval or respect. I'm not sure. All I can really concentrate on is getting closer to the door.

"You might wanna take the fight instead of Crew," he laughs, joining Jason on the other side of the room. "You fight better than he does. I'd even let you walk outta there just so we can have makeup sex later."

"Go to hell and you can take this with you." I shove the check at his chest, but he ignores it. My hands shake as I pull them back, watching the check flutter to the floor.

"She's a feisty one," he laughs, glancing at Jason. "I love it."

He grins mischievously and rubs his thumb against his forefinger. He brings his hand to his face, breathing in deeply, before licking his fingers. "Damn, I can see why these brothers passed her around."

"If you don't get out of here now, I don't care what the NAFL does, I'll have you reported for assault. *Get the fuck out of here!*"

"You aren't reporting shit," Davidson barks. "You won't risk the fight getting called off. All you are going to do is go back to that pussy of a man I'm about to break in half and tell him all about what just happened."

His eyes light up and I know that's exactly what he wants to happen.

"You'd love that, right? Well, you, Mr. Davidson, can go fuck yourself."

He takes a step towards me and Jason pulls on his shirt, drawing him back.

"Let's go, Hunter," Jason says and starts to the door.

Hunter follows but stops abruptly. "Tell Crew not to worry about ya after this fight. I'll take care of ya," he winks.

"Tell him yourself. See how that works out for you. *Again,*" I wink.

He shrugs like he doesn't really care one way or the other, but I can see I've irritated him. It's a small victory, but I'll take it.

"You've finished your *charity work* today, Hunter. Let's go," Jason says.

"My *charitable acts* . . ." He looks at Jason and busts out laughing, his anger sloshing beneath the surface of his tone. "My charitable acts can include the gift of orgasm, Miss Gentry. It's kind of a coveted thing by women, especially ones passed around. Like *you*. I'll leave the invitation open until after the fight. Your tune might change after I kill your boy."

His eyes shine like a tiger ready to pounce. "And I do mean *kill*."

JULIA

MY HAND SHAKES, the adrenaline still coursing through me minutes later as I dial Will's number. Although Hunter is gone, the room still smells like him. His energy is still in here, crawling over my skin. I shiver, waiting on Will to answer.

"Hello?" He asks, sounding distracted.

"Hey, Will. It's Julia."

"What's wrong?"

"I need to talk to you." I pace the floor from the door to the window, trying to burn off some of the energy I can't seem to rid myself of.

"Is Ever okay?"

"Yes. Ever's fine."

"Okay. What's up?"

"Will . . . Hunter Davidson just left here."

"What? He just left where?"

"The hospital. He showed up here with another guy, Jason Someone."

"What the fuck?"

"I don't know. They walked in here and gave me a check. It was all so weird."

He pauses, the line rife with tension. "Did he do anything else? Say anything else?"

I stop pacing. I look out the window and a part of me wishes I could just jump out of it. It would end the drama, the pain, the confusion.

"Yeah, he did. And I don't know what to say to Crew."

"What did he say?"

I laugh, my voice crackling with nervous energy. "It wasn't as much what he said, Will . . ."

"Did he touch you, Jules? Did he do something to Ever?"

"Ever's fine. She wasn't in here most of the time . . ."

"Look, I'm going to need you to be really honest with me here. You're gonna have to tell me what happened so I can help you."

"I don't want Crew to do something stupid," I whisper, my hands starting to shake.

Will exhales, the sound of his breath rippling through the phone. "If Davidson touched you, Crew will go to prison. Fact as fuck."

I sit on the sofa and bury my head in my free hand. I know Will is right. I can't blame Crew for wanting to go after him. But I can't let that happen. Not now.

"He pushed me against a wall, Will," I blurt out. "He grabbed me . . . you know . . ."

"Imma fucking kill him myself, stupid motherfucker!"

"Will! Stop! Listen to you!" I cry. "I can't tell Crew this if *you* are acting this way. I don't want to lie to him, but what do I do?"

He mutters a string of profanities under his breath, the sound of something slamming against something else bursts through the background. Finally, he says, "We can't tell him. We *can't*. He'll lose his head and probably shoot the cocksucker."

"So I lie?"

"No," he says, "you omit. You can tell him later, after the fight. But if you tell him now, his focus will be gone. Fighting is as much mental as it is physical and if he knows this, he'll lose the fight even *if* he manages not to go to prison."

"But—"

"No buts, Jules. If he gets pissed later, blame it on me. I'm going to the gym now to let Sal know if he hasn't heard about it already. I'll break it to Crew that he was there so you don't have to. But *do not* tell him the rest."

"Are you sure?"

"No," he laughs. I hear a door shut and a car engine start. "But I think this is our only option."

"Thanks, Will."

"Thank me later. Pray for me now that Crew doesn't kill me for being the messenger."

Chapter FIFTY

CREW

I FINISH MY round with Victor in the ring. This is the last time we'll spar before the fight.

"Hey, man," he says, sticking his glove out. I knock it with mine. "Good luck this weekend. You're ready."

"Thanks," I say, climbing over the rope. I take my gloves off and toss them on the floor. I search for Sal, who's strangely missing from the gym. I turn the corner to his office and see him sitting at his desk, Will across from it.

I lean against the door frame and watch them. I know something's going on. I see it on their faces. I feel it in my stomach.

Sal glances at Will and nods. He leans back in his chair and rubs his temple.

"What are you doing here?" I ask Will.

"How was training?"

"Shut up and tell me why you're here."

He looks to Sal one more time before pulling his phone out of his pocket. "Sal called me in here to talk about some stuff."

"What do the two of you need to talk about?"

"Have you heard from Jules today?" Will asks, narrowing his eyes.

"No. I just checked my phone before I got in the ring with Victor. Why? Is Everleigh okay?"

"Yeah, yeah, yeah. She's fine. They're on their way home, actually."

I breathe a little easier until I realize that not only has Will talked to Sal, but also to Julia.

Something's fucking wrong.

"The NAFL called this evening," Sal says, his chair rolling back as he stands. "Davidson donated a few thousand dollars to your niece's care today and they wanted to know if you wanted to make a statement."

"He did what?"

Sal shrugs. "It's a publicity stunt, gets him bonus points with some of the fans. I think his camp was a little taken aback by how many people are rooting for you in this fight. So this just makes him look a little better in the press."

"Fuck him," I say, still not sure I have the whole story. There's a bubble of uneasiness sitting in my stomach, threatening to burst.

"They've got this press release coming out about how generous he is, a modern day Robin Hood or some shit. They're spinning this whole thing and making him a saint. It's disgusting. I don't know how you want to respond," Sal says calmly, but I sense the uneasiness in his voice.

"What else?" I look between them, waiting for someone to start saying the things they aren't saying.

"What else what?" Will asks, not looking me in the eye.

"What else is going on? I'm not fucking stupid." I look at Sal. "Someone better talk."

Will jams his hands in his pockets. It's his nervous tick, the unconscious thing he does when he's uncomfortable. I've seen it a million times.

"Look, Crew . . ." Will blows out a breath before looking back at me. "Davidson showed up at the hospital today . . ."

"He did *what?*" I imagine him in the room with my girls, breathing the same air, his poison tainting the only pure thing I have. I can't handle it. *I'm going to fucking kill him.* "He showed up to the hospital? Did he talk to them? Did he hurt them? Did he—"

"Calm down," Sal says, his voice riding over mine. "Will talked to Julia and they're fine. They're on their way home, like he said."

My head snaps to Will. "You swear to me they're okay?"

He nods. "They're okay. I called Jules and she said Davidson was there but she was fine. She didn't know they were coming . . ."

"You know as well as I do that his little impromptu visit wasn't a fucking publicity stunt. There was more to it. There always is with that bastard," I say, looking at Sal. "If he even breathed on her, I'm going to rip his heart out and feed it to him. There will be no fight in the cage because I'll kill that motherfucker now."

"You're going to stick to the game plan, that's what you're gonna do," Sal says, marching across the room. "You are going to get your head straight and fucking remember what we've been training for. He's fucking with you and you're playing right into his hands by letting him get in your head."

"He—" "

"Do you want to win this fight or not?" he booms. "Do you want to win and save your niece's life or do you want to have a pissing match with this chump? Huh? Answer me, damn it, because I can guarantee which way he'd rather have this go!"

I glare at him and he steps within inches of my face.

"Answer me!"

"I'm gonna fucking win!" I shout but Sal doesn't flinch. "I'm gonna fucking win," I say quieter this time. "But God help me . . ."

"God doesn't help you win fights, Crew. That's up to you."

CREW

MY FOOT IS heavy on the accelerator. It feels like I'm barely moving, but I'm probably going way too fast . . . if I cared. And I don't.

With every passing mile, I don't feel any less like wanting to explode. The idea of that asshole with Jules and Ever . . .

I pound my palm off the steering wheel.

Fuck!

This little stunt isn't just about me and him; this is about *him* being near *them*.

I've seen a lot of worthless pieces of shit in my day, but Hunter beats them all. He was a wrestling standout at Iowa but has never won a match playing fair in his life. He talks all kinds of trash, gets into ridiculous situations and uses his parent's money and father's position on Wall Street to get him out of every predicament he's ever been in. He's a Five Alarm Fuck-Up, one that should never have been allowed to get near my girls.

I have Sal calling around to see who let them in and to make sure it doesn't happen again. Somebody's head better roll or I'll cut it off.

"Fuck!" I shout, my voice sounding over the lyrics of Nine Inch

SACRIFICE

Nails. I flip the radio off and steer the truck onto my road. My gut twists as my house comes into view, Jules' car parked in the driveway. It looks completely normal and that pisses me off. I've just had the sanctity of my private life literally touched by the fucking devil and everything looks like the image of a perfect life from out here.

I park the truck beside her car and get out. Before I get to the door, it opens and Jules comes out. Her eyes are wide and I know she's been crying. She runs to me and leaps into my arms, wrapping her arms around my neck.

She presses her face against my chest and I'm taken aback. I wrap her up in my arms and lean against the truck. I feel her body tremble,

I run my hands over her body, grasping, molding. I'm not sure what for, but it gives me some peace of mind that she's okay.

"Are you all right?" I ask, kissing the top of her head.

"Yes. We are all right."

"What the fuck happened today?" I hear the anger in my voice, even though I don't mean to sound mad. I don't know what happened in there for sure and I don't want to make assumptions. I know he was there and she didn't call me.

She sniffles and wipes her face with my shirt. I just watch her and try to keep my mouth shut before I lose my cool.

She looks at the ground and I see her struggle with the words she wants to say. She's biting her lip and I reach down and remove it from between her teeth.

"Jules . . ."

"We were sitting there and they just walked in."

"They just showed up? Who are *they*? And who let them in?"

"Hunter and a guy named Jason Drake," she says, her voice soft. "I didn't know who they were, Crew. I've been so busy with Ever that I never bothered to even look up who Hunter was or what he looked like."

Tears start to fill her eyes and I pull her to me again. I look at the sky and watch the clouds float by. I try to find some calming effect in them, try to tone myself down a couple of notches. "Tell me what happened."

"They said they were with the NAFL and that they had a check. They gave it to me and. . . . and then they left."

I lean back and look at her face. I know she's lying. "That's not all."

"What do you mean?"

"I mean he didn't just give you a check and leave. That's not how he operates, Jules."

"Well," she says, tucking a stray strand of hair behind her ear, "I'm fine. Ever's fine."

"You're fine," I say, tilting her chin so she's looking at me. "But are you okay? Two different things."

"Yeah," she breathes, resting her cheek against my shirt. "We are okay."

I hold her tight. I struggle with wanting to just keep holding her, to ask her more questions, and to get inside to see Everleigh and make sure she's okay, too.

"I'm gonna need to know what happened in there. What did he say to you? What did he do?"

"Well," she says and takes a long pause that disturbs me, "he was an asshole."

"Because . . ." I wait for a response but don't get one. "Jules, I'm not a patient man. I'm trying really hard to stay calm and do things the right way, but you can't pull this not talking bullshit."

"I'm sorry. He just . . . he basically insinuated that I was some kind of whore."

"He did what?" I roar, pulling her back so I can see into her face. "What the fuck did he say?"

My body is on alert, exactly how I feel when I'm ready to fight. Every sense is heightened, a viciousness barreling through my veins full speed ahead.

"He just said something about you and Gage passing me around or something."

I move her backwards and start to open the door to my truck.

"Crew, stop!" She grabs my arm and tugs on it. "Just stop!"

I turn to look at her. Her tear-stricken face is pale, her eyes wide, the panic in them brimming. Even as beautiful as she is, even though I want to carry her inside and gather her and Ever in my arms, I can't. Not now. Not yet.

"You think he's gonna say that shit to you, that he's gonna walk into Ever's fucking hospital room, and I'm gonna let that slide? Think again, Jules."

"That's exactly what he wants you to do! He wants you to lose your head and find him. Cause a scene. Maybe get the fight stopped because you are some kind of hothead. That'll clear his record, win him fans, and you lose . . . *in every sense of the word.*"

I drop my hand from the door.

SACRIFICE

In every sense of the word.

"Fuck!" I shout, garnering the attention of the neighbor lady out getting her mail. I know she's right and I hate it. He's put me in a position where I can't do anything because if I do, I lose the fight, the money . . . everything that matters to me.

I watch her silently implore me to stay calm, to fight the fight that needs fighting . . . and that isn't a brawl with Hunter for being a cocksucker today. It's the fight for Ever. For her. *For our family.*

I wrap my arms around her and pull her tightly against me. I can feel relief leave her body.

"Did he hurt you? Did he scare Ever?" I mumble, my face buried in her hair. I let her scent wash over me, use it to help me calm down.

"No, nothing like that. Ever was sleeping and then out for testing most of the time. He just tried to intimidate me, you know? I know he wanted me to panic and call you, but I'm not giving him any victories over you today."

She smiles sadly and my anger starts to dissipate.

"You should've called me," I groan. "Call me next time. You have to promise me you'll call me the next time you're in a position like that."

She lays a soft kiss to the center of my chest. "I promise. I love you, Crew."

I'll never get used to her saying that. I'll never get tired of hearing those words come out of her mouth.

"Don't let him get in your head. That's what he wants. The easy win."

"You're more of a fighter than me," I laugh.

"I don't want to think about this all night. I don't want that asshole impacting our time together."

"Tomorrow I have to get up early and go through the last minute stuff with Sal. Then I have a few things I need to take care of." I squeeze my eyes shut. "But tonight, I want to go inside and watch cartoons or whatever Ever wants to do. I want to curl up next to you in my bed and forget the world."

She looks at me, her eyes full of the same love I know she sees in mine. "Let's do that."

Chapter Fifty-One

JULIA

I CHECK ON Ever and she's sleeping peacefully. She had a rough day but is all cuddled in her bed, her face smooth and without pain. She has no idea that our world is going to shift, good or bad, in the next few days.

We watched cartoons tonight just like Crew said. We stretched out on the couch and just relaxed as best as we could. Ever laid on Crew's chest and the sight of the two of them just about broke my heart.

If Crew wins his fight the day after tomorrow, Ever will start her treatment the following Monday. It's the best case scenario.

If Crew loses and something goes wrong, I could be set up to lose them both.

I push it out of my mind. I can't go there. It's the first time in my life that I refuse to make plans, to consider the future. But I can't. I can't fathom losing either of them on top of having lost Gage, let alone the possibility of both of them.

There are so many things fighting for a spot in my brain.

What will happen if Ever gets the treatment? What if she doesn't? What if Crew wins? What if he doesn't? What if he gets hurt? Is it right to even let him do this? Am I right to let him make his own choice about it?

Am I wrong to not tell him I'm pregnant?

My hand goes flat against my stomach. I've only known for a couple of days. It's still so early, I'm just a few weeks along, and I lost a baby before and after Everleigh. There's no guarantee I won't miscarry this one. There never is a guarantee, of course, but I don't want to announce it and then have to explain that something's happened.

I know, too, that Crew has been worried sick about me on top of Everleigh and his fight. I don't want to add more pressure to him. A part of me thinks maybe I should tell him. He deserves to know before he fights. A part of me thinks I shouldn't tell him, that it'll only distract him. That he will fight anyway and this will be in the back of his mind and take his focus off the fight.

I'm torn. This is yet another thing for me to worry about. Although, at the end of the day, it's given me something to smile about in the midst of the madness. So many moments I just close my eyes and imagine us playing, as a family, together at the beach. Ever's hair blowing in the breeze, her giggle riding on top of the sound of waves crashing. A baby chasing her, its little feet imprinting in the sand behind her, while I sit with Crew and watch.

I slip out the door and down the hallway. I open the door to Crew's room. I haven't slept in here yet. It's not that I've been against it like I was before, but we've been home so infrequently. And the nights that we have, Crew's came in and fallen asleep while I've been caring for Ever and I don't want to wake him or Ever has wanted me to lay with her because of her nightmares.

He's lying on top of his sheets, his eyes closed. A white t-shirt is stretched over his torso, hinting of the lines of his chiseled stomach. He has on dark blue boxer briefs, the color of his eyes when he's worked up. I could just stand and watch him like this forever. He seems so peaceful, so carefree, which are two things he isn't in his real life very much. I wish I could give him those things every day.

Maybe, when this is behind us, I can.

I close the door and lock it behind me. I pad to the bed and slip in next to him. He rolls immediately to face me, his blue eyes popping open and seeing into my soul. We gaze at each other's exhausted, familiar faces and appreciate the peace in the air.

He grins a sleepy, lazy grin. "I've been waiting on you." He rolls on top of me, spreading my legs with his knee. He bends down and almost kisses me, but doesn't quite. His lips hover over mine, his eyes boring into mine.

"I love you," I whisper, my heart as full as it's ever been. I love this man so much, differently than I've ever loved anyone else. Crew has always been the ying to my yang, the black to my white. His weaknesses are my strengths and he's strong where I'm not.

We complete each other.

He moves and I see his skin on his left forearm is red and angry. I turn it over to see a dream catcher inked between his elbow and wrist. In the center is a "J" and sitting above it are the words "FOR EVER."

"Crew..."

He doesn't say anything, just gives me a shy smile that melts me.

"Make love to me, Crew," I whisper.

He pulls my shirt up, leaving it bunch under my chin. His face is full of tenderness, reverence. He kisses me gently, his full lips pressing softly against mine.

With one hand, he pushes my panties off and then his own boxers. He settles in between my legs again and I feel his hardness resting at my opening.

"I love you," I say, watching a wave of emotions rip through his eyes as the words pour over him. "I mean it, Crew. I love you. Every single piece of you."

His grin is lopsided as he blushes with the compliment. I raise and kiss him, taking the pressure off of him to respond.

"I love you," he whispers after I pull back. He brushes a strand of hair out of my face. "I always have."

"I have a confession to make," I whisper.

"Confessions make me nervous."

I laugh and touch his cheek. "Remember when you asked what you were to me?"

"Yeah."

"You're my everything," I say breathlessly.

A feeling of being wrapped up in a fleece blanket winds itself around my heart. In his eyes, I see his acceptance of my words. I see the forgiveness for how I've treated him in the past and the promise of a future. Most importantly, I see my love reflected back.

He pushes inside me, stretching me with his size. I'm wet for him, ready to give myself to him. I know this quiets him, centers him. It always has. I know he needs this from me and I'm more than willing to give it to him.

I need it, too.

"I've waited for this all day," he says, rocking in and out of me. I wrap my legs around him, aching for all the connection I can get. "I've waited for this for years."

I smile at the look on his face, one that I'm sure I'm the only one that's ever seen. I'm not a fool to think I'm the only one Crew's been with. But I do believe I'm the only one that he's ever loved.

He kisses me again, the sensuousness erasing all thoughts but his lips and body from my mind. My thoughts go blank, absorbed in the sensations given to me by the man I love. His tongue works against mine, his length stroking me, lighting me up from the inside out. His hands are all over me, carefully, slowly, worshipping me in his way.

I tighten myself around him, squeezing his cock. He groans against my mouth, the rawness of it quickening my orgasm threefold. He increases his tempo, drawing himself out just enough to touch my clit at the top. It's the most overwhelming, blissful feeling, and I close my eyes and just enjoy the moment of being in his arms and away from the world.

He builds me higher and higher, repeating beautiful things in my ear. His words melt over me and I try to concentrate, words like 'beautiful,' 'love,' and 'mine' are mixing together, swirling in the back of my brain. I feel so loved, so treasured, that I never want it to end.

I know it won't. Not with Crew. Not this time.

My legs begin to shake as my orgasm hits. They drop to the side and he increases his pace. The thrusts become deeper, quicker, and I tilt my hips and meet him movement for movement.

"Crew . . ." I try to warn, but he stops me with kisses. I grit my teeth and feel a smile against my mouth as I fall apart under him.

He pumps into me a few more times before pressing himself all the way inside and empties himself into me.

He rolls off to the side and pulls me into his chest. I try to stay awake, try to think about telling him we're having a baby, but the sweet words he's whispering in my ear, the warmth of his body, the cocooning effect of his arms is too much.

I drift into a peaceful slumber for the first time in forever.

Chapter Fifty-Two

CREW

I HAVEN'T BEEN here in years.

The water rolls in lazily. Seagulls squawk overhead. The sun is going down in the west.

I feel her here.

I sit on the grass at the edge of the sand, letting the final few rays of sun hit my face. It's been a peaceful day, starting with pancakes for breakfast and a run through with Sal. Will met me for lunch and then it was cartoons all afternoon.

Crazy that NickJr. is my idea of a perfect day.

I watch the birds circle over the water, flying around gracefully. Ma would've loved it. She loved simple things: a sunset, a good Red Sox game, a good pancake.

I smile. The beach is empty. It's just us.

"Hey, Ma," I say softly. "Long time no see, right?"

I scoop up a handful of sand from the beach at my feet and let it run through my fingers. "Well, I don't know if I'm fucking up again or if I'm finally doing the right thing."

The birds squawk again and I laugh.

"I feel like an idiot talking out loud right now. You better be listening because I can't promise it'll happen again." Another handful of sand flows through my fingers. "It took me a while to get what you meant when we talked last. I don't know if I just didn't get it or if I didn't want to get it. But now, I think I do."

I brush my hands off and lean back on my elbows.

"I'm sorry I caused you so much grief. Fuck, looking back, I don't know why you didn't just write me off. But you didn't." I think for a second. "No, that's not true. I know why you didn't because I wouldn't do that to Everleigh, either."

I smile. "You'd love her. She's so pretty and so smart. She's a lot like Gage and Jules, but I'd like to think some of me has rubbed off on her, too."

"I'm doing the best I can down here since you and my fucking brother decided to leave me alone. Funny that you two turned everything over to *me* . . . the one with no idea how to take care of myself, let alone other people. But I'm trying."

I blow out a breath, my chest feeling lighter. "You know, though, I get it now. I get what you were saying. I was pushing and sacrificing everything then for all the wrong reasons. I lost track of everything that mattered."

"What you said was right. Life is about the simple things. Fuck if I don't know that now more than anyone. It's about a good woman, that feeling you get when you walk in the door and you feel that happiness you can't explain. It's about health and pancakes and doing what you have to do to take care of those you love."

"I fight tomorrow. I act like I got this shit in the bag, but between you and me and the beach here, I don't know. My neck and back are hurting every day. Davidson has a vendetta against me that's fueling him. I have a huge mountain to climb and one leg to stand on. I hope to God this was the right answer, but I don't know that there was another one."

"When the opportunity came to do this, I didn't think twice. I've put some stuff together that I hope works out. Even if I don't come off that mat in one piece, it's worth it all as long as Ever has the chance at getting well. Because that is the real kicker . . . she doesn't even have a fucking chance without this therapy. I called the doctor's without Jules knowing and we had a frank conversation. She has to have this to even have a shot. I won't go through my life knowing there was something I could've done to give her that chance. She deserves a chance and I'm the only one that can give her that. If something bad is gonna come to one of us, it'll be me. I've fucked up so many times in my life that if anything should come of this fight, I probably deserve it. But Ever, she's innocent. She's perfect.

And I'll be damned if I don't give her a fighting chance."

I dust off the back of my pants. "Thank you for sacrificing your life for Gage and I. You killed yourself every day to make sure we had food. I may not have realized it then, but I get it now.

"Tell that brother of mine that I have his back. And as much as I love him, I hope to see him later than sooner."

With a final glance at the sun dipping behind the horizon, I turn and head to my truck.

Chapter Fifty-Three

JULIA

I'VE BEEN LYING in his bed for an hour. Ever is resting. The new meds they sent us home with make her sleep a lot. I need sleeping meds of my own, but then who will take care of everything?

I'm lying on his side, his scent surrounding me. I breathe it in and hold it in my lungs, letting it comfort me. My nerves are shot. Gone.

Tomorrow is the day of reckoning, the day the rest of my life either goes or stops. I feel so much apprehension, so much fear, that I haven't eaten in three days. If I let myself think about it too much, I dry heave. I also haven't decided whether to tell him about the baby before the fight. I'm so torn about it.

My body begins to relax and I nuzzle into his pillow, letting my mind go black.

I must've fallen asleep because when I open my eyes, Crew is sitting beside me. He's watching me sleep. The light from the street is coming through the open blinds, casting a glow over his handsome features.

"Hey," he whispers.

"Hi." I smile and he returns it. "How long have you been here?"

"Long enough."

"Where did you go?"

"I just had a few things to wrap up." He climbs over me and lies beside me. He pulls my back into his front.

His skin is still damp and he smells musky like his body wash. I rest my head on his bicep.

"Tomorrow's the day," he says quietly like I don't know, like it hasn't been consuming me. "I'll be gone when you get up."

"I won't see you before you leave?"

He shakes his head. "I gotta be out of here early. I need to have my head straight. And I know it sucks, but please don't call me tomorrow, okay? It'll make me lose focus because I'll be wondering what you and Everleigh are doing."

I still, knowing now that I can't tell him about the baby. I know he'll be happy, ecstatic even, but I also know it won't change his decision to fight. It'll only add to his worries . . . and distract him.

Can I let him go without knowing? What if . . .

I can't think that way. I have to be strong for him.

"I understand. I don't like the idea of not seeing or talking to you, but I get it."

"Good girl."

We lay quietly. I get the feeling he's got something on his mind and I give him space to work it out. He's told me before I'm his safe place and I want him to feel safe here, just like he makes Ever and I feel.

"Whatever happens tomorrow, I want you to know a few things."

I turn in his arms and face him. His features are creased, his eyes full of sincerity. It takes my breath away.

"There's never been a time in my life that I didn't love you. From the first time I saw you, you were the only girl for me."

"Crew . . ."

"No, let me finish. I need to say this." He brushes his thumb against my cheek thoughtfully. "I found the letter Gage wrote you the other day. I was looking for some papers and I ran across it. I probably shouldn't have read it but I did. And Gage was right, you know. On so many things."

I smile. "Gage was right all of the time."

"True. But he was right in what he said to you. First, about me never turning my back on you. Until I take my last breath on this earth, I will fight for you and Everleigh. Not just because of Gage, but because of you. You know that, right?"

I do, tears pricking my eyes.

"I'd give anything to make you two okay. And whatever happens tomorrow, I want you to know I went into it knowing the possible outcomes."

"Don't talk like this!" A sob works its way up my throat.

"Shh," he whispers, his eyes shining with tears, too. "Also, if something does happen in that cage—"

"Don't," I cry, burying my head in his chest. I can't listen to this.

"Jules, please," he pleads, tilting my chin so I'm facing him. Tears are rolling down my cheeks, soaking my shirt. "I need you to listen to me. I need to leave here tomorrow knowing you heard me."

I nod. As much as I don't want to listen, I will if it will help him in some way.

"If tomorrow doesn't end okay, I want you to keep Gage's letter. Read it. Because I agree with it all. You deserve to be happy. You deserve to have a good life. Take care of Ever and take care of yourself. Do what you have to do to survive."

"I can't live without you," I whisper. "I can't lose you, Crew. I can't even entertain the idea."

He pulls me in close and I breathe him in. His heart is pounding. Mine is breaking.

"I love you, Julia."

I pull back and look him in the eye. "I love you. With everything I am. When you get out of the cage tomorrow and Ever is better," I smile, watching him grin, "we are going to get married on the beach. Ever is going to be our flower girl and we will start our own family."

"I'd love that. I want that more than anything I've ever wanted."

"I love you," I whisper. I lean in and kiss him on the lips. "I love you so much. You were my first and last love. No one came before you and no one will come after you."

His eyes light up. "You are my *only* love. I've never loved anyone but you."

"Mommy?" I roll over to see Ever standing in the doorway with her monkey. I push away from Crew, not wanting her to see me in here like this. "Can I sleep with you and Daddy?"

"Oh, Ever! I'm not sleeping in here, baby girl. I'm just talking."

She walks across the room and climbs up in bed. Crew scoots over and she lies in between us, snuggling down in the blankets.

"You should sleep in here," she says, yawning. "Mommies and daddies are supposed to sleep together."

I look over her at Crew. He whispers, "Told you." I can't help but smile.

Everleigh cuddles up to Crew, her monkey pulled in tight. She reaches out and lays one hand on my cheek. "I love you both."

"Not as much as we love you," Crew tells her. "Now let's get some rest. We have a big day tomorrow."

"Will you tell me a story, Daddy?"

Crew beams at the title, just like he does every time she says it. "Stories aren't really my thing, you know."

She yawns again. "Tell me the one about the two princes."

I give him a puzzled look and he returns it with a sheepish smile.

"Let's save that one for later. How about Mommy tells us one tonight?"

"I think I want to hear this story," I say, smirking. I'm not sure what it is, but I get the feeling I would be entertained by it.

"It's a good one," Ever says, her voice heavy with sleep, "about two princes that both love a beautiful princess. They love her the same but different . . ."

She keeps talking but I don't hear her. All I can do is look into the eyes of the man across from me.

Chapter FIFTY-FOUR

CREW

I STAND IN the living room and take a look around. I don't want to leave because I know once I do, nothing will ever be the same one way or the other.

I grab my bag off the floor and take one final glance at the place I've finally felt like was home. I turn to go to the door when I hear something behind me.

"Daddy?"

I turn around. Ever's standing in the doorway in her Tinkerbell nightgown, watching me.

"Where are you going?" she asks.

This is what I wanted to avoid this morning. I drop to one knee and motion for her to come to me. She pads across the room and hugs me.

"I have to go to work today."

"Will you be home for dinner?"

"No, monkey, I won't. Not tonight."

"If I feel better tomorrow, can we go to the park? Mommy said on Monday I have to go back to the hospital." She frowns. "I miss going to the park with you."

I choke back tears. There's so much I want to say to her, so much I want her to know. I know she's too little and too fragile for me to say the things I want to. "Yeah, if you feel better tomorrow, we can go to the park."

She kisses my cheek and stands up.

"Monkey, I want you to promise me something, okay?"

She nods.

"Never forget that I love you."

"I know that," she says sassily.

"I'm glad you do. But sometimes things happen and as you get older, you forget that. You forget that what people did for you when you were little is because they loved you so much. And they knew what was best for you when you didn't."

"Okay," she smiles. "I'll remember."

I know she won't. She's too little.

"But you might have to remind me because that was a lot of words and my brain hurts from the medicine."

I kiss her bald little head. "You're my little fighter, Miss Everleigh."

"You're my big fighter, Mr. Daddy," she giggles.

Let's hope, Ever. Let's fucking hope.

Chapter FIFTY-FIVE

JULIA

I WAKE UP to the sound of a dog barking outside. I reach my hand across the bed and pat around. Emptiness.

I sit up quickly and look around. There's light pouring in the window and my heart leaps in my chest. Panic begins to set in.

Where are they?

I grab my robe and race out the door. Down the hall I go, rounding the corner to the living room. Ever is curled up on the couch, her cartoons playing softly on the television.

"Hey, baby girl. Where's Crew?" I ask, tying my robe snugly around my waist.

"Daddy left."

One hand goes to my throat and I choke back the tears.

He's gone. Oh my God. What if...

"How long?" I ask. "Before your show started or after?" I glance at the clock.

"I watched part of one and then all of this one."

A good forty-five minutes.

I smile as warmly as I can. "Okay. How are you feeling today?"

"Good. Daddy told me some secrets before he left. I can tell you one of them," she grins mischievously. "There is an envelope for you on the counter. Daddy said to make sure you see it and you don't spill your coffee on it."

My heart races, thumping against all the walls in my chest. I barrel into the kitchen and spot the manila envelope propped up against the toaster.

Jules is scribbled on the front in Crew's messy handwriting. I stare at it, almost afraid to touch it. But in the end, my curiosity wins out.

I pick it up and it's heavier than I expect. I pop open the metal tabs in the back and pull out a stack of papers. I set them on the counter and go to toss away the envelope when I feel something in the bottom. I turn it upside down and something falls to the counter, rolling across the surface until it comes to a stop beside the coffee maker.

I start to pick it up and freeze. My knees go weak, a sob escaping from my throat. With a trembling hand, I reach out and pick up my wedding ring from Gage. I hold it up and look at it, no worse for the wear. I clutch it in my palm and squeeze my eyes shut. I can't even process this right now.

Slipping it onto my right hand so I don't lose it, I relish the feeling of it back in my possession. I can't believe it's here, that I have it back.

I pick up the stack of papers. The top one is a note from Crew. I shuffle through the rest and drop them on the floor.

My God.

Dropping to my knees, I scoop them up and try to keep my tears from dotting them. They're the most beautiful, yet horrific, pages I've ever seen.

Life Insurance Policy No. 110302070202, Mr. Crew Michael Gentry. Pay On Death, Ms. Julia Nicole Gentry.

I'm afraid to touch them. I shove them back in the envelope like they're burning me. I never want to see them again.

With tears streaming down my cheeks, a heart beating so hard I think it might shatter, I pick up the note.

Jules,

First of all, yeah, I'm totally stealing this idea from Gage.

SACRIFICE

Whatever happens tonight, remember it was my decision and mine alone.

I intend on walking in the front door in the middle of the night. You should be in our bed waiting on me. There'll be no more of you sleeping elsewhere. After this is off my back, things will change a little bit. I'll be around more. I'll be able to help you with Ever. I'll try to be everything you ever need.

If things don't go as planned, there are papers in here. There's a business card in there somewhere. Call the guy listed and he'll take care of you. I knew him in college and he's a decent guy. If I don't make it home tonight, he'll make sure things are taken care of. He knows to pay for the therapy and then cut you a check for the rest. Everything else, call Will.

I know you're crying and you should stop.

I know you're scared and you shouldn't be. By the end of the night tonight, you'll have the money we need one way or the other. Because if I don't walk off that mat a winner, you can cash those life insurance papers in. That's the thing . . . we win either way. I promised you the money and you'll have it.

I love you. I'll love you until my last breath.

Crew

PS Your ring is in here, too. Keep it. It's yours.

I crumble onto the floor, unable to control the sobs escaping my throat.

I cry for Crew, for Ever, for me, for Gage.

I cry for the baby I'm carrying that I didn't get the chance to tell him about.

I cry for everything that's ever happened between us and everything that's going to.

It's going to be the longest day of my life.

Chapter FIFTY-SIX

CREW

THE MATS ARE cold against my skin as I go through my routine. I sit and stretch my legs, my back, my arms. I'm calm, focused on the task at hand, yet unfocused as well. I can't get too keyed up this early. I still have a few hours before anything really happens.

I watch Will and Victor carry shit out to the car. Victor was here when I arrived this morning and asked if there was anything he could do. Sal kind of left it up to me because each fighter has different preferences as to who he wants around when he's getting ready to brawl.

I like Victor. Our personalities mesh well. He knows his place and does his job. He defers to me, keeps his mouth shut, and works his fucking ass off. He's helping get things loaded now and he'll help me stay loose before the fight. I'm also having him run tickets over to Adam and Dane. I had Will give them a call a couple of days ago. This fight is happening because of their recording, after all.

My headphones are blasting Eminem. "Not Afraid" seems to be my anthem at the moment, although I'll have "Lose Yourself" going through my ears as I walk to the cage.

Sal walks across the mat, his gray track pants and "Believe" t-shirt on. I take my headphones off my head.

"You about ready?" he asks, standing in front of me.

"Sal? Have I ever not been ready for a fight?"

"This is your last chance to back out," he says with a smile.

I don't react.

"Okay. You weigh-in in three hours, so let's head on over to the green room and get situated. Things will start to go really fast when we get there. I hate this new same day weigh-in bullshit."

"Yeah, but it makes sense," I say. "Keeps guys from cutting weight crazy and then bulking up the day of."

"It just rushes everything," he says in disgust. "Anyway, that's for me to worry about. Let's get over there, get you weighed in, and do all the rule meetings and shit."

He starts to walk away but turns abruptly. "I just wanted to say . . ." His voice trails off with a crackle. He looks away and a quick brush of nervousness passes across his face.

It causes a lump to form in my throat. In all the years I've known Sal D'Amato, I've never seen him nervous.

"We'll chat later. Let's go."

JULIA

MY VOICE IS shaky. "It starts at ten," I tell Olivia.

"Do you want me to come stay with you? Or I could bring Everleigh here?"

I sigh, my head a mess, my heart even worse.

"Does she know what's happening?" Olivia asks.

"No, she has no idea. She thinks he's at work today and won't be home until late. I don't want her knowing."

"I'll just come pick her up if that's easier, Julia."

"I don't know what's easier. I don't want her to see the fight. I don't want her to see me a wreck, either, and I'm a train wreck already. But thinking I'm going to sit here by myself and watch this go down . . ." My stomach rolls. "What if this doesn't go the way he planned?"

"Stop thinking like that. Let him do his job. He knows what he's doing, sweetheart. I'll be over shortly for Everleigh. I'll have Rory come over and it'll be fun for them and give you some space to work this out."

"What would I do without you?"

"I'll be by soon."

Chapter FIFTY-SEVEN

CREW

THE FOCUS MITTS pop as I pepper them with punches. Victor moves and I hit them again.

I feel good. I feel strong. I feel quick.

Pop! Pop! Pop!

I tap the mitts lightly, getting my body ready to go.

"That's enough," Sal says, coming into the room. "I want you to rest for a little bit before we stretch you out. We have," he glances at his watch, "about two hours before we go."

Victor takes off the mitts and tosses them into a chair. He looks at Sal, waiting for instruction.

"You need some water?" Will asks from the corner. He's sitting in a chair, fielding calls and texts that are pouring in. He passes along a few well wishes every now and then. It makes me feel good that guys from the dock, from Shenanigan's, guys I haven't seen in years are pulling for me tonight.

"Yeah," I reply. I'm not really thirsty, but I know I need to be hydrated. I made weight easy this morning—185 pounds even, but I didn't drink a lot earlier just in case.

The room is warm from too many bodies in one small space. I feel edgy, unable to calm with all the people and chaos going on. I need a few minutes to myself, a few minutes away from everyone watching me like a gladiator going into the Coliseum.

I'm grateful for these guys. They've given me their dedication and support and loyalty. Without them, I never could've gotten ready. I never would've made it to this point. They've helped me get ready for the biggest fight of my life, but their attention is a little too much right now. I need to get my head together. Focus. Remember what's going, what I'm doing.

What I have to do.

"Can you guys do me a favor and get the fuck out of here for a while? I need to breathe," I say.

They exchange a glance and Will stands. "Sure."

Sal pops open the door and they all walk out. The door closes behind them. I watch it long after it shuts, waiting for someone to walk back in. Once I'm sure they won't, I lay down on the floor.

The tile is cold and hard. It cools my body and my mind. The ground is where I'm most comfortable, where I work. I extend my arms to the side and close my eyes.

I've pushed my brain to stop thinking all day . . . for days, actually. I've tried to stay focused, keep my thoughts uncomplicated. But I know I can't go out there without making peace with them.

I stand and walk to my gym bag tossed carelessly in the corner. I open the front pocket and pull out a picture I tucked in there last night. It's of me, Julia, and Ever taken by Olivia a couple of weeks ago. Ever and I, with our freshly shaven heads, are sticking our tongues out at the camera. Jules hated that I prompted her to do that; it wasn't lady-like. I laugh as I remember her gorgeous face looking all sternly at me.

I run my thumb across the photo, wishing it was Jules' skin I was touching. She's what grounds me, focuses me, makes me feel like everything is okay as long as I have her.

But that's not true.

Everything will be okay as long as tonight plays out all right.

I sit again and look at my daughter.

My daughter.

The thought makes me smile, brings tears to my eyes. She may not be mine biologically, but she sure as hell couldn't be anymore mine. I've loved this little girl since the first time I saw her. I walked into Julia's room at the hospital and Gage placed her in my arms. I remember the look on his face, beaming, as he touched her cheek. She opened her eyes and looked at me, wrapping her tiny fingers around my thumb.

"You realize how fucked we are?" I asked him, watching this perfect little

thing look back at me.

"Don't cuss around her," he said, making me laugh. "But, yes, I realize how much trouble this is going to be." He placed his hand on my shoulder. "You gotta help me keep her safe, Crew. It's gonna take the both of us."

"I've got your back, brother. Don't worry about it."

I hang my head, my hand holding the picture dropping to my side.

"Look," I say out loud, "I don't know if you hear me or if there is some kind of routine I have to go through to talk to you. I'm not even sure I really believe in you. If you're this kind, loving God, then why in the world have you let so many shitty things happen? Why did you take my brother away from Julia and Ever? Why did you let a baby girl get sick like this? That's all kinds of fucked up and, if you are listening, I'd really like to say fuck you right now. Because I don't understand this and I'm positive there is no way you'd be able to explain this to me."

"But let's say you are there and let's say you give a shit. I want to make a deal with you. I know my bargaining position isn't good because I've been to church only a handful of times in my life and I think I've tried to talk to you less than that. But I'd appreciate you hearing me out right now."

"There's nothing you can gain by taking Everleigh. You'd crush Julia, who is barely hanging on as we speak. You've already taken so much from her. So take me instead. Take whatever punishment or wrath you're throwing their way . . . take that out on me. Take my health. Take my life, damn it. I don't give a shit. Whatever the cost is, I'll pay it. Just let my girls be okay."

I stand and pace the room. "I hope you're listening to me right now. I'm about to walk into the room and face another one of your creations, Hunter Davidson. I'm not praying for a victory, I'm not asking for him to lose. All I ask of you is that you do with me whatever you need to in order to clear my girls of any more harm."

I slam my fist into the bag hanging in the corner.

"Did you hear me!? Do you? Take me! I'll be your sacrifice!"

I hold my arms out to the sides, my muscles twitching as the emotions become almost too much. I tilt my head to the ceiling and close my eyes.

"I'm right here. I give myself to you. Just let them be okay."

I take a deep breath and blow it out, a feeling of warmth settling over my soul.

"Please, God, *please,* let them be okay."

JULIA

"PLEASE, GOD, *PLEASE,* let him be okay."

I kneel in front of our bed, folding my hands in front of me. It reminds me of when I was a very little girl and my grandmother teaching me how to pray. It's not something I've done a whole lot of in my life, but something that has always made me feel comforted.

"I've been asking a whole lot of you lately," I say out loud, my voice echoing around the room. "It seems you think I'm a whole lot stronger than I am. Well, I'm *not!*"

I dip my head, resting it on my forearms. "I'm not strong, not strong enough to deal with *this!*"

My words are choked by my sobs. Tears drip steadily off my chin and onto the University of Minnesota Wrestling t-shirt I found and slipped on.

"Please don't abandon us tonight. Please keep your hand on him, God, and keep him safe. I need you to keep him safe. I've already given you Gage and am fighting to keep Everleigh. Why do you want to take everyone that I love?"

My entire body shakes, tears coming so powerfully, my sobs nearly ripping me in pieces.

"You can't have him! I won't give him up. I won't!" I wail. "If you're trying to punish me for something I've done, punish *me!* Give me cancer! Let me be in an accident! Take my legs and arms if you have to! But stop taking my heart and soul piece by piece! *Please!*"

I fall back onto the floor and lay flat, my hands on my heart. My chest shakes with the force of the sobs. I'm alone, terrified, and I know the worst is yet to come.

Chapter Fifty-Eight

CREW

WHEN THE DOOR swings open again, I can hear the roar of the crowd. Sal and Will come in and shut the door solidly behind them.

"You ready?" Sal asks, his voice stern.

I roll my neck and stretch my arms overhead. "Yeah."

Will nods, not really needing to say anything else. The look on his face explains it all. I nod back and the start of a grin begins on his face.

"Let's get to it," Sal says, opening the door again. The roar of the crowd pours into the room, music pumping through the stadium. The electricity is palpable, even from back here. It's obvious that this isn't just another fight for Hunter Davidson; this fight is a big deal . . . to all of us.

I take a step forward but Sal stops abruptly. He closes the door once again and turns to me.

"I just want to say something before we walk down that aisle." He watches me carefully, like he's searching for the words he wants to say.

"A number of years ago, I was driving passed Shaw's and saw a bunch of kids fighting. Out of all of them, there was one guy that caught my eye. I stopped and got out and approached him. He was cocky and tough-as-nails. I'm looking at that same guy right now. He's the toughest son-of-a-bitch I've ever met." He pauses and takes a deep breath. "Whatever happens after we open this door and walk down the aisle, don't forget who you are."

"When I open this door, you are gonna see things like you've never seen before. There's gonna be more people out there than at all of your NCAA wrestling meets combined. There's movie stars, politicians, models, CEO's and all of them will have something to say. But you worry about who Crew Gentry is. You remember what you're fighting for."

"You've gone from that unpolished kid with no direction into the man you are right now. A man that has more heart, sense, and loyalty in his little finger than most men have in their soul. It's easy to be a man when you are the man, when life is easy and you're shitting roses. But the true test of a man is how he handles things when life gets tough. When life throws you so many combinations that you can't slip them fast enough. Let me tell ya, kid, you already passed that test. Now let's go out there and finish this."

We're standing toe-to-toe. I can feel his energy, feel his support roll off of him. I absorb every bit of it I can and let it hit home, let his words marinate in my skull.

"You're the most natural kid I've ever trained. I want to see you go out there tonight and leave it all on the mat. Remember what I used to tell you: you only get one shot. Do not let your chance go by. If you don't leave it all out there," he pauses and I know exactly what he means, "you'll never forgive yourself."

I take a deep breath and blow it out. Will lays my headphones around my neck and grabs a white towel off of the bench behind me.

"Will . . ." I say, turning around.

"Ah, Crew. I know you love me. Do you want to have a group hug?"

"Fuck you, Will."

Will smiles. "Later. Let's go out there and knock this cocksucker out."

I nod to Sal who then opens the door. The crowd is going wild, Davidson's entrance song, Aloe Blacc's "The Man," buzzes throughout.

"Get your headphones on and block this shit out," Will says, pulling them up to my ears.

I roll my neck and shake my hands at my sides, trying to stay warm and loose. Victor is waiting for us in the hallway and joins our pack as we walk to the entranceway. The media and NAFL's cameramen see us coming and scramble into position. I put my head down and Will tosses the towel over my head.

The tunnel is in front of us, the crowd dying down as the lights dim. There's a black hole waiting for me and I take step after step towards it.

"You guys ready? I'm about to give you a show to remember," I say, peppering myself in the face a few times.

Will's hands are on my shoulders, working them back and forth.

I forgot this feeling. The buzz, the electricity that surrounds a fight is unmatchable.

I missed this shit. This is what I was born to do.

The adrenaline kisses my veins, rockets through my body. I feel invincible.

A smile spreads across my face and I bow my head so the cameras don't catch it. I turn my head to the side and make eye contact with Sal. He sees the look in my eyes and laughs.

"Killers aren't made. They're born," he says, loud enough for just me to hear. "You were born for this, kid. When you get out there, destroy him, Crew. Where you came from, there is no mercy. Show him none."

I click the button on my headphones, the first notes of "Lose Yourself" playing as we approach the mouth of the tunnel. I take a step through and the spotlight hits me. I glance up and every jumbotron in the building has my face on it, a barrage of flashes goes off in every direction.

All eyes on me.

JULIA

THE STATION GOES to commercial just as Hunter enters the cage. He looks larger, meaner, more evil than I even remember. In his red sparkly trunks and his hair manuvered into a perfect mohawk, he looks like the asshole I know he is.

I start to sit on the sofa when a knock raps on the door. I have no idea who it is, but I don't want to walk away from the television. Feeling torn, I yell, "Who is it?"

"Julia! It's me, Macie!"

"Macie?"

"Yes! From the hospital!"

"It's unlocked! Come in!"

I watch the end of a sports drink commercial before Macie comes around the corner. She sits her purse on the counter and smiles at me. "I hope I'm not bothering you, girlie, but I didn't think it was a good idea for you to be here alone. And Will thought it would be a good idea for me to come by . . ."

I smile gratefully. "Thank you. Maybe you being here will keep me from losing my mind."

She returns my smile and sits down beside me. "I would've been here earlier but my shift ran over. I got Will's texts as soon as I clocked out and hurried over here."

I shush her as the fight comes back on, pointing at the screen.

"I've never seen someone with no professional fights garner this much attention, Nate," the announcer on the television says. "Crew Gentry walks into the place tonight and the crowd is going wild. This is insane!"

I watch as the camera comes into focus. Crew is walking into the stadium, a towel over his head. A man is walking next to him, Will a few steps behind. The lights are shining directly on him, the crowd screaming like he's a rock star.

"I can't believe this," I whisper to Macie.

"The crowd is on its feet, acting like this is the main event! Don't forget, we have Love vs. Brusci following this fight," the announcer laughs.

"Marv, no one cares," Nate laughs. "This *is* the main event, whether it's billed that way or not."

"By watching this, you'd think the crowd agreed with you, Nate. The response to Gentry coming in is every bit as strong as what we heard for Davidson."

The towel slips just a bit and I see his eyes. He's looking forward, not towards the camera, not seeming to register the craziness the announcers are going on about.

"I've been doing this for years and I've never seen a fighter come into the cage with no entrance song," Marv remarks. "He's coming in with black shorts and no fanfare. His team is wearing black shirts with the word "Believe" across the front and a simple "Crew Gentry" across the back. Compare that to the red, flashy shorts and self-aggrandizing music of Davidson and we couldn't have more of a dichotomy in opponents!"

"That's what makes this fight so interesting, Marv."

Crew makes it to the opening of the cage. A man in a black suit steps in front of him. Crew shows him his mouth piece and his gloves. He nods at something the man says and steps through the metal links.

My stomach curls. As the station goes into their statistics, I run into the bathroom and lose the contents of my stomach into the toilet.

Chapter FIFTY-NINE

CREW

THE DOOR TO the cage clinks shut behind me. I look across the mat and I'm face-to-face with the motherfucker I've been dying to get my hands on again.

He's jumping up and down in a boyish attempt to be intimidating, hitting himself in the face and yelling. It sort of makes me laugh, but it sort of makes me want to beat the fuck out of him worse. I can't tell if he's doing it for the cameras or for me.

I shake my hands at my sides and bend a few times to loosen my legs, careful through this process not to remove my glare from his face. I don't need to jump up and down like a gymnast to intimidate him. I just need to let him see my eyes. That's all the intimidation I need because unlike him, I'm not a circus performer. I'm a fighter.

The referee walks into the center of the cage and motions for us to join him. Hunter grins his cocky little grin as he comes at me and I meet it with a cold, dead gaze. The same gaze I've been giving him since I got in the cage.

This isn't a game to me. This is a confluence of events, some shitty aligning of the stars, an opportunity for me to put things the way they should've been anyway.

The ref puts his hands between us and the mic lowers from the ceiling. The crowd is deafening, roaring with excitement. I look at Hunter's face across from me and the noise drowns out. It's just me and him.

"Gentlemen," the ref says, "I want a good clean fight. Listen to my commands and defend yourselves at all times. Touch gloves and go back to your corners."

Davidson extends his gloves and I touch them. He pushes back and flinches at me, acting like he's going to come across the invisible line and start the fight right fucking now. I hear him laugh. "Fuck, man, your girl tasted good. I can't wait to put my mouth on that little pussy of hers."

Pure rage soars through me. My arm immediately snaps forward, aiming at his face. Hunter's expecting it, though, and is already a few steps back and out of reach. I barrel forward, ready to end this motherfucker right now. The referee jumps between us, wrapping his arms around my waist.

"Gentry! Enough! Get to your corner!" he says, inches from my face.

"Yeah, I think I'll do that!" Davidson shouts across the mat. "I'll do that right after I bury you beside your dead brother."

I try to charge forward again, but the ref keeps pushing me back. "Just a minute, Gentry!"

Satisfied that I'm far enough away to not get to my opponent before the bell actually signals it's time for it, he turns to Davidson. "Keep it clean, Davidson!"

Only then do I register the voices of Sal and Will behind me, almost drowned out by the noise of the stadium. The room is hot, blisteringly hot, the energy curling through the air almost electric. The crowd feels the anticipation of what's to come, ready to see us end a vendetta years in the making.

"Gentry! You fuckin' listen to me!" Sal shouts behind me. I glance over my shoulder, his fingers laced through the fence. "You keep your head on your shoulders out there! Let his mouth fuel you, but don't let it make you fuckin' crazy! We have a plan and you better stick to it, kid!"

The ref is back in the center, his arms out in front of him. The bell dings and it's on.

JULIA

I LEAP TO my feet at the sound of the bell. I don't know whether to yell or cry, my wits strung so tightly I can barely even function at all. I lace my fingers together in front of my face. "Come on, Crew. Come on, baby," I mutter, watching him stalk towards Hunter.

"And here we go," the announcer says. "It's Hunter Davidson in the red trunks, Crew Gentry in the black."

Macie stands behind me, her hand resting on my shoulder. I can't take my eyes off the screen as Crew and Hunter paw at each other.

"They're feeling each other out," the announcer comments. "Neither of these two want to see this go to the ground already. You must remember, these were two decorated Division I NCAA wrestlers. This just might come down to the better striker."

"Come on, Crew." I don't know what else to say. I know very little about fighting. All I know is watching them circle each other is fraying my nerves one strand at a time.

"They're both trying to set up their game plans. Each getting the other in position . . . Woah! Did you see that kick?" The announcer's voice pierces the air.

My insides twist as Crew's body takes the impact. He throws a hand and Hunter deflects it. Hunter throws another kick and Crew steps to the side. They trade punches and I swear I can feel every one.

"Davidson is trying to work his way inside . . . he ate a big one there!"

Crew lands a huge punch on the side of Hunter's face and follows it up with barrage of shots. Hunter is knocked back a little but regains his composure quickly.

"Come on Crew!" I say, pacing in front of the television.

"He's got this, Jules. He's got this!" Macie says assuredly, but it does nothing to make me feel better.

Crew stalks Hunter around the cage before they land against the fence. Hunter's back is on the perimeter and Crew is against him, throwing punches against his body.

"Great hook by Gentry, but he got caught with a short shot from Davidson. Gentry appears to be the aggressor, Davidson the more reserved consummate professional, Nate. They're in the clench position now, Gentry looking for a possible take down."

"I'm really impressed, Marv, by Davidson's ability to stay calm. He's not playing into the grudge match we all expected."

When the announcer stops talking, you can hear the roar of the crowd. It's insane and I have no idea how either of them are even able to concentrate, but they seem to be. They're tangled up and I have no idea who is winning or what they're doing, the stillness in the action a bit of a relief, yet it feels like it's drawing out the inevitable . . . whatever that is.

"Davidson escapes," the announcer says as Hunter tosses Crew off him and makes his way back into the center of the mat. "Smart choice by Davidson to disengage."

The seconds tick on the clock on the bottom of the screen. Hunter throws a big hand that Crew barely misses as the bell rings, ending the round.

I blow out a breath in relief.

One round down.

Chapter SIXTY

CREW

I HEAD BACK to my corner and try to catch my breath. My nerves are settled down and I'm relieved that I fell back into the fight so naturally.

Will and Sal rush inside the cage, Will shoving a bottle of water at me. He smiles, his eyes alive. "Great job, man!"

"Crew, you look good out there. You have one round down. Davidson is hanging back and hasn't showed you anything yet. Watch for the takedown and watch for the right leg. He's gonna come out aggressive."

"Yeah," I say, wiping my face off with the towel handed to me by Will.

"How ya feeling, kid?"

"Good. Strong. I live for this shit," I say, smiling confidently.

"Good. Go out there and do your thing."

I give the bottle and towel to Sal. "I've got this."

He pats me on the shoulder as they leave me in the ring for round two. I hear the gate close behind me, the crowd's roar starting to build again as the referee comes back to the center of the mat. His hands go in front of him and we're off.

Hunter comes at me aggressively, just like Sal said he would. He throws a right-left, which I easily block off my elbows. I counter with an overhand right which lands solid but high on his head. Davidson turns as the punch crunches into him and I don't see the kick when it comes.

His foot smashes me in the back of the head, right beneath my skull. I bend a bit in response and he kicks again. It takes the wind out of me, sending a spiral of pain through my spine. My adrenaline is so high that I know I'm not registering all of it.

He starts to kick again, but I step inside and blister him with a few shots but I don't feel the same strength behind my punches.

Something's wrong.

He comes straight back at me again, smiling. We trade punches, half of them hitting, half not, but it makes for a good show because the crowd's noise amplifies. We begin to break when he pulls my head forward and slams his elbow against my spine.

Motherfucker.

"Get outta there!" Sal screams at me, his voice riding above the crowd. "That was illegal, ref! Come on! This isn't a back alley, this is a sanctioned fight!"

JULIA

"THAT STAGGERED HIM at a bit," the announcer comments as Crew wobbles a little as he backs away from Hunter. "You know, it really looks like Davidson is targeting Gentry's neck."

"If you recall, Nate, that's the exact location where Gentry was injured the first time they fought."

"Wow, I can't believe Davidson would stoop to that level!"

"Well, I don't think Davidson thought Gentry would be standing here for round two, either, Nate."

"Macie," I breathe, watching Crew get himself together again. She's at my side, holding on to me. We watch him stalk towards Hunter, but something seems off. Crew's stumbling and his arms aren't up as high as they were before. The announcers notice it, too.

"Gentry is a little slower this round, I think. I'm not sure if he's being more careful or if that kick to the back of his neck hurt him. You have to remember, Gentry hasn't been in a situation like this in years."

"Maybe ever," the other announcer says. "Right now, he's giving the naysayers fuel that said he shouldn't even be in the cage with a professional like Hunter Davidson."

"Fuck you!" I say to the announcer, tears starting to hit my eyes.

SACRIFICE

Watching this is torture. I want to close my eyes and not watch, but I can't bear to not see what happens.

Macie and I stand together, watching the action on the screen. Crew throws a couple of punches and misses. Hunter takes a step back and taunts him, his arms out to the side, his hips swaying back and forth. He says something to Crew, but I have no idea what. The crowd goes wild at Hunter's little show and he just plays it up more, like an actor on stage.

I watch with bated breath as Crew goes in for a takedown, something I've seen him do a million times. I watch as Davidson's foot in seemingly slow motion connects with Crew's face.

He drops to the mat. My stomach falls right along with it.

Chapter SIXTY-ONE

CREW

I'VE FELT THIS pain once before. Ironically, or not, it was against Davidson that time, too.

The back of my neck burns from the bottom of my head all the way down my shoulders. The pain pierces through the adrenaline that normally keeps any real discomfort at bay during a fight.

Hunter is on top of me within seconds. He throws punches at my face, which I'm able to block easily thanks to many rounds with Victor. He's on top of me, wailing away, and I know I gotta get outta here. This is not the place to be.

I try to roll him off, but the pain in my neck puts me back flat against the mat. My elbows are in tight, my hands in front of my face, and I'm rocking back and forth blocking everything I can.

I feel another burst of adrenaline hit, that almost dizzying feeling that accompanies the relief, hitting me hard. I know I have to use it to my advantage. I have a very small window of opportunity; it's do or die.

Hunter goes to take a side mount, landing huge right hands against my face. I feel the force of every blow, each slap of the leather jerking my neck back and forth.

Davidson's face is animated, his eyes blazing, sensing the kill. And I realize—that's exactly what's happening.

This guy's trying to kill me.

SACRIFICE

Fight or flight kicks in and a rush of memories flashes through my mind. I see Jules' smile, Ever's eyes, hear Gage's laugh. I've set everything up for this moment, the one where the girls will be okay regardless of how it ends.

I know what I gotta do.

The pain is insane. Everything starts to bleed together, everything one big, giant, fucked up, muffled mess. I strain to find something to focus on, something to keep me present. I hear Will at the side of the cage and I focus on his voice . . .

JULIA

"I CAN'T BELIEVE what's happening, Marv! In a matter of moments, the predator has become the prey!"

"That's why people love MMA, Nate! Everything can change in a heartbeat!"

"Yes, but how quickly did Davidson just take over? Crew's on the mat looking like a beaten man."

"Come on, baby!" I yell at the television. "Come on, Crew!"

"I don't know what's going on with Gentry, Nate. I'm not sure he's going to hold on!"

Tears are pouring down my cheeks. I glance quickly at Macie and tears are falling from her eyes, too. She reaches for my hand.

The camera gets a close-up of the two of them and I can see Crew's eyes. They're wide wild, *unfocused*, full of some sort of emotion that I'm too afraid to name.

CREW

I'M GETTING SLAMMED in the back of the head by illegal punches every time I turn my head.

I gotta blow or go.

This motherfucker wants a street fight, I can do that.

I relax just enough so Davidson smells blood. Being the impulsive prick I know him to be, he takes full mount.

I summon every last bit of strength I have. I only have a few seconds left and I'm going to finish this fight, one way or another, the way I know. The way that's not won me medals or accolades, but the way that's saved my life in the past.

Sal said to remember where I came from; I came from the streets. I'm going to finish this like a street fighter.

Davidson straddles me and I explode. I rare up and blast my head into Davidson's face, stunning him. I wrap my legs around him. I reach my arm over his neck and put my forearm under his chin, locking my hands together. As I rock back, basically trying to pull his head off his body in a Guillotine choke, I feel my own head spin. I yell out, the pain in my neck so intense I almost can't hold on.

I can feel the panic take over Davidson. He knows he's caught now and has a few moments to escape or this is over. His hands free, he rocks my body with punches from both sides, each blast only intensifying my pain. My neck is pressed between the mat and the corner of the cage, Hunter's 190-pound body pressing down onto one spot in my neck.

The pain is white-hot. Blinding. I can't see anything clearly.

Each impact feels like a bomb is going off inside me. He hits me again, a bunny shot that shouldn't even register, but it does. I flex my arms, squeezing harder to keep him still, and something cracks in my back. I can actually hear it over the blood pounding in my ears, over the crowd, over Sal, over Hunter's groans.

The pain is ridiculous. My body relaxes for a split second, my head feeling light, and Hunter starts to break free. Quickly, I crank it down again as hard as I can. As I do, flashes of black sweep through my vision.

JULIA

MY KNEES BUCKLE. My airway clenches as I watch the image on the screen. The announcers are shouting, bantering back and forth so quickly that I couldn't make sense of it if I wanted to. But I don't. I can't. I can't do anything but watch the man I love fight a battle not just for my daughter's life, but maybe for his own.

I fall to my knees, the image on the television blurry through the tears. He's struggling, I can see it. I can feel the panic through the screen. He's working to hold Hunter in place. The sweat on his body catches the light from above the cage and I can see his muscles flexing, pulling, grasping to end the fight. Hunter is trying to roll, pulling at Crew's arms to release but he manages to hold on.

"Hold on, baby! Hold on," I cry out, my voice splintering through the tears. "Please. Hold on . . ."

CREW

I PULL THE move in tight as everything starts to blur. The darkness is even heavier this time, the noises coming at me like I'm in a tunnel. I try to find Will's voice, or Sal's, but I can't make it out. I can't find anything to hold onto.

My entire body feels like it's on fire. I want to let go. I need a reprieve from the pain.

I feel Hunter starting to panic and I know that this is going to be the end for one of us. I'm either going to cinch this down and cut off his airway or he's going to get away and pound me into the mat. If I let him up, I know I won't be able to fight back.

My head starts to spin, my neck feeling I've been shot with a cannon. I, too, start to panic, my need to just sleep starting to overtake any other thoughts.

"Man up, little brother."

"It's going to take both of us to protect her."

The crowd becomes clear. I feel Hunter's body heavy on me. I feel his sweat drip off onto me, the smoothness of his gloves as they glance off my body.

I hear Will shouting at me to fight. I hear Sal telling me to remember what I need to do.

I grit my teeth and pull down on his neck as hard as I can, pulling his legs down and away from his body. He gurgles and I feel him swiping at me. I cinch down one final time with everything I have.

Pain sears every nerve in my body, causing me to yell out. I hear the crack that resonates through every fiber of my being rattle through my ears. The agony is unrelenting, but the black that follows it is welcome.

The darkness lures me with the promise of rest, a break from the fire. I know I have to hold on. I squeeze tighter, but the pressure I'm exerting isn't as strong as it was.

I bite down and yank one.

Final.

Time.

The last thing I feel is a tap on my shoulder and I float away into the darkness.

THE END

EPILOGUE

JULIA

Two years later

THE GRASS IS soft, still damp from the rain last night. The air is unseasonably warm, but the wind is very chilly. I smile as Ever races her way through the cemetery, heading for the stone in the back. She knows her way here like the back of her hand.

Michael babbles on my hip, laughing as a red bird dips in front of us and lands on a tree on the edge of the grass.

I approach the stone and smile. I don't cry here anymore. I used to sit and pour my heart out, ask him why he left us. But I don't do that anymore. It's not that I have things figured out; it's more that I've learned to have a little faith.

I look at Everleigh, pushing the slush off the bottom of the stone with her boot, telling her daddy stories about her recent adventures. She tells him a story about how we visited the pediatric oncology unit last week and delivered a bunch of games we collected in a fundraiser. The whole thing was her idea, a way to brighten the days of the kids in a precarious position she was in herself not long ago.

It's been almost a year since she was declared in remission. Almost a year since my world became right and I've been able to breathe. I know we aren't completely out of the woods and there is a chance of side effects later or of the cancer returning. But I've learned a few things in this process. To enjoy each and every day like it's your last. That life throws you curveballs, that it brings people in and out of your life as it sees fit. You just have to go with it and find a way to move on.

A key to moving on is to realize that you can't let your experiences go in vain. You have to use what you've been through to make a difference to someone else. You have to use the trials and tribulations, losses and devastations, to make someone else's life better somehow.

"I've been taking swimming lessons, Daddy!" Everleigh says, playing with the flowers in the urn. "I can hold my breath practically forever! I can't wait to go surfing this summer. I have your old board in my room, propped against the wall. Mommy says it's too big, but I'm going to try it anyway. She also says I have to use a life jacket, no matter how good I can swim. If she catches me without one, she says I'll never be allowed to go to the beach again."

"I'm not kidding about that," I remind her.

"I know," she pouts. "I miss you a lot. You wouldn't believe how tall I'm getting! And you should see Michael! He can say Everleigh now. Well, he says something like "Ewerwee," but it's close enough!"

"Ewerwee!" Michael blurts, making us all laugh.

"See?" Ever says, leaning against the stone. "We can't stay long today because we have to go to this fundraiser thing. I don't even know what that means, really, but Mommy has been really excited about it all week."

Ever circles the stone again and plants a kiss on the top. "I love you, Daddy."

"Wub you, Da-da," Michael repeats.

I choke back a sob.

"Ever, why don't you take Michael and head back to the car. I'll be right up."

"Okay!" She takes Michael from my hip and places him on hers. He gives her a open-mouthed kiss on her cheeks and she giggles. I watch them make their way back the way they came before turning my attention back to the stone.

"I miss you," I whisper. I run my hand along the stone. "I miss you so much."

Birds chatter in the tree-line and it breaks the stillness.

"I wish you were here to go with us today. You'd be proud of what we've created. Taking inner city kids and giving them a place to go. You'd like that, I think." I sniffle. "We've gotten tons of support from the community and Sal is going to spend a few hours a week over there as a mentor. You wouldn't believe the people that want to be a part of this."

I wrap my sweater tightly against my body and plant a kiss on the top of the stone like Ever did. "I love you. Always."

A hand touches my shoulder and I smile. I know he hates coming

SACRIFICE

here and I understand why. It's hard for him, too.

"You ready?" he asks.

I turn to see his smiling face. "Yes. Let's go, Will."

EPILOGUE 2

JULIA

WE WALK INTO the building, Will carrying Michael and Ever holding my hand. There is a crowd of people seated in folding chairs facing a collapsible stage along the back wall. They turn as we walk in. Some of them smile, some walk over and shake our hands and introduce themselves.

We take our seats at the front of the room next to Olivia, Macie, Mrs. Ficht, Victor, Brett, Adam, and Dane. I personally asked them all to come. They each were instrumental, in their own way, in getting us *here*.

I look at my smiling daughter.

She's beautiful in her little yellow dress, her hair now to her chin. The sparkle is back in her blue eyes, just like her daddy's. And her mischievous grin is so reminiscent of her other daddy, it makes my heart clinch.

Her life is a mixture of two of the greatest men I've ever known.

She opens her little purse and takes out a piece of Laffy Taffy, something I'm certain she's addicted to at this point. She nibbles on the candy, swinging her legs back and forth.

I feel Will move at my side. I look at him, but his eyes are trained on Macie. She gives him a tight grin and he smiles brightly in return. She shakes her head and crosses her arms and turns back to the stage. I have no idea what's going on between them, but that's nothing unusual. I think Will's met his match with her.

The room erupts in applause as Sal takes the stage. He taps the mic and waits for everyone to settle. As Sal begins to speak, Michael scrambles off Will's lap and tries to climb the stage. I start towards him and Sal laughs. He waves me off and scoops up my son. Michael jabbers while Sal situates himself behind the podium once again.

SACRIFICE

"Ladies and gentlemen, I want to thank you all for joining us today. I'm so proud to be a part of this organization."

He readjusts the microphone and clears his throat.

"A few years ago, I was driving to Providence when I stumbled upon a group of boys fighting behind a supermarket. Two of them caught my eye right away. They were tough, street smart, and had a spark about them that's hard to find. I invited them to train at the Blackrock Gym and they became regulars. They became students. They became friends."

"The Gentry boys came from the inner city. They had no father and a working mother. They had, to put it bluntly, no future. But what they did have was potential."

Michael twists in Sal's arms and he sets him down. He makes a beeline to his favorite person. "Will!" he screeches. Will heads to the stage and catches my son. They sit next to me, Michael playing with Will's keys.

"Gage and Crew Gentry were given the opportunity to make something of themselves. By coming to the gym, they stayed out of a lot of trouble. They stayed off the streets, off drugs. They were given the chance to better themselves . . . and they did. Both kids grew up to be men worthy of respect."

"When Julia Gentry came to me a few months ago with her idea, I knew I had to be involved. This program will give countless kids in the same position as the Gentry boys the same opportunities and more. They'll be given a place to go, something to turn to besides the evils of the streets. They'll learn about discipline, respect, and giving back to others. I'm honored to attach my name to this project."

"Now," he says, a smile on his face, "without further ado, I give you the man that brought this full-circle, Mr. Crew Gentry, everyone!"

The crowd leaps to their feet, clapping enthusiastically. We watch him make his way across the stage. He comes across briskly, rolling his wheelchair like it's an Indy car. He looks at me and winks.

He's getting stronger every day. For weeks, he lay in the hospital bed, unable to move. They said he'd never walk again. They said to prepare myself, that Crew would be an invalid. The doctors would walk out and Crew would tell me they were full of shit. He promised me he'd walk again.

And Crew doesn't break his promises. Not anymore.

He gets to the podium and stands. He rests his forearms on the wood, taking the weight off his back. He's been more active than usual, trying to oversee the construction of the building and helping with Michael.

He still tries to do everything he could before and some days it's just too much. He's learned to let Will take some of the pressure off, like taking me to the cemetery this morning. When he gets back on his feet, because I'm sure he will, he'll make up for lost time.

He's so handsome. He smiles at the crowd and it takes my breath away. If you just saw him standing there, you'd never know he was almost completely paralyzed. You'd never know he spent weeks in the hospital, unable to move at all. You'd never know the fight he made to get his legs working again. You'd never see the struggle that it still is every morning, when his body is tight and he has to force himself out of bed. But he does it. And he never complains. He just says he'd do it all over again because it saved Everleigh. The money he won from the fight by beating Hunter Davidson got our daughter into the therapy that destroyed the cancer in her little body.

"I want to thank you all for coming." He looks around the room, taking in the supporters, media, mentors and guests. Finally, his gaze rests on me. "Today is the anniversary of my brother, Gage's, death and it seemed like a fitting day to open the for-EVER en-GAGE Foundation. It's the brainstorm of my wife, Julia, and is in memory of my brother and in celebration of our daughter, Everleigh."

He shifts his weight and I know he's hurting. But he's going to say what he has to say; he won't let the pain stop him.

"Our goal is to engage the bodies and minds of the kids of Boston, kids like my brother and I growing up. We will give them opportunities to see what they're capable of, to develop their interests and talents, to give them a place to go instead of the alleyways of the city."

"One key area we want to focus on is community involvement. It's our goal to show the youth that they are a part of a larger collective, that they can and should make a difference in our communities and to those that are less fortunate."

He glances down at Ever and pauses. "We will create funds through our Red Slipper Initiative to support families that are going through medical emergencies. We will raise money for research for many causes, but especially neuroblastoma, a cause close to our hearts." His voice begins to break.

"No matter what the kids that come into our building have been through, no matter what they've already done, they'll get another chance. I'm a firm believer in second chances."

"Getting this foundation up and running is not going to be easy. But

SACRIFICE

I'll tell you something that I know from personal experience. When things seem unbeatable, you have to keep pressing forward. Because no matter how bad they look, you can always win. You always have the power. You just have to realize it."

Crew glances at Ever. She's smiling adoringly at her dad, nodding her approval of him using a reference to their favorite movie. He beams and I've never felt more blessed.

"The best things in life don't come easy, but those things are the ones worth the sacrifice. This is something I can promise you. And this foundation is worth all of our time and energy."

I grab my daughter's hand and squeeze it, my heart bursting with so much gratitude. I watch my husband's lips turn up, the corners touching his sparkling blue eyes.

"I love you," I whisper. I know he reads my lips because his face lights up. He winks and knocks gently against the podium four times.

Crew Gentry has been my prince this whole time after all.

Acknowledgements

I ALWAYS IMAGINED writers kicking back with a glass of champagne as they wrote their acknowledgements; that's so far from the truth. At least with me, anyway.

I just wrapped my third novel in less than a year. It's been a crazy ride. I've learned so much about myself, publishing, marketing, and friendship.

There are so many people that have made this entire thing possible. It's humbling to think of all the people, most of which I've never met, that have read my books, encouraged me, pushed me, and taken time out of their day to message me. I know I will inadvertently forget someone's name after I send this to formatting and I'll kick myself for weeks over it. So if you don't see your name and you should, I ask for your forgiveness now.

First and foremost, I want to thank the Creator of the Universe. It might sound cheesy, but I'm eternally grateful to whoever it is that created me and blessed me with so much in life. My life isn't perfect and my journey hasn't been without bumps, but I'm smart enough to realize how very blessed and undeserving I am.

None of this would be possible without the support of my family. Mr. Locke and the Littles shock me with their enthusiasm for my work. My mother, Mandy, and in-laws Rob and Peggy cheer me on endlessly. Simply put, they are the backbone of this endeavor.

Actually writing the book is only a part of the battle. I've managed to put together the very best team of professionals to bring my words to the world. Kari at K23 Designs took my vague description of what I had in mind for the cover and nailed it! Ashley with Escapist Freelance Editing didn't kill me and tightened my manuscript with a smile. Christine with Perfectly Publishable took my words and made them beautiful. Jen with

KinkyGirls Book Obsessions read early and supplied me with more teasers and enthusiasm than I ever dreamed! Kylie with Give Me Books put the word out and gathered such an amazing group of bloggers to review and spread the word. Sacrifice was marked as much by these brilliant ladies as it was by me. Thank you all for going on this journey by my side.

I owe more than a thank you to the girls that helped me plot this book. They let me cry on their shoulder and kept me focused. Heather P, Jennifer C, Kari, Mandi, Michele, and Susan—without you, I'd still be mulling over the concept (and probably be trying to back out). Thank you for pushing me and telling me all the things I needed to hear when I needed to hear them, whether I liked it or not.

Ninfa, Laura, Jillian, Lara, Macie, Joy, Jen P, Jen O, Tiffany L, and Jessica walked in with sharp eyes and willing hearts and tore into this book. Thank you girls for your time, energy, and friendship. It means the world to me.

Julie, Mary Lee, Mary Ruth, Kristi, Christy, Tiffany C, Selja, and Selma have all made me smile each and every day. Sometimes with a simple hello and sometimes with a video or a picture, they provided me with a grin while I battled through Crew. Thank you for all that you did and continue to do.

The hundreds of supportive souls in Books by Adriana Locke have been so encouraging. You've pushed me, fought over my characters (sometimes before knowing them! LOL), followed me to parties, and been the best group I could ever have imagined. Thank you from the bottom of my heart.

Robin, Chandra, Christy, Julie "Jules," Misty, Heather C, Holly, Lisa, Chelsia, Sherry, Kristi, Laura H, Shely, Mix, and Analia make me smile every day with their tags, posts, and help in getting my books out there. You ladies are the sweetest, most selfless women I've ever known. Thank you for all you do for me.

Indie Chicks Rock, Keshia, Angie, Suzie, Kristy, Gail, SE, Emersyn, Lauren, Beverly, Tori, and Seraphina are my brilliant peers that never fail to stop and answer questions. They always make me feel like a part of the writing world and cannot possibly know how much that means to me.

And how could I forget my Instagram girls? :) nalledecvz, cozy_dita, kinkygirlsbookobsessions, readingwhore, thefiftyshadesqueen, lovekellankyle, heatherlynb1988, tiffany.the.bibliophile, thereadingruth, nicks_biggest_fann, charliehunnamforever, book.whores, innergoddess_booklover, bookobsessedgirl, book_ish_life, laker124vr, jenifrmthebloc, bitcheslovvveit, readsbyrose, macie.reads, kshadows, jengare, catherinemark13, booksandbandanas, authorellymarin, most_beautifulmen, tmunn396, mg_herrera, fixtion_fangirl, sucker_for_books, love50shadesx, bookangels_, bookit18, criceeiscute, reader_luv_books, girlwiththeghibitattoos, crazybook_lovers, reading_is_sexyy, 73jem, tina_the-bookworm, smuttybooklover. You rock my socks. That is all. <3

Jaseland and their fearless leader, Virginia, are the most distracting, fun, kind (and did I say distracting?) group on Facebook. Because of them, this book was almost delayed. (But it would've been worth it.) ;) Thank you for welcoming me with open arms. Jaseland is seriously a little piece of heaven on Earth.

To each and every blogger that gives their time and energy so willingly for next to nothing in return—THANK YOU. You give so many of us a chance to succeed by helping get our words to readers. I know it's a thankless job much of the time, but I want you to know that I appreciate each and every single one of you.

Last but so certainly not least, thank YOU. It is not beyond me that you have a million titles to choose from. The fact that you chose mine means the world to me. Thank you for selecting my book. I hope you enjoyed it and I'd love to hear your thoughts about it.

I love you all.

xo,

Addy

About the Author

ADRIANA LOCKE LIVES and breathes books. After years of slightly obsessive relationships with the flawed bad boys created by other authors, Adriana has created her own.

Adriana resides in the Midwest with her family. She spends a large amount of time playing with her kids, drinking coffee, and cooking. She loves to be in the sunshine and always has a piece of candy in her pocket.

Besides cinnamon gummy bears and random quotes, her next favorite thing is chatting with other readers. She'd love to hear from you.

CONTACT ADRIANA

www.adrianalocke.com

Facebook
Twitter
Instagram
Goodreads
Spotify
Pinterest

Continue on for a preview of The Exception, available now.

THE EXCEPTION
BY ADRIANA LOCKE

CANE

IF I CLOSE my eyes, maybe she'll disappear.

"That was amazing. So good, Cane."

Maybe not.

The woman nestled against me, her hand draping across my body. She stroked my skin, the intimacy of the action curling my stomach.

I switched on the bedside lamp, letting my eyes adjust to the bright light. Glancing at the clock, I pushed her hand away.

It's not too late. She can still go home.

Sitting up, I swung my legs over the side of the bed; my body groaned in response. I stretched my arms overhead in an attempt to work some life back into my exhausted muscles.

This girl was a decent choice for a last minute decision. Memories of her contorted in a variety of wicked ways, screaming my name, made my dick harden again.

"Do you want me to get us something to eat?"

Her nails grazed down my back and I moved out of her reach. Her touch, like her voice, was more annoying than I remembered it being a few hours earlier.

That's because I just dumped a load.

I twisted around. Her blonde hair was spread across my pillows, black makeup smeared across her face. A part of me wanted to tell her she looked like hell, but a bigger part of me didn't care enough to point it out. I just needed her gone.

She rolled onto her back, cheap perfume wafting through the air.

I'm going to have to do laundry. Hell, I'll probably just have to burn these sheets to get rid of that smell.

"I was thinking I would grab us some hamburgers. I could pick up some things for breakfast while I'm out."

I cringed at the implications saturating her voice. "You're going to need to tone that shit down."

"What are you talking about?"

"Look, I have things to do tonight." Her face was familiar but her name—not so much.

"Oh, that's fine. I can just wait here while you do what you need to do." She flashed me her biggest smile and settled back into the sheets, looking way too comfortable in my bed.

"No. You're going to need to get up, get dressed, and go home." I massaged my temples with my fingertips, a migraine inching its way into my skull.

For fuck's sake! Why isn't this ever as easy as they make it out to be? Maybe I should get them to sign some shit, a 'This is a Fuck and Only a Fuck' disclaimer or something.

"I really have no plans for tomorrow, Cane."

"We discussed this. We fuck. You leave. You know this." She had the nerve to look hurt.

"I didn't think you were going to say that once we were done."

"It was amazing. It is always amazing with me." I flashed her a grin and literally watched her swoon.

That never gets old.

"Look, I don't do this 'sex and a sandwich' thing, but that is not a newsflash."

"But Cane!"

"Why does it feel like we've been here before?" Frustration took over and I took a deep breath, trying to keep myself calm. All I needed was a hot little body to dump my stress into for a little while and I had made no illusions otherwise. She agreed to this before she followed me home.

Why does it have to be complicated now? I ran my fingers through my short blond hair, scrubbing my scalp in annoyance.

"When I was here a few months ago, we had lunch, too. Remember? We sat out on the patio."

Remember her face. Do not triple dip this one.

"You don't understand how this works." I glanced at her reclining against my pillows and fought hard to not sound as brusque as I felt. "I have a bunch of shit to do. You really need to go."

She sighed dramatically as she got up and found her jeans on the floor. I watched her ass jiggle as she pulled them on slowly, undoubtedly for my benefit.

It worked.

I had to restrain myself from grabbing her and fucking her one more time, just for good measure. That would only make getting her out of my house even harder and she simply wasn't good enough to waste any more time on.

Instead, I sat and enjoyed the show. She turned to face me as she pulled her shirt over her head, her eyes never leaving mine. She tucked her bra in her purse.

With a final glance over her shoulder, presumably to give me time to change my mind, she was gone.

And I was alone again—just the way I liked it.

AVAILABLE NOW

DO YOU WANT TO CONTINUE YOUR CONTEMPORARY ROMANCE LOVE?

How about delving into these contemporary romance authors and their novels?

Casey Clipper
Silent Love

Former Navy SEAL Sean Millen has been perfectly fine with his bachelorhood until recently, when he realizes he's unhappy with his single status. Unfortunately, his playboy reputation doesn't offer him the type of woman that could fulfill his days and nights as well as settle into the specific life he envisions. Four years ago, Beth Connors' world was entirely altered. Beth spends her days trying to remain invisible in order to avoid unwanted attention. Each night she sheds grief-filled tears over the former life she once led but will never be able to regain. When Beth literally runs into HIM. Doctor Sean Millen. A force of nature. A rock. A reputable heartbreaker, who takes an immediate interest in her, there's no place for her to hide. But Beth's natural instinct to push Sean away to save herself and him from the difficult task of adjusting their lives to her shortcomings is always front and center. Yet, Beth secretly longs for love. Is she strong enough to tear down the walls of her self-imposed prison? Sean finds himself falling for a woman who is determined to reject his every advance and deny their surprisingly deep connection. Can Sean push past Beth's concrete walls that she refuses to destroy? Or will Beth's shocking revelation of her past prevent them from finding the love they both deserve? Or will a tragic accident pull Sean and Beth apart permanently?

Isabella Norse
The Purrfect Partner

Lorelei Stevens, newly certified veterinary technician, faces the future with a mix of excitement and dread. Freedom from the meddling of her well-intentioned friends is finally within reach. All she has to do is spend Valentine's weekend dodging the unwanted attentions of strangers during the annual singles gathering at The Lodge. In return, her friends promise to never, ever set her up on another blind date.

Dalton Freeman, laid-back rancher, receives a getaway to The Lodge as a gift from his brothers. The catch? The gift is only good during Valentine's weekend. So what if all of his attempts at online dating have failed miserably? There's no reason for his brothers to play Cupid. Really.

When these two strangers pretend to be a couple for a weekend, will it be a disaster or will fate - and a half-frozen kitten - lead them to the purrfect partner?

Amy L. Gale
Blissful Valentine

Straight-laced 19-year-old Brooke Powers has two goals: First, avoid the party scene and all the drama and disaster that go along with it. Second, focus on attaining her Marketing and Business degrees. When her roommate begs her to attend a fraternity party she reluctantly obliges, but gets more than she bargained for when she meets enticingly charismatic fraternity brother, Dean Parker. After a mishap causes her to wake up in the worst possible place she can imagine, she vows to stay away from anything or anyone fraternity related. Staying away from Dean is a daily battle, one she's slowly losing. When her feelings conjure up old demons from the past, her strategically planned future turns into chaos. Brooke is desperate to keep herself on track. Will Dean be her downfall or is he exactly what she needs?

Valentine's Day isn't always complete bliss.

Susie Warren
The Exiled Jeweler

Emilia Berceto's beauty captures the attention of a well-known Italian billionaire, Alex Armanti, when she attends a gala at his mansion in Los Angeles. Images secretly captured of her partially nude are released to the tabloids and her overly protective family sends her far away.
Four years later, Emilia continues to live a secluded life designing custom jewelry for the wealthy. Her family needs her to return home to California when their jewelry empire is near bankruptcy. When she returns, she must face the man who caused her downfall and is threatening to reveal her secret if she is to save her family's jewelry empire.

Nicki Rae
Damaged Perfection Book One of The Perfection Series

Guilt. It rules my life. I am riddled with it. After fifteen years, you would think it would lessen. It hasn't. Drugs numb it. Women relieve it. But it always returns, stronger and heavier. Always. The light, it is refreshing It gets closer and I reach for it. But it is always just out of my grasp. Always.

Christina Tetreault
The Billionaire Playboy

Legendary playboy Jake Sherbrooke arrives in North Salem with one thing in mind, helping the town recover from a devastating hurricane. Once there though he meets Charlotte "Charlie" O'Brien, a doctor in the US Navy, and he cannot help but be attracted to her. But can a relationship between a billionaire playboy and a woman afraid to let any man get to close survive his reputation?

Printed in Great Britain
by Amazon.co.uk, Ltd.,
Marston Gate.